BOARDWALK BABYLON

A Mickey Cleary Novel

BOARDWALK BABYLON

A Mickey Cleary Novel

Daniel J. Waters

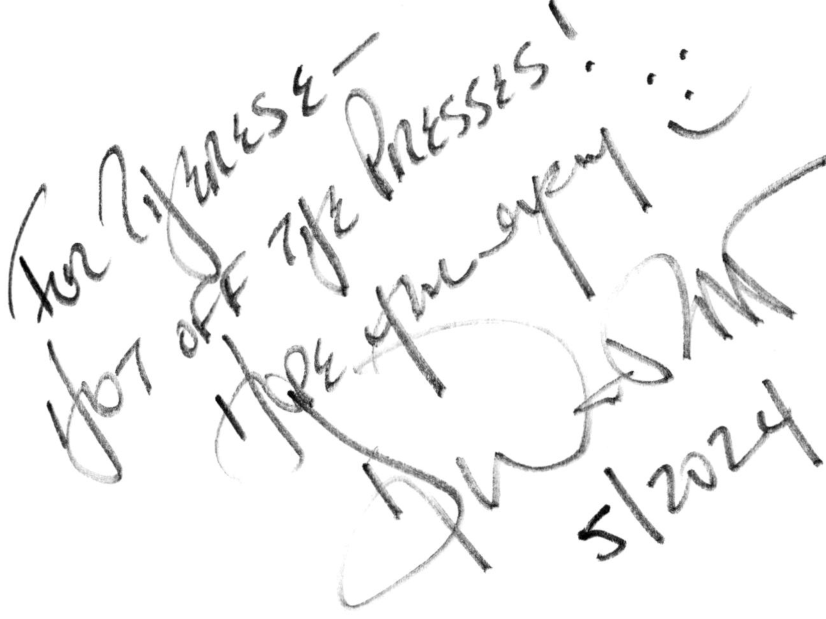

This is a work of fiction. Names, characters, places, organizations, events, and incidents are either products of the author's imagination or are used fictitiously. Any resemblance of fictional characters to actual persons, living or dead, is purely coincidental and unintentional. Actual historical or public figures are used in a fictional context with what the author hopes the reader will recognize as respect and genuine affection.

Text © 2024 Daniel J. Waters — *All Rights Reserved*

No part of this publication may be reproduced, stored in a retrieval system, or transmitted in any form or by any means, electronic, mechanical, recording, or otherwise, without the prior written permission of the author.

Cover Design by James Zach / *zGrafix* Design, Mason City, Iowa

Cover image: iStockphoto (Getty Images) used by permission.
Author Photo by Jean Poland Photography, Clear Lake, Iowa

FRIEND OF THE DEVIL

Words by ROBERT HUNTER Music by JERRY GARCIA and JOHN DAWSON

© 1970 (Renewed) ICE NINE PUBLISHING CO., INC. — *All Rights Reserved*

SHE'S NOT THERE

Words and Music by Rod Argent Copyright © 1964 Marquis Music Co. Ltd. Copyright

Renewed International Copyright Secured — *All Rights Reserved* — Reprinted by Permission of Hal Leonard LLC

Reprinted by Permission of Hal Leonard LLC

JERSEY SHORE MAP

Courtesy of Ryan Martz & Doug McCarthy / Fire & Pine, Bluffton, South Carolina

www.fireandpine.com— Used by Permission

BARNEGAT LIGHT & INLET CHART

Office of Coast Survey, NOAA Historical Map & Chart Collection; Chart 12324 Folio; Sandy Hook to Little Egg Harbor 1977; historicalcharts.noaa.gov

For Pam, Jessica, Michael, John,
and Samson
More stories that await telling...

Long Beach Island
Beach Haven
Atlantic City
Ocean City
N
NW
NE
W
E
SW
SE
S
Cape May

Barnegat Light & Inlet

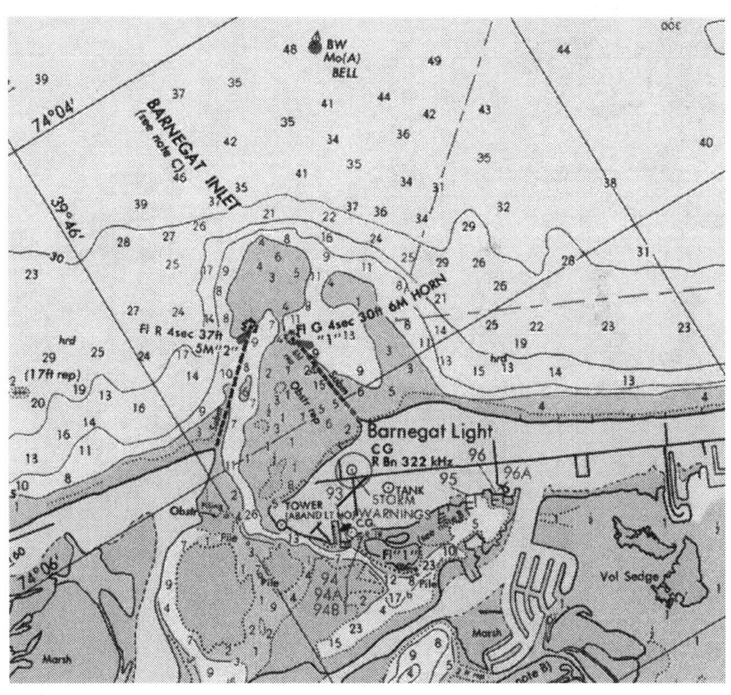

"A friend of the devil
is a friend of mine"

Friend of the Devil
The Grateful Dead
(1970)

ONE

MAY 1978

Steel Pier, Atlantic City

TIMMY MULHOLLAND WAS ONLY eight, but he was a brave eight.

He was demonstrating this fortitude by fiercely resisting every attempt by Grandma Siobhan to hold his sweaty-palmed hand. They were packed tight in the line, only three bodies from the front, waiting to board the World Famous Submarine Diving Bell for its first voyage of the day into the briny depths of the Atlantic Ocean, which lapped menacingly at the pier's massive wooden pilings.

Timmy's mother had made him wait until after the Memorial Day weekend was over. She said the crowds would be smaller then.

She had been mistaken.

There was a salty, sticky breeze blowing, but everyone around Timmy was taller and wider than he was so he got none of the balmy benefits. Making matters worse, his mother had insisted he wear his "nice" clothes because Atlantic City and its aging boardwalk were, in her mind, fancy places where celebrities visited and mingled. She told him to keep an eye out in case Frankie Avalon or Bobby Rydell were strolling the boards and to try to get her an autograph. She even made him take a new Bic pen, which was lodged uncomfortably in the right side pocket of his Montgomery Ward shorts. The collared shirt she'd bought to go with them, now soaked-through at both armpits, did not have a breast pocket.

Timothy Michael Mulholland looked down at his Buster Brown school shoes and dress socks and decided he was the only living boy in Atlantic City not wearing sneakers or flip-flops. At least he'd steadfastly refused to wear the dorky sun hat she'd bought to keep deadly solar rays from touching his pale and freckled face.

"All Mulhollands are redheads," she'd reminded him. "We don't tan, Timmy boy. We just burn." A Coppertone kid, Timmy knew, he was not.

A little ripple went through the crowd as a lanky teenager skirted the edge of the line and made his way toward the boarding platform. Timmy's legs shook in anticipation.

"I think we'll be getting on soon," his grandmother said, again reaching for his hand. Timmy jammed his fingers in his left pocket and stepped forward a little.

"Going aboard, you mean," Timmy corrected her. One of the books he'd studied was on naval jargon.

The large man in front of him reached down to pick something up, giving Timmy his first real glimpse of the Submarine Diving Bell. Rather than the sleek vessel of his imagination, he saw, with some measure of disappointment, something that looked more like a popped tin can with a ring of round porthole windows around the top. They looked so high up that he wondered how he'd be able to see out of any of them. If his grandmother had to pick him up, he was certain he would just croak from embarrassment. He hoped they had stools or benches inside it.

A scratchy voice came out of a loudspeaker somewhere overhead. Timmy couldn't understand any of what was said but then the line began to move. Batting away several more grandmotherly hand-grasps, he pushed forward up a small wooden riser and then stepped into the submersible bell, primed and ready for his deep-sea adventure.

Beck Barton watched the suckers cram themselves into "the can," as he called it, counting heads using a silver clicker he kept looped to his belt. He'd been working amusement rides on the Steel Pier since he was twelve, in violation of several child labor laws and even more workplace safety statutes. But he was eighteen now, old enough to drink legally in any Jersey Shore dive bar from Manasquan to Cape May. A few of the patrons were pretty fat, so he stopped the line two patrons shy of the usual twelve-person capacity. He enjoyed wielding a little power. Not like his days at the Duck Pond or, worse, at The Scrambler, where he'd had to mop up fresh puke at least ten times a day. No one ever heaved on the can. They maybe got a little panicky or claustrophobic, but it didn't sway enough to make anyone seasick.

He'd only had to surface it emergently once in the three years he'd been working it, when a pregnant lady freaked out and screamed she was having the baby while it was still submerged. Most riders didn't realize the mechanism in the round tower above didn't lower the Bell. Instead, it powerfully pushed it down to the not exactly deep-sea depth of eighteen feet, well below the undulating surface and the blue-green swells. When this downward force was suddenly released, the can's natural buoyancy shot it to the surface in less than five seconds. He had to admit it was quite a sight. People definitely got their one dollar's worth of excitement.

Beck swung the watertight door on its spring-balanced hinge, turned the large red locking wheel with both hands, and then hopped back on his stool. He picked up the microphone and started his spiel, assuring the passengers of their safety and the rules against smoking and encouraging them to shout out "messages from the deep" to their friends and loved ones waiting topside on the creaking boards. He checked the few simple gauges in front of him and flipped a toggle switch which sent the powerful hydraulics above him into groaning motion.

This was the Submarine Diving Bell's fiftieth summer and, if what he'd heard whispered was right, quite possibly its last. The Steel Pier had been bought by new owners, and rumor was that sweeping renovations were being planned. The word "cutbacks" was used a lot, and apparently, the new owners were nitpicking the profitability of each and every amusement on the pier, along with their potential liability. The tattoo guy said he'd definitely get the boot, and Bart figured that if the Bell went, the Diving Horse and probably the high-ladder platform divers would be gone along with it. About once a week, he could hear protestors shouting things about animal cruelty whenever one of the horses mounted the elevated chute. And the guys who returned each summer to swan dive from the dizzying heights weren't getting any younger.

The volume of excited voices rose as the bell descended. Bart had learned to tune most of it out. He looked down at the churning green water and the curtain of bubbles that rose as the bell's dome disappeared. He wondered how he would feel when he sent it down for its final descent and where it would go afterward. He hoped it wasn't the scrap yard.

Each trip lasted for exactly seven minutes, at which point the mechanism was supposed to release automatically. A little analog chronometer was ticking off the time. Beck's dad had served on submarines during the Second World War. He'd told the boy that seven minutes underwater was an eternity and that when the *USS Thresher* sank in sixty-three, those guys probably endured seven minutes of knowing they were about to die horribly as the sub sank to crush depth and then imploded. Beck stopped riding the bell himself because of that story.

He peeked at the timer again. When it reached six minutes, he would get back on the horn and warn the passengers to brace themselves for the rapid ascent. This advisory was always accompanied by squeals and screams, but he'd learned to tune those out as well. Beck Barton listened as the whirring stopped and the Bell reached its maximum plunge depth. He knew he would submerge and surface the can nineteen, maybe twenty more times before his shift was over.

He was bored already.

Bruxelles Bombay Hotel & Casino
Boardwalk, Atlantic City, NJ

Mickey Cleary patted her hip for the gun she wasn't wearing.

Having left the state trooper's life behind for that of a detective, she now had actual days off during which she was not required to carry her official or any personal sidearm. Her holster and badge, however, remained on her belt.

It was an old habit. She was doing better but she couldn't seem to shake it. Especially when she was someplace unfamiliar. And Benny Bruxelles' garishly opulent monument to himself and the ever-malleable Garden State politicos who'd made it a reality was definitely unfamiliar territory.

At the moment, Mickey was lost, having made one turn too many in the labyrinth of deeply carpeted hallways. The casino had been open for only a few days, but it already smelled like the bottom of a bus depot ashtray. Several turns back, the casino gaming floor had almost overwhelmed her with its constant and cacophonous din, its crush of humanity, and its omnipresent haze of cigarette and cigar smoke.

Mickey had never been to Las Vegas, but in her mind, it was all glitz, glamour, guiltless sin, and movie stars. What she'd seen so far was a far cry from any of that. A dress code seemed non-existent and the local gamblers' daytime uniform seemed to be either housecoats or bathrobes for women and sleeveless t-shirts with cutoff blue jeans for male patrons. The wafting blue tobacco smoke was locked in fierce competition with the pungent aroma of body odor up and down the narrow, serpentine rows of slot machines, blackjack and craps tables, and clattering roulette wheels she'd negotiated.

Mickey had caught glimpses of what she thought might be some high-roller tables behind red velvet ropes. But so far, she had not spied a single black tuxedo, white dinner jacket, or an evening gown with a plunging neckline anywhere. Even the cocktail waitresses and the cashiers seemed sadly beleaguered, as if they realized that this was not the glamorous jet-set crowd they'd signed up to serve. The new casino industry was being hailed as nothing less than a savior to Atlantic City's desperately depressed economy. So far, Mickey wasn't buying it.

The noise level was receding, as was the level of ambient illumination. Turning yet another dark corner, she saw a light emanating from what looked like it might be an alcove up ahead. She headed for it. As she approached, Mickey was surprised to see that it was actually a small lounge. Empty red leather booths lined the walls, and a polished marble bar jutted from the darkness. On every mirrored and backlit shelf, there were sparkling bottles and decanters. The varying colors of the spirits and liqueurs residing within caught and refracted the upturned lights like dozens of competing prisms. Now *this*, Mickey thought, this felt a little more like Las Vegas.

Drawing closer, she saw only two patrons seated at the bar. One had his back toward her, and the other was concealed in a shadow. A sole bartender seemed to be keeping a respectful distance at the far end near a glimmering gold cash register. Mickey stepped across the lounge's threshold, noting that the carpeting gave way to a sprawling Oriental rug laid over pink marble tiles.

She was two steps inside when four shapes rose from the darkened recesses of the booths and moved toward her. Instinctively, she went to her hip. She saw that the four shapes—burly men in dark suits, she realized—all did the same. Mickey raised her hands.

"Hey, hey, easy now boys," Mickey said in as calm a voice as she could. "Just asking directions."

"Private party," one of the men said in an accent that sounded Italian. "I'm afraid you need to le-"

"It's OK," a strangely familiar voice from the bar called. "She's a friend. A very good friend, I might add. Carlo, you and the boys get back in your cages."

The familiar voice leaned out from the shadow.

"So, like the song goes, what's a nice girl like you doing in a place like this?"

Jim Frichionne rose from his barstool and extended his arms.

For a moment, Mickey was too dumbfounded to speak. The other man at the bar, seemingly unperturbed by her arrival, tilted his head slightly but did not turn around.

"Jimmy the Fixer," Mickey finally said. "Of all the gin joints in all the towns in all the world."

"You walk into *mine*," Frichionne shot back, completing the famous Humphrey Bogart line from *Casablanca*.

"Yours?" Mickey asked.

"Ah, you know me," Frichionne said. "I'm always somebody's silent partner. This little spot is one of my better perks. An oasis in the desert, if you will—far from the madding, not to mention the aromatic crowd." He grasped her hands. "How you doin', kid? Have a seat. I'd like to introduce you to someone."

The man on the barstool sipped his drink and then turned slowly toward her.

Mickey was about to utter a practiced greeting when, as her old friend Father Feeney used to say, she was struck as dumb as Zechariah in the presence of the Angel Gabriel.

"Nice to meet you," the man said with a transfixing smile. "I'm Francis Albert. You can call me Frank."

TWO

The Diving Bell
Steel Pier, Atlantic City, NJ

THE SIX VERTICAL STEEL poles inside the diving bell had small circular platforms, each one wide enough for a child to stand on. Timothy Mulholland had quickly escaped his grandmother's grasp and alertly scampered up onto one as soon as he'd boarded. This put him at eye level with one of twelve circular portholes. Two teenage girls were in front of him, close to the bell's outer wall, but he was able to squeeze his head between their shoulders for an unobstructed, if somewhat uncomfortable, view of the briny deep. They both smelled really good, he noticed.

At first, all there was to see was murky water and swirling sand. As the bell went lower, Timmy could start to make out the giant wooden pilings that held up the supposedly all-steel pier. They were covered in a greenish slime with what he guessed were barnacles. The young lady librarian in Surf City had shown him three books to check out in preparation for his own voyage to the bottom of the sea. He was hoping he'd spot a shark or maybe an octopus, but so far, all he'd caught sight of was a blowfish paddling by. Flounder lay flat on the bottom, he knew from reading, but the weird, reddish sea robins or some swimming crabs might make an appearance.

The two young girls hardly glanced out the portholes, which annoyed Timmy to no end. They were too busy talking about some boy named Lance who had tried to feel up both of them on a school trip to Willow Grove Amusement Park. Timmy didn't know what feel up meant, and he couldn't really tell if they were happy or mad about it. Either way, their chattering was interfering with his undersea experience. He leaned in a little more. That's when he saw it. It was only a flash but he definitely saw something slip by the little round window. And he was pretty sure he knew what it was.

Timmy pulled his head back and pushed around the shorter girl's outer shoulder for a better look.

"Hey, squirt," she said with a snap of her gum, "Do you mind?"

"I want to see," Timmy said. "There's somebody out there. I saw him. I did."

The girl inched closer to her friend. "Okay, right, but don't, like, drool on me or do anything gross or disgusting," she said. Timmy stretched his freckled neck as far as he could.

He saw it again.

"Hey! Look! It's a skin diver!" Timmy shouted. "Or maybe a deep sea diver. Look! He's waving! Wow, this is so cool!"

A leg drifted across the porthole. The two girls stopped talking about getting felt up and edged closer to the little window. Other passengers crowded toward the remaining ones, causing the bell to shudder slightly.

"Oh, I see him, too!" a woman yelled. "He's right outside."

"I don't think he's a skin diver," a man's voice somewhere behind Timmy said.

A face floated in the window right in front of Timmy. But it wasn't a friendly face, and it wasn't wearing a mask or a helmet. It was all swollen, and it looked like maybe one eye was sticking out.

Whatever Timmy Mulholland wanted to say was stuck deep down in his throat, and it refused to come out.

The girls in front of him had no such problem. Their piercing screams echoed so loudly in the enclosed metal space that it made Timmy's ears ache. The yell that was trapped in his own throat finally found its way to his lips as the distorted face pushed hard up against the porthole glass, the pressure of the surrounding current making it even more grotesque in appearance.

His and the girls' screams were part of a deafening chorus as the remaining passengers caught glimpses of the floating specter. Timmy felt the bell teeter as shock and panic spread within its sealed confines. He looked around for his grandmother but couldn't spy her. He was fully convinced that they were headed straight for the ocean floor like the sailors on a doomed submarine his cousin had told him about. Timmy closed his eyes tightly and clasped the St. Christopher's medal his mother had insisted he wear on such a dangerous adventure.

There was now so much noise and commotion that he couldn't tell if he was still screaming.

Beck Barton's eyes and attention quickly wandered to the girl wearing the tube top and hot pants in the next boarding group. They were only at the four-minute mark of the dive when he'd last checked, but he noticed that the expressions on the faces of the patrons waiting on the pier had suddenly changed. He was used to shouts, screams, and even occasional profanity from the bell's riders, but that usually didn't occur until the ascent.

Something was different this time. He cocked an ear in the direction of the loudspeaker. The sounds were definitely not the excited or scared chirpings of happy patrons. These were the sounds of people who were genuinely terrified.

His immediate thoughts were that water had leaked into the can or someone had suffered some sort of emergency, like a heart attack. But the screaming was getting louder. It sounded almost incoherent. Beck had never heard anything quite like it before.

The World Famous Submarine Diving Bell's maximum plunge depth was so shallow that the surrounding water pressure wouldn't dent an empty aluminum soda can. And the Bell, Beck knew, wasn't actually fifty years old. Only the attraction was. The original Bell, built by a welder named Edward Martine in the late twenties, had been damaged and repaired in 1944. But then it was lost at sea in the Ash Wednesday Storm of 1962. This Diving Bell wasn't even as old as he was.

It didn't have any fancy sensors or alarms inside that could read pressure to tell him if there was water leaking in or air leaking out. So Beck did the only thing he knew. The only thing his meager training had taught him to do. He tilted back the plastic cover over the red Emergency button and hit it as hard as he could with the bottom of his closed fist.

There was a decompressive hiss as the hydraulic latches released. Beck jumped off his stool and moved to the edge of the enclosed square of seawater.

The Bell popped to the surface with a shudder. It bobbed several times and then leveled itself in a boiling circle of seawater. The passengers were banging madly on the walls of the steel capsule. As the vessel very slowly rose back to its launching position, he beheld a sight that would haunt him until he was an old man. Tangled in the rubber air and electrical conduit hose beside the main center support was a body, hanging upside down with its head dangling over one of the portholes.

The banging on the cylinder's hull from inside grew louder and more frantic.

For an instant, Beck found himself unable to move or even breathe. The crowd on the pier was roaring as well. The massive boards shook under his feet and a wall of noise completely surrounded him. Almost in a trance, he moved to the gangplank and turned the locking wheel clockwise. As the door creaked open, the trapped riders began forcefully pushing out, the heavy door nearly knocking him into the still-bubbling seawater below.

As they rushed by him, Beck Barton realized something.

He was screaming as well.

THREE

Bruxelles Bombay Hotel & Casino

FRANCIS ALBERT WASN'T SIMPLY dazzling, Mickey realized. He was positively mesmerizing.

It was more than the sky-blue eyes and the velvet voice. He spoke to her as if he'd known her for years. She grasped what the term star-struck meant.

"If I were your husband," Sinatra said, "I don't think I'd wander too far away from you, honey. What's that Buffet kid's song? Something about fins and bait?"

Mickey glanced down at the bar. A tiny puddle of condensation caught the light from the bulbs overhead, splitting it into a quivering rainbow.

"It's my late husband, I'm afraid," Mickey said. "But I'm sure he's keeping watch over me as we speak."

Sinatra grimaced. "I'm sorry, doll. Not the damn war, I hope. You know, Jack once told me he got bullied into that one – the price he paid for youth, I guess. He said with our government, you can never be sure who's really pulling the strings."

It took Mickey a second to process that the "Jack" Sinatra was referring to was the late and beloved president, John F. Kennedy.

"Or the trigger, I guess," Mickey blurted out and then wished she hadn't.

Sinatra sipped his drink. "Or the trigger. It's a damn dirty world," he said, staring straight ahead. "Did he make it home? Your husband?"

"Oh, yeah," Mickey said. "He made it home. I met him after he got back, actually. But it, the war, it never went away. At least not for him."

"Please don't say he - "

"No," Mickey said. "He didn't, but several guys he served with did. No, it was more like Agent Orange reached out and grabbed him ten years later. Have you ever heard of Agent Orange?"

"The weed killer," Jimmy the Fixer interjected. "Jesus, Francis, they sprayed that shit on the whole freakin' jungle over there. Buckets of it."

Sinatra shook his head. "I'm sorry, kid. You have little ones?"

Mickey nodded. "Two. A precocious little girl. Six going on sixteen. And my son, smack dab in the middle of the Terrible Two's. Every day is an adventure."

Sinatra smiled.

"My darling daughter," Mickey continued, "puts on her daddy's combat boots and sings along to your daughter Nancy's record. I mean, she belts it right out there. It's quite a sight."

"I'll bet," Sinatra said. "You know, Lee Hazelwood wrote that song for her based on a line I had in a movie, *Four for Texas*. Except the original line I said was, 'These boots *weren't* made for walking.'"

"So, did the State Police give you the day off?" Jimmy the Fixer asked Mickey.

Sinatra's face registered surprise. "You're a cop?"

"Actually," Mickey answered, "I'm a detective. And I'm no longer with the New Jersey State Police. Something my friend Jimmy here knows very well."

"Right. And I forgot to mention, Francis, she also can't hold a job," Jimmy said with a grin. "So, can we buy you a drink, *Detective* Cleary?" He waved the bartender over. "On the house."

"We're in a casino," Mickey shot back. "That means the house always wins, right."

"*Usually* wins," Jimmy corrected.

"*Always* wins," Sinatra said. He swirled his drink.

The bartender came over. Mickey thought he looked familiar. Another joint at another time, maybe. His name tag said "Lloyd."

"What can I pour you, miss?" Lloyd asked.

"I'll have what Mr. Sinatra's having," Mickey told him. "Say, Lloyd, didn't you used to pour drinks at Mae's Tavern over in Seabreeze? It would be a few years back. Three, four, maybe?" He didn't appear a day older if it was the same person.

"Oh, I've poured a great many drinks at a great many establishments, miss. And for a very long time," Lloyd said. "Bartenders tend to be, shall we say, overlooked, and each one seems very much like every other one, I'm afraid. One Rusty Nail, coming right up." He pointed at Sinatra's glass. "Another for you, Mr. Sinatra?"

The singer nodded.

Mickey noticed that Lloyd hadn't answered her question but decided she'd let it go. She looked at Jimmy.

"Don't ask me," Jimmy said. "Benny says it's like he appeared behind the bar when the lights came on. They're still trying to track down who hired him and his paperwork. Union regs, you know?"

The cocktails appeared. Lloyd retreated to the shadowy end of the bar.

"Have you ever met Mr. Bruxelles, Detective?" Sinatra asked.

Mickey looked at the light amber liquid in her glass. A perfect spiral of lemon rind draped over the side. She took a tentative sip and answered.

"Not in any official capacity, if that's what you mean," Mickey said. "But let's say I'm quite familiar with him. Can't tell the players without a scorecard, as they say at the ballpark."

She licked her lips and continued.

"German mother, from *Niedersachsen* - Lower Saxony. It's like one of our states. She's the one who named him Benno—Belgian father, supposedly a distant relative of King Leopold. Benny Bruxelles grew up with more money than God, although the source of it is a mystery. He fancies himself a real estate tycoon, but he seems to be constantly teetering on the brink of bankruptcy, at least according to the newspapers. How he ever managed to snag the first gaming license from the New Jersey Casino Control Commission is beyond me. I'm guessing it was because his name didn't end in a vowel." She winked at Sinatra. "Mmmm. This is good. Doesn't taste like either rust or nails. What's in it?"

"From what I hear about the Commission, that's probably truer than you think," Sinatra replied with a broad grin. "And as far as the booze goes, it's Drambuie liqueur with some excellent and very old Scotch. I started drinking these at P.J. Clarke's club in New York City."

Mickey took a longer sip. The single ice cube, which was large and perfectly square on every side, lightly kissed her lips.

"So," Sinatra continued, "I'm guessing you're not here on business. I mean, you're not actively detecting anything presently, I presume. And that our meeting is purely by chance."

"Well, again, we are in a gambling casino," Mickey said. "Doesn't everything here happen strictly by chance?"

Sinatra chuckled. "Dollface, take it from me. Chance is just an illusion. Never believe it's anything else. And luck, despite composer Frank Loesser's contention, ain't no lady." He put his glass to his mouth and drained half the drink. "And what does my old neighborhood friend James here mean by suggesting you can't hold a job?"

"First, I'm not here on any police business," Mickey said. "As to my employment history, I started as a beat cop in North Philly. I saw some very bad stuff and took a year off out west. Then I decided to come back, and I became a beach cop over in Surf City. That was the summer of '67."

"Correction," Jimmy chimed in. "She was the Chief of Police in Surf City, the first woman police chief in New Jersey."

"Old news," Mickey went on. "Anyway, I did that for a few years. Then, I enrolled at the State Police Academy in Sea Girt. Not the very first woman there, but one of them. Spent a couple of years as a Road Trooper. But when Ronnie, who was my husband, died, I knew I needed something where I could stay closer to the kids. I loved being a trooper. I really did. And I was good at it. But riding the Jersey Turnpike, pulling over heavily armed drug runners with broken tail lights and tinted windows wasn't going to be the answer. I'm less likely to get shot on Long Beach Island. Drown, maybe, since I'm not a great swimmer. But not shot."

Mickey paused and swirled her drink. The huge ice cube had melted to half its original size but had retained its symmetry.

"But, gotta keep working," she continued with a shrug. "Ronnie's military pension and what he gets from the New Jersey Forest Fire Service help, but it isn't enough with two little ones who go through clothes the way we go through Kleenex. You used to be able to live on Long Beach Island for a song. Not anymore. The big money out-of-towners and the real estate barracudas have discovered it. And with Atlantic City and legalized gambling a dice throw down the road, you can do the arithmetic. Our property taxes alone have gone through the roof."

"You were a State Trooper?" Sinatra asked, seeming surprised. "I'm impressed. One thing James and I learned as kids growing up in North Jersey is that you do *not* mess with a New Jersey State Trooper."

"No, sir, Mr. Sinatra, you most certainly do not," Mickey agreed. "It was great training and even greater experience. A little hair-raising at times, for sure, but I can't imagine a situation that I couldn't handle. I was sad to leave, but the little towns and boroughs on LBI all got together and offered me the job of being a detective working alongside their PDs. I already know the territory, and I certainly know the players. I couldn't turn it down. Better money, and I get time off now and then to come check out fun places like this."

Sinatra looked around and shook his glass. "It ain't exactly Vegas, is it?"

"You tell me," Mickey replied. "Never been there. I thought about stopping on my drive out to California. But I didn't."

"Trust me, babe. This isn't Vegas," Sinatra said. "And it never will be. Las Vegas is isolated, mysterious, way out there in the desert. That's the real key to its success. It has a sense of separation, which is a big part of its allure. Not everyone can get there. And if it happens in the desert, well, then it often stays in the desert. Sometimes, it literally *stays* in the desert."

Sinatra cocked an eyebrow.

"So, you're saying no charter buses packed with senior citizens in bathrobes and hair curlers toting buckets of nickels like I saw on my way in?" Mickey asked.

"Gamblers are an economically diverse crowd by nature," Sinatra continued. "Most of them are losing money they don't have. But enough of them have so much money that they keep the casinos churning. Add a tux or a sexy gown, flash a fat roll of C-Notes, throw in a comped suite and liquor, and the A-Listers will show up—for a while, anyway."

He set down his glass.

"Oh, don't get me wrong. It'll be fun here for a while," Sinatra said. "I kinda get a kick out of it. It's like my whole life story in one place. Out front, it's the Jersey Shore, which I loved as a kid. Inside, it's Las Vegas. One block out the back door, it's Hoboken. And not the nice part of Hoboken, either. Once the novelty wears off, though, I guess we'll have to see how long it takes for that to happen."

"So, are you performing here?" Mickey asked.

Jimmy the Fixer coughed at the question.

"That, my dear, remains to be seen," Sinatra answered and shot Jimmy a glance. "I've got a gig coming up at the A.C. Convention Center. I don't owe this *yutz* Benny any favors. So, like I said, we'll have to see. I can do more for him and his casino than he can ever do for me. My lifelong friend James and I were discussing the subject when you wandered in."

The singer finished his drink.

"I'm sorry about your husband, kid. I am. Jack would have gotten us out of that crazy Asian war if he'd lived long enough." Sinatra seemed lost in thought for a moment. Then he continued. "How about I do a song in your husband's honor at one of my shows? Does he – did he - have a favorite?"

Mickey tried to remind herself that this was the world's most famous and most popular singer, not a WFIL Boss Jock or Casey Kasem, asking her if she had a radio dedication.

"Well, wouldn't that be something?" Mickey said. "When I first met Ronnie, he sang 'How Can I Be Sure?' to me on the beach. He had a beautiful voice, though he always said he was no Felix Cavaliere."

"The Rascals," Sinatra said with a smile. "I like those kids – they're from Garfield. Did you know that? That's only about fifteen minutes north of

Hoboken. And they've done well for themselves. Maybe not as well as Frankie and Tommy DeVito, but a voice like Valli's comes along maybe once in a lifetime. Although, that Carpenter chick might be another one. So pure. I keep askin' Valli how the hell he's going to hit those notes when he's my age. He laughs. Says he'll hire someone to hit them for him."

Sinatra paused and cleared his throat.

"Sure, kid. I'll do it for you. I'll have to run it by Nelson. Nelson Riddle, he's my arranger. But I'm sure he'll go along. And, so that you know, Felix Cavaliere did not sing lead on "How Can I Be Sure." Eddie Brigati, that's whose voice you're hearing. Eddie started out with Joey D and the Starliters. I think they still play down here. Over at The Dunes, maybe. Eddie replaced his brother David. What do they call that style – Blue-Eyed Soul?" Sinatra pointed to one eye. "Sounds like the song for me. I'll let James here know and make sure you have front-row seats and backstage passes. And let me see if I can get Nancy to autograph a picture for your little girl. What's her name?"

"Eileen," Mickey answered. Sinatra drew a sleek silver pen from his sports jacket and grabbed a cocktail napkin. Mickey turned to Jimmy the Fixer. "Why, James, I don't think I've seen you this quiet since we met."

Jimmy smiled. "When Francis Albert talks, my dear Detective, people listen."

"I thought that was E.F. Hutton," Mickey responded.

Jimmy arched an eyebrow. "When Francis Albert talks," he said and then paused. "E.F. Hutton listens."

Sinatra jotted something down and tucked the napkin and the pen in the pocket of his jacket.

"Any other requests?" he asked

"My dad, he was a Philly cop. He and my mom loved 'Beyond the Sea.' They would dance to it in what passed for our living room in Northeast Philly. We lived in a row home, so it always seemed like a dream to me to go somewhere on a boat."

"I think that one might already be on the setlist, but I'll make sure," the crooner told her.

"You know," Mickey said, "No one on earth is ever going to believe this conversation happened."

"Then don't tell them," Sinatra replied. "I mean, I won't if you won't." He looked over at the Fixer. "James, old pal, you need to have more friends like this one."

A faint buzzing sound punctuated the statement. Mickey reached for her belt.

"I thought you said you were off-duty," Jimmy remarked.

"I am. But I try not to be out of touch for too long. Probably the babysitter. It's only an answering service. Maybe someday someone will invent a phone you can carry on your hip." Mickey looked around the bar. "I need to find a place to take this."

Jimmy the Fixer put a hand to the side of his head, his thumb and pinky extended in the universal gesture for a telephone. Lloyd glided to their end of the bar and pulled a sleek white Bell Telephone unit from a dark recess underneath its polished marble top. He set it in front of Mickey.

"We promise not to listen," Jimmy said with a wink. Lloyd removed and refilled Sinatra's drink.

Mickey dialed the memorized number, which connected her to a secure exchange. She'd made up the babysitter part. When the operator clicked on, she intoned, "Detective Cleary, Charles-Lincoln-Edward-Adam-Robert-Young, zero-four-two-five-six." She heard a series of faint beeps as the call connected.

Mickey tried to keep her facial expression blank as the person on the other end began speaking. She nodded a few times and murmured some obligatory uh-huh's. Then she signed off with, "I'm not very far away, as it turns out. This isn't anywhere near my jurisdiction, though, so we're clear about that up front." She hung up the receiver and downed her drink.

"Kids OK?" Frichionne asked.

"The kids are alright. Work-related matter," Mickey answered. "Well, gentlemen, it's been a pleasure," Mickey said. "Thank you for the drink and the conversation. Rusty Nail, you said?"

Sinatra nodded. "It was very nice to meet you, Detective Cleary." He tapped his jacket. "I always keep my promises."

"An honor meeting you, Francis Albert," Mickey replied with a smile. "I'm sure you do."

"Hey," Frichionne protested. "What am I here? Chopped liver?"

Mickey touched him on the shoulder. "Ah, Jimmy. Maybe not caviar, but definitely not chopped liver," she said. "And somehow, I'm sure I'll be seeing you again." She turned to Sinatra.

"Do you remember a gentleman named Hyman Levine?"

Sinatra looked surprised. "Hyman? Yeah. Sure I do—the Cardozo Hotel in Miami Beach. We shot a movie there a long, long time ago. Nice man. Good-looking kids. Gorgeous wife."

"He built a new hotel on Long Beach Island. We're friends. Is it OK if I mention we met?"

"Sure. And tell him I send warmest regards," Sinatra said. "You know something, Detective Cleary? You get more interesting all the time."

"You can call me Mickey."

"Mickey Cleary," Sinatra said. "Mickey Cleary. You know? That's a good name for a detective. Maybe not as good as Tony Rome, mind you. But still pretty damn good. I have a friend who's a movie producer in L.A. He's off mountain climbing in Nepal right now. Annapurna, I think. I'll mention it to Stephen when he gets back."

Mickey's pager buzzed again.

"Jeez. What now, kid?" Sinatra asked. "Somebody heist a sack of hot peanuts over at Planter's?"

"Steel Pier, actually," Mickey answered. "You ever ride the Diving Bell?"

"Once, when I was a kid," Sinatra said, "I couldn't see a thing. It was the worst thirty-five cents I ever spent. And back then, thirty-five cents was a fortune."

"I bet," Mickey said. "But it doesn't sound like that was the case today." She surveyed the dark hallway outside the lounge's entrance and looked at Jimmy. "I didn't think to leave a trail of bread crumbs. Think maybe one of the boys over there could show me the way out?"

"The *bulvans* are required to stay with Francis at all times, I'm afraid," Jimmy answered. "It's a dangerous world."

"That's certainly been my experience," Mickey shot back.

"But, if you don't mind slipping discreetly out a side door, I'll gladly show you the way." Jimmy rose from his barstool and took her arm.

"See you at the show," Mickey called to Sinatra over her shoulder.

"Yeah? How can I be sure?" Sinatra replied with a grin.

Jimmy the Fixer whisked her away before she had time to answer.

FOUR

The Ozymandias Suite

Top Floor, Bruxelles Bombay Hotel and Casino

OF ALL THE FEATURES he'd chosen personally, the windows were his favorite.

Benno Wilhelm Bruxelles sat with his back to his desk and beheld the vista below and beyond, stretching east to the horizon. Given a powerful enough lens, he mused, he could see all the way to Western Europe, the land of conquerors, the land of his heritage.

The continuous slab of optical quality plate glass had been manufactured by Bendheim in New York City. He'd chosen the company because it was founded by a German couple from his mother's native village, Margaret and Sem Bendheim. They'd started in a Greenwich Village storefront in 1927, importing and distributing art glass from Europe.

The huge, unbroken mass had been poured, cured, and polished in a single gigantic mold at the company's foundry in Passaic and shipped to the construction site in Atlantic City at a dizzying cost and with nearly insurmountable logistics. Four massive cranes and a Sikorsky Sky Horse helicopter leased from McGuire Air Force Base placed it atop the casino like a crown.

Bruxelles considered himself a man who was and would always remain unbroken. He wanted his view of his empire – his kingdom - to be the same.

He was middle-named after a Kaiser. His cultural roots ran thick and deep with despots and dictators. He understood wealth and the power that accompanied it. He intended to accrue a fortune so vast that he could wield the accompanying power with absolute impunity. Money, he'd learned early on, made you immune to almost everything.

A phone buzzed, but he was so enthralled by the view that he ignored it.

The massive desk behind him was mahogany, a down-to-the-millimeter and scrollwork replica of the Resolute Desk, which sat in the Oval Office at the White House. He had been born on American soil, and even if his allegiances were subject to the whims of foreign flags and influences, he was solidly a citizen, if not necessarily a solid citizen. His birthplace was the first thing his enemies had challenged when he sought the gaming license, going so far as to float a doctored birth certificate from, of all places, Kenya. On the far wall, the largest television screen obtainable was showing a *Star Trek* rerun. James T. Kirk, now there was someone who understood what it meant to run a tight ship.

Although it had been suggested more than once, Benny knew politics wasn't ready for someone like him. Not yet. But he believed there would come a day when his domain would extend to the sea in the opposite direction. He wasn't interested in governing. He wanted to rule. But for now, he could wait, collecting the craven politicians, their sleazy, sycophantic minions, and their opaque moneymen, secretly stacking them like so many markers to be cashed in when he was ready.

Benno Bruxelles reached into his pocket and withdrew the casino chip he'd had minted long before the wrecking ball had demolished the grand old hotel that had graced the boardwalk for decades. When his personal pleasure dome was only a dream and a secret set of architectural blueprints. The chip was solid ivory, smuggled from the dark heart of what had once been the Belgian Congo. He kept it with him at all times, like a talisman—another reminder of his colonial lineage. A mighty jungle elephant had given its life, needlessly perhaps, for the baker's dozen of them he'd had made. But Benno Bruxelles had his sights set on another big game trophy. And it wasn't over in Margate.

The phone buzzed again. Bruxelles swiveled around and depressed the Answer button.

"Mr. Rigger is here, Mr. Bruxelles," a voice with a faint Teutonic edge said. "Wonders if he could have a moment. Feels it's rather important."

Rigger was a ruthless, amoral, pussy-chasing prick. That's precisely why he'd hired him. Who better than someone drummed out of the State Police like Chuck Connors was drummed out of the Army on *Branded*? Someone with a standing grudge against any and all law enforcement agents and agencies? Before the casino had even opened, Benno had enough secretly recorded video of him *schtupping* underage girls, waitresses, and hookers to keep him doing his bidding forever or, if necessary, putting him away for the same period.

"Tell him he may enter," Bruxelles said.

The double wooden doors clicked and buzzed and then opened, whispering over the marble entry tiles.

"Sorry to intrude, Mr. Bruxelles," Jack Rigger said. His head gave a tiny but noticeable bow of supplication. "Eye-in-the-Sky on the casino floor picked up something I'd like you to see. May I?"

Bruxelles nodded. Rigger advanced to a table to his left and cued up an array of video screens. He manipulated a joystick controller to select one, then punched a button at the top of the joystick. The image enlarged. Bruxelles leaned toward it.

"Someone I should know?"

"No," Rigger said. "But she's someone who knows you and more than a bit about you. She's someone I know. Someone who may or may not mean trouble."

Bruxelles' gaze narrowed.

"Where did she go?"

"We never see her anywhere else. We don't even see her leave. There are still a few blind spots – planned accommodations we made for our true VIPs. But she couldn't and shouldn't have had access to those areas. I have the grunts scouring every one of the hourly feeds right now."

"Well, she certainly doesn't look very threatening," Bruxelles said and sat back. "Rather attractive, actually. She moves like a gazelle through that crowd."

Rigger shifted uncomfortably on his feet. He watched the video as it looped, the striding figure covering the same carpeted ground over and over.

"She is, and she does," Rigger said. "But she's cold as a stone and twice as hard. I'll ask you to take my word on that."

Benno Bruxelles chuckled. "Very well. But do try to remember, Mr. Rigger, that *is* the Atlantic Ocean out there," he said with a wave of his hand. "Where a stone of any weight, by its very nature, must eventually sink to the bottom."

Rigger clicked the video screen off and cleared his throat. "Is the gentleman at Ilsa's desk one of our VIP guests? If I may ask?"

"You may not. Ask, that is," Bruxelles replied. "There are certain things and people you need to know and certain ones I need to know. They are not always mutual."

Rigger took the hint and backed out of the room.

Standing outside what he privately referred to as the Throne Room, Rigger glanced sideways at the waiting man.

"Thanks, love," the man said to Ilsa, Benny's private secretary and personal assistant. "I was worried I'd be havin' to stall the ball a fair bit longer than this."

The man rose from his seat, glanced back almost imperceptibly at Rigger, and disappeared inside Bruxelles' office. The doors closed behind him.

Rigger walked the few paces to the private elevator, certain the figure he'd seen on the video was Mickey Cleary. She was still a pebble in his shoe, still a potential threat, still a failed conquest who had not only spurned his advances but had the brass balls to threaten him in the process. She was unfinished business, and Jack Rigger never left business unfinished.

He mused on Bruxelles's words as the gilt-and-glass elevator doors glided open. For a guy who dropped his deuces in a platinum-plated toilet, his boss might just end up being right.

Boardwalk, Atlantic City

The sun was so bright that it hurt Mickey's eyes. She heard the heavy metal door click shut behind her and noticed that there were no handles on the outside.

Mickey fumbled in her shirt pocket for her Wayfarers. She walked toward the sound of the ocean and stood outside the casino's glassy main entrance, almost blinded. Shapes moved gauzily in front of her, but they had little defining detail. It was almost disorienting. Finally, the sunglasses were in her grasp. As she hurried to put them on, a voice called to her from what sounded like not far away.

"Cleary! Jesus, Cleary, is that you, Mickey Cleary? For God's sake, Cleary, I can't believe it."

Her battered Wayfarer frames, with their recently placed bifocal lenses, finally settled on the bridge of her nose.

"Yo, Cleary. You, OK? Did they comp you one too many Mai-Tai's in there, or what?"

Mickey put two fingers to each temple to stop the throbbing. Then, she turned her head to locate the source of the voice.

"Cleary, hey. You havin' a stroke there or what?"

The face that went with the voice slowly came into focus.

"Schassau? Shit, Darwin Schassau, what the hell are you doing out here?" Mickey asked.

"I thought that was you. Been what, two years? Jesus. Mickey fricking Cleary. You sure you're OK?"

When he finally came into focus, Mickey saw that he was in uniform.

"Wait. You're a cop?" she asked him.

"Yeah. Sort of," Darwin Schassau answered. "Head of casino security. Well, technically, Head of Perimeter Security. So, are you slumming or simply trying to supplement that shit State Police retirement fund by playing a little high-stakes poker?"

"Just seeing the sights, Darwin." Mickey considered their checkered history at the State Police academy for a moment. "What are you, I mean, what have you been doing since-"

"Since they let me graduate and then cut me loose, you mean?"

"Yeah, I guess. I never did hear the whole story," Mickey said.

Schassau shuffled his feet. "Well, it wasn't pretty. And I'm sorry about all the grief I caused you when we were classmates. I was a complete turd. But I'm not like that anymore, I'm happy to say. I know that sounds stupid and fake, but it's true. As it turned out, the girl who made all that trouble for me ended up doing me the biggest favor of my life. I heard she married a bartender from The Dunes, and now she runs the makeup counter at Strawbridge and Clothier."

Mickey laughed at the thought of Jacquie DiBenedetto and her unlikely adventure in the Pine Barrens with Mickey's friend, Sister Marian.

"It's Bamberger's, and she's their Head Cosmetics and Fragrance Buyer," Mickey told him. "She has a kid now, drives a Datsun 280-Z, and lives in some ritzy part of Moorestown, last time I heard. Her husband, the bartender, bought a bar in Cherry Hill, spruced it up, and renamed it an Ale House. I guess you can't get a seat at the bar or a table on the weekends. He's raking in a fortune. Go figure, right?"

"Well, good for them, but don't tell her you seen me. You wouldn't know this, but she sent two guys from her neighborhood to, uh, visit me and deliver a message." Schassau lifted his mirrored aviators. He pointed to a scar on his cheek and a small dent in his forehead.

"Looks like it came Special Delivery," Mickey said.

"Yeah, it did. Hand-delivered, you might say. For a minute, I thought they were going to, you know, emacerate me. That got my attention."

Mickey ignored the mangled term, but it did remind her of her first summer as Chief in Surf City and the gruesome genital carving that befell poor Frankie Numbers. She still felt partly responsible for that one.

"Please don't say you found Jesus," Mickey said.

Schassau laughed. "Nah. But I did lose Johnnie Walker. They don't call it demon alcohol for nothing. I heard your husband died," he continued. "I am sorry about that. I would have said something or sent a card, but, you know, I didn't think it would have meant much coming from me."

He seemed so different from the shitbag Mickey remembered. She wasn't sure it was possible, but even if he was faking sincerity, he was faking it exceptionally well.

"How do you like this security gig?" Mickey asked, shifting the conversation away from the past and the personal.

"So far, so good," Schassau said, slipping his aviators back on his face. "You won't believe who the actual Head of Casino Security is, though. Go on. Take a guess."

"No idea," Mickey said. "Bobby Black Fingers Rocca? Some newly-discovered bastard son of Danny Rags or maybe Little Nicky?"

Schassau laughed. "No, not quite. But you remember John Rigger from the State Police academy?"

Mickey had to catch her breath. Shit, did she have a crossways history with *everyone* at the Jersey Shore?

"Rigger Mortis?" she asked.

Schassau laughed again. "The one and the same. And it still fits. Talk about walking around with a perpetual stiffie. I gotta watch what I say on account of him being my boss, but for a guy who stepped in such deep shit, he came up smelling like a dozen roses."

"I heard the SP canned him," Mickey said. "What do they call it now? Sexual harassment? They were pretty tight-lipped about it is all I know."

"I don't ask questions, but I think that was it. Although in the end, I think it came down to witness tampering. The women who were set to testify against him. I'll say that for a guy who likes to dip his wick, he could not have landed in a place with more inkwells than this casino."

Mickey was making quick mental notes. She'd made enemies in her decade on the Island, some still around and still dangerous, but most were relatively easy to keep tabs on or avoid altogether. It bothered her that individuals who had worked hard to discredit her or derail her career were still part of the local mix.

"Well," she said, "Then don't tell him *I* said hi. Don't even tell him you met me. I'll have to remember to wear a disguise if I ever come back here. I never formally reported him, but I'm sure he still holds more than a grudge."

"I can do that for you," Schassau answered. "I owe you that. And more, I know. Hey, that door I saw you come out of only opens out and from a restricted part of the casino. How did you – what were you doing in -"

"I got lost," Mickey lied. "Luckily, a couple of nice fellas in suits and earpieces were happy to show me the way out."

"Yeah, I'm sure they were," Schassau said. "This place has more secret rooms and passageways and more surveillance technology than the friggin' CIA. And I only know about some of it." Mickey watched him look out at the boardwalk and the ocean beyond. "Must be some commotion going on over at the Pier. Any idea what it is?"

"Nope," Mickey lied again. "I was on my way to grab some Planter's Peanuts, some Fralinger's salt water taffy, maybe an Italian Water Ice for myself, and head home to my kids. I'm glad things are better for you now, Darwin. I truly am."

"Remember Thurgood Patterson, the Black guy in our recruit class?" Schassau asked. "He used to say that I wasn't very evolved for a guy named Darwin. I hope I've made at least a little progress since then."

"Seems like you have," Mickey said. "And Patterson, so you know, he's a sergeant on the fast track to being a detective. Anyway, good to see you. And good luck with this casino gig. I still predict Rigger ends up capped in mid-screw by a jealous husband, an enraged father, or an angry pimp. There might be an opening for you to apply for in the future."

Schassau smiled at her. "Well, at least he'll die doing something he loves."

Now it was Mickey's turn to laugh. "Get back to work, Darwin," she said. "The perimeter of this monstrosity isn't going to guard itself."

Mickey turned and walked toward the ocean, glittering green and silver over the salt-sanded boardwalk rails. She paused to let a motorized wicker jitney carrying two white-haired women roll by, then strode toward the bustling entrance to the World Famous Steel Pier. All she'd been told on the phone was that there was a situation that had a direct connection to Surf City, and they would appreciate it if she could check it out.

Two teenage boys jostled her as she shouldered her way into the swelling crowd. As they passed, she heard one of them say the two words she didn't want to hear. The ones that had set the tone for her whole career on the Island. The ones that had almost gotten her killed. She thought of the pure ivory betting chip tucked away in her underwear drawer, wondering if she should have thrown it into the "damned Atlantic Ocean out there" when she had the chance, as her late friend Doc Guidice had strongly advised her.

Despite the simmering heat, a chill ran up Mickey's neck. She mouthed the two words the boys had said under her breath as she hustled along.

"Dead body."

FIVE

The Steel Pier

THROUGH THE CROWD, MICKEY saw what looked to be most of the Atlantic City Police Department herding shocked tourists back through the narrow walkway that led away from the Diving Bell. It didn't look like they were taking any witness statements.

Mickey angled her torso, using her shoulder to cleave the densely packed throng shuffling toward her in the opposite direction.

"Wrong way, sweetheart," a sunburned man in a tie-dyed Grateful Dead tank top yelled at her. Then a hand roughly grabbed her trailing arm by the wrist.

"Turn around, ma'am," a young ACPD officer said. "And I mean right now."

Mickey reached for her empty holster and badge and realized immediately it was a mistake.

"OK. Hands where I can see 'em, now," the young cop said.

She saw him reach for his sidearm. Mickey had a brief flashback to her first deputy, Kalen Fairbrother, who'd drawn his sidearm on a fleeing thirteen-year-old theft suspect in Surf City.

"Easy there, Officer. It's OK. I'm a cop," Mickey shouted to him. "Just getting my badge."

"I said let me see your hands!" he shouted back. "Do not, I repeat, do not move!"

Mickey guessed the number of days since he'd graduated from the police academy might still be in the single digits. His weapon was out, but he hadn't pointed it at her.

Yet.

"OK, OK, OK," Mickey said, raising her hands to shoulder level. "But please, put your weapon back in your holster before something bad happens here."

The young man's face flushed crimson. "You, you...you do not tell me what to do. Now get on the ground!"

Mickey raised her hands a little higher. She was not getting on the ground.

"I said down. Now!"

His voice was quivering and an audible pitch higher. The tight crowd around her had separated and become very quiet. What had she said to Sinatra about her chances of getting shot?

"Stand down, Officer Lamb," a male voice said sharply. "Unless you want your picture on the front page of *The Press* for shooting one of local law enforcement's living legends."

The young cop looked confused but shakily did as he was ordered.

"Get back to your post now." For the third time in an hour, the voice belonged to someone she knew.

"Thanks, Rich," Mickey said. "I mean, thank you, Captain Rodriguez."

"Jesus, Mick," Rich Rodriguez asked. "Was I that jumpy when I came to work for you?"

Mickey shook her head and extended her hand.

"You seriously left a cushy gig at Rehoboth Beach for this craziness?"

Rodriguez grabbed her forearm with both hands and squeezed affectionately.

"Yeah. That sounds silly, I know, but I did a lot of security detail work for the junior senator from Delaware. Mr. Biden. Nice guy. Loved the beach. Lost his family in a car accident shopping for a Christmas tree five or six years ago. He commutes from home to D.C. every day on Amtrak. It got to be all I did was ride the Metroliner between Wilmington and Union Station and make small talk with the Capitol Police and the Secret Service guys. I realized I needed more scumbags and lowlifes in my day. I have to say, A.C. certainly has a bumper crop of both now. I did briefly consider applying to the Capitol Police. Now that's a cushy gig. It's not like anyone's going to storm the Capitol, right?"

Mickey laughed. "And here you are. Can I assume I have you personally to thank for pulling me into whatever mess this is sure to be?" She waved at the crowd of uniforms surrounding the Diving Bell. "I didn't realize that I was the - what was the message again? The direct connection to Surf City."

"Yeah, well, you know. We never talk anymore," Rodriguez answered with a smile. "It was as good an excuse as any, I figured."

"I do hope you're kidding," Mickey said. Rodriguez hooked her arm. The murmuring crowd parted as he led her toward the enclosed square of the green ocean. "I'm a long way from home, Rich. Maybe not in miles, but certainly in jurisdiction."

Mickey remembered when Rodriguez told her he was leaving Surf City for Delaware. She knew it was a good career move, and she'd wished him well. But she recalled feeling like someone had sawed off one of the legs of her chair when he was gone. He'd been a rock for her back then. If he needed something, she'd try to deliver.

"How are Colombia and the kids?" she asked.

"Good. Real good," Rodriguez said as they neared the narrow entrance to the World Famous Submarine Diving Bell. "Teenagers are so much worse than rugrats. Hey, I heard Bu-"

A middle-aged officer approached them, cutting short the pleasantries.

"Dive team's almost finished, Captain," he said. Mickey figured him for a sergeant.

"Dive team?" Mickey asked.

Rodriguez adjusted his hat. "Yup. Easier when they wash up on the beach, right?" He winked at Mickey.

"Yeah, right," Mickey answered. "You're certainly asking that question to the wrong person."

"Ah, you did real good on that one, Mick," Rodriguez countered. "And it ended up paving the way for everything else you've accomplished, like hitting a homer in your first big league at-bat."

"Yeah, if you just ignore the getting kidnapped and almost raped and murdered while rounding third part," Mickey shot back. "ACPD has a dive team?"

"Nah," Rodriguez said. "But the FD Rescue Squad does. The Diving Bell is technically, kind of, sort of, offshore, so that's who I called. I guess the NJSP has one too now, but they weren't as close and -"

"And," Mickey interrupted, "They would have caught the case, not you." It was her turn to wink.

"My decision was purely a matter of logistics, manpower, and proximity, Detective Cleary," Rodriguez answered. "I leave any police politics to my superiors."

"They're not going to be too happy about this up in Trenton, Rich," Mickey said. "The new Commander is a hard-ass. Worse, he's a hard-ass with major political ambitions."

"Detective," Rodriguez said. "Everybody around here has political ambitions. I'm sure the guy who runs the Ferris Wheel has political ambitions. And see? This is another good reason to have you on board. You left the State Police on good terms—I might need some of that goodwill depending on what this turns out to be."

"I think *you* already think it's going to be something."

Rodriguez did not reply.

They finally arrived at the planked gangway that led to the Bell. Mickey watched as three men in wetsuits awkwardly struggled with a nearly naked male corpse, almost dropping it twice. They laid it on top of a black, unzipped body bag. Peering over the wooden railing, Mickey spied another diver in the water around the Bell, a circular curtain of bubbles surrounding him.

"Wow. Looks like an episode of *Sea Hunt*," Mickey cracked.

"Yeah, I liked that show," Rodriguez said, "even if it was in black and white. Although it did seem like Mike Nelson either got his air hose cut or somebody shot a spear gun at him every week."

Rodriguez led Mickey around to where the dripping body now lay. They crouched simultaneously for a closer look. The three divers crowded around them, their wetsuits dripping on the salt-stained boards. From the corner of her eye, Mickey saw the fourth diver clambering sideways up a rusty ladder that appeared tenuously attached to a piling. His single scuba tank clanged against it as he did.

Neither Mickey nor Rodriguez spoke for several minutes. Occasionally, they exchanged glances. Their unwritten rule, stretching back to Mickey's days as chief in Surf City, was not to discuss their impressions in front of other law enforcement personnel. Each had learned the hard way that whatever they said would be on the wire within the hour.

"Fellas, can you tilt him up so we can check out the B-Side?" Mickey asked.

Two of the dive team members did as she requested, pelting her neck with droplets of cold seawater. Mickey wiped them away and said nothing.

"OK. That's good," she told them after exchanging a confirmatory look with Rodriguez.

"Atlantic County Medical Examiner's office has been notified," a heavyset diver said. "They said they'll try and find someone to send out, but it could be a while. Bag it and tag it for now?"

"Yes. Show the uniforms how to do it," Rodriguez replied. "With the casino open, I'm sure they could use the practice."

He and Mickey stood up, Rodriguez giving a little grunt in the process.

"Come on, old man," Mickey clucked. "Walk me to your squad car. I'm assuming you saw what I saw."

"Yes, I did," Rodriguez answered. "I saw it when I first arrived on the scene. That's why I bothered you. Do you still have any cred with those boys?"

Mickey noticed that the Diving Bell crowd of onlookers had been almost completely dispersed. Bright yellow Crime Scene tape snapped and fluttered in the freshening offshore breeze.

"Not like I did," Mickey said. "If I needed a sit-down, I'd take an escort these days."

"Haystacks and the LT, maybe?

Mickey nodded. "Yeah. Probably both. Maybe Filisky and Garufi, as well. I heard they're bouncers at a strip club somewhere around here now. They might still have the cred. And the history. But the Sons of Satan aren't a rogue's gallery of disaffected Vietnam vets anymore. The entrance exam now requires a prison stint - a nickel at a minimum unless it's a violent crime. Then you can get in with a trey. The club officers all have manslaughter raps or worse except, I think, the new president and one of the old Vietnam vets. But they're running their game inside the walls and out now. Rahway and Yardville are the hotspots, but they're itching for that new prison to open in Bridgeton. It's right in their backyards, so you know that'll be their new inside-the-wire command center—and minor league feeder system. Triple-A baseball for criminals.

"For the SP," Mickey continued, "they were, and I assume they still are, Public Enemy Number One—and vice versa. And they might have access to better artillery. What about A.C.'s detectives? Don't step on too many toes here at once, Rich."

"Ah, I'll let them wet their beaks a little. But I'm not letting them in on our little arrangement." Rodriguez paused. "I'm looping you in as a consultant, not as an active investigator."

"Oh. So, we have an arrangement now?" Mickey said, chuckling at *The Godfather* line.

They crossed the bustling Boardwalk, dodging bicycles, strollers, and the occasional moped, which was technically forbidden. Rodriguez slowed to let Mickey go down the railed wooden ramp leading to the terminus of South Pennsylvania Avenue. His ACPD unit was parked less than twenty feet away. The asphalt appeared ready to melt.

"I hope you locked it," Mickey said as she walked to the passenger side. "This isn't Surf City." Rodriguez held up his keys.

He unlocked his door, hopped in, and started the engine. Mickey heard the other door lock pop and opened her side. A blast of hot air shot out. Rodriguez got back out and leaned on the squad car's white roof. Mickey did the same from her side. They were more or less alone for the moment, so Rodriguez continued their conversation behind the light bar.

"What did you make of the tattoos?" he asked Mickey.

"One definitely suggests Sons of Satan," she answered. "But it wasn't the full patch. So, not a member. A Prospect, maybe? And the others were kind of faded, did you notice?"

"Yeah, but wouldn't a day or two marinating in the briny deep do that?" Rodriguez countered. "Somehow, I can't believe they'd get rid of someone, especially one of their own, any place but the Pine Barrens. And they're not exactly known for their recreational boating skills."

Rodriguez took off his hat and ran a hand through his dark locks. Mickey noted the graying temples and pointed to her own.

"The job give you those?" she asked.

"Nope. The teenagers did. You just wait. Your turn is coming." He replaced his hat. "Look, I know this doesn't involve you or Long Beach Island, Mick, but you have friends in places I don't. You have backdoors where I don't even have a front door. Can you help me out here – for old time's sake?"

"Can't do it, Solly," Mickey said, trying her best to keep a straight face.

A young couple pushing an umbrella stroller came down the ramp. Rodriguez tipped his cap. "Enjoy the sunshine, folks," he said to them. "It's still free."

"Hey, we heard there was a body stuck to the Diving Bell," the man called. He was wearing a black Iowa basketball jersey with a gold number twenty-two. "So, was it a murder? Like a mob hit? Somebody got whacked at the Steel Pier?" His wife, a tall, lithe brunette, adjusted the little umbrella attached to an arm of the spindly stroller.

Rodriguez shook his head. "Not likely. People come to Atlantic City for fun. Probably fell off of a boat or a dock. You folks have a good afternoon. Cute baby. What's her name?"

"He's a boy," the woman replied. "His name is Sam, short for Samson."

"Got it. Well. Stay away from women barbers then, I guess," Rodriguez said with a wave. The couple started walking again. He paused to let them pass. "*Dios mio*. It never fails, does it?"

"What never fails?" Mickey asked.

"Call a baby a girl, and it's a boy. And vice versa. So much for my keen powers of observation." He squashed a giant greenhead fly that had landed on the light bar. "At least I still have my lightning-quick reflexes. Iowa. That's potatoes, right?"

"Pretty sure that's Idaho," Mickey answered.

"Hmm, so I wonder who Twenty-Two is. He's got to be their big guy. Big guy or point guard. I watch the Big Five and the Sixers."

"I follow St. Joe's," Mickey said. "Out of my deep affection for Father Feeney. They need to play that Valderas kid more. And who says Twenty-Two is a guy? Ever heard of women's basketball? My little Leenie works on her layups every night."

"Right," Rodriguez said dismissively. "A guy wearing a girl player's number. May God let both of us live long enough to see that." He checked to make sure the little family was well out of earshot. "If I simply rule it an accident, our lives will be much simpler. Another dumbshit's death by misadventure."

"And if old Doc Guidice were still alive and still a coroner," Mickey said, "that is exactly what he'd advise you to do. I didn't listen to him in '67. You know how that turned out."

"Mick, come on. You were brand new. And the first woman chief. I would have done exactly what you did. Any good cop would have done what you did. Shit, they should have put you on a Wheaties box for what you did. Do you miss him? The doc?"

"The Juice? You bet I do," Mickey said, using the old physician's boyhood nickname. "The cancer got him quickly, but he was razor sharp right up until the day he said he needed to take a little nap and never woke up. Even lying in the casket at the viewing, I swear he had that crinkly little smile - along with loafers with no socks. Old Doc, he was a true original. So, who is your M.E. here now? In all the excitement I kind of lost track myself."

"Been vacant for eight months. Gene Galasso does some freelancing when we need him. Your buddy Dale Andreas is still with the State Police, but-"

"But," Mickey interrupted, "The SP will freeze you out if you send the DB to him. That's too bad. Dr. Dale is the best I ever worked with. A real-life *Quincy*. But I get it."

Rodriguez smiled. "And, if I ever hope to follow in the footsteps of the legendary Mickey Cleary, I need a big case. A big case, say, like this one maybe."

"OK. Then try to get Galasso," Mickey said after a moment of thought. "Then I won't have to go through layers of inquisitive channels to get the skinny on something if I need it."

"I'll try," Rodriguez responded. "That is If I can pry him away from his pizza oven. He's making New York-style pizza for the invaders over in Margate these days. I'm sure oregano and baking dough smell a lot better than formaldehyde and decomp. But you said you wouldn't -"

"Of course, I'll do it," Mickey told him. "Be glad I'm your friend and not your *consiglieri*. And you haven't tried to whack anybody I know."

Rodriguez let out a feigned sigh of relief and smiled at Mickey. "You never answered me on how things were going since Bu-"

"Captain! Hey, Captain!"

They turned their heads in the direction of the shout.

"Captain Rodriguez. Great, sir, you haven't left." The officer who had accosted Mickey came galloping down the ramp toward them. He was panting when he arrived at the squad car and paused to catch his breath.

"Jesus, Lamb, how in God's name did you ever pass the physical?" Rodriguez asked. The young man was bent at the waist, hands on his knees. "Come on, Lamb. Spit it out for Christ's sake," Rodriguez implored him.

Officer C.J. Lamb stood upright, his pale face now bright pink and dripping with sweat.

"You need to come back up, sir," he said, his panting voice dry and hoarse. "Right away, sir. Now, sir."

"Good Christ on a crutch, Lamb," Rodriguez said, "Whatever it is, take care of it. And if it's something you can't handle, well...handle it. You know. act like a law enforcement professional, son. Take charge of the situation."

"Captain," Lamb said slowly. "With all due respect, sir, you need to come back up to the Pier. Sir."

When the young officer hesitated, Mickey suddenly got a very bad feeling. The vibe, Ronnie always called it.

"Lamb," Rodriguez said. "This is not the time for silence. Tell me what's going on up there?"

The young cop glanced at Mickey and then back at his superior.

"Sir. There's, there's...sir, there's another body."

SIX

Sons of Satan Motorcycle Club
The New Jersey Pine Barrens

OWEN "DEAD DOG" PETTIGREW was not a particularly happy camper.

With the departure of the club's last original member a month earlier, the new president had tasked Pettigrew with going through the aging, ramshackle structure and disposing of any vestiges of the MC's former military identity. He thought this was perhaps not a great idea, but he was only the Sergeant-at-Arms and thus had no choice but to carry out the order.

He'd served two tours in Vietnam, one of the last grunts out when Saigon fell to the commies. He'd watched the smoke rise from the safety of a Navy helicopter that had plucked him and four other exhausted soldiers off a leaking fishing boat bobbing in the South China Sea. When the last chopper had departed the U.S. Embassy roof, stranding them outside the walls, they'd abandoned all their possessions, shed their uniforms, and hoofed it overland, keeping southeast to avoid the swarm streaming down from the North.

They'd been forced to swim across the *Dinh* River, where huge, man-eating saltwater crocs prowled the brackish estuaries. Pettigrew was still so unnerved by the experience that he wouldn't voluntarily enter a natural body of water bigger than a puddle.

They looked like castaways by the time they finally reached the beach at *Vung Tau*. They commandeered an old and severely degraded *thung chai*, a giant woven bamboo boat shaped like a bowl. It usually carried only a lone fisherman and his catch. The combined weight of the five Americans put the gunnels only inches above the rolling swells.

What was making Pettigrew most unhappy was that he was doing the assigned chore himself. He'd assigned it to a club Prospect, Donny "Scooch" Pascucci, who was currently nowhere to be found. To make matters worse, Scooch was supposed to be initiated into full membership that night, something that was rarely disclosed to a Prospect beforehand.

Pettigrew was the kid's sponsor, and he knew he would lose significant credibility if Scooch couldn't be located or didn't show up to get patched in. He was one of the few veterans left in the ranks. To him. an order was an order, so he'd pulled out dusty drawers and rummaged in cluttered closets, hoping no one would notice.

The MC's new president, a career criminal named Walker White, seemed intent on weeding out the remaining guys with service backgrounds or combat experience. This also seemed to Pettigrew like a genuinely bad idea. He assumed that his future with Walker White wielding the gavel was, at best, uncertain. Even the Old Ladies were different now. Mostly young runaways, often abused - happy to be Properties and nothing more. The push to allow a female to be a member had ended a few years before when the only woman ever to come close died in a Pine Barrens forest fire.

Walker White's order included the directive that any traces of Margaret Mayday Minette that turned up be consigned to the burn barrel. Pettigrew found a few things of hers tucked deep in a drawer in what had been Ronnie Stopper's bedroom. Minette had been his old lady and was herself a Vietnam vet, working as an O.R. nurse in a surgical field station. At the moment, Stopper was doing a dime at the State Prison in Trenton for aggravated manslaughter.

A big crystal meth transaction involving some Russians from Little Odessa up on Coney Island had gone south. Worse, the buy was raided by the State Police, who clearly had been tipped. A child walking outside the stash house was wounded in the crossfire and later died. Stopper swore on his mother that he had never fired a shot and that the bullets could only have come from the troopers. But the State Police's in-house medical examiner swore otherwise, although the ballistics evidence had been inexplicably and permanently misplaced.

Stopper had been defended *pro bono* by A. Louis Petroni, Jr., the Philly mob's primary attorney. Petroni's father, a previous mob mouthpiece himself, had disappeared mysteriously back in the late sixties, although Pettigrew didn't know the details. Junior was cocky and brash, almost strutting before the bar on the days Pettigrew had ridden out to sit in solidarity in the courtroom gallery with the defendant. It seemed like the kid was doing everything he could to piss off the lady judge, who was having none of it. The big-shot columnist at the *Philadelphia Inquirer* found Ronnie guilty in the newspaper before the trial was even halfway over. The jury took less than three hours to agree.

Pettigrew assumed that A. Louis Petroni, Jr., knew from the beginning that Stopper was toast and only took the case to trial to raise his profile in the papers and on local television. Pettigrew recalled that the Philadelphia and the New York media ate him up.

Pettigrew had visited Stopper a few weeks after his weakly worded appeal was denied. The decrepit and decaying State Prison was on Federal Street in Trenton. Its original construction dated back to 1798, and it housed the Garden State penal system's worst and most violent offenders within its walls. Inmate assaults and murders were predictably commonplace. It was, Pettigrew learned from a C.O., where the guy who kidnapped and killed Charles Lindbergh's baby had been incarcerated and then electrocuted.

Stopper was in for a child's murder, and, as far as Pettigrew knew, he was still in Gen Pop. Prison justice, in his experience, was usually swift and always terrible. And the more gruesome or inventive the attack, he knew, the better for the assailant's prison cred. He figured the only way Ronnie Stopper was ever leaving the place was on a toe-tag parole.

Pettigrew rummaged in his pocket for the few things of Maggie Minette's he'd managed to locate—the things she carried when she got home from the war. There were some combat ribbons, a rusty hemostat, an Army Nurse Corps pin, and a Purple Heart medal that was still attached to its ribbon but missing the clasp and the ceremonial case that usually came with it.

Pettigrew's identical decoration was safely tucked away in a strongbox at his sister's house in Toms River with instructions that it be pinned on him again only when he was in his casket. This assumed that he would not run afoul of the club's new order and would end up in at least a cheap box and not, like some unlucky others, buried in a shallow pit somewhere in the swampy wasteland that was the Pine Barrens.

Reflecting on the MC's new leadership and attitude, Pettigrew wondered if Scooch had somehow gotten wind of his imminent initiation, been spooked, and decided to disappear along with the young thing who would automatically become both his and club Property. Or, considering the brutal initiation requirements now required of Properties, maybe it was her idea to disappear. Pettigrew never thought she looked like a gangbang type of girl.

He slipped the items back into the pocket of his leather vest and decided he'd ride the perimeter again to see if Scooch had turned up. As he passed the small room where the MC's officers met to discuss club business, he thought of Walker White's new rallying cry.

"Make no mistake," White had said after the votes were counted, the keg tapped, and the celebratory methamphetamine distributed. "We are not... noble warriors. We are the Sons of Satan. From now on, we are...apex...fucking...predators."

SEVEN

The Steel Pier

EVEN FLASHING THEIR BADGES and barking the whole way, Mickey and Rodriguez's trip back to the Diving Bell took twice as long. Word of the second body had spread like a virus, forcing them to wade through an even more agitated crowd than the one they'd left.

The crush of bodies reeked of body odor and suntan lotion as they made their way through it. Those close by peppered them with questions and the occasional harangue about police incompetence. Mindful that she was on Rodriguez's turf, Mickey resisted her instinct to respond and slipped in behind her former deputy, a maneuver which moved them ahead more efficiently. She kept a close eye on Rodriguez's sidearm, making sure no unseen hand made a grab for it.

C.J. Lamb had been briefly in sight several feet ahead of them but he had quickly gotten swallowed up in the swarm. Mickey felt like a human bumper car.

Finally, they reached the cordoned-off entrance to the Diving Bell. Some of the Crime Scene tape was already in tatters and had been replaced with what looked like docking ropes festooned with yellow bows. The sappy Tony Orlando song, "Tie a Yellow Ribbon," played briefly in her head. Uniformed officers stood like sentries at each of the massive wooden pilings that held the Bell's supporting platform in place.

Mickey noticed that the body bag was now zippered shut, and three of the divers were back in the water. The fourth, a rather obese middle-aged man who appeared to have been poured into his wetsuit and now threatened to burst out of it at any minute, had his arm hooked around the increasingly suspect ladder. Rodriguez motioned to him, and he hauled himself up with more than a little apparent difficulty. The Diving Bell was now entirely out of the water. The heavyset diver doffed his swim fins and approached them, his bare feet slapping in the puddles on the sagging boards.

“I didn’t miss it, Captain,” the diver said before Rodriguez could speak. “I couldn’t have. It must have floated in after I got out.” He pulled off his neoprene dive hood. It made a sucking sound, and again, Mickey got sprayed with droplets of brine.

“Nobody said you did, Cal,” Rodriguez said. “Man or woman?”

The diver looked down. “Female. Young Woman. Late twenties, maybe.”

Mickey looked over the rickety wooden railing and watched as the three men still in the ocean pulled the body toward the ladder like a swamped sailboat. She gazed out toward the ocean and then down at the water swirling past the barnacle-encrusted pilings.

“Tide’s coming in,” she said. “That’s why it showed up now.”

“Since when did you become a seafarer?” Rodriguez asked with a smile. “I thought you were scared shitless of boats and open water.”

Mickey took off her Wayfarers and tapped them.

“Polarized lenses,” she said. “Cuts down on the glare off the surface. Plus, I have a friend in the fishing fleet who lets me do a ride-along every now and then and takes me out when the seas are small. I’m getting better, although losing sight of land still gives me the willies. Anyway, look down at the pilings. See how the water is pushing around them straight toward the shore. It’s an old sailor’s trick that tells you which direction the tide or a current is moving.”

“I’ll have to remember that,” Rodriguez said. “Polarized lenses, huh? Do they work anything like those X-ray glasses you can send for from the back of comic books?”

Mickey smiled. “Well, they don’t let me see through people’s clothes, if that’s what you’re wondering,” she said. “But they do let me peer into people’s souls. It's pretty dark in there, Rich. You should think about maybe going to church occasionally.”

Rodriguez shook his head.

The body was now halfway up the ladder, with one dive team member pushing from below and the other two pulling from above with their hands hooked under the dead girl’s shoulders. Something looked off with her arms, Mickey thought, and so she walked over to where the divers on the pier were still huffing and grunting as they tugged and hauled. Rodriguez followed her. As the men finally heaved the lifeless form up onto the pier, it turned halfway around. Mickey could now see that a fraying length of yellow rope tied the girl's hands together.

“Ah, shit,” Rodriguez muttered.

The male body, they’d both silently noticed earlier, had ligature marks on its wrists and ankles. The two victims, Mickey surmised, had gone down together, with or without the ship. And not of their own accord.

“Well, Captain,” Mickey said, “Unless you believe in cosmic coincidences, here’s your big case. What did Doc Guidice always say - be careful what you wish for?”

“Yeah, no kidding. You’ll still help me, though, right?”

Mickey looked down at the girl’s body, which now lay prone and dripping on the boards. She tried not to dwell on the damage the saltwater and various toothed or clawed sea creatures had done to it. Instead, she focused on a tattoo, a blooming rose encircled by a ring of interlaced knots, perfectly centered between the two small breasts. The color was still vibrant, indicating it was a recent acquisition.

The design tickled something in Mickey’s memory. A story her mother might have told her or a picture she might have shown her when she was little.

“Mean anything special?” Rodriguez asked.

"Not sure yet," Mickey answered. "Maybe. Tell your crime scene guys to get good close-ups of it and any ink anywhere else on the male body. And to look closely for something that might have faded or been bleached out."

"Roger that," Rodriguez said. "I know there's a tattoo guy on the Pier. Been here for years, I guess. If it does close after this summer, he'll have to move his operation. I'll show him the pictures when we get them. Maybe something will ring a bell."

Mickey nodded, still searching for the childhood memory that eluded her—something about a Rose Tattoo. She looked again at the bright red ink.

"What?" Rodriguez asked her. "I can see the wheels turning up there. What are you thinking?"

"Just recalling an old saying," Mickey answered, then fell silent.

"Which is?" Rodriguez prodded after an extended pause.

Mickey gazed again at the incoming ocean. The foamy breakers were now growing in height.

"True love will never fade," she said before turning away.

EIGHT

Federal Bureau of Investigation Field Office
One Gateway Center, Newark, NJ

"TELL ME AGAIN WHY the FBI's Resident Agency in Atlantic City is administrated all the way up here in Newark instead of in Philly or Cherry Hill?"

The question was posed by a tall man in an impeccably tailored khaki suit.

"It remains one of life's great mysteries, Director," answered Evan Driscoll, who was seated at the long teakwood conference table. He swiveled in his leather chair and looked out the windows at the view of the Passaic River from their ninth floor vantage point.

The khaki suit took a seat across from him.

"Driscoll," FBI Director J.J. Durkin said. "Why am I here, not in D.C., engaging in mortal combat with clueless congressional committees? I realize it's a question I should never have to ask. And if you tell me that's also a mystery, you'll be checking beach tags in Barnegat by the end of the day."

Driscoll slipped a hand into the pocket of his blue blazer and fished something out, obscuring it in his palm. He then extended his hand toward his Director, dropped the object in front of him, and withdrew his arm. J.J. Durkin eyed the flat, white disc and then picked it up.

After examining it briefly, Durkin said, "It's a chip from an Atlantic City casino. There is probably a truckload of them in play right now. I don't see a dollar value or why it's important."

"It's a one-hundred-thousand-dollar marker. At least that's what it's worth today," Driscoll responded. "Next week, it could be twice that."

"No doubt, another wise expenditure of Bureau funds," Durkin responded. "And its significance? Tell me it does have some."

Evan Driscoll leaned in. He and Durkin had climbed the ranks in synchrony, and he was comfortable keeping his demeanor familiar yet still respectful.

"It's one of only thirteen chips that were made before gambling in New Jersey was even on the ballot. Pure elephant ivory from the old Belgian Congo. Which is illegal even to possess now. They were given, secretly, to politicians, bankers, and a few union leaders to assure that the referendum would pass, and that this particular casino would get built first."

"Then why do we, the nation's most powerful law enforcement agency, possess it?" Durkin queried. "And, I have to ask, why thirteen of them?"

"Technically, we don't possess it if you ignore the nine-tenths rule," Driscoll answered. "It's on loan to us, courtesy of a member of the Garda Siochana. Our guess is that it was a Baker's Dozen, thirteen being an otherwise odd and unlucky choice for a gambling venture. We believe we know where twelve of them are."

"The Irish National Police and a missing marker. OK, now you've got my interest." Durkin placed the chip on the table between them. "Evan, my jet back to Andrews doesn't leave Newark International until four. That's not a great deal of time." He pushed the chip toward Driscoll the way a poker player would ante-up. "Let's not waste it."

Surf City, NJ

There was music playing inside.

The man at the front door of the tidy bungalow two blocks off Long Beach Boulevard thought the voice sounded like Nancy Sinatra. The song was "It Ain't Me Babe," by Bob Dylan, although he recalled that the Turtles had a big radio hit with it. He waited until it began to fade out and knocked again. A new song started up, the familiar *decrescendo* guitar riff of "These Boots Were Made for

Walkin’,” followed by what sounded like real boots stomping on a wooden floor inside.

“Hellooo,” the man called through an open screen window next to the door. “Mickey? Mickey, are you home? Mickey, it’s Mike Kase from ShoreMax Realty. I have some truly exceptional news. I think you’ll want to hear it.”

The music and the stomping persisted. Kase thought the volume might have even been turned up. He tried knocking on the door again. Then he felt a hand grip his shoulder.

“She won’t answer if she’s in there by herself? She’s not allowed.”

The hand on his shoulder belonged to a younger man with sun-bleached blond hair and a weather-beaten complexion. He sported a grimy gray cutoff sweatshirt, ragged canvas pants, and rubber boots.

“Mickey?” Kase asked.

“No, the little one. Eileen.” He let go of Kase’s shoulder and dropped his hand to shake. “Christian Hansen,” he said. “Folks usually call me Helly.”

“Mike Kase. ShoreMax Realty.” Kase whipped out a business card from inside his sport coat. Hansen took it, glanced at the printing, and quickly handed it back.

“I’m still paying off my fishing trawler,” Helly replied. “I’m afraid that’s all the real estate I can afford right now.”

Kase palmed the card. “Well, when you’re ready to toss out your anchor, now you know who to call. I have something to fit every budget.”

“Only a Sunday sailor tosses his anchor, Mr. Kase,” Helly said. “Always drop it straight down. Unless you want it to drag.”

“I’m not much of a boater, but I’ll try to remember that,” Kase answered. “Thanks - Helly, did you say?” Kase thought for a few seconds. “Oh, I get it. Helly Hansen. Like the pricey raincoats.”

“Pricey because it’s the best wet weather gear you can get. It’s a working man’s rain suit, Mr. Kase. Don’t let L.L. Bean and that fancy catalog of his fool you. That’s for rich college kids. And my name comes stamped on mine right from the factory.” Helly gave Kase a broad smile and released his hand.

“So you must run, what, like a charter fishing boat?” Kase asked him.

"Shit, no," Helly said. "I'm not any good with the public. Seasick drunks all complaining they didn't hook a trophy marlin? Not for me. No sir, I'm a dour Norwegian fisherman like my father and his father. There have been pound fishermen on this island for over a hundred years."

"What's a poundfish?"

Helly laughed out loud. "Jeez, man, it's not a fish. Pound fishing is an old way of *catching* fish with nets staked to long poles stuck in the bottom offshore. They call the set-up the pound, not the fish. And if it's out there within a mile of shore, it would end up in the net. Everything from blowfish to sea robins."

"You still do that?"

"Not anymore," Helly said. "We changed with the times, like everyone else. But I am thinking of putting a couple of slot machines on my boat if I can get a gambling license from the CCC."

"Seriously? You can legally do-"

Helly interrupted him. "Nah. I'm only tugging on your bobber, Mr. Kase," he said, putting his hand flat on the house's weathered strake-board siding. Kase could see his skin was chapped and raw. "She won't sell," Helly went on. "She won't. This place means a lot to her. So does this island. She won't sell it to you or anyone else. Might be best if you let it lay for a while. Give her and her kids some peace. Been a tough year for all of them."

Kase took a step back. "I do have some personal history with her, so I understand exactly what you're saying. But some of these offers are, frankly, well, staggering for this little square of land. These buyers don't care about the house, I know. They only care about where it sits. I'd be truly remiss if I didn't let her know what they're willing to pay her for it. It could be, what do they say now? It could be life-changing. She could buy or maybe even build a place twice this size. With cash left over for the kids to go to college."

"I know you're doing your job," Helly said in a slightly darker tone. "But, the thing is, *she* cares about this house. It's home to her. I won't cast doubt on your good intentions, Mr. Kase. It might be the right thing, but it for sure isn't the right time if you want my honest opinion."

Kase regarded the earnest, if somewhat scruffy, individual before him. "So, are you close friends with Mickey?"

"Close enough," Helly said. "We've both lost someone dear to us."

"So, you're... seeing each other?"

Helly laughed and shook his head. "No, sir. We are most definitely not romantically involved. It's not the right time for that. For either of us. I'm here at the moment to see if she wants to take a little boat ride. She says the only thing that's ever scared her is open water. And she wants to learn the ropes, so to speak, and how to handle a simple boat in a fair breeze and an ocean swell." He looked off toward the horizon. "It'll be slack tide in a couple of hours. Best time to run the Barnegat Inlet, given the wind direction today. It can get pretty wavy when the tide is running against the breeze."

Kase was puzzled. When he'd amicably departed Jimmy the Fixer's employment as his bodyguard, he'd fallen into the real estate racket on the island just as it was heating up with an influx of new money Philly suburbanites and frustrated New Yorkers who couldn't afford The Hamptons. Kase knew the territory. But, he now realized, he knew Long Beach Island but very little about the water that surrounded it or the locals who worked it.

"And who knows, Mr. Kase," Helly said. "If she were to come into a windfall like you say is out there, she might decide to buy herself a boat instead—right next to all those fancy yachts down in Holgate. If you know Mickey like you say, you know she likes to have her hands on the wheel. And she's a born skipper, by my reckoning. She simply needs to get her sea legs under her."

Helly removed his hand from the boards and brushed off some flakes of peeling paint.

"It looks like she'll need help repainting the place before the summer's out," Helly said, rubbing his palms together.

"I, I feel like I do have to tell her about interested buyers," Kase reiterated. "It's part of my ethical responsibility."

"Funny," Helly said, cocking his head to one side, "I don't see a 'For Sale' sign anywhere. I suspect you can't buy what's not being offered."

Mike Kase knew that selling to any one of the several motivated buyers he'd been cagily stringing along would yield a commission large enough for him to buy a boat. But having known Mickey Cleary in their former professional lives, he fully understood the young fisherman's concern. He worried that working for Jim Frichionne had hardened any soft spot he'd once possessed, but he realized that with Mickey Cleary, it was different. He decided to take a less aggressive approach.

"OK, I'll go with what you've told me. You don't happen to have a real estate license, do you?"

Helly grinned. "I have only a driver's license and a commercial fishing license. Scout's honor."

"Would you at least tell her I dropped by?" Kase asked. "And if the time comes that she's interested, she should call me. I only want to help her and her kids."

"I believe that, Mr. Kase," Helly said. "I do. And I will tell her. She said she'd be home by now."

Kase noticed the music inside was still going, but the stomping had abated. "Flowers on the Wall" was now playing. A surprisingly strong child's voice was singing along, word for word.

Both men leaned in a little.

"Great song," Helly commented. "I like the Statler Brothers version a little better. Belts it out there for a little thing, though, doesn't she?"

"That she does. Mickey used to call her Beach Baby," Kase said. "You know, like the song?"

"If you do, that little spitfire will tell you she's not a baby anymore and to call her Eileen," Helly replied. "Fair warning to you."

Kase was about to answer when someone called to them from the sidewalk.

"Hey! Who you guys? Huh? What you want? What you doing on our porch?"

Kase and Hansen stopped their conversation and turned around.

"Oh, hey, Helly," the girl said.

A slender young woman approached. She was pushing an umbrella stroller with a scaled-down striped umbrella attached to its frame. Beneath it, a toddler lolled, head to one side, sleeping blissfully.

Kase noted the girl's straight black hair and soft Asian features.

"Who this mook?" she asked Helly

"Hey, Bunny," Helly said. "This is Mister..." He paused

"Kase," the realtor interjected. "Mike Kase. ShoreMax Realty." He automatically reached for his card and then stopped himself.

"Mickey-san house not for sale," Bunny told him. "You go away."

She gently bumped the stroller up the wooden steps. The little boy, in its faded sling, yawned but did not wake.

"I wanted to talk to Mickey about -"

"Not for sale," Bunny said again. "No need talk. Go away. Go buy somebody else house. Mickey stay. Now move away from door."

Kase noted Helly's big grin.

"Bunny," Helly said, "Mike is a friend of Mickey-san. You be nice to him, OK?" He turned to Kase. "Mr. Kase, this is Bunny Tran. She and Mickey go way back. Like *waaaayyy* way back. She's young but, shall we say, she is rather formidable."

Bunny eyed Kase suspiciously.

"It's nice to meet you, Miss Tran," Kase said, extending his hand. She kept both of hers on the thin C-shaped stroller handles.

"You open door before Michael wake up," Bunny commanded him.

Kase complied, pulling on the worn screen door and then pushing the inner wooden one open to allow the young girl and the stroller egress. He couldn't tell how old she was, but he guessed maybe mid or possibly late teens. Bunny rolled the stroller over the scuffed aluminum sill and into the bungalow.

"Mickey home quickie-quick, I hope," Bunny said to Helly. "You wait?"

"No," Helly replied. "Tell her it might have to be another day." He looked at Kase. "If we miss slack tide, it won't be much fun for a greenhorn." Then he turned to Bunny. "Tell Mickey-san I'll check the weather and the tide table and let her know."

Bunny nodded. "OK. See you, Helly." She glanced at Kase. "You go away. No come back. House not for sale. Leave Mickey-san alone. She no sell house." The girl disappeared inside, but not before peeking back at Kase one more time, "Close door. Don't slam. You wake Michael up, everybody mad at you. Very grumpy child if no long nap."

Mike Kase promptly did as he was told. Helly must have seen the look of puzzlement on his face.

"Like I said, Mike. Formidable."

"Chinese?" Kase asked.

"Vietnamese," Helly responded. "Long story, I guess. And I only know a small part of it. Mickey says she showed up in Surf City nine, maybe ten years ago with a note pinned to her sweater. Mickey's name was on the note."

"War orphan?"

"Yes and no, I guess," Helly said. He looked at his watch. "Long and very complicated story. If I see you around the docks, you can buy me a beer and tell you the part I know. But right now, I should probably help my dad process some nice poundfish. Nice meeting you."

Helly hopped down the three sandy steps and climbed into what Kase recognized as a Chevy C10 square-body pickup. He guessed maybe the 1974 model. The truck's paint had faded, but it still sported enough of its original orange color to match most traffic cones. Various nets, poles, and gaffes sprouted from its bed. Stenciled in block letters on the door was

HANSEN FISH Co.

Viking Village, Barnegat Light

(609) HY5-3474

Kase instantly memorized the information, noting the outdated HY for Hyacinth exchange designation and the amusing fact that the last four numbers spelled out F-I-S-H on a telephone's buttons. He wasn't sure if he'd need a commercial fisherman anytime soon. But he figured it couldn't hurt to have the number of a local seafaring Viking in his Rolodex.

NINE

Steel Pier

WORD OF A SECOND dead body had swelled the crowd even further. It made Mickey think of sharks and a feeding frenzy. A cordon of uniforms escorted her and Rodriguez across the boardwalk, down the ramp, and all the way to his cruiser. She had heard the sounds of a helicopter overhead and assumed it belonged to one of the Philly TV news stations.

They slid into the front seats. The uniforms cleared a path for the car to exit the small access street.

"Have you given a news conference yet?" Mickey asked Rodriguez.

"And steal the ACPD Chief's thunder?" he answered. "Thank you. No. I'll prep him thoroughly when I get back. Then, I'll stand to the side and glance confidently at him while he speaks to the press. He'll handle it much better than I could."

As the cruiser passed the last uniformed officer, a tap on the trunk signaled they were clear. Rodriguez turned right on Pacific Avenue and then pulled over.

"Where'd you park, and what are you driving?" he asked. "Wait. Don't tell me. One of those, what do they call them – minivans I read about, right? My oldest daughter said if we ever got one, she'd run away from home in embarrassment."

"Nope," Mickey said with a chuckle. "And my car guy said those won't be out for a few more years, so you're safe for a while. He said I had choices, though. An actual van, a big boat sedan, or a station wagon."

"So what did you get?"

"I got a station wagon, of course."

"Wood on the side?"

"What do you think?"

Rodriguez turned down the car's fan.

"But, you know me and cars," Mickey continued. "Not just any station wagon. I bought an old Chevy Brookwood off a summer kid—a nineteen-sixty Brookwood. I did some fairly heavy work on it to get it back in shape. I'm telling you, I could drive that thing into battle. It is truly a tank."

"You know, I think I ticketed that kid," Rodriguez said with evident surprise. "Way long time ago in Surf City. I'm sure of it."

"Same one," Mickey answered. "Get this. He's going to law school—he's doing something called an internship at the Bombay Casino, no less. He even had a name for the beast. The Green Dragon. Once Leenie heard that, there was no going back."

Rodriguez dropped the fan another notch.

"OK. But what are you *actually* driving? The Mickey Cleary I know does *not* roll up to a crime scene in a '60 Chevy wagon."

"No, she most certainly does not," Mickey said. "So, you know how it goes in Jersey. I ask a guy if he knows a guy. He says, no, but he knows a guy who knows another guy and – *bada-bing*! I get lucky."

"Corvette, right? It's a freaking Stingray. Tell me it's a freaking Corvette Stingray."

"Better."

"Better? What's better than a Corvette Stingray?"

"You ever see the movie *Bullitt*?"

Rodriguez removed his aviators and rubbed his forehead.

"Oh. Wait. No. No way," he finally said. "You are totally bullshitting me now, Detective Cleary."

"I am totally *not* bullshitting you, Captain Rodriguez," Mickey retorted. "1968 Ford Mustang GT 390 Fastback."

"Tell me it's green. It's gotta be green."

"Highland Green. Be nice, and we'll do a pursuit through the dusty beach roads of LBI after the season ends. I'll even let you be Steve McQueen." Mickey pursed her lips. "It's in the Bombay parking lot. I did take up two spaces, so you might have to write me up."

"California plates?"

Mickey shook her head. "No. But I have an in at the DMV, so I was able to get Jersey plates that say **JJZ-109**. Luckily, California uses the same letter and number system we do. Thanks to me, some lady in Teterboro, or maybe it was Totowa, got brand new plates."

"Jeez, I shoulda known," Rodriguez said. "OK. Colombia's homemade tacos at our house if you can tell me what the other car was."

"Rich," Mickey said with a grin. "Who are you talking to? They showed us *Bullitt* one night after supper at the academy. There was a pop quiz when it ended. I got out of a week's perimeter guard duty for being the only recruit to know the make, model, *and* the plate number."

"I don't believe it."

"'68 Dodge Charger 440 Magnum, Black, California license plate **RDR-838**." She cocked her head. "Middle-aged Caucasian male driver and front seat passenger. The driver wore black glasses. But that part was easy."

Rodriguez beamed in admiration. "OK, OK, you win. But you let me drive it one time when this is all over, and I'll owe you forever. Jesus, Mick, how did you ever find it much as less buy it?"

"Hey, we're in Jersey," Mickey responded. "Anything is obtainable with the right connections." She winked. "But let's get back to what we both saw and what we're thinking while it's still fresh. Then you can drop me off. I'll even let you drool on the hood for a minute. Or I could walk."

Rodriguez frowned. "You know, I'm not sure what it says about us. We saw two dead – two *murdered* – young people. And the first thing we want to talk about is cars."

"It says that we've both been cops for a long time."

Mickey paused for an extended moment and then continued. "OK. So we agree on that. They're both homicides. Now. First question. Who are they, and why were they killed together?"

Rodriguez rubbed his chin and then pinched the skin beneath it. "Drug deal gone bad. Or semi-regular or maybe not-so-regular citizens who saw something, did something, or showed up someplace they shouldn't."

"Yes. Good," said Mickey, "But the tats are bugging me. The female's was recent and done by a pro. Lotta detail and – and it was her only one unless I missed something. That pattern means something. I can't place it right now, but it'll come to me. And the male's – some of his were faded, but it was like they were *too* faded. Like maybe they weren't real to begin with."

"You mean, like the ones that kids get at carnivals?"

"Yeah," Mickey responded. "Like those. They use henna. It comes from a plant. Eileen has one on her arm right now. She got it at Funtown U.S.A. up in Seaside Heights. They usually only last about three weeks. And there are two kinds of henna—black and brown. Black will hang around much longer. It might also have been professionally done, but what parlor or self-respecting tattoo artist would dare use henna?"

"Prison ink, maybe?" Rodriguez asked. "I mean, there is not exactly a lot of quality control going on there."

Mickey pondered the question. "That's a thought. Inside, they use tap water, alcohol, and soot to make the ink. The blacker, the better. But it usually doesn't fade. Like, ever." She drummed her fingers on the dashboard. "And who gives or gets a henna tat in prison?"

They both fell silent.

"All right,' Mickey finally said. "Next question. Were they killed and then dumped, or were they heaved overboard still breathing to drown? Nobody does cement shoes anymore. If it's the latter, where are the weights? If it's the former, where are the wounds?"

Rodriguez pondered the question. "I'm going with tossed alive and kicking into the drink," he said. "Definitely. The lig marks on both of them were wide and they were fresh. They definitely struggled. And I think they struggled for a while. If they were in the water, that had to be awful."

"I agree," Mickey said. "The autopsy will tell us more, although the actual C.O.D. doesn't matter that much right now, other than it tells us the perp or perps probably had access to a boat. That's a pretty big crowd around these parts."

"Also agreed," Rodriguez responded. "Opportunity? That doesn't matter for the same reason. A thousand boats go in and out along this little stretch of coast five hundred times a day. Where would you even start looking?"

Mickey's eyes narrowed. "You've seen your share of floaters. When did you put their T.O.D.?"

"Twenty-four to forty-eight, given the relatively low amount of predation. And did you notice? They both still had their eyes. Meaning they probably didn't spend much, if any, time on the bottom. Bottom feeders, like crabs, they always go for the eyes first."

"Right," Mickey responded with a nod. "So you're going to need to find someone who's constantly aware of the wind, the tide, and the offshore currents. Ask if they can backtrack twenty-four to forty-eight hours. Then try to make an educated guess as to where they might have entered the water."

"That would be a start," Rodriguez answered. "And you wouldn't happen to know a guy who knows such a guy, would you?"

Mickey slid her Wayfarers back on. "Better. I happen to know such a guy. Let's go. I have to get back to Surf City. Shit. What time is it?"

Rodriguez glanced at his watch. "Going to Surf City? Oh. Then it's two to one."

"That doesn't sound ri-" Mickey stopped herself. "Oh. OK. I get it. Smartass. So are you Jan or Dean?"

Rodriguez grinned and shifted the cruiser into Drive. "C'mon, you have to admit, that was pretty good on short notice," he said as they pulled away from the curb.

"OK. It was," Mickey said. "But promise you'll stay away from Dead Man's Curve on the way there."

Bombay Hotel & Casino
Room 2512

Ilsa Schoenweiss wiped the sweat from between her naked breasts with the linen comforter. The Egyptian cotton sheets lay in a mangled mess, bunched at the foot of the bed. Her boss would tolerate her indiscretions as long as they contributed to the overall good or the financial gain of the Bruxelles Organization. She wasn't sure yet if this had achieved either aim. Ilsa, however, considered herself more than satisfied.

Her parents had emigrated to the United States from Bavaria in the late 1940s. They had always and still considered themselves Bavarians first and Germans second. They told her that Bavaria had once been a kingdom all to itself until the despised Otto von Bismarck forced its incorporation into the German state. Americans seemed to associate it with chocolate, cuckoo clocks, and little else.

Ilsa, like her parents and most Bavarians, was a staunch Catholic, her promiscuity and her papally proscribed birth-control pills notwithstanding. Mama and Papa had been born in Algau, a day's ride from Neuschwanstein Castle, a lineage that Mama claimed had isolated them from the evils of the Second World War and the brutal Nazi regime. But when Ilsa learned in high school history class that the infamous Dachau concentration camp had been only a two-hour bus ride away from her parents' village, she began questioning the story.

Ilsa had been born at a Catholic hospital in Camden. She considered herself a real American and was deeply hurt when she realized that for many people in the United States, German-Americans still somehow walked around with an invisible swastika. "Hogan's Heroes" hadn't done much to dispel the myth, and she understood why her parents had forbidden the show from ever appearing in their home.

Mama had known her boss's *mutter*, Hannah, from their shared girlhood in the village. Ilsa had gotten the job as Bruxelles' personal assistant without even interviewing when he learned where her family was from and that she could speak fluent German, which he often asked her to do. Mama expressed some concern when Ilsa announced her new employer, muttering darkly about Hannah Munternacht's papa, calling him a *mitfauer* who grew wealthy by appropriating the homes and shops, and all the possessions within, of displaced Jewish families in and around Munich.

It was rumored that he'd smuggled out millions of dollars worth of art, sculpture, and precious jewelry before *Die Familie Munternacht* hastily departed for New York, a half-step ahead of the Nuremberg investigators.

The source of Benno's fortune was a *verboten* topic, but Ilsa assumed his mother's family had provided most, and perhaps all, of it. Benno was unfailingly pleasant and courtly toward Ilsa. His respectful treatment of women was beyond reproach, and rarely, if ever, did she hear him swear or use uncouth language. He asked her opinion and often took her advice on personal matters. It was Ilsa who'd talked him out of a very bad hairpiece and suggested that his bald pate was not only more handsome but more intimidating.

Benno cultivated the Hugh Hefner playboy image, but Ilsa saw someone different hiding underneath. She wondered if he'd been a lonely child. Ilsa made it her mission to shield him from the scheming gold diggers and the malignant sycophants who flocked to the casino like birds to a water hole. After she warned off one particularly persistent harridan, Benno put Ilsa in complete control of his social calendar.

But she simply could not see him as either a hard worker or a business genius. She often found herself making what seemed to be high-level fiscal decisions on his behalf, sometimes having to forge his signature on financial disclosures, bank loan applications, and even mortgages. His ego and his business acumen, she decided, were in direct and opposite proportions to each other.

But it was a great job, and for a twenty-five-year-old graduate of the Rutgers Business School in New Brunswick, it was a dream fulfilled. She'd stopped shy of the credits needed for an M.B.A. but calculated that with her lavish casino paycheck and perks package, she could return in a few years to comfortably complete the degree requirements. She might never own the Bombay, she often thought, but that didn't mean she'd never run it.

The *schussing* sound of the shower had stopped.

Ilsa's voracious sexual appetite and proclivity had always been her parents' greatest concern. But she'd never embarrassed them or herself, never gotten pregnant, and had learned to choose her partners carefully and with Teutonic precision. She'd never slept with a real Irishman before. His lilting brogue and his hard body had made him as intoxicating as catnip in the few minutes he'd sat next to her, waiting for the odious Jack Rigger to conclude his business with Bruxelles.

Ilsa had gotten Gaetano Galliardi, "Gus" to his coworkers, his coveted position as the hotel's Chief Concierge, elevating him from an entry-level blackjack dealer. In return, Gus assured that Room 2512, with its commanding view of the ocean and its constantly replenished bar, always appeared as **RESERVED** or **OCCUPIED** at the reservations desk and that Ilsa had the only working key. When she departed later, she would leave the door slightly ajar and a crisp twenty-dollar bill on the nightstand. The hotel's housekeeping supervisor, whom Gus had personally promoted from chambermaid to management, would tidy up the mess.

Her Irishman had oddly declined to remove his t-shirt during their hot and sweaty tryst, even after she'd asked him several times. He'd physically stopped her on one occasion from doing it herself. His lovemaking certainly didn't indicate any lack of self-confidence, and she hadn't felt any disfiguring lumps, bumps, or humps, so she could only muse about what he might be concealing.

"Ah," he'd said to her between thrusts and grunts, "We all have our past indiscretions to account for, love, don't we now?" She didn't ask him again.

The bathroom door opened, and Ilsa's new friend stepped out. Still wearing the t-shirt, she noticed. He'd politely turned down her offer to shower together.

"There, that's a bit better, isn't it?" he said. "I was a bit manky after all that lovely rolling around. It's all yours, love. I even put the seat on the jacks down for you."

Ilsa laughed. “I don’t understand half of what you say. And the nice thing is, I don’t need to understand any of it.” She pushed the comforter away. "There’s plenty of hot water. Are you sure you don’t want to roll around some more before you go?”

He flashed the smile that had captivated Ilsa when he first walked into her office. His eyes were a color of green she never recalled seeing before.

“Sure and I would, and cleanliness is truly right next to godliness, but I’m afraid I’ve got a pressing bit of business I must attend to straight away.” He pulled on his boxers and reached for a pair of khaki pants slung over the club chair near the window. He stopped dressing for a moment to look out. “One can never tire of gazin’ out across the sea, can they? It’s something only a free man can do, now, isn’t it?”

The remark struck Ilsa as odd, but she let it slide. She watched as he picked up a religious medal on a chain lying on the writing desk. He looped it around his neck and tucked it inside the tight, white undershirt.

“Saint Christopher?” Ilsa inquired. “He is the patron Saint of travelers. You certainly qualify as a traveler.”

He reached next for his Oxford dress shirt and slipped it on.

“This would be the good Saint Brendan, my dear,” he said, tapping his chest. “Brendan of Clonfert. Patron Saint of sailors and voyagers. I like to think of myself as a bit o’ both.” He buttoned the shirt, tucked it in, and slipped on the blue blazer, deftly dropping the folded silk necktie into a flapped side pocket. “I’ll be much looking forward to seeing you again if that’d be something to your liking.”

Ilsa opened her legs slightly and ran a perfectly manicured fingernail from her moist mons all the way to her lower lip.

“That would be very much to my liking,” she said. “Use the number I gave you. I’ll be the only one who picks up.” She swung her legs over and off the mattress. “You know, you don’t look like an Archibald, Mr. Graham. What *were* your parents thinking when they named you?”

Archibald Graham smiled. “My sainted mum, she was a Scot, and her deddy was named Archie as was his deddy before him. Me own poor da, he was given no say in the matter whatsoever, mind you. It may not be royal, but I suppose it'll have to do for the present."

He leaned forward and kissed her lightly on the cheek.

"And they say chivalry is dead," Ilsa deadpanned.

"*Slan go foil*," Graham said. "Gaelic. It means goodbye...but only for now." He left the room without turning around.

Ilsa never found herself troubled by what one of her biz school classmates waggishly referred to as 'fornicators' remorse." She'd never taken a walk of shame. Here, she'd gotten what she craved with little effort and at no cost to herself. Benno Bruxelles said there was an element of art in every business deal. Ilsa had come to believe him. Her latest conquest indicated he'd only be in the country for a short time. It couldn't get any cleaner, Ilsa mused.

But she was already thinking about how it could get dirtier.

TEN

Garden State Parkway Northbound
Bass River, NJ

IT TOOK EVERYTHING MICKEY had in her not to let all three hundred and ninety horses take off at full gallop. But she knew this was maybe the one vehicle that could actually get away from her.

She pictured the faces of Eileen and Michael and let up on the accelerator, double-clutched, and downshifted from sixth gear to fourth. The stretch of the Parkway where she and Ronnie had once crossed the median in her patrol car, barreling northbound in the southbound lanes, was not far ahead. They had raced home from a quiet dinner at the Tuckahoe Inn when Eileen had inexplicably gone missing.

Mickey saw the sign for the Highway 9 exit and downshifted again. The old two-lane would present her with much less of a temptation.

The vintage Mustang's six-speed manual transmission had taken a little getting used to when the car first arrived. She'd read that Steve McQueen did hours of his own driving to produce the eleven-minute scene that appeared in the movie's final cut. On her last birthday, her friend April had given her a blue turtleneck, and Charlie Higgins had somehow managed to track down a Safariland Model 19 double-shoulder holster. She had yet to wear them out in public, but she had modeled them for herself in the bedroom mirror.

She liked the look but found, to her disappointment, that the holster that accommodated the fictional Frank Bullitt's Colt Diamondback snub-nosed .38 Special onscreen, would not securely retain her new Smith and Wesson Model 60. Luckily, Mr. Pace, Long Beach Island's elderly and lone working cobbler, said he was sure he could add some stitching to rectify that once the summer was over. Mickey said she could wait.

The exit ramp to Highway 9 was a three-hundred-and-sixty-degree asphalt corkscrew. Mickey took it at fifteen miles an hour over the sign-recommended speed strictly for fun. The Mustang's tires stayed glued to the road. Once she slid smoothly onto the bumpier macadam of the older State Road, she cruised right at the posted limit.

Mickey assumed she had already missed Helly Hansen and his offer to take her out on the ocean again. Her trepidation with leaving the safety of dry land had lessened appreciably after the first few "Driver's Ed" trips. However, Helly had kept the *Rachel* within sight of the shoreline or, at least, where she could still see the top of Barnegat Light. Dr. Mary Beth Harman, who had become both friend and family physician to Mickey and the kids, said she suffered from something called thalassophobia – a paralyzing fear of wide open spaces. Dr. Harman told her that if she got dropped in the middle of a Nebraska cornfield or a Kansas prairie, the level of terror would be about the same.

The Mustang's suspension was so good, and its ride was so smooth that Mickey worried she might nod off, so she rolled down the driver's side window all the way. Every newer car she'd looked at had power windows, but she decided it was a trivial inconvenience. The wind blew back her hair, and she turned up the volume on the car's original AM radio. She was still waiting for the LBI PDs to decide who would pay for the police radio that sat boxed on her desk. She offered to install it herself.

Her musical tastes had continued to change. "Matured" is how Loretta LaMarro, still her closest friend despite their age difference, described it. After she put the kids to bed, Mickey enjoyed listening to the Nightbird, Allison Steele, on WNEW on her FM tuner. But soft and sultry would not do for a trip back to the beach on a sun-bleached afternoon.

Mickey fiddled with the station dial and punched all the preset buttons, unable to land on anything that fit her mood. She was waiting for the AM stations to start playing Bruce Springsteen finally. Doug Doucette, who'd stumbled upon the singer sweeping floors at Tony Marts, said his songs ran too long for AM radio executives and programmers and were too musically complex for many listeners in the AM market demographic.

He explained that people liked Phil Spector and his bombastic Wall of Sound, they wanted Bob Dylan's melodies and his beat poetry lyrics, and they were starting to like Jim Steinman and Meat Loaf's operatic storytelling. They weren't ready for all three rolled into one, which, he said, was what made Springsteen and his band so unique. Mickey thought about "It's Hard to Be a Saint in the City" and "I Came for You" and had to agree. If her life had been one long, anything, she thought, it was an emergency.

Double D reminded Mickey that airplay wasn't about musical artistry but about selling advertising. Still, she couldn't understand why one of the best singers and songwriters to come out of New Jersey couldn't crack the local AM playlists. Doucette said AM music was on its last legs anyway and electronics companies had already phased out transistor radios. The future, he said, was in whole albums you could listen to anywhere, including the beach.

Mickey had resisted the suggestion to upgrade the late sixties-era dashboard with an AM/FM radio or a cassette tape deck. Doucette had cautioned her that 8-track tapes would soon go the way of the transistor radio. He hadn't been wrong yet.

She knew she needed to change her push-button presets, as all her long-time favorites had switched formats. WFIL was still around at 560, but its once raucous crew of Boss Jocks was reduced to playing a tepid slate of syrupy ballads they called Adult Contemporary. WIBG 99, her beloved Wibbage, had disappeared altogether. It was now renamed WZZD and called itself The Wizard. It aired a similar mix of forgettable soundalikes and, to her horror, more than a bit of disco. Mickey was sure that Hy Lit, once the king of the Philly DJs, was pulling his hair out somewhere.

Rodriguez had told Mickey not to put his request for her assistance ahead of her caseload. She had almost laughed at the thought. Her load at the moment was anything but taxing. The detective's gig allowed her more time to look after her children, which was the ultimate luxury in law enforcement. It also mostly removed her from the line of fire and dramatically dropped the odds of orphaning them on a lonely stretch of dark road. With her mom and dad both gone, Mickey thought one orphan in the family was enough.

But that safety came with a price. Her professional life had never been boring. Her friend Mike Gannon, now the lead investigative reporter at *The Inquirer*, had once described her in a newspaper story as a "lovely lass of the law with adventures that rival the Perils of Pauline." He'd also once commented that Angie Dickinson's Pepper Anderson character in *Police Woman* seemed an awful lot like Mickey Cleary. That show, perhaps ironically, had been canceled only a few months earlier.

The chance to be even peripherally involved in what looked to be a complicated murder case struck her as anything but a burden. It was a gift. And if she could find Steppenwolf's "Born to Be Wild" anywhere on the dial, she'd crank it up all the way because she was definitely ready to get her motor running.

Mickey ran the little red tuning bar up and down the dial twice. When the braying trumpets of the "Macho Man'" intro blared, she switched the radio off altogether. It seemed sadly appropriate that she hadn't touched the stick shifter once since she'd hit Highway 9. The Mustang wasn't fuel-injected, but it was chrome-wheeled, and she decided it was time to step out over the line.

The two lanes ahead were devoid of traffic. A sure sign from God, Mickey assumed. She clutched, shifted from third to fourth, and pressed the gas pedal. As she was ready to shift again, she heard the pager's bumble bee buzz. She tried looking down several times but couldn't quite see the red numbers she knew were flashing in sequence.

A loud horn blast startled her.

An ancient-looking flatbed, almost overflowing with ripe melons, was bearing straight down on her. She hadn't stepped out over the line so much as drifted there. Mickey downshifted again, braking and clutching rapidly now to maintain control. The truck passed by, its occupants gesticulating and cursing at her in what she guessed was Spanish. She had missed its oversized side mirror by mere inches.

Out of the corner of her eye, Mickey saw a battered red-and-silver New Jersey Bell telephone booth on the opposite side of the road. It still had a wire droopily looping from its roof to a nearby pole. The farm truck was now well in her rearview mirror, and she saw no other cars. The mandatory high-speed pursuit course at the State Police academy still ranked as one of her favorite experiences. The instructors had given her high marks at the end, even going so far as to note on the record that if she ever left police work, she should consider becoming a race car driver. She wasn't sure it was meant as a compliment, but she took it as one anyway.

Mickey checked her mirrors again. Few things were more fun in her mind than a high-speed J-turn, so she goosed the gas even harder. A second later, with her right hand, she pulled up hard on the emergency brake handle but kept her foot completely away from the brake pedal. At the same time, with her left hand, she violently yanked the steering wheel to the left.

The delightful sound of rubber screeching and stuttering on macadam was better than anything the old radio had offered. Within three seconds, the shimmying hood was pointing in the opposite direction. Mickey released the emergency brake, straightened the wheel, and gunned the car forward toward the old booth, which, she observed now, was tilted a few degrees to one side. The Leaning Phone Booth of Hammonton, she thought with a smile.

She briefly hit the gas, shifted out of gear, and then jammed the brake pedal until it almost met the floorboard.

The Mustang shivered to a stop in a hail of dust and gravel, enveloped by an aromatic cloud of gasoline vapor. Its front bumper was barely three feet from the booth's slightly open accordion door. Frank Bullitt, Mickey thought with a grin as she got out and inhaled the fumes, would have been proud. She approached the battered silver box and noticed something odd.

The phone inside was ringing.

FBI Field Office
Newark, NJ

A thin line of cold perspiration had formed on Evan Driscoll's forehead.

Director Durkin had his back to him, gazing out the window into the afternoon sun. Driscoll used the moment to withdraw his handkerchief and blot it dry discreetly.

His calls to two carefully selected phone booths at the prearranged time had gone unanswered. Driscoll then took the extraordinary step of going to their fail-safe option. The nice woman at the Paramount Air Service office had not even questioned the unusual request. Barbara Tomalino's father, Andre, Driscoll knew, was a World War II veteran, having flown both fighters and gliders over Europe. When he came home, he'd established the aerial advertising business with a partner in the mid-nineteen-forties. When Driscoll inquired, he had been more than willing to "help my government." Even more importantly, he tacitly understood what a "sensitive" assignment meant and asked no questions when the details were disclosed.

Paramount's planes towed advertising banners up and down the coastline from Mother's Day until Labor Day, flying low just offshore for the captive audience of beachgoers and boardwalkers. At Driscoll's request, one plane would turn inland, towing a specific banner, PARAMOUNT AIR SERVICE, over a particular location on a specific compass heading, before returning to the company's private airfield in Cape May County. Andre Tomalino had personally selected the pilot, a Vietnam War scout plane veteran. This was the signal for Driscoll's contact to contact him ASAP. If the banner read DUNES TIL DAWN, the operation was aborted, and the extraction protocol immediately went into effect.

Finally, J.J. Durkin turned around.

"I don't think I ever recall seeing you sweat before, Evan," Driscoll said. Then he realized Durkin could watch his reflection in the window glass.

"This is, I admit, worrisome," Driscoll said evenly. "If there'd been a delay in transit, I would have been alerted. The alternate plan was a call to this number," he pointed at the phone resting silently on the conference table, "or the Resident Agency in Linwood. No one has heard anything."

Durkin adjusted his necktie. "Your next step then?"

Driscoll stood. "I'll leave immediately for the R.A. If the operation has been compromised, best to have my boots on the ground close by." He was expecting to face the Director's wrath and was surprised by Durkin's next question.

"Atlantic City has a local airport, as I recall from our previous sojourn," Durkin said.

"Yes, sir. Bader Field is a Muni, but it's fully capable and operational. I don't thi -"

Durkin raised his hand. "Arrange for a car from the R.A. to meet you. I am the Director of the FBI, at least until a certain in-over-his-head Georgia peanut farmer decides otherwise. The jet waiting for me will go where I tell the pilots it needs to go. I will tell them to plan a long touch-and-go in Atlantic City. Hell, going to D.C., it's not even out of the way. If anyone asks, I'll say a warning light came on or some such avionics nonsense and that we landed briefly to have it checked out. You won't appear on the passenger manifest, so if we crash on the way, I'm afraid you'll be forever MIA."

"Thank you, Director. That certainly would be -"

Durkin didn't let him finish. "I trust you still have contacts in the A.C. area?"

"The field agents at the Resident Agency there are top-notch, Director Durkin. I've known all of them for ye-"

Durkin stopped him again. "Yes, I'm certain they are. What I'm asking, Evan, is if you still have a reliable source you can tap into when you get there. You're going on a hunting expedition. You'll have considerably better luck if you use a local guide."

Driscoll fumbled for an answer, unsure where the conversation was going.

"Evan," Durkin continued, "I'm not going to go on record as having made any direct recommendations here. But if I said you always should wear pinstripes for a trip to the Bronx, would that help?"

Driscoll looked down at his navy blue slacks and suit jacket. The Bronx? Then it came to him: the Bronx, pinstripes, Yankees.

"Yes, sir," he answered. "I understand. And yes, sir, I believe a guide with extensive knowledge of the terrain and prior encounters with the local, uh, local wildlife could be a great advantage in this situation."

"I thought you might," Durkin said with a barely perceptible smile. "Do give my regards, won't you? Now, push that phone over this way. I'll inform the pilots it's time to kick the tires and light the fires."

Driscoll reminded himself that his Director had been a Navy combat pilot during the Korean War.

Durkin picked up the receiver but then paused before punching in the numbers. "Hmmph. The local wildlife. I like that one, Evan. Very clever. I'm going to use it from now on. Without attribution, of course."

Driscoll grabbed his briefcase and mentally started planning his next few hours. The trip from Newark International Airport to Atlantic City should take a little over twenty minutes, wheels up to touchdown. He wanted to be locked and loaded once he got there. He might have lost touch with Chief Mickey Cleary over the last decade.

But that did not mean he'd forgotten her.

ELEVEN

Surf City, NJ

MICKEY DECIDED THAT IF she had snuck out with one of the portable bag phones the State Police had issued her, her life would be much easier. At the moment, she was inching over the Causeway bridge, unable to use anything but first gear and neutral, the Mustang's tachometer mocking her with its pathetic trembling at the low end of the rpm gauge.

Looking out over the guardrail as she approached the span's apex, Mickey couldn't help but remember Kalen Fairbrother's rapturous tourist brochure description of the upcoming visual panorama accompanied by the visceral rush of salt air wafting through open windows.

The new model cars that bracketed her in every direction had their windows rolled up tight, their air conditioners no doubt working overtime to keep the interiors at a frosty sixty-eight degrees. Mickey was sure Jimmy Carter's thermostat recommendation was meant for furnaces in January, not luxury sedans in July.

She crawled along for a while longer and could now see the delay from the dreaded rubbernecking phenomenon. Drivers were slowing to gawk at a not-bad-looking wooden boat that had gone hard aground, its bow wedged against a bridge support. Mickey was a little disappointed that there were no Ship Bottom boys in blue there, hand-directing the traffic jam, but she also knew the backup would take pressure off the local roads for a while, so she gave them a pass.

Even Mickey guiltily paused to have a look as she approached the bottom of the bridge. She thought the boat looked familiar, maybe one she'd seen when Helly had taken her to his boat on the docks at Viking Village, up island near Old Barney. The vessel's stern was pointed toward the bay, but Mickey wondered if it might be the *Virginia Jean*, an older but still smart-looking wooden boat Helly had pointed out to her because its owner had left it behind and had vanished to parts unknown.

Mickey knew the New Jersey laws for abandoned and derelict vehicles to the letter, but she never thought of boats as motor vehicles. Helly had informed her that boats were required to register like cars with the universally despised DMV. The *Virginia Jean* was a serviceable and seaworthy vessel, Helly had told her. If it remained unused and uninhabited, and if she waited the required thirty days and filed the proper salvage paperwork, it would be hers simply for the asking.

She thought someone must have had a similar idea as she finally shifted into second gear. Joyriding in a stolen car was rare, but it happened on the Island a few times every season. She wasn't sure if the same held true for joyriding in a boat. It struck her that no one had ever stolen a boat on her watch on LBI.

Helly Hansen had imparted to her a surprising amount of practical knowledge in the half dozen times they'd gone out. It was a personal seamanship class, like the one offered by the Barnegat Bay Power Squadron, but it was on the water and not in a musty old hall.

Mickey turned left and motored up Long Beach Boulevard. Ron Dimenna's little Ron-Jon Surf Shop had customers lined up out the door, LBI having developed its own cabal of dedicated surfers now.

She passed by Bill's Luncheonette and smiled at the sandwich board sign out front.

NOW WE SERVING GREEK CHEESESTEAKS
YOU COME TRY SOON!

Mickey wasn't sure whether either she or the summer populace was quite ready for a lamb version of the Philly staple, but she loved owner Bill Kuriakos.

And Bill loved her, along with Greece, where he'd emigrated from two decades earlier. He'd sell Greek Coca-Cola if he could find a way, she once told him.

"Sure," he'd answered her, unaware she was kidding him. "I call it Greekola!"

Bill was mostly out front with the patrons now at the little diner, his nephew Nick having taken over the cooking and managing duties. One afternoon, while she was having a burger, Nick had casually asked Mickey how long American women were required to mourn their husbands.

"Forever," she'd answered.

A knot of laughing teenagers on the sidewalk gave her a thumbs-up, recognizing the car and not her, Mickey assumed. She revved the engine and tapped the horn in response. Normally, she would cruise down the boulevard so she could drive past the beach shack where she'd first encountered Ronald Dunn. But it had been leveled in March, and a boxy three-story condo now stood in its place. She was glad Ronnie never had to see it.

Whenever the sadness threatened to settle in, Mickey learned to think of their children. She even devised a trick - she said their names out loud three times as she drove.

"Eileen Johanna Michaela Dunn. Michael Patrick Francis Dunn."

She repeated it twice more, a little louder each time. "Eileen Johanna Michaela Dunn. Michael Patrick Francis Dunn." Eileen loved *Schoolhouse Rock* and informed Mickey that three was a magic number.

The lapping wave of grief receded. For the moment, anyway. She hoped this A.C. case would help occupy her mind. It would be challenging, but then again, it wasn't her case. No brass or politicians would be dogging her to solve it or asking for progress reports twice a day. She'd overstated the financial pressure she was under, but not by a lot. The thought of selling their house, modest as it was judging by the new construction around her, made her physically ill. Leenie and Michael's father had been torn from their lives. She would not let the only house they'd ever known as a family be next. The money be damned.

Mickey signaled and made another left, taking her past the Surf City Police Department. She saw that four of the now five cruisers were parked there. Charlie Higgins' Chief's car was the one missing. They were all late models, maybe a little boxy, but still sporty enough to get her approval. She'd broken the mold with her first cruiser, a Danube Blue '65 Chevelle SS, which she paid for and tuned up herself. The one and only Zeke from Manahawkin had hand-painted the SCPD insignias for her. Zeke had quit chopping cars, she'd heard, when one slipped off a jack and almost flattened him. Mickey wasn't sure what he was up to now.

Her own small office was in a building across from the PD. Its prior occupant was a CPA who absconded with several hundred thousand dollars of his client's tax refunds. Mickey had been working out of a corner desk at the SCPD, which proved to be awkward. Even Charlie Higgins kept calling her Chief, and he was the Chief. She tracked the accountant to the Sea Spray Motel in Long Beach, where he'd signed in under the unfortunately chosen alias Charles P. Atwater. She almost missed it, but he'd had to initial something on the room registration form. The CPA is what caught her attention.

Charlie had wanted her to meet his latest hire. He said she was fresh out of the academy, but she reminded him so much of a young Mickey Cleary that he worried he might not be Chief very much longer. Her name got stuck in Mickey's head – Margherita DellaDonna. She wondered what Sinatra would think of that one.

The call from the phone booth to Rich had been brief. She told him they'd regroup later and to let her know when it was taco night. She said Tuesdays worked best for her. She could visit the PD tomorrow when Charlie was there. Mickey knew she was late, but Bunny wouldn't care. The girl had become less of a babysitter and more of a nanny since Ronnie's death. Charlie and Barbara had begun the formal adoption process when her parents disappeared for the second time. Charlie nicknamed their family The Mod Squad – one Black, one white, one Vietnamese. Bunny said it was cool being Peggy Lipton's Julie, but she stopped short at the idea of dyeing her jet-black hair blonde. Charlie swore he was a dead ringer for Lincoln Hayes. Barbara was unsure how she felt about being Mike.

Mickey checked her watch.

She knew it was time to click her clunky rubber heels together three times and turn herself back into Mrs. Dunn. As she rolled to a stop, she did truly believe there was no place like home.

The Pine Barrens

"Haven't seen Scooch or his Property around," Walker White said. "The old ladies want some time to, you know, help her get ready for her big night."

Someone had once told Pettigrew that men could be mean to women, but never to the degree that women seemed to enjoy being mean to other women. The initiations he had witnessed bore that statement out. Walker had revised the brutal proceedings. In the not-so-distant past, by the time the new member's Property staggered into the main room of the clubhouse, she'd already been sexually assaulted in ways even he found stomach-turning.

Pettigrew had patronized the brothels in Saigon more than once during his tours. He thought he'd never again see acts so depraved. He had been wrong. No Property had ever died, but some had come close. And if any of them got pregnant or got the clap, then a defrocked doc from Tabernacle was summoned to make either problem go away. It reminded Pettigrew of the town he'd read about in a biography of Wild Bill Hickok.

Walker White's edict did away with most, but not all, of the worst behavior. He seemed to sense that the ritual was a dead-end road and only created more problems within the ranks. Disease had decimated the Indians, whose ground they occupied. Walker White told him that new venereal diseases were on the horizon. Deadly ones. Ones that could wipe out the MC in six months, he'd said. Walker White kept the humiliating public copulation of the new Patch and his Property, but the requirement for pulling a train was quietly dropped.

Pettigrew had had the clap more than once in country. The memory of the two giant syringes full of 10W-30 grade penicillin the medic injected in each butt cheek was enough incentive for him to stay on the straight and narrow ever since.

"Job's all done, so I told him to be back here in an hour," Pettigrew lied. "We didn't find much."

"Did you burn it?" White asked. "Burning is the best way to clear out dead wood."

"On my way to do just that," Pettigrew said. "Figured that part was my responsibility."

"Until he's patched in, Scooch and his little slut are your responsibility," Walker said. "I'd worry more about them if I was you. Everybody looks forward to this. I certainly am. A drunk and disorderly crowd, well, that's one thing. But a drunk and disappointed crowd, now, that is quite another. Make sure they turn up. Too late now for cold feet."

Pettigrew decided not to answer. He simply nodded in assent.

His plan was to ride out and see if he could track the pair down. He assumed they were together. Mayday Minette's meager belongings were in his pocket, and he wanted to hide them somewhere outside the wire. The idea that one soldier would destroy another soldier's decorations and mementos was simply beyond his comprehension.

Pettigrew hustled outside and looked around. It wasn't a clubhouse—he'd known that the day he rode up—it was a hideout. And if he couldn't produce Scooch and the girl, he wasn't sure where he would be able to hide out.

If they were already gone, he'd need to know. And he'd need to know pretty goddamn soon.

TWELVE

Surf City

MICKEY PULLED TO A stop in the little driveway and shut off the engine.

In the long, painful crawl across the Causeway, she hadn't found one tolerable song to listen to, and now, just as she was ready to get out, she turned the radio back on and checked the presets one more time. The turgid and severely overdone "Sometimes When We Touch" was mercifully ending. Overlapping it was a catchy bass line she recognized instantly. Mickey flipped the ignition collar to the accessory position. She twisted the volume knob until it wouldn't turn any farther.

Colin Blunstone started to tell his story.

When "She's Not There" hit the "But it's too late to say you're sorry" line in the first verse, Mickey started singing along and tapping her palms on the steering wheel, her wedding ring pinging the plastic each time.

She didn't stop when Eileen came bounding down the front steps, and she didn't stop when the child started banging on her door. She mouthed, "Sing!" through the open window, and the little girl matched her lyrics.

How should I know? Why should I care?

When The Zombies finally segued into the jazz organ solo, Mickey shouted, "Dance!"

Eileen broke into what looked like a combination of The Watusi, The Twist, The Bristol Stomp, and something she thought might be from *Saturday Night*

Fever. Mickey laughed and clapped until the verse repeated. Then they both started singing again, Mickey bouncing in the bucket seat like a teenager.

But it's too late to say you're sorry,

How should I know? Why should I care?

Please don't bother trying to find her

Bunny came out the front door with a worried look. She was holding Michael in her arms. Mickey's little boy seemed unimpressed by the noisy commotion, and the teenager walked carefully down the steps with him. Eileen was twirling wildly now and nearly knocked them both down.

"You crazy sometime, Mickey-san," Bunny yelled over the music. "She," Bunny double-pointed to Eileen, "she like you. She crazy. You both crazy. You thank God Michael not crazy."

Eileen had now danced herself into utter exhaustion or twirled herself into violent vertigo, quite possibly both. She crumpled into a heap on the crushed seashell front lawn. Mickey bobbed her head, waited until the song faded out, and turned the ignition ring to Off.

She got out and walked over to the little girl.

"You OK there, Leenie Meanie Chili Beanie?"

Eileen got up, a little wobbly at first, and then wrapped her arms around Mickey's waist.

Bunny shook her head. "Dinner not ready yet," she said. "Michael is having a very good day! We play all day since he wake up. Make me tired."

"Did he talk?" Mickey asked.

"I tell you later. Yes. But no. But yes. I tell you later."

Mickey was worried about Michael's verbal delay, but Dr. Harman assured her some children were later talkers than others. The little boy, she said, had hit all his other developmental milestones, and she was confident he'd catch up to this one quickly, joking that with "Little Miss Loquacious" for a sister, he might not be able to get a word in edgewise when he did start. If he didn't, Mickey worried, pricey specialists and expensive tests might be more than she could afford. Mike Kase had left a card at her office. She'd never called him.

Eileen grabbed Mickey's hand as she closed the car door. They headed toward the porch. Bunny walked two steps ahead. She stopped and turned around.

"I'm sorry dinner not ready, but you late. Helly, he come but have to leave. Michael was so happy to play, I think better good not to stop. So sorry, Mickey-san."

Mickey looked down at Eileen and grinned.

"Ready?" she asked the child.

"Ready," Eileen answered.

They launched into a shaky, off-key duet again.

"But it's too late to say you're sorry," they sing-shouted and pointed at Bunny.

Bunny just shook her head again and mounted the steps, holding tight to Michael. "Like I say, you both *dinky dao*. Yeah. You both *boo-coo dinky dao*."

Mickey and Eileen were still singing when the front door closed behind them.

The Claridge Hotel
123 South Indiana Avenue, Atlantic City

Three suitcases, each a different color, lay on the barely disturbed twin bed closest to the door. Only two were open.

He checked again to make sure all of Archibald Graham's and only Archibald Graham's accouterments and papers, including the sweat-stained t-shirt, were in the white one in the center. He'd tucked the undershirt in a plastic bag the hotel had thoughtfully supplied for laundry or dry cleaning, or maybe vomiting. Americans, in his limited experience, were a bit of a funny lot when it came to gawking. And though the Claridge Hotel was old - a plaque in the ornate lobby said it opened in 1930 - it was clearly no kip, so maybe they attended to every possibility. He also noticed on the elevator that there was no thirteenth floor.

His parents had never been ones for serious notions, so fancy digs, as a rule, had not been part of his upbringing. Unless he counted the clinkers and the graybars where the front desk men knew him by his Christian name. A name, with any decent Irish luck, he'd not be using his own self ever again once he departed.

The open green case on the left held the documents and belongings of the individual he was about to become. He'd showered again, it being less of an exercise to wash away any lingering traces of Ilsa's loamy, not-unpleasant musk than it was to clear his head and help him reset his story.

The third suitcase was one he'd found in a second-hand shop in Belfast. The store clerk asked him if he was sure he truly wanted a "Proddy Orange" Samsonite. He'd told the man it was for a bomb and was charged half of the marked price. It was the only one of the three he'd leave with. Tucked inside it, along with the dullest wardrobe he could put together, was a Lufthansa Airlines ticket from Philadelphia to Madrid.

The Backing of Warrants act and the Extradition Act were still being batted around by the Irish courts as to what constituted a political offense and was, therefore, non-extraditable. If, by bad luck or trouble, his fingerprints or picture did come up, he'd be safely beyond the reach of the Garda. A few compatriots were there already there, laying low. They planned to leave The Troubles and the struggle for unification to younger guns and thought they might open Madrid's first real Irish pub. Spaniards liked their beer cold, his mates reported, but maybe they could change that.

The money and the weapons were his ticket out of the life. He'd know his stepmother, who'd loved him as if he was her own, was avenged, even if he wasn't there to witness it. He planned on being in the U.S. only another two days and figured one more bounce with Ilsa and she'd open the vault as quickly as she opened her legs. He knew something unexpected could always materialize to stand in his way, but he was prepared to neutralize any threat to his sacred mission.

He planned to ask Driscoll for the chip back straightaway. It had been proof of his *bona fides*, even if the story of its provenance was pure fiction. Once safely in his pocket, it was almost all but done.

He walked to the mirror. Ilsa had shown unusual persistence in trying to get him bare-chested. Next time, he'd tell her he had an ugly birthmark and couldn't perform if he knew it was visible. He wished he'd thought of it sooner, but no harm had come of it. He turned so he could see his reflection. On his back was inked

Easter Rising 1916

with its intricate and symbolic portraiture below. He could explain that one away as being religious in nature.

But he needed to hide the one on his chest. The one he'd gotten in Long Kesh on the first night of his incarceration, the date forever memorialized above it.

Ilsa could see a lot and still be allowed to live.

But not the rose tattoo.

FOURTEEN

Surf City

MICKEY HAD BEEN MORE than a little skeptical about a Vietnamese teenager cooking southern fried chicken and hominy grits. Right up until she'd taken her first bite.

Bunny Tran had replicated Charlie Higgins' mama's recipe perfectly.

Mickey went to the kitchen for extra napkins, her fingers a greasy mess. She tapped Bunny on the shoulder on her way back to the table.

"I'll clean up," she said. "You've done enough. Thank you, honey, that was delicious."

"Charlie-san say I make good as his mama," Bunny beamed. "He say Colonel Sanders go back to Kentucky once he taste mine." That made Mickey laugh.

"OK, now scoot," Mickey told her. "Charlie and Barbara will think you ran away."

Bunny shook her head. "I stay. I call them and ask. Barbara say it OK. I think they want time for *nuk-nuk.*" She started to insert one index finger into the curled fingers of her other hand until Mickey stopped her.

"Bunny," she said. "What did we talk about?"

"It's OK, Mama," Eileen chirped. "Bunny told me what it means."

Mickey glared at the teenager.

"And what exactly did Bunny tell you it means?"

Eileen folded her hands in her lap. "Nook-nook is a big hug that only people who are married are allowed to do. But they hafta be laying down."

Mickey processed the answer, inhaled deeply, and relaxed.

"That sounds about right," she said. "But we only call it that inside this house. Understood?"

Eileen nodded. Mickey looked at Bunny.

"Yeah. Sure. You big boss, Mickey-san. Big hug from now on. OK?"

Mickey chuckled. "OK. Big hug. That's our password now, too. Got it?"

The two girls bounced their heads in agreement.

"Anyway," Mickey said, "Take the kids and go watch TV. This is my job."

The scuffling of wooden chairs on the wooden floor initially muffled the knock at the door. When it came again louder, Mickey put down her handful of plates and went to investigate.

Eileen beat her to it.

"Halt!" the child said with a sentry's practiced conviction. "Who goes there? Identify yourself."

There was laughter outside the door.

"Hey, it's me. It's Helly. Can I come in, please?"

"Advance and be recognized," Eileen commanded before running off to the living room. Mickey thought that if the academy were ever to have its first female D.I., it might be Leenie.

"Come on in," Mickey said as Helly Hansen eased through the doorway. "I'm on K.P. Want to help?"

"Maybe later," Helly said. "Weather looks perfect for a few hours. Want to go for a ride? Sunset cruise, like the tourists overpay for every night."

Mickey looked at the table and the mess in the kitchen. "Man, Helly, I'd love to but I've been gone all day and -"

Bunny popped her head in. "You go with Helly. Me and Eileen, we clean up. How much you pay?"

"Uhhhh," Mickey stammered. "I don't know. Five bucks?"

"Seven-fifty," Bunny shot back. "Enough we get ice cream. Michael love ice cream. Black Raspberry. One scoop. He eat all gone every time."

"Tell you what, Bunny," chimed Helly. "Make it ten. I'll throw in half."

"See?" Bunny said. "Good deal for everybody. We rich now and you go on boat with Helly. Everybody happy. You get changed, Mickey-san. *Didi-mau*."

"Remind me to hire her to run my business when she's old enough," Helly said.

"Do I need a jacket?" Mickey asked him.

"Maybe bring a sweater or a sweatshirt for the trip back. A fresh breeze underway can make it feel ten degrees cooler."

"Aye, aye, cap'n," Mickey said and hustled to find different clothes.

Bunny peeked her head around from the other room and gave Helly an enthusiastic thumbs-up.

Bader Field
Atlantic City Municipal Airport

The Cessna 500 *Citation I/SP* was FAA-certified for one-pilot flight, but government protocols required a fully vetted military pilot and co-pilot when ferrying dignitaries, members of Congress, or high-ranking federal appointees and bureaucrats.

The cockpit doors had remained shut, and neither pilot appeared in the cabin. There was no attendant. *All the better not to see you with*, Evan Driscoll thought to himself. J.J. Durkin had pointed out that the jet they were on had been introduced in 1976 and cost American taxpayers somewhere upward of seven hundred thousand dollars. It was an enhanced version of the 500 *Citation I*, sporting a longer forty-seven-foot wingspan while retaining the two Pratt & Whitney turbofan engines with the addition of a reverse thruster.

Evan Driscoll's aviation expertise extended to balsa wood gliders and the occasional asymmetric paper airplane, but the Director went on with a former stick jockey's enthusiasm and intricate knowledge, so the flying time passed quickly. Driscoll asked him if he'd ever piloted it.

"God, wouldn't I love to," Durkin had replied. "If only they'd let me. But I think they're afraid I might buzz the boys over in Langley."

In Driscoll's experience, J.J. Durkin rarely let his guard down. But once in the air, he'd been as relaxed and amiable as Driscoll had ever seen him. He mentioned that with its turbofan engines, as opposed to turbojets, and its straight instead of swept-wing configuration, it flew a little slower, leading aviation industry wags to dub it the Nearjet or the Slowtation. They'd arrived in Atlantic City a full ten minutes ahead of schedule and Durkin said the nicknames were purely the results of corporate jealousy.

As he climbed into the car with Special Agent Walt Stenkewiecz, the plane was already rolling toward the runway. Driscoll doubted the tires had time to cool off.

"Stosh," Driscoll said as he buckled up. "Tell me they showed up. And with garbage bags full of evidence."

Stenkewiecz shifted into Drive and bee-lined off the tarmac just in time to avoid a Piper Cub that was wobbling its way to a shaky touchdown.

"No Joy, sir," he said as he navigated the blue-lamped runway access and then cut sharply across a grassy field toward a line of unbroken chain-link fence. "We left word at the dead-drop, but that's still untouched as of thirty minutes ago. They're both good agents, sir. The girl – the woman – this was her first field assignment under deep cover. She basically bullied them into giving it to her. She devised her own cover story and even went and got herself a real tattoo – the kind that hurts to get and that you have forever. I mean, there's commitment," he paused, "And then there's *commitment*. I'm praying they couldn't chance an extraction and are either on the move or are waiting it out, holed up someplace cozy in the Pine Barrens, hoping the cavalry arrives soon."

"Johanna," Driscoll replied. "That was – is – her name, right? Johanna?"

"Yes, sir. Johanna Colleen Tierney. Her dad's an NYPD lieutenant. Top of her class at Quantico. Her thesis at Wharton, she has an MBA, was on the monetary barriers to peace in Northern Ireland."

"Monetary barriers? What was her conclusion?"

"That the two sides doing the actual fighting and the killing don't want peace at all. That a civil war is big business for both. That there is no money, no profit, in any temporary, much less any permanent peace or even a cease-fire."

Driscoll thought about that. "No John Lennon song either."

"No, sir. I doubt 'Give War a Chance' would break the Billboard Top 40."

The sedan, a black, unmarked 1978 Plymouth Fury, jounced along the fence line until it reached an opening that looked only inches wider than the car. Stenkewiecz hit the bullseye and zoomed through with what Driscoll guessed was a quarter-inch of clearance on each side. He looked over at his driver. Stenkewiecz shrugged.

"I do a little stock-car racing and some stunt-driving in my spare time," he said. "Over at the ATCO Dragway. Helps me relax."

Driscoll laughed. "Yeah. Certainly sounds relaxing. You ever see *Bullitt*?"

Stenkewiecz turned onto a paved frontage road and accelerated.

"Sir. That movie is ten years old, and it gets better every time I watch it. I bought myself a dark blue turtleneck because of it. My wife says, as much as she loves me, I'm not Steve McQueen. Crackers in bed and all that. Like to know where he got that shoulder holster, though. I could pull off that look, I'm pretty sure."

The frontage road became an uneven two-lane, and Driscoll settled in. "Who do you have searching?"

"Our guys and everybody they could spare from the F.O. in Cherry Hill. I still can't believe that isn't our Field Office. Did you know the Director lived in Cherry Hill for quite a while?"

"Yes," Driscoll answered. "While his girls were in high school. I believe they're both in college now."

"The older one's in law school down in Delaware. Should be graduating next Spring – might be a good career builder to remember that."

Driscoll smiled. "Yes, it might. Stosh, what do you know about my kids?"

"You don't have any children, sir," Stenkewiecz said and turned down the car's fan. "And I hope you find the right woman soon. Or she finds you. That would be a good career move as well, if you look at it in a certain light."

"Because people wonder why a man in his late thirties is still a bachelor and they think maybe he's got a secret?" Driscoll said. "Any juicy back chatter you want to let me in on, Agent Stenkewiecz?"

"None to speak of, Mr. Driscoll," Stenkewiecz said. "Simply an observation. Anyway, I also tapped into a couple of local poachers I've used as assets before. They know the Pine Barrens like the backs of their grimy hands. But those bikers, they're like Clifton Clowers on Wolverton Mountain – I swear the goddamn birds and the bears let them know the minute a stranger shows up."

"There aren't any bears in the Pine Barrens, Stosh."

"I know. sir. But it works with the song. One of them, the poachers, he said he thinks the MC might have its own surveillance camera or even cameras now. They deal in a lot of stolen electronics, so it sounds plausible enough. They're like a virus – they adapt to threats. That's what's scary about them. This new head honcho, he's no dummy."

Driscoll considered the possibility and the analogy. "You're quite the philosophical thinker, aren't you, Stosh?"

"I'm a true detective, sir," Stenkewiecz answered. "And you can thank the good Jesuit fathers for any philosophical bent I might possibly possess. Three semesters. Required. And I was a business major."

"So maybe we should talk about religion instead?" Driscoll asked.

"Three semesters of Theology. Also required."

"History?" Driscoll queried.

"Two semesters of U.S. History. Taught by the incomparable Professor James V. Lennon. Don't confuse a college degree, Mr. Driscoll, with a college education."

"Have you thought about being a contestant on *Jeopardy*, Agent Stenkewiecz?"

"I'm terrible when it comes to Geography. I try to help my kids with their homework, but the names of all the cool-sounding countries have changed. Madagascar, Mozambique, Ceylon? All different now. And boring. At least Ivory Coast is still hanging in there. And Lake Tanganyika. For the moment."

"Know much about the Congo?" Driscoll asked.

"I read *Heart of Darkness*, which is about the ivory trade and how the Belgians basically made the whole country their private plantation and the Congolese natives their slaves."

Driscoll thought of the chip in his pocket. "Speaking of Belgium. Dare I ask?"

"One of the Benelux countries is what I remember from sixth grade. Belgium, the Netherlands and Luxembourg. I'm sure that's outdated now as well. Their king, Leopold, he got hold of the Congo somehow and raped it for decades. There aren't very many famous Belgians. Jacky Ickx, the Formula One race car driver, he's Belgian. His real first name is Jacques. French is one of Belgium's three official languages. Dutch and German are the other two."

"Well, I know Emerson Fittipaldi is Italian," Driscoll offered.

"Emerson Fittipaldi is actually Brazilian, sir. Watch *Wide World of Sports*. Jim MacKay will tell you everything you need to know about Formula One racing in one afternoon. Is there any significance to Belgium? It's not a common question, you'll admit."

"The owner of the new casino has Belgian roots," Driscoll said. "We're still a young enough country that our ancestors who washed ashore here are still very much in our hearts and minds. We all salute the flag and recite the Pledge of Allegiance, but something older still tugs at us, still influences us - even blinds us sometimes."

"Who's being philosophical now, sir?"

They drove in silence for several minutes. Then Stenkewiecz piped up.

"You asked, have I seen *Bullitt*? Mr. Driscoll, I saw *Bullitt* in the theater when it first came out in 1968. I've seen it at the Manahawkin Drive-In, alone, so I wouldn't miss anything. I have it on Betamax, Laserdisc, and VHS. If it comes out on a school film strip or a GAF View-Master, I'll buy that. So yeah, I have watched it a few times."

The Plymouth rumbled over a gaping pothole, swerved slightly, and then settled back in the left lane.

"Sorry about that," Stenkewiecz said and then continued on with his side of the conversation. "Did you know that the chase scene lasts for ten minutes and fifty-three seconds? And McQueen did all his own driving? And that the wheelman in the Charger with the black glasses? He's a professional Hollywood stunt driver."

"Stosh," Driscoll said, "I did not know any of those things. But now I do. And in the last ninety minutes, my knowledge of business jets, Lieutenant Frank Bullitt, history, geography, and Formula One racing have all increased exponentially."

"Proud to be of service, sir," Stenkewiecz said.

He pulled the Fury off the road onto the crumbling shoulder.

"But you did know that Bullitt's name was Frank and that he was a Lieutenant. That's impressive. Tell me the Mustang's plate number, and I will spring for sirloin steaks at Zaberer's."

"OK. Now you're sandbagging me, Stosh," Driscoll replied dryly.

"Sir, I try not to assume anything, but I assume we're heading to the R.A.? If so, I'll need to turn up ahead here."

"Stosh, how long a drive is it to Long Beach Island?" Driscoll asked.

"It depends. There is only one bridge on or off it and only one main road up and down it. Where on LBI exactly? If it's Barnegat Light or Holgate, it'll be twice as long as, say, Ship Bottom, which is right in the center."

"Surf City," Driscoll replied.

"May I ask, sir, what's in Surf City? I know they sell some nice boards at the Ron-Jon."

Driscoll thought for a moment and then answered.

"The Ron-Jon is actually in Ship Bottom. And it's not what's in Surf City, Stosh."

He paused.

"It's who."

FIFTEEN

Borough of Barnegat Light, NJ

THE *RACHEL* WAS A twenty-six-foot lapstrake hull ocean skiff built in 1964 by the Henry Luhrs Boat Company in Morgan, N.J.

Mickey had no idea where Morgan was, and Helly had described it to her this way: New Jersey looked kind of like the silhouette of Alfred Hitchcock on his old black-and-white TV show. Morgan, he said, was tucked in a nook right at the nape of Hitchcock's neck, inland from the Atlantic and dead even with the imaginary offshore demarcation line between New York and New Jersey's waters.

On their first trip to the dock, Mickey mistakenly thought they were going aboard the fishing trawler, The *Hans N.* When she asked what the N stood for, he'd stared at her.

"Hans N. Hans N," she'd repeated. "Hans-en. Hansen. OK, now I get it, Duh."

That first afternoon Mickey had been surprised when they kept walking past the *Hans N* to what, in comparison, looked considerably smaller.

"Aren't we gonna need a bigger boat?" She'd blurted out when Helly pointed out the *Rachel*, bobbing in the swell.

When he finally stopped laughing, he'd said, "I guess you police chiefs are all the same."

On previous trips on the *Rachel*, Mickey hadn't done much but sightsee. Helly taught her how to handle and coil the lines, scolding her when she called them ropes. He showed her a few basic seamen's knots so she'd be able to tie up securely and cast off easily. He went over some terminology like port and starboard, fore and aft, stern and bow, and tried to explain how to read and steer a magnetic compass heading from a simple chart. He also demanded Mickey call the boat "she" not "it."

On this trip, he said he wanted to show her how to read the channel markers, how to lower and retrieve the anchor, and how to handle the boat in a mild swell.

Traffic was light for a summer evening, but the trip to the docks at Viking Village was still taking a little time.

As they motored along up Long Beach Boulevard toward Barnegat Light, Helly was playing a cassette tape he'd cobbled together from songs off the radio. The sound was a little fuzzy, but with enough volume, it worked well enough. Jimmy Buffet's "Son of a Son of a Sailor," was playing. Helly pointed to the tape deck and then at himself with a grin.

When they stopped at a red light, Mickey asked him how the boat had come into his possession. She didn't think it looked like a fishing boat. He turned down the volume.

He explained that the boat had originally been purchased by a wealthy doctor in Stone Harbor. Helly's father, who was also named Christian but who went by Hans, was hired to motor it down to Long Beach Island, something he did on weekends for extra money. The trip had not been uneventful, Helly remembered, having been brought along to crew.

A large group of pedestrians pushing bicycles and dragging rafts, boogie boards and beach umbrellas clogged the crosswalk long after the light had changed.

"So," Helly said. "We're nicely waking way south, cruising about a half-mile from shore when, literally out of nowhere, this summer thunderstorm kicks up as we're passing Lavallette. We didn't know how far out to sea the front extended. Back then, we didn't have radar or reliable weather radio. And even though it was a brand new boat, twenty-six feet is about as small as you want to be out on the ocean. Plus, it didn't have enough power for us to turn into the wind so we could take the waves head-on."

"Why would you ever want to take waves head-on?" Mickey asked.

" 'Cause," Helly replied, "the bow is shaped like a V for a reason. So it cuts through them. If they hit you broadside – he pointed to her door - the boat can start to wallow in the troughs and could roll over and capsize if another big wave comes along and catches it leaning."

"So why not just head straight for shore."

"Yeah, that's the idea, but if you head straight in, then the waves are directly behind you. It's called a following sea. They slam into the stern, which is flat. It's like a hammer hitting an anvil. And, if the seas are big enough, you can take enough water over the transom to swamp you."

"But not sink?"

"Well, not right away. But when you swamp, water floods the engines, so you lose power, and you lose steerage. You're basically just a waterlogged cork at the mercy of the wind and the waves."

"So what did you do?" Mickey asked.

The line of cars was moving again, but not very fast.

"Well," Helly went on, "Dad knows every anchorage and harbor there is from Manasquan to Cape May. He climbs down from the flying bridge -"

"That's the steering wheel place up on top of the cabin?"

"Yeah, I guess you could call it that. So Dad says we'll make a run for shelter in Seaside Heights until it blows past. I remember they had this amusement park. Sticks right out into the ocean."

"Funtown U.S.A.," Mickey interjected. "They still do, and it still does. Leenie and I were just there. She got a mermaid tattoo."

Helly looked at her funny.

"A fake one. Jeez."

Helly nodded. "Ya, I sure hope so. Anyways, Dad goes throttle wide open as far as he can and slides us in on the lee side of a pier. Jesus, could he handle a boat back then. We tie her up, and as we set foot on the pier, *boom*, the storm arrives. 'Bout blew us both off the dock. Lightning's hittin' all around, buzzing the topmasts of the big sailboats. Dad still swears he saw St. Elmo's Fire dancing on one of them."

"What's St. Elmo's Fire?" Mickey asked, intrigued by the name as much as the story.

"Old sailor's legend, but a true phenomenon. It's a green glow you see sometimes when the air is heavily saturated with electrical charges. Watch the old 'Moby Dick' movie, the one with Gregory Peck as Ahab. They did a pretty good job showing what it looks like. But if you ever experience it during a storm on the water, lay down flat in the boat or even jump overboard."

"Why would you do that?"

"Because there's a good chance a lightning strike is imminent. And nobody wins an argument with a lightning bolt."

Mickey spied a sign for Viking Village with an arrow.

"I'll make the rest quick," Helly said as the cars ahead pulled away.

"So we hoof it up to the boardwalk and duck inside the first door we see. It's a pizza place—Leone's, I think. Great pizza. It was the first time I ever had it right out of the oven and not a cardboard box. Dad disappears for a couple of minutes and comes back with two bottles of beer. My first one ever, now, you have to understand—Miller High Life. It sure tasted like champagne to me."

That made Mickey chortle. "Okay. You got two minutes," she chided. "Wrap it up, Popeye."

"OK, OK," Helly said. "So the thunderboomer, like Jim O'Brien would say, it's come and gone in like ten minutes. We hustle back down to the pier, hoping this brand-new boat's not damaged because Dad's afraid he'll be on the hook for any repairs. It wasn't, but as we're firing up the engine this big guy comes rumbling down the dock yelling and screaming at us. He tells Dad he's blocking his slip and that he's already notified the cops and the Coast Guard. Maybe the Marines, too, I can't remember. My dad is not one for foul language, so he grabs a boat pole, walks over to the rail, and points it right at the guy. 'Go back to your fancy yacht club, Commodore,' he says. Y'ain't never heard the expression 'any port in a storm?' *Uff da*, what a magnificent moron you are. You should name your boat the *Idiyacht*."

"OK, stop for a second," Mickey said. "What's with this *uff da*? I know I've heard you say it more than once."

"It's Norwegian – means, well, it's an expression of frustration or surprise at a bad or even an unusual situation. Hey, Sven, I heard your brand new boat sank. *Uff da*."

"Better than 'holy shit' I guess," Mickey said. "I might try that one around our house. You get another two minutes for me interrupting, but we're almost there, so..."

"So we shove off and haul ass back to the docks here. It's now almost dark, so we tuck her in and meet the guy, the new owner, the next day. Dad watches him take her out and winks at me. Sure enough, a month later, the guy calls Dad and asks if he wants to buy the boat. He says it's too small for the ocean, and he's buying a bigger one. Figures he'll get more from Dad than he would in trade."

"See!" Mickey yelped.

Helly shook her off. "So, Dad, he buys the boat. Tells me it's mine, for a fair price, when I turn eighteen. Every cent I made from then on, crewing, cleaning fish, scrubbing decks, pumping out bilges and overhauling engines, it all went into the bank."

"Cool story," Mickey said as they pulled into a parking space. "Long. But cool." A fleet of battered pickups, all with some fisherman's name or business stenciled on the door, crowded the lot.

Helly got out and pulled a small cooler from the truck's bed.

"What's in there?" Mickey asked. "And don't say baitfish. I am not biting the head off a herring for luck."

"No, not bait," Helly replied. "It's a little reward for when we get back, but you'll have to earn it."

"Well, that sounds worrisome," Mickey said. She slammed her door shut.

They walked down toward the *Rachel*, past the big scallopers, the longliners, and the drag boats. Smaller day boats, ones belonging to members of the commercial fleet, dotted the spaces in between. Seagulls squawked and fought each other fiercely over scraps in the evening haze. The smell of salt air and decaying fish was somehow anything but unpleasant.

She looked out at the endless expanse of water and reminded herself she wasn't going out or coming back on it alone.

"Ladies first," Helly said as he ushered her aboard.

SIXTEEN

The Pine Barrens

HE'D BEEN PUSHING THE thought out of his mind all day, but Owen Pettigrew knew there was another worrisome explanation for Scooch's disappearing act. He refused to believe it was possible. The girl, now that was an outside possibility, but not Scooch. His story was airtight, and more guys than Pettigrew had checked it. The link to a buyer for the stolen weapons had come from him and it had also checked out six ways from Sunday.

If there was a rat, Pettigrew believed, it would have to be the girl. Scooch seemed to care about her, and that would certainly make him an easy mark if she wasn't who she said she was.

But it didn't matter if it was one, both, or neither of them. A no-show would fall squarely on his head. He'd sensed that Walker White was gunning for him from Day One. Pettigrew did whatever he could to diminish himself as a threat, but Walker was like a guy with a bug up his ass most of the time anyway. The folder he'd hidden in the lining of his club vest was the insurance policy he'd need if he ever found himself jammed up.

He kicked the bike into life and headed down the gravel path. The camera he knew was mounted high above him was recording. But he also knew that someone would have to climb the tree that held it to get to the tape.

So Owen Pettigrew rode out, knowing if he didn't find Scooch or the girl, one option was to keep on riding.

Surf City

Evan Driscoll had first met Mickey Cleary formally in 1967. She and the events that followed were still burned into his memory. He'd kept loose tabs on her career, noting with not a great deal of surprise that she'd survived the New Jersey State Police academy, which had a reputation for being tougher than Marine boot camp and the Army Ranger school. Learning that she'd recently departed the State Police did pique his interest. There was a file on her in the Atlantic City Resident Office, and he'd asked Stosh to bring it along.

The Fury growled, stuck at embarrassingly low rpms as they made their way up Long Beach Boulevard. Driscoll saw Wally's Restaurant, the place where he'd met Mickey for lunch. Their specialty dish, he recalled, was corned beef hash on toast, the classic "shit on a shingle."

"OK," Stenkewiecz said. "Should be this next light and then two blocks back."

Driscoll closed the folder. "Wow. She's a widow," he said. "Two little kids. That's why she quit the Staties."

The streets were crowded, the days were lengthening, and the sun was still shining even though it was past suppertime. Stenkewiecz made the turn, drove two blocks, and then turned again.

"Should be just...up...here," he said, checking the house numbers. "Next to the – oh holy shit!"

"What?" Driscoll exclaimed as the Plymouth braked hard.

"There it is. Jesus Christ, I can't believe it, but there it is."

"The house?" Driscoll asked, peering out his window. "What's so spe -"

"No, sir. Not the house. The car. I cannot believe it."

Driscoll cranked his neck to look. "Is that the same car as -"

"Yes, it is," Stenkewiecz said as he shifted the Plymouth into Park. "Yes, sir. It sure as shit is."

Both men got out. Stenkewiecz immediately went to the Mustang, running his hand along the fastback louvers and then sticking his head in through the open driver's side window.

Driscoll laughed at the sight as he took the three front steps in one bound. He looked for a doorbell or a knocker. Seeing neither, he knocked three times on the screen door, rattling it loudly in the process.

When no one answered, he knocked again. With still no response, he walked the length of the small front porch and peered in each of the double-hung windows. They were all open, he noted. Gauzy white curtains inside swayed slightly in the late-day breeze.

"Mickey. Mickey Cleary," Driscoll called in through the one nearest the front door. He tried using the least intimidating tone of voice he could muster. "Mickey. It's Evan Driscoll from the F – from a well-known government agency and television show. I'm in town for a meeting and thought I'd stop by. It's been a long time." He felt the porch sag as Stenkewiecz joined him.

"Ask her about the car," Stenkewiecz prodded.

Driscoll straightened up. "Well, Stosh, it looks like the lights are on, but nobody's home," he said. "Sort of like your last performance report."

"I'll take that as a compliment, Deputy Director," Stenkewiecz replied amiably. "Do you think she'd mind if I sat in the car? Two minutes with my hands on the wheel, imagining I'm Frank Bullitt. That's all I ask."

"Sure, Stosh," Driscoll deadpanned. "And if we stop at the PD, maybe the nice policeman will let you wear his hat. Then we'll get you some ice cream on the way home. With sprinkles."

Stenkewiecz was unfazed. "That would be great, Deputy Director. But they're jimmies down this way."

"What...are Jimmies?"

"Sprinkles. That's what they call them. Usually chocolate. Ask for sprinkles, and they'll look at you funny. Like if you order a hero instead of a hoagie at a deli."

"I once ordered a cheesesteak with no cheese," Driscoll said.

"That is a felony in three states, if I'm not mistaken. You're lucky you got away with it."

Driscoll chuckled. "The Director said I'd do well to arrange for a local guide. I didn't realize he was referring to you."

"My pleasure to help you deal with the natives," Stenkewiecz said. "Their dialect and their unique tribal customs can be a bit tricky to navigate. Where are we off to next? Or were you planning on waiting?"

"No," Driscoll said. "I'll come back tomorrow. And yes, you can come along and ask her if you can sit in the car. Just don't ask to drive it, OK. Not yet."

"You are the quintessential party pooper, sir. I respect that."

As they turned and headed for the steps, the front door squeaked open. A young girl stuck her head through the narrow aperture.

"Why you knock so loud?" she said, clearly perturbed. "You almost wake baby up. What you want? Who you are?"

"Does Mickey Cleary live here?" Driscoll asked.

"Maybe. You tell me who you are, first."

Driscoll guessed her at about fifteen, but with her soft Asian features and thin frame, it was difficult to tell.

"I'm Evan Driscoll. I work for the – I work in law enforcement like she does."

"You cops?"

"We work for the government," Stenkewiecz interjected. Driscoll gave him a withering look.

"Which government?" the girl asked warily.

"Our government," Driscoll said as soothingly as he could. "The one in Washington."

The girl's eyes narrowed. "So, what, you CIA? Army CID? INS? I have papers. You check. Come back tomorrow. I show."

"No, no, no," Driscoll answered her. "None of those things. Listen, I know her, I know Mickey. We worked together a long time ago. On police business. Right here in Surf City. She'll know who I am. Can I leave my card?" He reached for his credentials wallet and slipped it out

The girl seemed to waver on the decision. “OK. Leave card. Then go. I tell her.”

Driscoll thumbed his business cards. He pulled out his official Bureau one and then slid it back in. He withdrew a beige card stamped with a government seal, a vague title, and a nonsense address and phone number. Pulling out a pen, he jotted a number on its back.

“Please make sure she gets it when she returns. Promise?”

The girl nodded, took the card, and disappeared. Driscoll heard the rattle of a chain lock.

“That went well,” Stenkewiecz said.

The two men walked back toward the Fury.

“Let’s do a quick touch-and-go at the PD,” Driscoll said. “I’ll leave a card there. Maybe someone can give us a heads-up on her whereabouts. You think they’re still open, right?”

“I think they’re like 7-Eleven, sir. Open twenty-four hours now. This would be a lot faster,” Stenkewiecz mugged. He nodded at the Mustang.

Driscoll shook his head and kept on walking.

Lebanon Forest

The Pine Barrens

Pettigrew checked the lonely asphalt road for traffic, then his beat-up but still dead-accurate G.I. watch for the time. He was at a fork in the road in more ways than one. And the sun was going down.

The Barrens looked impenetrable and unknowable to outsiders, but people had lived tucked away off its trails for generations. A born-and-bred Piney native could navigate miles of it comfortably at night, even with no moon. Pettigrew was not a Piney, but he knew the trails and the hidey-holes almost as well, and he felt like he’d just ridden all of them.

There would be no raucous initiation. But there would be plenty of questions. All of them directed at him. The MC didn’t deal in excuses. It didn’t put much stock in explanations, either. An assumption or even a simple plausible but unprovable suspicion was sometimes enough to buy you a dirt nap. He knew undercover cops and federal agents had a lot of leeway. But he also knew they all had a line they were forbidden to cross. They couldn't commit or participate in a murder or an assault. A rat was possible. But it wasn't a certainty. The plan did not call for anyone to be killed.

He reached inside his vest and patted the concealed folder one more time.

The money for weapons deal was going to mean an influx of untraceable cash larger than any drug buy or murder-for-hire in the MC's dark and troubled history. Having lifted them from an Army cargo shipment that arrived at McGuire Air Force Base, anyone pinched would do Federal time. Very possibly a lifetime of it.

If the imminent swap were compromised or canceled, the consequences for anyone deemed to be complicit or merely negligent would be dire. Scooch's induction had been fast-tracked so he could complete the transaction. Pettigrew was supposed to be his backup, guardian, and the club's monitor.

Owen Pettigrew revved his idling Harley, aimed the front forks to the right, and roared off.

The *Dinh* River swim, he thought as he shifted gears, had been easy in comparison to what was coming next.

SEVENTEEN

Atlantic Ocean
1.5 NM E of Barnegat Lighthouse

"I LOVE THIS SONG," Mickey said as the *Rachel* rocked slowly in the gentle swell. "Did she come with a tape deck?"

The Beach Boys' "Sloop John B" piped out of a Realistic brand speaker mounted under the cabin roof. Helly sat in the captain's swivel chair, futzing with something near the wheel.

"It should have. Luhrs named this model of their skiff the Sedan, if you can believe that. All I can figure is they hoped newbie boat buyers would think it was like a car you could drive on the water. No tape decks in sixty-four, remember?"

It looked to Mickey like they were the only boat out there.

"The original song is old," Helly said, "Old like nineteen-fifteen or sixteen. It was a folk song from the Bahamas. Somebody got hold of it and translated the lyrics. Brain Wilson heard about it, added a little rock beat, and did his usual amazing vocal arrangement. That boy is a musical genius."

The song ended, and complete stillness followed. The only sound was the waves lapping at the boat's wooden chines. Mickey heard the tap-tap of something plastic and then a click. Helly was flipping the tape, she realized.

"The B side is for the trip home. You do want to go home, right?" he asked.

"I don't know," Mickey said. "I guess maybe I don't feel so broke up." A new opening note played, but then she heard the click of a button, and it stopped. "Rigging for silent running?"

"Pop quiz, and then we'll head in. With soundtrack."

"Shoot, professor," Mickey said. She moved to the edge of the cabin, steadying herself with a hand on the lip of the roof.

"What did you learn this evening?" Helly asked.

"The lubber line on the compass tells you the magnetic heading direction - where the bow is pointing."

"Correct."

"You need five feet of anchor line for every foot of water underneath you. And with a hinged anchor, like a Danforth, you need ten feet of chain attached directly to the anchor. You attach the rope to the chain and the chain to the anchor. Otherwise, it won't lay down and dig into the bottom properly."

"Correct again," Helly said, smiling. "We'll have you taking the exam for your Captain's Certificate in no time. What else?"

"You can get to most places by dead reckoning."

"Because?"

"Because," Mickey paused for a moment to think. "Because all you need to know is your speed on the water, your magnetic heading, the point where you started, and the point you're heading toward."

"And what about timing the inlet?" Helly put his hand on the Play button.

"If there's no to light winds, five knots or less, you can do it under power regardless of the tide. In anything heavier, slack tide is always safest, even if you have to wait. Avoid running it when the tide is going one way, and the wind is going the other. Unless you're an experienced fisherman Like Helly Hansen."

"Great," Helly said. "I'll teach you one more critical thing while you're taking us in."

"Wait," Mickey said. "Wait. What? *I'm* taking us in?"

"It's a Perfect night to learn. Don't worry, I'll be right next to you. But you'll have the wheel and the throttle. She's a good boat. You'll have to try extra hard to sink her."

Helly depressed the Play button. The opening vocal harmony of Looking Glass's "Brandy You're a Fine Girl" tumbled out. He switched places with Mickey, settled her into the Captain's seat, and started the bilge blower, and then the engines.

"You're sure about this?" she asked.

"*Uff da*," he replied with a grin. "We're right here. The land is over there. Now, drive the boat already."

Surf City Police Department

"Told you," Stenkewiecz chirped as they walked up to the station door. "They even left the light on for us."

"I do appreciate your rapier-like wit, Stosh," Driscoll said. "I can't tell if we're supposed to be Joe Friday and Bill Gannon or Christine Cagney and Mary Beth Lacey?"

"Honestly?" Stenkewiecz shot back. "I was thinking more along the lines of Starsky and Hutch. I'd be Hutch, of course."

"Of course," Driscoll said and hit the buzzer. He looked up into an unconcealed camera above him.

"Can we help you?" a woman's voice said.

"Evan Driscoll and Walter Stenkewiecz. FBI. May we come in for a moment, please? Official business, but this won't take long." Driscoll whipped out his credentials wallet, displayed his badge and ID, and held it up to the camera. A quick series of clicks followed and then a brief buzz. They heard the door lock release.

Stenkewiecz opened it slowly and pushed inside. Driscoll followed.

A woman in a crisp, dark blue uniform greeted them. Her pants had gold piping. The inverted triangle insignia patch reminded him of the New Jersey State Police one. Driscoll pegged her at about five-five with bobbed blond hair, an athletic frame, and weighing maybe around a buck-twenty, twenty-five tops. She had what he sometimes referred to as a "don't mess with me" presence about her. Her gold-plated name pin said MD DONNA.

She extended her hand and shook aggressively with both of them.

"Thanks for allowing us in, Officer...Donna." Driscoll said politely. "What does the MD stand for? Are you a doctor, too?"

The officer waved them toward her desk and pulled over a second chair.

"I am not," she said as they all sat down. "It's a misprint. Margherita DellaDonna. Rita, for short. Although, I did deliver a baby last week. Little boy, six-pounds-seven ounces."

"Where did that happen?" Stenkewiecz asked.

"Back seat of my cruiser. Just over the Causeway Bridge in Mud City. I was pedal to the metal Code 4 trying to get the mom to Shore Memorial after her water broke. It was her fifth kid, so I don't even think she even bothered to push. Hiccupped, maybe."

"A boy. Too bad she couldn't name him after you," Driscoll added.

"Well, she kind of did – Martin Donal. They're Irish, I guess. If they call him Marty and you say them together real fast, it's Martydonal. Close enough for government work. Now, gentlemen, to what does SCPD owe the pleasure of a drop-in visit from the FBI?"

"We apologize for the lack of notice but we're looking for Mickey Cleary, er, Chief, no, I mean Detective Mickey Cleary. We stopped at her home, but she wasn't there. Took a flier since we were in the neighborhood."

"Surf City is all of one square mile, gentlemen, so it's pretty hard *not* to be in the neighborhood," DellaDonna said in reply.

"So, do you know where she is or where, say, she might be?" Stenkewiecz asked.

"If she's working, the Island is eighteen miles long and anywhere from a half-mile to a mile wide, with lots and lots of nooks and crannies like an English muffin. I thought the duty roster said she was off today, but she usually doesn't stray too far off-Island during the week."

"Can you contact her?" Driscoll queried.

"Are you officially asking me to contact her, Agent Driscoll?"

He looked at Stenkewiecz before answering. "No. I don't think we need to intrude if she's not on duty, Officer DellaDonna. But we would very much like to talk to her. If I leave my card, can you make certain that she gets it? The sooner, the better, if at all possible. I've worked with her before, but it's been a few years. She should recognize my name."

Driscoll handed her his personal card. DellaDonna looked it over and tucked it in the pocket of her uniform blouse.

"I'll make sure she gets it first thing in the morning. She's usually in her office by 0730, sometimes earlier."

"Then...her office isn't here in your shop?" Stenkewiecz asked.

"No, sir. She has her own office. It's actually across the street on the back side of the station. It belonged to a tax guy she busted for grand larceny – pocketed all his clients' IRS refunds, then tried to boogie oogie oogie out of the country with proceeds. Talk about *karma*, right? It's a funny story, how she ended up collaring him. Ask her about it."

"We will," Driscoll said and rose from his chair. Stenkewiecz did the same.

"Can I ask a question?"

"Sure, Agent..."

"Stenkewiecz. Spelled exactly like it sounds."

DellaDonna laughed. "Yeah, I get it. My boyfriend's Polish. His last name has one vowel. And five bucks says your nickname is Stosh. But go ahead, ask your question."

"Detective Cleary. Is that her car, the one - "

"Ha!" DellaDonna said. "You bet your puss in boots it is. I mean, it's not the actual one from the movie. At least I don't think it is. It could be, I suppose. But it is the exact same make, model, and year as the one Steve McQueen drove in *Bullitt*. Did you notice the plates?"

"I know they were Jersey plates," Stenkewiecz said. "And some people," he glanced over at Driscoll, "some people do insist on calling me Stosh. Very good, Officer DellaDonna. I'm suitably impressed." He patted his pockets. "But I'm afraid I don't-"

"No sweat. You can leave it on my desk when you come back in the morning. And, don't let a light on in her office fool you. She's got an electronics guy installing something for her after hours. She won't say what it is, but I don't think it's a BOSE 901 sound system. As for the Mustang, she did say she'd let me drive it sometime, but not until way after Labor Day."

Stenkewiecz turned to Driscoll and raised his eyebrows.

"Mickey Cleary," DellaDonna added. "You agents do know she's a legend, right? I mean, she's like Supergirl, only badass-ier. She's the reason I became a cop."

"Thank you, Officer," Driscoll said as they backed away. "You've been most helpful. And yes, we're quite aware of Mi – of Detective Cleary's hard-earned reputation. One last thing. Any place we can grab a quick bite nearby? It's been a bit of a long day."

"Bill's Diner," DellaDonna responded without hesitating. "No liquor, but good food for the money. If you have an, uh, an adventurous palate, try the Greek cheesesteak."

"Thank you again, Officer. We'll show ourselves out," Driscoll said. Margherita DellaDonna stood but remained behind her desk.

When they were outside, Driscoll turned to Stenkewiecz. "What's a Greek cheesesteak?"

"No idea," the agent replied. "Special seasonings, maybe? Mint jelly? And she said Cleary was badass-ier. Is badass-ier an actual word?"

Driscoll laughed. "It is now, Stosh. It is now."

As they turned, the door clicked and buzzed. Then it opened. Margherita DellaDonna stepped out, propping it with her leg.

"Can I ask a question?"

"I guess that depends on what the question is, Officer DellaDonna," Driscoll replied. "Go ahead."

"You guys and Detective Cleary. Does this have anything to do with that shit show over at the Steel Pier today?"

"Um," Driscoll said, trying to mask his surprise. "I'm afraid that is one question we can't answer. At least not until we've had the opportunity to speak with Detective Cleary."

"Got it," DellaDonna said. "I figured as much. And don't forget the fiver, Agent Stosh." She slipped back inside, and the door latch clicked again.

"Shit show at the Steel Pier?" Driscoll said. "Any idea what she's talking about?"

"No sir," Stenkewiecz answered. "But the radio in the Fury isn't exactly working. It'll broadcast but won't receive. I thought we were heading directly to the R.A. from the airfield, so-"

"OK. It doesn't matter now. Let's go," Driscoll said. "And you have my official permission to drive like Steve McQueen. Or Emerson Fittipaldi. Your choice."

EIGHTEEN

F.B.I. Resident Agency
Linwood, NJ

"I'M NOT SURE WHY they're still not answering," Agent Robert Marino said to the man seated in front of Stosh Stenkewiecz's empty desk. "Deputy Director Driscoll's plane landed several hours ago, so something must have come up. Do you mind waiting, Mr. Kilderry? I know this meeting is important."

"That's quite a meaty mouthful, now isn't it?" Kilderry said. "Deputy Director Driscoll. A real three-D character, in a manner of speakin'. Does this Deputy Director perhaps have a first name I might use? I'll be tongue-tied for a week if I have to repeat that all the long day. And if you tell me it's Dennis, I'll be departing back to Ireland directly."

He flashed Marino a big smile.

"Evan," Marino replied. "You can probably call him that. We can't."

"Evan'll have to do then, assuming he'll not be richly offended by my familiarity."

"I don't think he will, Mr. Kilderry. Should I call you mister? Officer? Agent? I don't know how the ranks in the *Garda Siochana* are organized. Am I even pronouncing it right?"

"It's a bit tricky in Gaelic," Kilderry said, "But try this - *Gard-a She-oh-hanna*."

"Gar-da See."

"She," Kilderry corrected. "Gar-da She."

"Gar-da She...oh-hanna," Marino said slowly. "Garda Sheo-hanna."

"Ah. Spoken like true Dubliner, Mr. Marino," Kilderry told him. "It means Guardians of the Peace. Everyone at home refers to it as The Guards."

"Thank you," Marino beamed. "Garda Sheohanna. And your rank in The Guards?"

"I'm a working man like you, Agent Marino. An Inspector with aspirations to become a Superintendent. That's the equal of your Captain rank, I'm supposing. Like that Furillo fella of yours on the telly. *Hill Street Blues*, isn't it? I work out of the Dublin Metropolitan District. It's a carve-out of the Eastern Region like your District of Columbia is a carve-out. Ireland's still quite a rural country, Mr. Marino. Has more sheep than shopkeepers. But a great mob of the Paddy's it does have that live in and around Dublin."

"I'd love to see it someday," Marino answered.

"Ring me up when you do, then. I'll be happy to give you the grand tour."

The phone on Marino's desk rang. "Maybe some news," he said cheerfully as he answered it. After a series of "Uh-huhs" and "Yessir's," interspersed with several "I understand's" and "Copy that," a funny look came over his face.

Kilderry didn't miss it.

"No," Marino said slowly into the receiver. "There's nothing like that on this end. Schreiber should be back any time now, though. I'll ask him if he's heard anything. Roger. Understood. Yes, sir, he's here. He's been here for about an hour. Would you like to speak to him? Roger. I'll relay the message. Yes, sir. Yes, sir, the Parkway is definitely faster. See you when you arrive."

He looked up at Kilderry.

"They're en route now, Inspector Kilderry. ETA about forty, maybe fifty minutes if they hit traffic. Can I get you anything? I can have Agent Schreiber pick you up a sandwich and a Coke if you'd like."

"That's all right, lad," Kilderry replied. "I'm doubtin' there's a good shepherd's pie and a pint to be had nearby. Troubles afoot? You looked a might concerned there for a sec."

Marino paused before answering. Again, Kilderry caught it.

"No. Nothing," Marino answered.

The sound of a car engine approaching caused them both to turn their heads. Two minutes later, Agent Denny Schreiber walked through the door carrying a newspaper and a thermos.

"Greetings," Schreiber said and walked to his desk. "This must be our long-awaited guest from the Auld Sod." He gave a little salute. "Dennis Schreiber, Special Agent in Charge here."

"Denny, this is Inspector Kilderry. Connor Kilderry."

"Schreiber," Kilderry said with a grin. "Now that's a right Irish name for you."

Schreiber chuckled. "My mother was a Muldoon, and her mother was a Fitzwater. They hailed from County Mayo. At least that's how the family story goes."

"County Mayo is on the Atlantic Coast, Connacht Province," Kilderry said. "My own humble forebears came from County Kildare. That's in Leinster, farther to the East but still a bit inland from the Irish Sea."

"Like Doctor Kildare. The old TV show," Marino piped up.

Kilderry was unfamiliar with the reference. "The one and the same," he replied, hoping it would end there.

"Your file said something about Antrim. That's up in the North, isn't it?"

Kilderry shifted in his chair. "'Tis indeed, Special Agent. Right in the beatin', bleedin' heart of The Troubles. I worked up there for nearly two years. The blendin' in with the local ruffians kind of work, if you take my meaning."

Schreiber nodded. "Undercover or deep cover. It didn't say."

"As deep as I ever want to be in that shite, truth be told," Kilderry answered. "And thus the reason for my visit to your fair shores."

"I'm sorry we don't have a more comfortable seat to offer you, Inspector." Schreiber tossed him the tightly rolled copy of *The Evening Bulletin*. "A little light reading to pass the time. Something happened on the Boardwalk today but I haven't had time to look at a newspaper. If there was something on the radio, I didn't catch it. Maybe it made it into that late edition. Let me know if you see anything interesting."

Kilderry scanned the front page and saw nothing unusual for a city like Philadelphia – violent crime, desperate politics, and racial strife. When he opened it, though, he had to catch his breath. He rattled the pages to distract from the sound.

"That's funny," Marino chimed in. "The DD asked-" He stopped himself.

"Asked what?" Schreiber queried.

"Nothing important. I'll tell you later," Marino answered.

"How long did you say Mr. Driscoll might be, mate?" Kilderry asked. His thoughts were racing, but he willed himself to slow down and think logically.

"Forty minutes at least from when I put down the phone," Marino said.

Kilderry looked at his watch. "I'm afraid I do have a related engagement that I mustn't be late for," he said. "Tell Mr. Driscoll I'll ring him up first thing in the morning, and we'll meet then. I'm not much for breakfast, but someplace with good, strong coffee and a splash of cream would be grand. Let's say eight o'clock. I'll get the pertinent details from you in the morning. Tell Driscoll if he brings a flask of Jamieson, we can have Irish Coffee."

He winked and rose unhurriedly from his chair, making it a point to tuck the newspaper under his arm as discreetly as he could.

"Apologies, gentlemen," Kilderry said, "But as you might appreciate, a delicate operation like this has more than a few moving parts, and I can't - we can't - afford to gum up the works, as you like to say over here. Now, if you'll excuse me."

Kilderry again forced himself to tamp down the adrenaline surge that was hammering at his brain. He could feel his pulse pounding in his fingertips. When he stepped outside, he realized that although he now had some serious work to do, Ilsa Schoenweiss would be impatiently waiting for him.

And Archibald Graham could well not afford to disappoint her right now.

The Pine Barrens

Walker White called the officers into the meeting room and closed the door.

"Something's rotten," he snarled. "And last time I looked, we aren't in Denmark." Blank stares greeted the Shakespeare reference.

Walker White had been an outstanding high school student destined, perhaps, for an Ivy campus and a full academic ride, his counselors told his parents. Then, on a weekend visit to Williams College in Massachusetts, his student chaperone introduced him to LSD. When he returned to Cherry Hill East High School, he was a substantially altered individual. The South Jersey suburbs were becoming more affluent, and with both his parents being highly paid professionals, affording a candy store assortment of intoxicants was not an issue.

Until it was.

The relatively sedate and chronically sedated life of an upper-middle-class drug addict - he thought Billy Joel's "Captain Jack" could have been written about him – started to fall apart when his physical cravings fell out of sync with his cash supply.

He started dealing to his classmates. Then to kids in his neighborhood. His grades cratered, and he spent more time locked in his room listening to Pink Floyd's "Dark Side of the Moon." It was more than the needle and the damage it was doing – every waking moment was spent either consuming drugs or scrounging the money to buy them. Any profits from his deals went up his nose or in his progressively sclerotic veins.

The Whites of Old Tavistock finally kicked him out of their house after he failed to graduate. The next two months were spent living out of a tent he'd managed to get from Bristow's Sporting Goods in Westmont by giving the kid who worked there a dime bag to sell. He moved almost every night. As soon as word spread that a skinny white boy was camped under the Walt Whitman Bridge, it didn't take long for the vultures to find him. When he stabbed one in the eye, his entry into the criminal justice system was rapid. He was over eighteen, an unfortunate calendar accident of only three days, and the overloaded Camden County Public Defender pleaded him out as self-defense. But he still did jail time.

Starving and strung out, he was an easy mark for predators, even at the medium-security Camden County Correctional Facility on Federal Street. A biker awaiting sentencing for braining a rival with a pool cue in a Pennsauken bar called The Rusty Nail took pity on him and protected him behind the shield of the Sons of Satan Motorcycle Club. Walker had never even sat on a motorcycle until the MC picked him up at the gate and spirited him away to the Pine Barrens. He'd only seen the Barrens from the back seat of his parents' Mercury Montego on the way to their beach house in Stone Harbor.

The old guard at the MC was departing, and Walker White, with an IQ twice that of the average member, slipped into the void. He was a shitty fighter, but a whiz with financial schemes that netted the MC more cash than it had ever seen. Walker White knew that the way the world was going, drugs, low-level paid hits, and retail theft were not the path forward. Guns and ammo, like the name of the popular magazine, were where he planned to go next.

He started small, handguns, shotguns they sawed off themselves, and some construction-grade explosives. Weeks ago, he'd started selling cocaine to a Supply Sergeant at McGuire. An offhand mention that weapons and ordnance for the Army at Fort Dix came through McGuire AFB first piqued his fertile imagination. After the Vietnam War ended, literal planeloads of surplus, high-powered armaments were constantly on the move. A missing case here and there, the sergeant assured him, would easily escape detection

Test runs on a couple of small shipments of shoulder arms were used to beef up the MC's arsenal. When the sergeant said he would be willing to alter paperwork on higher-grade weaponry in exchange for higher-quality coke, Walker White went looking for buyers. Scooch Pascucci said he had a contact, but it would be tricky because it wasn't an American. The deal was now only a day away, and bringing Scooch into membership to seal his allegiance had been fast-tracked.

Now he and his sweet young thing were both missing. His Sergeant-at-Arms hadn't checked in since earlier in the day. Walker White was a genius at running simultaneous scenarios and permutations. The plausible, worrisome explanations greatly outnumbered the benign ones.

"Everybody rides," White told what passed for the MC's brain trust. "Put the old ladies in the bitch seats. If they run, shoot to disable. I need to know exactly what is up here. From them."

The group grunted and snorted various assents and headed for their Harleys.

Walker White remained in his chair. The amount of money on the line, all of it in cash, was astronomical.

He was not about to let it slip away.

NINETEEN

Atlantic Ocean, Off Barnegat Inlet

MICKEY GRIPPED THE WHEEL in both hands. She leaned forward, trying to see through the slowly growing darkness ahead of her. Helly tapped her on the shoulder. He had paused the music.

"It's not the Turnpike at rush hour," he said. "You see any other boats around us?"

"No," Mickey admitted.

"Then just relax. We're almost home. You could back it in from here if you wanted."

"That might be easier. I keep trying to see over the bow."

"Then don't. Steer using that cleat to starboard. Starboard. To the right. Remember, the captain is the star of the show, so his side of the boat is the star-board side."

"A car is easier," Mickey said with a grimace. "There are lanes and lines."

"There are out here, too," Helly told her. "The lane is the channel, and the ATONs are the lines."

"Aids to navigation. Daymarks and buoys."

"Exactly." Helly put a section of a folded and salt-spattered nautical chart in front of her and pointed. "We're right here, so just ahead, we'll be looking for Marker BW – BW means it has Black and White stripes."

Mickey looked down at the chart. “How can I tell if it’s got stripes in the dark?”

“See these other marks?” Helly said. “M, O, A, and Bell? So we’ll listen for the bell and watch for the flash. We passed very wide of it on our way out. I should have pointed it out.”

“What does M-O-and the A in parentheses mean?”

“It means,” Helly answered, “That the light will flash the Morse Code signal for the letter ‘A.’ Which is?”

“Are you kidding me?” Mickey asked. “Now I need to know Morse Code?”

“Only the first few letters,” Helly told her. “And maybe the Mayday signal. Anyway, the letter ‘A’ in Morse is one short flash followed by one long flash. One Short – One Long. Got it?”

“Got it,” Mickey said.

“There’s a method to the madness out here. Thanks to the U.S. Coast Guard which places and maintains the navigation aids, and NOAA, who makes and approves the charts.”

“Noah? Like in Noah’s Ark?”

“NOAA, like in the government agency – N-O-A-A.”

“OK. I think I see the mark. And there’s the flash. How close should I be?”

“At least the width of the boat you’re driving away is a good rule. Two widths if you have room. If you think you’re too close, don’t turn the bow away suddenly. Remember, if the bow goes one way, the stern goes the other. You’ll slam it into the mark. Better to scrape by it than hit it. It’s not an iceberg.”

Mickey straightened up. “OK, we should be coming up to it with plenty of room. Wait, it’s not a signpost, it’s a floaty thing. But not a red or green one.”

“It’s not a floaty thing, it’s a buoy. And ifit was red, it would be shaped like a-”

“A nun. Or a nun’s habit. I remember now. A nun buoy. The green ones are can buoys. Shaped like a tin can.”

“But this one will be?”

“BW – Black and White. Which way do the stripes go?”

"Always vertical," Helly said. "And those stripes mean you do not go between the mark and the nearest land because you'll hit something if you do."

"What? Like a shipwreck?" Mickey asked. "Oh, now I can hear the bell, I think.""It means an obstruction. Could be a wreck. Could be a reef or a sandbar or rocks. Doesn't matter – just understand and obey what it's telling you."

Mickey sailed them past the bobbing marker. The white flashing light blinked at them.

"Shouldn't the light be red or green?"

"If it was a channel marker, it would be," Helly said. "But it's not a channel marker way out here. It's there to keep you out of trouble."

"But I need to find the channel markers to get into the Inlet."

"Atta girl," Helly said approvingly. "So now we start looking for what marker?"

"I don't know," Mickey answered. "Let me see the map."

"Chart," Helly corrected.

"Right. Let me see the chart. Hey, what's that up there?"

"You tell me."

"I see red and green flashers. Which one do I steer towards?"

"Remember the R's," Helly said. "Red Right Returning. Keep the Red ATNs on your right, your side of the boat, coming from the ocean toward land."

Mickey checked the chart again.

"What do all these other letters mean?" she asked.

"They describe the characteristics of the markers at the ends of the jetties. "Helly answered.

"But you said red and green, go between. So I should head right in the middle?"

"No, you should not," Helly said. "Slow down for a second."

Mickey eased the throttle back.

"The Inlet is tricky and the jetties don't help. They were built like an arrowhead. They almost come to a point at the entrance. They should have built them parallel to each other. Maybe they'll fix that someday."

"Great," Mickey deadpanned.

"So here's where you need what they refer to as Local Knowledge. The letters and numbers on the red mark tell you that it's Number 2, it flashes Red every four seconds, that it's thirty-seven feet tall, and that it should be visible at a distance of five miles."

Helly pointed at the chart.

"The other jetty marker, the south one, flashes Green every 4 seconds and has a horn. Stay away from anything with a horn."

"So, you're a local who, I assume, has knowledge. Where do I go here?"

"You're going to take us inside the Red flasher. Keep it on your right, but not too close. The rocks are underwater even at low tide so you can't see them. You have to know they're there. You can throttle up now. The channel kind of hugs that north jetty. Keep a respectful distance but follow it in."

"You sure you don't want to drive?" Mickey asked.

"I'm positive," Helly said. "I wouldn't give you the wheel of my boat if I didn't think you were capable."

Mickey took a deep breath.

"OK. Here we go. So now-"

A breeze kicked up a little swell. Mickey reflexively turned the wheel. Helly turned it back.

"Mickey. It's not a car," Helly said gently. "Don't oversteer. Just stay on this line, and you'll be fine. Once in a blue moon, you'll get a flat sea, but not often. You have to learn to roll with it. Just stay the course."

Mickey nodded her understanding. The *Rachel* passed by the flashing red light on the fixed marker. Mickey heard the horn from the green flashing marker off to port.

"So we're OK, right?" Mickey asked. She felt like she had a death grip on the wheel.

"What am I doing here?" Helly said. "You don't need me aboard, Skipper. There are no boats coming out so you can stay where we are. If there were traffic, you'd cheat to your side to give them leeway. But don't stop, or you'll drift into the jetty, which will be off the starboard beam all the way into the bay. Here. Now take the wheel with one hand and put your other one on the throttle."

Mickey complied, peering intently ahead through the cabin's windshield.

The boat rocked several times. Helly grabbed Mickey around the waist. "Did I do that?" she asked.

"Nope," he said. "Lots of boats wrecked around here because of the shoals and the currents at the mouth of the inlet. That's why they built the lighthouse where they did. That's why they put the rock jetties where they did, although Dad says the jetties made things worse. Like I said, they can be extremely tricky to navigate some days. OK, now ease off the throttle, but not too much, otherwise the current will tell the boat where to go instead of you."

Mickey throttled down. She realized she was starting to feel slightly more comfortable. That, she reminded herself, could also be dangerous.

"Am I far enough over to port?" she asked.

Helly showed her the chart again. "We're right here, so you're dead solid perfect. Great job, Cappy Mick."

Mickey steered the *Rachel* smoothly past the base of the jetty and let out an audible sigh of relief.

"Why don't you let me take her from here," Helly said. Mickey did not argue with him. "The Bay has all kinds of sandbars, unlit and even submerged islands. We'll work on that when it's light out. The channel gets very narrow, and the water gets skinny real quick."

"Skinny? That means shallow."

"It does. And it gets skinnier than Twiggy on a diet in some places. Every boater has or will run aground at some point. You don't want to make a habit out of it. And the inlet is an especially bad spot to have it happen."

Mickey grabbed the lip of the cabin roof with both hands this time as they motored forward. The faint aroma of diesel exhaust followed them. Realizing she'd navigated the feared Barnegat Inlet, Mickey allowed a small but pleasant sense of accomplishment to wash over her. Watching Helly steer through the rapidly disappearing light, she realized she still had a long way to go.

"I know what I wanted to ask," Mickey said. "Why is the compass thing on the chart tilted like that. Isn't north always north?"

"No, it isn't," Helly said. "The magnetic north pole moves around and it's different at different latitudes. Every chart has a – it's called the Compass Rose – it shows you where north is on this chart. That tilt is what your compass is seeing. Don't get fooled or you can end up out in the middle of the ocean."

"Compass Rose. I like that. Sounds like a rock band. Now, begging the captain's pardon, but maybe we could have some music?" Mickey asked.

"Sorry," Helly said. "I didn't want you to have any distractions." He punched the Play button on the tape deck.

The Beach Boys were back, this time with "Sail On, Sailor." The water in Barnegat Bay was calm. The lighthouse, whose lamp and Fresnel glass lens had been removed fifty-one years earlier, glowed faintly in the dark, a looming apparition illuminated by a ring of upturned ground lights.

Mickey started to sing along with Blondie Chaplin, a South African who Ronnie once told her sang lead on the cut, even though he wasn't a full-time member of the band. Mickey swayed gently to the tune's pulsing rhythm, musing that she already had two adventures involving Old Barney under her belt.

Gazing up at it from the dark water, she decided that two was enough.

Garden State Parkway Southbound
Port Republic, Atlantic County, NJ

"We gotta get one of those portable phones like the State Police have," Evan Driscoll said as they barreled along in the left lane. "For Christ's sake, we're the Federal Government, the Department of Justice, the freaking FBI. And we have to call our office from a phone booth?"

Walter Stenkewiecz said nothing. He wanted to mention that the equipment upgrade funding for the Bureau was buried deep in an appropriations bill now before the House. Republicans wanted it to fail rather than give the Carter Administration any kind of win they could make political hay with during the next election cycle. He thought it best to let the DD vent.

"I'm not blaming you, Stosh," Driscoll went on, "But do let me know next time if we're riding in a car that is unintentionally observing radio silence."

"Roger that, sir," Stenkewiecz said as he weaved in and out of the passing lane, trying his best to make up time lost when two semis had decided to have what the truck drivers referred to as an Elephant Race.

"Jesus. This asset travels all the way from frigging Ireland, and we keep him waiting," Driscoll continued. "We have two of our agents UTL and we have to presume MIA. We have no established lines of communication with any of our supposed law enforcement brethren. Not the Atlantic County Sheriff's Office, not the State Police, not even the ACPD." He paused for a breath. "Not even the goddamn City of Linwood cop shop. This guy could be working with the CIA and nobody would tell us. You know, if the radio worked, I would call Griffin Freaking Bell myself and tell him, that, with all due respect Mister Attorney General, this is no way to run an airline."

"I feel your pain, sir," Stenkewiecz responded. "I could try to patch you through to McGarrett if that helps."

Driscoll laughed out loud, breaking the tension. "I was always a bigger fan of Zulu, or maybe it was it Kono."

Stenkewiecz leaned on the horn. The car in the left lane ahead of them was doing, at best, forty. When it finally did move over, the driver flipped them the bird. Driscoll responded by flashing his badge as they pulled briefly alongside. He laughed again as the shaken driver, who looked to be at least seventy, immediately pulled off onto the shoulder.

"AMF," Driscoll said and exhaled loudly. "Adios, Mother Fletcher."

"Feeling better, sir?" Stenkewiecz asked.

"Much better, Stosh. Much better." Driscoll looked at his watch. "I don't suppose we have a roof flasher. You know, like the blue one Theo Kojak had?"

"We do not, sir," Stenkewiecz told him. "I could turn on the emergency four-ways if you'd like. And there might be a lollipop in the glove box."

Driscoll ran a hand over his face and slumped in his seat. "Wake me when we're five minutes out."

He folded his arms across his chest and closed his eyes.

Surf City

Mickey was surprised at how good the ice-cold Miller High Life's from Helly's cooler had tasted. She realized, with a touch of sadness, that they were the first beers she'd had since Ronnie had passed away. Maybe it was a small step. Or maybe it was just two beers in glass bottles on a summer night.

They'd sat on the Chevy's dented tailgate and watched as the few nighttime fishing boats straggled in. Mickey was amazed at how a captain could slip a seventy-six-foot metal-hulled scalloper into a berth as effortlessly as if he were parallel parking a VW Bug.

Helly had dropped her off, at her request, at the corner of Long Beach Boulevard. She wanted to feel the cool night air and solid ground under her feet. She also thought a little walk would do her good, the High Life's hitting a little harder than she expected. The result of the long abstinence, she assumed.

Mickey could see dancing blue shadows through the curtains as she approached the tidy bungalow. Deciding to leave the Mustang's window open overnight, she glided up the steps and into the house. Bunny was sprawled on the couch.

"What'cha watching?" Mickey asked.

"Starsky and Hutch," Bunny said. Mickey noticed a tin pan of Jiffy-Pop popcorn on the table, it's ballooned-out aluminum skin peeled open like a blooming flower. "They have cool car. You get that car next."

"That's a 1976 Gran Torino," Mickey said. "I would look pretty cool in it, wouldn't I?"

"You buy and then and you give me Mustang. I look pretty cool driving that."

Mickey plopped herself down in the recliner. When Ronnie could no longer lay flat and breathe comfortably at the same time, the little living room became their refuge. Sometimes, she imagined, she could still smell him on it.

"How your date with Helly?" Bunny asked, staring straight at the TV. David Soul was hip-sliding across the hood of the Torino.

"It wasn't a date and you know it, so quit that," Mickey said. "He's teaching me how to drive a boat. Be nice and you can come along some time."

"You like Helly. Helly like you. So. Date. When I take Driver Ed?"

"Maybe next year," Mickey told her. "After Sister Marian says your reading and English are better."

"Hey," Bunny said, "I read good. My English good. Maybe you teach me to drive. In Mustang."

Sister Marian Carlton had become a close friend and confidante. The local priests had offered prayers and platitudes but they pretty much disappeared after Ronnie's funeral. Marian came and sat with Mickey on many of the lonely nights that followed, reminding her that Ronnie was still there and still present in their children. And she'd tough-loved her with one memorable line.

"Listen to me. 'Cleary's don't cry' is complete, utter, absolute, and total fucking bullshit," Marian had said with a glint of anger in her voice.

And she'd been right. The creed that had been drummed into Mickey by her father, Patsy, had taught her strength and resilience, but it had also handcuffed her emotional well-being for years. She couldn't hug her kids in handcuffs, Marian reminded her.

Mickey did not know for how many hours after that she'd sobbed uncontrollably in the young nun's arms, but they'd gone to Wally's for breakfast right afterward. Mickey wore her Wayfarers to hide her red and swollen eyes. The good Sister Marian swore like a sailor in private and, although devoutly celibate, also freely shared how much she missed physical intimacy.

"Did you know it's technically not a sin to pray for an orgasm?" she'd said while they ate. "It doesn't even need to be immaculate."

That made Mickey laugh so hard she nearly started crying again. She might not have gotten through the ordeal without her.

"Why I have to have Sister Marian teach me?" Bunny asked.

"Because you'll be more successful if you can speak better and read better," Mickey said patiently. "You'll want to go to college someday. Listen. I'll make you a deal. If you work hard and do well with Marian, I'll teach you to drive this summer. But we start in the Green Dragon."

"Deal!" Bunny chirped and sat up. "You bet. I like station wagon. Like Army APC. *Boo-coo* strong. Just need fifty cal on roof."

It occurred to Mickey that Armored Personnel Carrier was maybe the best description of the old Chevy Brookwood she'd ever heard.

Charlie Higgins and his wife Barbara had taken Bunny in when she straggled back into Surf City six months earlier. The adoption process had been fraught. Bunny's parents, an American soldier Ronnie had known, and Bunny's Vietnamese mother, had supposedly moved with her to Arkansas. Neither Ronnie nor Mickey had ever been able to track them down after that, even with Mickey's contacts in law enforcement.

From what Mickey could piece together, they had quickly fled with the girl back to Southeast Asia to avoid an Army dragnet that was busting up a major heroin smuggling ring. The same one, she realized, that had murdered Charlie's brother Darnell with a morphine injection as he lay in a VA hospital bed after being wounded in combat.

They weren't legally dead, but they clearly did not want to be found.

Charlie believed Bunny's return was part of "God's plan" for them all. Despite years of trying, Barbara couldn't conceive and Bunny's unexpected presence in their lives did seem like an answered prayer. But they all agreed the girl must have rarely needed to speak English during the intervening years. Bunny was supposed to start school in the fall and they worried she'd be bullied and ridiculed if her English didn't improve. Sister Marian volunteered to tutor her.

"What were you going to tell me about Michael?" Mickey asked.

"Oh, Michael. He talk. I hear him talking – what Charlie say? Blue streak?"

"To who?" Mickey asked, trying to hide her surprise and her relief. "To you?"

"To Eileen. I hear him. It sound like he talking Chinese but she understand him. She tell me he want Cheerios. I give him Cheerios. Then he talk some more. Eileen say he want milk. So I give him milk. He very happy."

"You sure Eileen didn't want milk and Cheerios?"

"She don't touch. She like Lucky Charms. Magically delicious. And OJ."

Mickey was going to need to give Dr. Harman a call when she got back from her honeymoon, she realized. Harman had shocked everyone by eloping with Tom, her receptionist.

"Well, Bunny, that's good to know. Where do you want to sleep?"

"I sleep your bed. You snore?"

Mickey chuckled. "I don't think so. OK. Did you bring pajamas?"

"I sleep no clothes," Bunny replied. "Get too hot."

"Uhhhh, nope, that's not going to fly. I will loan you some PJs for tonight."

"How I brush teeth?"

"I'll give you a toothbrush as well. We'll have a little kit here that'll be yours if you have to stay over again."

"I like stay with you. Watch lots more TV."

"I bet you do," Mickey said.

"*TV Guide* say good movie on after news. *Voyage to Bottom of Sea*. We watch together."

"*We* are going to bed, young lady," Mickey said. "Kids go to sleep OK?"

"Yesssss. I read them book. *Everyone Poops*. Michael laugh a lot. Then he poop."

Dr. Harman told her that if Michael seemed to comprehend other people's speech, his would soon follow. She encouraged her to read to him at every opportunity.

"Interesting choice, but OK," Mickey said.

She pushed herself up and out of the recliner.

"Oh. Some men stop by," Bunny said. "Two men. Right after you leave for date with Helly. One say he knows you. Say you work with him long time ago. He leave card." She fumbled to find it, finally plucking it from between the couch cushions. "He say you call him tomorrow. Say important. He *dep trai*, too. Ummmm, in English is...good-looking?"

Seeing Evan Driscoll's name on the card opened a floodgate of memories. Mickey wondered what he needed from her this time. She'd managed to push the bodies at the Steel Pier out of her mind for a few hours. They probably weren't related to anything Evan Driscoll wanted to know, she told herself. But a fuzzy thought started nibbling at her brain. She knew she'd lay awake until it took shape. The wheels would be turning for a while. And, she now realized, she'd completely forgotten to ask Helly about the boat under the bridge or the winds and the tide.

She really hoped Bunny didn't snore.

TWENTY

Bombay Hotel and Casino
Room 2512

ILSA SCHOENWEISS WAS MOANING, guttural sounds escaping from somewhere deep within as she ground her pelvis in circles above him.

Her engorged nipples poked out like thumbs, inches from his face. Straddling him like a cowgirl, she wetly whispered things in his ear in German that he assumed were filthy. In any other moment, he'd be struggling to hold back.

But this was not any other moment.

In this one, he was struggling to stay stiff.

"*Ich bin gut zu vögeln,*" she panted. "*Ich bin gut zu vögeln. Ja*?"

"Ya. Ya," the Archibald Graham version of him grunted in reply, having no idea what she was saying. He desperately wanted her to finish. He had business that needed his swift and personal attention.

"Du machst mich so geil," Ilsa said. She leaned forward and buried her tongue in his mouth. *"Machst mich so geil. So geil."*

"Ya, Ya," he said again, unable to think of anything else and hoping this meant she was getting close.

Ilsa put her hands on his shoulders and bounced even harder. She was going to put his spine out of place if she kept it up. She threw her head back, arched *her* spine, and then – she abruptly stopped.

Ilsa smiled down at him, her sweat-soaked hair plastered to her face, and dismounted. She grabbed his hand and pulled him to a sitting position. Then, in one smooth rolling motion, she got on her knees.

"*Nimm mich von hinten,*" she commanded him. "From behind, *ja*?"

Sweet Jesus, Mary, and Joseph, he thought, this better do it. He gave a couple of tugs to return his softening lad to full attention and went back to work. Ilsa was saying something. But she had her head almost buried in one of the fluffy down pillows, and he couldn't make it out.

She reached a hand back and provided manual assistance.

He'd been mostly successful in sealing off the dark memories of Long Kesh, the H-Blocks, and the things that went on behind the walls. It was almost four years since they'd smuggled him out in a body bag.

"*Bitte,*" Ilsa pleaded. "*Bitte*, baby."

In thirty-six hours, he'd be on a plane. Ilsa was the key to making certain he wouldn't be leaving empty-handed. He took a deep breath, pulled back, and placed his hands on her hip bones.

He hoped this wouldn't take long.

The Ozymandias Suite

Benno loved *Hogan's Heroes*.

He'd hired Ilsa Schoenweiss as much for her resemblance to Cynthia Lynn, the actress who portrayed the show's Fraulein Helga, as on the strength of her resume`. But the characterization of every male German character as a dolt or a dupe bothered him. Werner Klemperer, who played the clueless Colonel Wilhelm Klink, was an accomplished singer as well as a respected actor. His father had been a symphony conductor, even leading the Los Angeles Philharmonic for several years after the family emigrated in the early nineteen-thirties.

Benno Bruxelles knew that he would one day erase these comic caricatures of his ancestors, as well as their persistent branding as barbarians and sadistic, bloodthirsty ghouls.

His phone had buzzed several times, but Ilsa had left early and his attention was focused on the TV screen and the program presently re-running. Benno knew that there was a certain amount of secret snickering about his infatuation with TV, his constant references to shows and characters. On occasion, he'd make phone calls identifying himself with inverted names like Kirk James or Gordon Artemis. But, for all its value as entertainment, Benno believed the much-maligned "boob tube" was poised to become the most powerful weapon in any arsenal on earth. Show people a fiction long enough and often enough and it would cease in their minds, in their subconscious minds, most importantly, to be a fiction. It would be a reality. And that reality could be shaped and packaged in any way one wanted.

Mission Impossible was on next. He enjoyed the part in every episode where Martin Landau peeled off a rubber mask to reveal his true identity as Rollin Hand. Benno Bruxelles believed wholeheartedly that the mission he was contemplating was anything but impossible. In fact, it would be easier than anyone could ever imagine. He believed you could fool, maybe not all of the people, but certainly enough of them. And you could keep them fooled all of the time.

Forty stories below him, thousands of them were swarming like mindless ants, literally donating their money directly to him, almost handing it to him personally. Money only a very small few could comfortably afford to part with. Children would go hungry. Bills would go unpaid. Child support payments would stop coming. Alimony checks would evaporate.

All for him.

They might as well be dropping gold bars straight into his pocket, he thought with not a small measure of satisfaction. That morning's *Philadelphia Inquirer* noted that the U.S. population had surpassed two-hundred-and twenty million, and it was only the end of May. P.T. Barnum was wrong, he calculated, but he was getting righter. An American sucker was now born every six minutes.

He stared at the ivory chip, its polished bone-white even brighter against the green felt of the desk blotter. He was collecting his markers now, before their value inflated even more. Only two were formally unaccounted for, but that didn't worry him.

Benno Bruxelles was not a gambler. The two chips were out there, burning holes in the pockets of two unknown subjects. It was only a matter of time before they escaped and succeeded in making their way back to him. He had plenty of money, and he had plenty of time.

He could well afford to wait.

Surf City

Bunny was snoring. Loudly.

Mickey gently rolled her onto her side. The volume dropped immediately, but the low rumble continued with every exhalation.

She tried to reconcile in her head the gangly girl lying next to her with the image of the little one she'd found sitting primly, hands folded in her lap, in the front seat of her Surf City patrol car, Mickey's name scrawled on a note pinned to her sweater. Bonnenuit Tran was her given name, a nod to the beautiful night her mother, Yvette, had delivered her into the world on a moonlit beach in South Vietnam. A few years later, the two would escape, purely by luck, the raid by U.S. soldiers on their village - the now infamous My Lai Massacre. They were off gathering firewood when the soldiers arrived and were spared only because a helicopter pilot landed his gunship and ordered his crew to train their weapons on their own advancing troops.

Mickey always tried to think like a true detective, searching in what appeared to be the purely random for hidden patterns, connections, and intersections. Bunny's journey was more of a circle, a complete one that had brought her back to Mickey's side. To the same spot in the same bed where she'd slept that first night years earlier.

Her mother used to tell Mickey, "Sure, and the Lord works in mysterious ways, and often, you'll find, in quite unsettling ones."

Mickey smiled. The memory of her mother's lilting Irish brogue could bring her to tears. Patsy had worked hard to lose any trace of his. But her mother never did. Never even tried. In what would turn out to be the last words she'd say to Mickey before downing what the doctor described as enough liquor and sleeping pills to kill a horse, she'd told Mickey to remember one thing. "Even if you can't see me, my little love, always know that I'm there, always right by your side."

A tear trickled slowly down her cheek, and she wiped it away.

Bunny snuffled, yawned, and turned so that now she was completely on her side. She kicked off some imaginary covers, mumbled something unintelligible, and then wiggled her back over toward Mickey until the two were touching.

It seemed appropriate, Mickey thought. Perhaps she and Bunny were somehow cosmically joined at the hip.

Mickey willed the wheels in her head to stop turning and closed her eyes. If Bunny were still snoring, she could no longer hear it.

National Wildlife Refuge
Brigantine Division, Galloway, NJ

The irony of the marshy spot where Owen Pettigrew sat contemplating his future was not lost on him. The area had been dedicated as a wildlife refuge way back in 1939, the same year Hitler rose to power. He reflected that most of his life had been the very definition of wild and that he was there, at least for the moment, because he needed refuge.

The dark had already settled in, and the sounds of the night, subdued at first, were gradually increasing in volume.

He'd had to visit three phone booths along old Highway 9 before he found one past Oceanview that still had a telephone book attached to its plastic binder There was, he saw in the blue Government Listings pages, an FBI office in Linwood. But it was attached to an 800 area code, and so he assumed calling would be of little help to him. No address was listed, but he knew Linwood was fairly small, increasing the odds he could find it without drawing attention to himself. He doubted the FBI would invest in a neon sign or a line of roadside Burma Shave placards.

Pettigrew figured Walker White would be sweating his old lady right about now for his whereabouts. All she knew was that he had a sister in Toms River. That, he hoped, would at least send them searching in the opposite direction.

He'd slept in worse places and with more worry during his desperate trek to the South China Sea. His present surroundings were tranquil and the Sons, for all their bluster, would have been no match for either the NVA or the Viet Cong. Not to mention the predatory crocodiles.

The Harley had pretty much stopped making its usual assortment of post-ride pings, pops, and metallic groans.

Pettigrew rested in a small stand of trees. The refuge was primarily marshland, spreading out beneath one of the busiest avian migratory flyways in the country. He was no botanist, but he recognized pitch pines, sassafras trees, and the occasional red oak.

He chose the oak to rest his back against. He'd filled up at a dilapidated, one-pump ARCO station and stuffed his pockets with TastyKake Kandy Kakes and Drake's Devil Dogs. He grabbed four bottles of Dr. Pepper to wash them down with.

A piping plover perched not far away in the marsh grass.

Pettigrew considered that both he and it were now migratory species.

"Move over, little plover," he said and stretched out. "Big bird is here for the night."

It was the first time he'd smiled all day.

TWENTY-ONE

Surf City

MICKEY WAS SURPRISED TO see the light on in her office. She was up even earlier this morning, and only one other person had a key unless the former tenant had made a break from the new low-security federal prison in Hopewell, Virginia.

She approached the door cautiously and found it not only unlocked, but slightly ajar. Her "major cases" were a string of beach tag thefts from swimsuits left hanging on clotheslines and a woman convinced her husband had been abducted by Arab terrorists. It was hardly a group likely to come looking for her. After the first ten minutes of interviewing the woman, Mickey was pretty certain she understood why the husband had vanished and that he very well might prefer the company of the terrorists.

She turned the knob and eased open the door.

There were some scuffling sounds, like boxes or cases being slid along the tired linoleum tile. The office was small, and she'd kept it intentionally non-descript inside and out. The CPA's cubicle dividers remained but were rearranged to provide her direct sight lines to the windows and the front door. She had kept the simple wooden desk she'd used as Chief, several credenzas she'd snagged at a furniture liquidation sale, and a wall of half-filled wooden filing cabinets that had belonged to the accountant. She also had a bulky electric typewriter on a separate metal table for filling out reports.

"OK, Goldilocks," she said to whoever was there. "Mama Bear has arrived. Who's been sleeping in my office?"

A head popped out from the side of one of the carpeted dividers.

"Oh, hi! I didn't hear you come in."

Mickey's hand rested lightly on her holster, and after seeing the face, she felt a little silly.

"You should have one of those *Men At Work* signs," she said. "Good morning, Mr. Nepp."

Mark Nepp stepped out from behind the divider. Dust was on his pants, and he held a screwdriver in one hand.

"Great news," he told Mickey. "As of yesterday, it's officially *Doctor* Nepp."

Mickey knew he'd been working on a Ph.D. in something called Computer Science at Penn.

"Well, congratulations - Doctor Nepp."

"Thanks," Nepp said. "I still have to walk the walk and pick up my parchment, but my dissertation was accepted. Finally, my mother can say, 'Meet my son, the *dok-tah*.'"

Mickey laughed.

"I'm sure she's quite proud. The dissertation, that's like the final exam?"

"It's final, but it's not an exam—not like a test you take. You write this very long paper detailing your research and your conclusions, and then three particularly persnickety professors pelt you with questions, trying to trip you up or find flaws in your reasoning. It's called defending your thesis. I handled everything they threw at me like Mike Schmidt with a hanging curveball."

"OK, Schmidty," Mickey asked, "What was your dis-, your dissertation about?"

Nepp smiled. "Funny you should ask, Chief, I mean Detective Cleary. I actually used the little project I'm doing for you as the basis for my thesis, although it's probably best if we don't tell anyone that yet. They were pretty impressed I had a working model, even if they assumed it was in an electronics lab somewhere on campus. The title of mine was 'The Feasibility of Packet-Switched Nodal Networks in Linked Databases.'"

"That is exactly what I would have called it. And it's not, I assume, in any lab," Mickey said. "Packets – you mean like...ketchup packets?"

"They're exactly like ketchup packets," Nepp beamed. "Except instead of ketchup, they contain information in a very compressed form. And there are way more than fifty-seven varieties, I can assure you."

She closed the door and joined him behind the divider in the rectangular space she referred to as her personal office.

"Ta-da!" Nepp said with a flourish and a bow. "I was just finishing connecting the cables."

Ph.D. or not, Mickey mused, Mark Nepp had a certain boyish enthusiasm that made him virtually impossible not to like. She saw that two of the worn credenzas were crammed to their edges with boxy-looking contraptions, all of them housed in the same beige-colored plastic.

"I did the initial assembly in my garage," Nepp said, "and then brought it all over here last night. One of the police officers from across the way poked her head in and asked me what it was. I told her you liked music and I was putting in a killer sound system for you. She acted a little suspicious until I mentioned BOSE 901 speakers. That seemed to satisfy her."

"Short, blonde, looks like she could take most guys in a fight?"

"That's her. Very nice, though. Very personable."

"DellaDonna. They say she's a pill. So you mean I'm not getting-"

"No," Nepp replied. "You are not getting BOSE 901s. But I believe what I'm about to finish up installing will be music to your ears."

Mickey walked around the credenzas, running her hands over the odd-looking equipment.

"Any idea what this is going to end up costing?" Mickey asked. "I'll have to find a way to disguise it in the budget."

"Call it...call it...call it information technology. It's probably a stupid name, but it's boring enough that no one will bother to ask what it is. And there's no cost - none at all."

"Now, how can you do-"

"You got me my doctorate, Detective Cleary," Nepp said. "I should probably pay you."

Mickey shook her head. "You said we'd be able to access public information like newspapers without having to go to the library or a newsstand."

"And we can, or rather, we will," Nepp said, twirling the screwdriver in his fingers. "But not the Philly or the South Jersey papers. If this works the way I think it will, we can look up newspapers from around the world. Paris, Rome, Dublin, Istanbul – gosh, maybe even Moscow if you like. See what Brezhnev had for breakfast.

"Many of them print English-language versions. It's early, but they're starting to store them as computer files rather than paper copies in their morgues. And, luckily for us, they're keeping those files in the equivalent of unlocked cabinets. If we can open the drawer, we can browse through whatever's in there."

"And we're all legal, right? I mean, me being an actual cop and all."

"This is all so new, there are no legal restrictions. Think of it like this – there are no Zoning Laws on the moon, right? So, until there's a property dispute in the Sea of Tranquility – and here we would be talking about protected information, and intellectual property at some point – there's nothing on the books to prevent us."

Mickey considered the possibilities. "So I could check a Dublin newspaper to see who won the Irish Sweepstakes?"

Nepp nodded. "Theoretically, you could check a Dublin newspaper. But, and I can't wait to test this out, we might even be able to access some law-enforcement agency databases. Instead of sending away for something in the mail or getting a crappy telecopy of a picture, you could look at it on this. He tapped what looked like a small portable television, but one without its antennas.

"A TV?" Mickey asked.

"It's called a monitor, but yes, it's kind of like a TV. But no channels. I can't wait to fire it up. Oh. How many phone lines do you have here?"

"Only the one that I know of," Mickey said.

"You'll need to request a second one. Like for a Bat Phone, maybe. You'll use your telephone line to dial into a network to use this. While you're doing that, you won't be able to make or receive phone calls."

Mickey nodded, although the information was coming at her so fast she was having a hard time processing it.

Nepp flipped the screwdriver and caught it in his palm. He was on a high and on a roll, Mickey figured. She'd let him enjoy them both.

"By lunchtime, if all goes well, I'll have you connected and we'll go what they call on-line."

"On what line?" Mickey asked.

"It's an expression. Means you have access to a network and all the terminals on it."

Mickey scratched her head. "Wait. So all these, these...terminals, they could have access to me?"

"Again, theoretically, yes. But you don't have any stored data. You don't have a, a filing cabinet. Plus, I'm working on something I call encryption, which means even if they somehow know you're there, they won't know who you are. Cool, right?"

"Whoopie doopie, Dr. Nepp," Mickey said. "You'um genius."

Nepp smiled broadly. "Believe me, this is literally the dawning of a new age."

"And it sure ain't Aquarius, Dr. Nepp."

"It most definitely is not Aquarius, Detective Cleary," Nepp said. "I need about two more hours, maybe three and - "

They stopped when they heard the door open. Mickey had left the accountant's quaint little bell attached to its top.

"Mickey? It's Charlie. Charlie Higgins. You back there? Mick. I saw the li - "

Mickey stepped back out.

"Good morning, Chief Higgins," she said. "Stick around. In a little while we're going to blast 'In a Gadda Da Vida' so loud it'll create cracks in the plaster. "

"Hmmm. You know, I think I'll pass," Charlie Higgins said. "Hoping to hold off on Beltones for a few more years at least. Bunny wasn't too much trouble, was she?"

"No," Mickey answered. "It was nice to have the help. She snores like a freight train. You knew that, right?"

"Oh, my. All too well," Charlie replied in his deep baritone. "Doc Harman says might be tonsils, even at her age. Go figure that. You heard about the mess over in A.C.?"

Charlie rubbed at his graying temples.

"Poor Rich," he continued. "Back less than a month, and he catches that one. You know their brass and the papers will be breathing down his neck and, excuse my language, crawling up his butt until it's solved. Shame. Two young people. I pray it was an accident."

Mickey realized that in all the years she'd known him, she had never lied to Charlie Higgins or hidden anything from him. She was about to do both.

"Yeah, it sounds kind of odd. Rich is top-notch, though. He always was. Maybe this will be his time to shine."

Charlie pulled a card from his breast pocket.

"Margherita said two guys stopped in and left this for you last night. They were Feds. She says they seemed pretty intent on finding you." He chuckled. "Although she did say one of them seemed far more interested in your Mustang than in you. The number to call is written on the back."

"It wouldn't be the first time," Mickey said, taking the card from him. She looked down at it. Evan Driscoll was clearly making more than a social call. "Thanks, Charlie. I'll follow up. How's DellaDonna doing, by the way?"

Charlie laughed out loud. "Runs on a full tank of piss and vinegar. Just like her idol."

"Shit, Charlie," Mickey said. "I'm still too young to be anyone's idol. Could I be a role model for a while, maybe?"

"She's doing well. Delivered a baby in the back of her unit last week over in Mud City. No training, simply winged it, I guess. Fearless, that's what that girl is. Just fearless."

"Well, you teach her how to be smart first and fearless second. She'll be around longer that way."

"Come over for coffee sometime," Charlie said, moving toward the door. "You can tell her yourself. See ya, Mick."

"See you, Charlie."

The little bell tinkled again when he closed the door. Mickey slipped back behind the divider and found Nepp under a table muttering to himself.

"OK if I use my phone right now?" she asked.

"Sure," Nepp answered. "Give me a few hours and we'll do a test drive. It worked in my garage. We'll see how it does here."

Mickey slipped behind her desk and sat down.

She studied the card. The vibe was buzzing a little, but it wasn't strong. It was like static electricity. What had Helly said to her about a lightning strike? And if Evan Driscoll wanted to meet, she realized, it couldn't be here.

As she picked up the phone and began to dial the scribbled number, the opening lines of Buffalo Springfield's "For What It's Worth" rocked and rolled gently in her ear. She agreed with Stephen Stills.

Whatever was happening here, it was anything but clear.

TWENTY-TWO

Bombay Hotel & Casino
Room 2512

ARCHIBALD GRAHAM HAD TO look twice at the sleek digital clock radio on the bedside table. The sun was blasting through the East-facing windows. Ilsa was sprawled almost completely on top of him. The room smelled like the middle of a forest at dusk. His face felt like a glazed donut.

He slid her leg off his hip.

"Wake up, love," he said. "It was a grand time but we've things to do today."

Ilsa mumbled and reached down for his willy which, after four tosses, was less of a weapon and more of an appendage at the moment.

Graham brushed her away.

"Ah, none of that now. You promised if I stayed the whole night with you we'd attend to business first thing."

"Once more," Ilsa said sleepily. "That's all, I promise. *Bitte*?"

"Jaysus," Graham said. "If I were bleedin' Superman I don't think I could."

"You were Superman," Ilsa cooed. "And I don't see any kryptonite."

"You've rubbed the shine off my shillelagh, darlin'. Give a man a day to recuperate and we'll have at it again. I promise you."

Ilsa pouted and rolled off him.

"OK," she said. "But at least show me what's under that t-shirt."

Graham used the opportunity to free himself from the bed. "Ah, that'd put an end to all the mystery, now, wouldn't it? Maybe tonight. But a peek is all you'll be gettin'."

He poked her shoulder.

"You go first," he said and pointed to the open bathroom door. "Can't afford to have you lollygagging in bed while the day slips away. And be a love. Have them send up a pot or two, would you? Strong as they can make it. *Cuppa tae* won't cut it, I'm afraid. It's going to be one grand day."

Surf City Beach Patrol
South 2nd Street Lifeguard Stand

When Mickey pulled up and onto the beach access in the Mustang, the knot of LG's immediately came apart and trotted up the sand to greet her. One familiar face came and stood next to the rolled down driver's side window.

"Well, well," he said addressing Eileen, who sat unbuckled in the passenger side bucket seat. "Here's our honorary Lifeguard-in-Training. How you doin', sport? You ready to take us out today?"

The wooden, strake-construction SCBP dory was resting on its thick keel down near the waterline, its two long white oars shipped.

"Can I row one side?" Eileen asked excitedly.

"Maybe," Greg Gause said. "How about you start out by skippering, if that's OK." He looked at Mickey for silent permission. She winked. "Hey, I like your tattoo." Gause pointed to the fading henna on the little girl's left shoulder. "Figured you as more of a shark or a Jolly Roger kind of girl, though. Why'd you pick a mermaid?"

Eileen looked down at the drawing.

"Mermaids can go all the way under the water and not get drownded," she proclaimed without hesitation.

"Well, that is a truly excellent reason," Gause said. He turned his gaze to Mickey. "Nice to see you, Chief. It's still Chief, right? Cool car, by the way. Does McQueen know it's missing?"

"Not yet," Mickey told him. "And I never thought I'd see you wearing a whistle again. Shouldn't you be on the Supreme Court or something by now?"

"Law school wasn't for me, it turned out," Gause replied. "I switched back to graduate school. Studying Government and International Relations. I think I might concentrate on the Middle East." He kicked at the beach beneath his feet. "Something about sand, I guess."

"And I'm a detective now," Mickey said. "It's been a good change for me, too."

"You coming back to pick her up later?" Gause asked. "Can't very well be letting her hop into a car with some stranger, now, can I?"

"I do still have to work on occasion," Mickey said. "Probably it'll be Nancy – Miss Donahue. You ever meet her?"

"I did," Gause said. "Librarian, if I remember right. Pretty girl. She still single?"

Mickey laughed. "She is, but not for long, I don't think. You know, that whole 'engaged to be engaged' thing."

"Well, it's a long summer," Gause answered. "A lot can happen between now and Labor Day." Now it was his turn to wink.

"Take care of my little Leenie," Mickey said in a more serious tone. "Make sure she doesn't think that tattoo gives her magical mermaid powers."

Mickey heard the Mustang's familiar metallic creak as Eileen pushed her door open and got out.

"Jeez, Mama," the child said, rolling her eyes. Then she shoved it closed.

"I made sure we have a Coast Guard Type One life jacket that'll fit her," Gause said. "She'll hate it. It's bulky and it has the big, square pillow collar. But if you go in, it'll turn you right side up and keep your chin above the water. Even if you're unconscious. Closest thing I have to mermaid powers."

"Thank you," Mickey answered. "Try and keep her in the boat, would you?"

"Rule Number One. It's always better to stay in the boat," Gause said. "Good to see you again." He gave a little tweet on his silver whistle and walked away.

Mickey watched Eileen reach up and take his hand as they moved toward to the beach. A lump formed in her throat. She had to swallow hard twice to push it back down.

After the ordeal of the funeral, Mayor Billy Tunell had taken her aside. There was an African proverb, he told her, and it said, "It takes a village to raise a child." Then he'd put his arms around her and whispered, "What better village could you ask for than this one?"

Mickey started the Mustang up and shifted it into Reverse. Watching as the silhouetted Mutt and Jeff figures slowly dissolved in the bright morning haze, she knew she couldn't ask for a better one on earth.

Bombay Hotel & Casino
Room 212

Last night had been a close shave, as his father always liked to say. A whisker away, was more like it, is what he thought.

Jeffrey Silverman had been awake most of the night, shuffling and sorting the Xeroxed papers laid out on the bed. He'd rang the top floor several times without answer and had almost peed himself when he heard the door to Benno Bruxelles' private suite of offices start to open.

Luckily, his secretary's spacious desk had afforded him more than ample room to conceal himself. He could have taken a nap under there undetected, he figured. The secretary's unlocked file drawers had not yielded anything like a smoking gun. But, with his fingers toner-stained and still tingling from the static electricity generated by the photocopier, he'd happened, essentially by chance, upon a Dividend Statement from an overseas company and a wire transfer from a European bank that appeared to have no links to the casino, the hotel or anything else he could surmise. Filed along with and attached to it were numerous older, heavier papers, many with large sums noted, each followed by the abbreviation ***R.M.*** Jeffrey would need to research that one.

He decided he'd copy them all.

Heidi Abramowitz, the girl he had pursued since his early teen years, had preferred to stay in Cherry Hill with her parents since they were tenaciously opposed to the mere notion of their presumably virginal daughter "shacking up" before they stood beneath the *chuppah*.

Jeffrey's interest in Benno Bruxelles had been piqued by an article in *The Press of Atlantic City* when his gaming license had been granted and his plans for "The Seventh Wonder of the Boardwalk" were finally unveiled to the public. Jeffrey had been tracking along to practice corporate law when a friend of his father's pointed out that in International Banking and Finance, the laws that governed it were going to be the new legal frontier as corporations and conglomerates became multi-national.

"This is 'One word - plastics' and you're Benjamin Braddock," Joe Bottalico had told him one night during a neighborhood barbecue at the Croft Farm. The knowledge that Joey Bottles, whom his father once described as a recovering wiseguy, was driving a Chrysler New Yorker Brougham made Jeffrey all the more confident he'd done well to take his advice.

But Jeffrey had experienced something of a personal epiphany when his beloved *bubby*, Matya, had passed away. He'd only recently learned that she was not, in fact, his grandmother, but, in truth, his aunt. Matya had been shipped on a cattle car to Dachau along with her husband Eitan and their three daughters. She had been the only one of them to make it to liberation. She'd lived the rest of her life with her brother and his family when she got to the States.

At the funeral, Jeffrey made the rounds of the mourners and was surprised at the number of Holocaust survivors in attendance. He did not consider himself sentimental or passionate about his ancestors or their history, but there was something about the experience, about seeing the indelibly tattooed forearms, that profoundly moved him.

The internship in the Legal Affairs Department at the Bombay had not been his smartest or even his best offer. He'd turned down an opportunity to clerk for the Honorable Richard Hughes, Chief Justice of the New Jersey Supreme Court, who had also been the state's governor for two terms. His career advisor at Seton Hall thought he was crazy and almost dropped him, but Jeffrey felt the stirrings of a cultural conscience and decided to follow its lead.

He still had no idea if he could find anything that would prove his suspicions. But it was not a time-sensitive subject. If it took him ten days, ten months, or ten years, the end result would be the same. He even had two reporters picked out if he succeeded in discovering the link he was looking for. In his mind, he would be the mysterious and still unidentified Deep Throat, and they would be Woodward and Bernstein, although neither of them had a Jewish last name.

Jeffrey looked at his wrist and noted the time. Heidi had given him the engraved watch, an all-stainless-steel, solar-powered Citizen Crystron as an engagement present. He placed the copies in a file folder and dropped them into his attaché case.

He would spend the next eight hours protecting the interests of Benno Bruxelles and his fortress. After that, Jeffrey decided, his time was his own.

Jeffrey had been intrigued by the intricately constructed large-scale model in the foyer of the Ozymandias Suite. It was a detailed replica of the Hanging Gardens of Babylon, replete with miniature trees, ferns, and vines. A small attached plaque read:

"Seventh Wonder of the Ancient World"

Jeffrey had read somewhere that the Hanging Gardens were the only one of the original Seven Wonders whose existence could not be definitively proven, as no physical traces had ever been found. Most antiquities scholars doubted it was anything more than a legend. The model didn't look much like the 3-D pictures on the GAF View-Master slide wheel he'd gotten as a child at Hanukah. But when something wasn't real, he guessed you could make it look like whatever you wanted.

The Bombay was real, Jeffrey thought. But what it was built on might be another story altogether.

TWENTY-THREE

McLean's Restaurant
Beach Haven Crest, Long Beach Island

THE RESTAURANT DIDN'T TECHNICALLY open until 4 p.m., but Mickey had done a small favor for the owner back when she was chief in Surf City, tracking down some chronic check-bolters. She'd assured him that they wouldn't be dining, but said that a couple of pots of strong coffee would be appreciated.

Mickey had arrived first. She handed the young girl who'd come in early a five-dollar bill for her trouble. Sitting at a table near the window, she saw that the fiver would neatly cover the "Everything Dinner Special" listed on the oversized plastic menu. Mickey fished in her pocket and pulled out a quarter. With the five, it would match the cost of the "Full Course Steak Dinner" listed directly below it.

The girl, dressed in cutoff sweatpants and a **KELLY FOR BRICKWORK** t-shirt, returned holding two glass Bunn coffee decanters and two white and one orange ceramic mugs. The mugs were chipped but clean. Mickey laid the quarter on the wooden tabletop.

"Now you can get the steak dinner," Mickey told her. "Says it even includes the salad bar."

The girl set the decanters down and smiled. She arranged the mugs around the four-person table.

"Need cream and sugar?" she asked.

"Sure," Mickey said. "Not sure how my guests take it."

"I'll bring some spoons and napkins, then, too," the girl replied.

"Thanks...uh," Mickey looked but did not see a nameplate, then remembered she was not officially working a scheduled shift.

"Melissa," the girl answered. "Like the Allman Brothers' song."

"Cool," Mickey told her. "Greg Allman wrote that song about a little girl he saw with her grandmother at an all-night grocery store." Mickey remained dedicated to keeping Ronnie's love of the history and lore of rock music alive.

"Even cooler," Melissa said.

"What's your last name? So I can say good things about you to your boss."

"Summerfield," the girl told her. "Good name for a beach town waitress, right? Oh, I think maybe your friends have arrived." Melissa Summerfield looked over her shoulder. "I'll bring another mug."

Mickey turned her chair.

Approaching her were three men, not the two she had anticipated.

Evan Driscoll looked older, but he hadn't changed much. The second man was clearly another Fed. Side part and glasses. Mickey had learned to spot one a mile away with her eyes closed. The third one, however, was very clearly not a Fed. Too pressed out, she thought, too nattily dressed. White linen blazer, pastel shirt with no tie, and blue trousers. Nope, definitely not a Fed. She recognized his mirrored aviator sunglasses from a magazine advertisement - Cool-Ray Silver Clouds.

Mickey thought about it but decided not to stand up. They were coming to see her, she figured. Melissa returned with the fourth mug. A green one this time. The three politely waited for her to wander far enough away and then seated themselves.

"Long time, no see," Evan Driscoll said. "You haven't changed a bit, Detective. Wish I could say the same for myself. This is Agent Stenkewiecz. He's from the local agency in Linwood."

The man held out his hand. "Stan," he said. "Heard a lot about you, Detective. All very impressive. Gotta say, your Bureau file reads like an Elmore Leonard novel. I hope you'll feel that comparison is justified."

She saw Driscoll shoot him a disapproving glance. She assumed they'd been keeping a file on her since they'd shown up on what was essentially a local law-enforcement manner back in 1967. It didn't bother her, so she decided to ease Stan's mind.

"Don't believe everything you read, Agent Stenkewiecz. There are probably more than a few wannabe novelists writing reports at the FBI."

Stenkewiecz nodded and smiled. His expression telegraphed his appreciation - he knew she had covered him.

Driscoll continued the introductions. "And I hope you don't mind that I brought someone along. I think you'll find what he has to say rather interesting."

Mickey noticed that the man in question did not remove his Cool-Rays. He extended his hand.

"Connor," he said. "Connor Kilderry."

His brogue was thick and lovely. He said something after his name, but Mickey realized that she couldn't have repeated the words if you paid her.

The Pine Barrens

The old ladies had been harder on Rhonda Petty than Walker White would have liked. Especially since they'd gotten nothing out of her despite their rather concerted effort. The girl looked like a dishrag when they dragged her into the little meeting room after a night of what Walker suggested to them should be "enhanced" interrogation.

"Bitch either doesn't know anything or she's the toughest piece of ass on the planet," said Sally Springer, the undisputed boss of the club's female retinue. "Springs" was senior only to "Shocks," DeAnna Shockley, his Road Captain's property. In an MC, the old ladies - Walker refused to use the "ole" modifier - were right below the bikes in the hierarchy. It didn't need to be imposed or enforced, it was simply accepted. It was a life and a lifestyle most of them not only chose but sought out and then fully embraced.

"Anything you want to tell me, Rhonda?"

"Toms River is all I know," the girl answered thickly. "Sister. S'all I know."

Walker White was satisfied. "Clean her up, get four Percs from Rabbit, and give them to her with a shot of whiskey. Then put her in a bed. Check every once in a while to make sure she's breathing. If she buys it, you two are digging the hole."

Rhonda Petty was helped to her feet and escorted, perhaps a little more gently now, out of the room.

The Patches, the Prospects, and the Officers were all due back by five, with the exception of Melk, who was sent to scope out the sister's house in Toms River.

Walker White had a decision to make. He ran and reran the scenarios in his head, swiftly noting the comparative risks. It was like he was looking at the rows and columns of an accounting ledger in his mind. The decision seemed obvious.

The deal was still on.

TWENTY-FOUR

Surf City

MICKEY PARKED THE MUSTANG and walked the short distance to the former offices of **Refunds 'R' Us,** a name stolen and repurposed from a U.S. Trademark and Copyright Office application filed by a newly incorporated toy retailer. The clerk who processed it was the imprisoned accountant's brother-in-law.

Dr. Nepp was still at work, judging by the amusingly mild profanity issuing from behind the dividers.

Mickey shook the door as she entered, rattling the bell above.

"Just me," she shouted. "How goes the struggle?"

Nepp stood up from his crouch and wiped his forehead.

"All good but the monitor. Nothing matters if you can't see what's there. And it is there. But I'm reconfiguring the input circuit – I'm hoping that will do it."

"Can I use my phone for a while?"

"Sure," Nepp answered. "This will take a few minutes. Do you want me to step out?"

"Nah, that's OK," Mickey told him. "I've granted you unofficial security clearance. Simply by thinking it."

Nepp went back to work, fiddling with the monitor. Mickey sat down and picked up the phone. She'd also taken her chair and its well-worn cushion from the SCPD at Charlie's insistence. She'd become intimately familiar with its particular series of squeaks and creaks, to the point where she'd stopped using 3-in-One oil on its springs.

Mickey dialed the number of the exchange, was quickly connected and, as she expected, Rich Rodriguez picked up.

"What have you got for me, Amigo?" she asked.

"A little," Rodriguez said, "But not a lot. Can we meet someplace?"

"I need to stick around here today," Mickey answered. "Can you do Bill's Diner in, say, an hour."

"That old *Grick*?" he said, using Bill's pronunciation. "Sure, be there in thirty. Maybe twenty."

"It'll take you at least forty," Mickey countered.

"I still have lights and a siren, even if you don't. Twenty."

"Hey, I put in a requisition for one of those blue roof flashers that plugs into the cigarette lighter. It isn't here yet," Mickey said.

"Oh, OK, Theo," Rodriguez deadpanned. ""I'll bring the lollipops. See you in twenty. Crocker out." He hung up.

Mickey checked the ornate and ancient clock hanging on the wall, another holdover from the prior tenant. It was a German cuckoo clock with a working, if rather annoying, cuckoo. Carved wooden figures stood on a balcony below the cuckoo's door. The three weights that hung below it on chains looked like skinny pine cones. Mickey finally figured out how to wind it but couldn't find a way to silence the cuckoo, whose odd and strident three-note chirp sounded disturbingly like *Heil Hitler.* A faded and peeling label on the back of the clock listed the maker as Adolf Herr from Bavaria. She'd been meaning to replace it.

"Finally!" Nepp exclaimed. "Come see."

Mickey wheeled over in her chair to the credenza where the monitor sat. In front of it was what looked like a disconnected typewriter keyboard.

"What's that for?"

"It's how you tell the machine what to do, what to look for. I'll write down some basic commands. I don't think we can get it all done today, though. If you give me two hours tomorrow, though, I'll show you how to search for things yourself."

"OK," Mickey answered. "I can do that."

"First, I need the phone. Just the receiver, please."

Mickey untangled the curlicue cord and handed it to him.

He placed it in a smaller rectangular thing that looked like the bottom half of what might have once been a Princess Phone.

Nepp's fingers tapped on the keys. Odd green letters and phrases popped up on the screen.

"Ready?"

"I guess," Mickey said.

He tapped another key and picture appeared on the screen. It looked like the front page of a newspaper.

Nepp beamed. "You said the *Irish Times*, right? Shall we check today's issue? They're five hours ahead of us."

"Yeah. See if I won the Sweepstakes. My late dad entered me every year, so I've kept up the tradition and bought a ticket myself."

He fingered a few more keys and the image enlarged. Mickey could read the headlines now. **Water rationing may be imposed in Dublin** one of the larger ones read. The byline credited a reporter named Eugene McEldowney. The name made Mickey smile.

Nepp messed with the keys a little more, then showed Mickey how to move the image around to see more of the page and also how to use arrows to turn to another page.

"You built this?" she asked Nepp.

"I did."

"In your garage?"

"In my garage."

"I once built a Pinewood Derby car in our basement and thought I'd done well. They wouldn't let me race it because they said I was a girl and not a real Cub Scout. I said I didn't want any ribbons. I only wanted to see how fast it would go.

I would'a won." Mickey checked the cuckoo clock's white hands. "I'm gonna have to scoot, Dr. Nepp – stay as long as you want. I'll check back in later."

"OK," Nepp answered. "Hey – does that cuckoo sound like he's saying –"

"*Ja wohl* he does," Mickey said. The sparse amount of German she knew came from watching *Hogan's Heroes*. She rose and slid her chair back to its spot behind her desk.

"If I'm not back when you leave, please lock the door on your way out."

Nepp smiled and gave a bent-elbow Third Reich salute. "Don't tell *mamenyu* I did that, please."

Mickey put a finger to her lips. "See you later, Dr. Nepp."

She twirled her key ring and headed for the door.

Bill's Greek-American Diner
Surf City

Mickey was surprised to see Rodriguez seated in a booth with a Coke in front of him when she walked in. He grinned at her.

Before she could take another step, Bill Kuriakos rushed to greet her.

"Cheef Mee-kee," he said. "So good you come. Whole new menu I have. I make special something for you. You say hi to Nick."

Nick Kuriakos was enveloped in a veil of steam, busily working two silver spatulas on the flattop grill. He raised one of the utensils in a mock salute.

"Is it still forever? What I asked you?" he called to her with a smile.

'Still forever, Nick," Mickey replied as kindly as she could.

"Nicky," Bill said in a near whisper. "He's a good boy. Work hard. Make someone a good husband." Bill winked at Mickey. She leaned down and kissed him on his balding pate. "What you like?" Bill continued. "Burger? Chiz-steak? New *Grick* chiz-steak?'

"How about fries and a Coke," Mickey answered.

"I make you special *Grick* fries," Bill said. "Forget those Frenchies. Use special *Grick* seasons. Even Colonel Sanders wants recipe."

Mickey was shaking her head as she sat down. Rodriguez pulled a brown envelope from his lap and laid it between them.

Mickey took it, slid her finger under the seal and withdrew the contents, which were only a few printed pages and some photographs.

As she did, Bill arrived with a steaming plate of fries. "Tell me how you like."

Mickey nodded. Bill stood by the table and Mickey realized he was waiting for instant feedback. Mickey took one of the smaller fries, blew on it and popped it in her mouth. The taste was not exactly what she was expecting.

"Good," she said, reaching for the Coke he'd also delivered. She took a long sip.

Bill Kuriakos smiled broadly. "You want more, you ask me. Free for Chief Mee-kee."

He waddled back toward the kitchen.

"A little taste of Greece?" Rodriguez asked her.

Mickey reached for the napkin dispenser. "Grease is right," she said, wiping her fingers and showing him the oily residue stuck to the paper. "I'll have to figure out a way to ditch these before we go," she continued.

When she was sure her hands were clean she shuffled the papers and the pictures around.

"Anything look familiar?" Rodriguez asked her.

"The female's tattoo – it's common in Ireland. Means solidarity with the unification, I'm pretty sure. Usually signifies a Catholic allegiance."

Rodriguez gave her a puzzling look. "I thought Ireland was all Catholic."

"We're talking Northern Ireland here. A country within a country. Protestants loyal to the British on one side and Catholics who want the British back on their side of the English Channel at any cost on the other."

"They're big on bombs, right?"

"That they are," Mickey countered. "But the IRA, the Irish Republican Army, it has what it calls its Paramilitary Wing. Basically a militia or, if you're the RUC, a terrorist organization seeking to overthrow the royal and legal English government."

"What's the RUC?" Rodriguez asked

"Royal Ulster Constabulary. British boots on Irish ground. Think of New Jersey if Cornwallis was still here. The nickname for this raging conflict is The Troubles. Maybe the most understated description of a civil war in world history. I don't know how many men, women and children have been shot, blown up, or kidnapped and murdered strictly on the basis of what church they attend or where they chose to take a stroll or hold hands with on a certain day. There literally are no civilians in this one."

Rodriguez drank half his coke in one swallow, ignoring the straw.

"Why would a woman connected to the IRA join a dirtball MC?"

"No idea," Mickey said. "Makes no sense on the face of it, does it? Maybe she's a sympathizer. What about the male? Not much here that I can see."

Rodriguez drew in a breath. "Funny thing about the male. Got a hit on his prints and a name to go with them. But only a name. No clue to what agency obtained them, stored them or even why they had them. It's like his record didn't exist or it was scrubbed clean."

"What's his name?" Mickey asked.

"Marty Quinn," Rodriguez said. "Martin Quinn if we're being formal. No MI, again, something odd. But despite having prints on file with somebody, so far we cannot find another bleeping shred of personal information. It's like the guy is a ghost. No birth certificate, no schools, no social, no military papers, nothing."

Mickey considered the information.

"Martin Quinn is an Irish name. And this tattoo, the black rose, that may have political significance as well."

"Could they both be foreign nationals?" Rodriguez queried. "I don't know. Maybe stowed away together on a rusty steamer some dark night and ended up at the Port of Philadelphia? An MC would be a good place to hide out until you could establish yourself. Especially if you were running from something or somebody. Like a foreign government or a terrorist organization. But his tat, it doesn't say Sons of Satan."

"Gotta be a Prospect, then," Mickey said. "I'll show it to the LT to make sure, but I think it's kind of an entry level one – you can get several before you get patched in. Some of these tats, the smaller ones on the fingers and the crook of the thumb- they're either prison ones or gang ones. There's this whole complex code as to what they mean. They're like, um, like the Merit Badges you get in Scouts. Except they're for murders or assaults and other notable accomplishments your parents would be proud of. And see - they're just a little bit faded as well. Something's not quite right here."

Mickey paused and downed more of her Coke. The single heavily seasoned fry had managed to make her mouth parched all by itself.

"Anything else?" she asked.

"Yeah. Galasso, he's doing the autopsies. He found some tiny yellow plastic fibers embedded in the ligature marks. Probably what was used to tie them up," Rodriguez told her. "I'll let you know if he can positively ID what or where they came from."

"OK. Can I take these?" Mickey asked. "I'll swing by *The SandPaper* office and see if Stellwag is there. April Everheart is still in Monaco. She went to the Formula One Grand Prix. Her family and Grace Kelly's go way back, apparently. She's been on a yacht for the last three weeks, no doubt doing the horizontal mambo with the rich and famous of both sexes.

"You do know an interesting assortment of people, Mick. I'll say that for you."

Mickey recalled the brief but intriguing conversation she'd had with Evan Driscoll's guest during their sit-down at McLean's. He'd given her a card and asked if he could stop by later, after he'd had a chance to, as he put it, "beat the bleedin' bushes a bit more."

Driscoll was keeping his cards unusually close to his vest this time around. It was what she called a Paul Harvey Moment. Except she didn't yet know the rest of the story.

Rodriguez slipped out of the booth. He grabbed the paper boat with the fries.

"I'll take these along with me," he said. "Save you the embarrassment. You can keep those." He pointed to the documents and photographs. "I don't need them back. Mick, I'm pushing as many buttons and pulling as many levers as I know how right now. But if you come up with something – anything – call me. They're rattling my cage from all four sides and the top. Next they'll be reaching through the bars for my neck."

"Will do, Rich," Mickey said as he departed.

Bill returned and looked at the empty table. "See? I tell you, you love them. You must be part *Grick*. Stay here, I tell Nick to make you more – for the road."

Before Mickey could protest he was gone.

She very much wanted to stop home and spend some time with Michael and Eileen. Nancy Donahue, technically Nancy Croce after the adoption was formalized, challenged and then formalized again, watched the children on her afternoons off from the library. Bunny was due to start English and Grammar lessons with Marian as soon as school let out. Mickey knew she was going to have to rearrange her childcare jigsaw puzzle yet again.

Bill Kuriakos came toddling back. He handed Mickey a brown paper bag. Oil stains were already saturating parts of it, she could see.

"Mee-kee look very busy today," he said. "So I make you To Go bag. You come back soon. Bring the children. Now I have *Grick* yogurt. Better than Mr. Softee ice cream. Healthy too. Make everybody poop *ischyros*. That's *Grick* for strong." He showed her a tightly clenched fist to accentuate his point.

Mickey took the bag and wandered out the door.

Standing by the Mustang, she thought about the charming but decidedly opaque Connor Kilderry. His story was engaging but it had, to Mickey's ear, at least some of the blarney of a practiced Irish storyteller.

Was it simply his way or was someone, as Patsy used to say, being intentionally stingy with the truth? Evan and his agent, Stan, were running back to Atlantic City to chase down some leads he'd given them. Kilderry said he wanted to meet with Mickey again before the day was out. She'd been non-committal in her reply. But if he called, she was thinking now she might agree. Maybe he'd have something Rich could use.

Plus, the suspense, she realized with some amusement, was killing her.

TWENTY-FIVE

The Claridge Hotel, Boardwalk

HE LOOKED AT THE suitcases. With so many back-and-forth changes in one day, he tried a new mental trick. At the moment he was Mister White, the things that made him so stacked in the suitcase of the same color. Soon, he'd close the lid on Mr. White forever and assume, for several hours, the identity of Mr. Green. An identity that would also last but a few hours, before that lid was closed on it for good. By tomorrow he would be Mr. Orange. But that didn't sound right so he reset. Tomorrow, and until he was safely out of U.S. airspace, he would be The Orange Man. It seemed silly and juvenile, like a character in a Roald Dahl book. But it would also allow him to claim, if anyone asked about his luggage, that he was a proud Ulsterman. If that left an impression, at least it would be the wrong one.

He felt again for the smooth, white chip in his pocket and pictured the stack of ornate certificates bearing James Monroe's stern visage, each one worth five thousand dollars, it would soon become. A bit of monetary transubstantiation it was, like wine into blood, or bread into flesh, as the Missionary Sisters at the Assumption Grammar School in County Down had beaten into him with their mighty arsenal of metal-edged rulers and hickory pointers.

Ilsa had sweetened the pot upon his empty promise of another tryst. There were still things she wanted to try, she'd said. What further contortions or unnatural acts still remained, he couldn't quite fathom and he was relieved he'd not have to endure more depravity than he already had.

Hidden in the lining of the Ulsterman's kit were pockets for the Bearer Bonds. Ilsa was presently removing them from Benno Bruxelles' private vault. The ivory chip, if one were to be ignorant of its provenance, would fetch $125,000 U.S. Dollars. A hundred thousand of that would purchase the RPG V7 rocket launchers and the ordnance to go with them the local degenerate bikies had lifted from right under the nose of some drug-addicted military quartermaster.

The one useful thing Long Kesh had taught him was how to sniff out a snitch. He should have seen that the lad and his molly were a bit too conveniently Irish, their story a bit too pat. Never kid a kidder, his da' used to say. He knew what real hatred of the fecking Prots felt like. The boy got close, but unless your own dear mother had been carted away, screaming, in the middle of the night for the sin of being kind to a Protestant widow, her beaten and bloodied body left on the marble front steps that were her pride the next morning as a warning to the neighbors, well, then, the best you could hope to manage was perhaps a pale and pitiful imitation.

He didn't feel any remorse. Soldiers, they were. Them doing their jobs and him doing his. Drowning wasn't a particularly valorous end, but it was still in the line of duty. By the time the Feddies pieced the whole thing together, he'd be behind a grand olivewood bar, patiently pouring a pint of Guinness for some tipsy *tourista*. The extra twenty-five, safely deposited in *Banco d'Espana's* Main Branch on the *Paseo del Prado,* was going to see to that. He still didn't understand why they hadn't stayed on the bottom. He'd grown up a lighthouse keeper's son. Rope, knots and weights were his stock-in-trade.

Ilsa, he considered with a fair bit of humor, wouldn't even be stealing. Two chips remained outstanding, she'd shared. His was one of them, and Benno Bruxelles would be elated when she placed it in his palm. And, she told him, she was counting on a sizable bonus for her own self for delivering it back to him.

The woman at the restaurant, Cleary, she'd bothered him, though. He needed to circle back around to gauge what she knew and what, if anything, she might suspect. The dead ones, they were making a splash in the papers. He wanted to make sure there were no ties to him that could be discovered before he stepped on a plane.

But at the moment, Archibald Graham had some U.S. Treasury Bearer Bonds to pick up. Ilsa had suggested her room for the exchange. He'd slipped his neck out of that noose by telling her he needed to immediately deliver them to a safe place and that he'd return following that for a dinner of freshly caught fish and an extended evening of further fornication.

He slipped on Mr. White's coat and tie then sat on the edge of the twin bed to collect his thoughts. He worried that he was laying on the brogue and the blarney a bit thick. Americans got their impressions of foreigners not from travel, but from television. He was trying to fall somewhere in between a cereal leprechaun and a soap commercial and drew the line at uttering "Saints be praised," "Top o'the mornin' to ya," or "Sure and begorrah."

Details, he believed, were like the loose ends on a Keeper's wool sweater. If someone pulled on the right one, it wouldn't take but a minute for the whole bleedin' garment to unravel.

He wasn't sure yet if Mickey Cleary was the type to pull on such a thread. But there was something about her, the way she'd looked him over, sending a silent signal that she wasn't someone to be trifled with.

Once he'd bid Ilsa a quick fare-thee-well, he'd have to make sure.

Definitively sure.

The SandPaper *Offices*
Surf City

Mickey knocked on the door, turned the knob and pushed it open.

"Out in a sec," a man's voice called.

Mickey had first run into Claude Stellwag on one of Surf City's dark and dusty beach roads. Looking back now, she often laughed at the particulars of their encounter – more of a face-off than a confrontation. She'd been Chief less than a month and the run-in could have easily gone south. But they'd somehow respected each other's swagger, Mickey recalling they had her outnumbered three to one, unless she counted the two terrified underage girls with them. Stellwag had asked her if she was a Meter Maid, she remembered.

It established a sort of détente and, within only a few weeks, that uneasy eyeing of one another somehow evolved into a friendship of sorts and, eventually, an alliance.

Stellwag, 'The LT' to everyone but his boss and live-in lover April Everheart, had been the president and one of the founding members of the Sons of Satan, back when the MC's requirement for membership was a combat tour and a war wound. Eleven years had erased any semblance of the original club, and the present version of the Sons made the Corleone Family look honorable in comparison.

Mickey waited. A minute later Stellwag emerged sporting a brown vinyl apron and wiping his ink-stained hands on a towel that had clearly seen better days.

"Bobby Black Fingers Rocca would be proud," Mickey said.

Stellwag look up and smiled. "Hey," he said. "Seems like it's been forever, Mickey. What brings you around?"

"Semi-professional courtesy visit," Mickey answered. "You do the typesetting now, too?"

Stellwag motioned her to a chair.

"Nice career arc, huh?" he said. "From Son of Satan to Printer's Devil." He balled up the towel and laid it on the desk next to an ancient Underwood typewriter. "I was just talking to Haystacks and Garufi. We're thinking of starting up a more, uh, socially acceptable kind of MC. You know, weekend rides, maybe a little charity work. No bike chains or brass knuckles. Garufi wants to call it 'Weekend Warriors MC Original.' Me and Haystacks, we really should call him Everett, we favor 'Fortunate Sons.' You know, like the Creedence Clearwater song. No senators' sons, allowed."

"I like it, LT," Mickey replied. I think I'd go with 'Fortunate Sons,' though. It's hard to beat a CCR reference. How's Filisky feeling?"

"Physically? He's better now that they put him on that regulating medicine. He says his heartbeat only races when he sees a girl in a swimsuit. If he ever sees one of those thong bikinis, he'll have a heart attack. I think I have him talked into 'Fortunate Sons,' though. It's who we were and what we are. Fortunate, that is."

"Kind of why I'm here," Mickey said. "You got a Coke or anything? I tried some of Bill's Grick fries. Nothing like grease from Greece."

"Only Tab and Fresca," Stellwag said. "April never changes. Although now she's into something called sparkling water. That hasn't made it out of our hacienda yet."

"Tab sounds good," Mickey said.

Stellwag disappeared behind a wall. Mickey heard the clink of glass bottles and the "pop" of two caps. He reappeared holding the bottles and handed her one.

"She ever going to sell this rag?" Mickey asked and then took a swig of the Tab.

"God, no," Stellwag replied, knocking back a healthy swallow of his Fresca. "It gives her some weird kind of legitimacy with her dear mummy and daddy, not to mention the rest of the Everheart aristocrats. Something to brag about at The Peale Club during wedding receptions. They talk about her like she's Katherine Graham and Nellie Bly rolled into one."

Mickey rolled her eyes.

"Sorry, I'm not trying to be a pedantic jerk. Katherine Graham owns the *Washington Post* and published 'The Pentagon Papers' despite being directly threatened by the Nixon White House. Nellie Bly was maybe the first undercover newspaper reporter. Got herself intentionally admitted to an insane asylum for women on what's now Roosevelt Island, out near Lady Liberty, and then wrote about it. This was like ninety or a hundred years ago. The owner of *that* newspaper, I think it was the *New York World*, was Joseph Pulitzer."

"Mike Gannon would be proud," Mickey said after another sip. "Or quite possibly appalled. At the comparison, I mean. But at least *you're* a real journalist."

"I am. Even finished my degree through Rutgers Night School. I'm working on something, maybe a story, maybe a book. About having my chopper shot down in Vietnam during that second tour and managing to make it out."

"Yeah," Mickey laughed. "I went to the wake the Sons held for you, remember?"

Stellwag smiled. "Mike Gannon was in here a week, maybe two weeks ago. With his Girl Friday – the one that used to work here."

"Candy? Candy Catanzariti?" Mickey said, a bit shocked.

"Yeah. Guess she shortened it, so it's just Catan now. They're like Woodward and Bernstein. The girl, Candy, she tracked some radical bomber chick from the sixties all the way to Crookston, Minnesota. I guess you can spit into Canada from there. Thought she might find the kid who tried to fly his plane into the lighthouse with her. But I guess she didn't."

Or didn't want to. She let it lie.

"You're not going to ask me to go undercover with the old MC, are you, Mick?"

Mickey smiled at the thought. "No, but do you have anybody still on the inside? I could use some intel – maybe even a friendly face-to-face. Mae's Tavern, maybe? That would be a neutral corner. I'll buy the beers. I'd do a visit out to Cartoon Corners, but only if you, Haystacks, Garufi *and* Filisky went along. I could saddle up Ronnie's Enfield if it would help. It's not a rice-burner."

"Some troubles on LBI with the Sons?" Stellwag asked. "That would literally be news to me."

"No," Mickey said and finished her Tab. "Rich asked me to bird-dog anything I could find on that mess he caught at the Steel Pier. Can I show you some Eyes-Only info and a few pictures?"

She pulled the envelope from her beltline behind her back. Stellwag slipped the contents out and looked them over.

"Jeez," he said.

"Recognize the ink?"

"One, on the guy, that's definitely club ink. Almost certainly he was a Prospect. No clue about the girl's, though. Nice work, whoever did it."

"What about the paperwork?"

"Martin Quinn," Stellwag said and handed the contents and the envelope back to Mickey. "OK. That's funny."

"What's funny?"

"The name. Martin Quinn. Once you've been in the military, in your head you think of names in reverse, the way you're taught to repeat your name, rank and serial number. So, Martin Quinn becomes Quinn, comma, Martin. Quinn Martin. Like I said. Funny. Or really odd, if it's a true coincidence."

"Why would it be odd?"

"Mick, you gotta watch more television," he said. "Quinn Martin. Like half the cop shows are," Stellwag dropped his pitch to a dramatic register, "'A *Quinn Martin Production*'."

"I am a cop," Mickey said, "I don't watch cop shows. They're so fake."

"I run a newspaper and I watch *Lou Grant*," Stellwag countered. "You know what they say - Art imitates Life. So fiction imitates reality. Especially on television. Ed Asner gets letters from people asking if they can be reporters for the non-existent *Los Angeles Tribune*. Mick, put it on TV and you wouldn't believe how many people will assume it's real. Scary, if you think about it."

"So, anyone still in the MC we could try to tap for something useful?"

Stellwag shook his head.

"Dead Dog's still in. That's a possibility. Stopper's doing a dime at the joint in Camden. Even money on whether he survives that. Jailhouse visits are tricky. They – you – listen to every word. That's pretty much it for me. One by one they've pushed the ex-military members out. I can ask the other guys, but they're a different club than the one they, you or I knew. And from what I hear, this new president, Walker White, he's no Michael Corleone. He has no plans to take the Sons of Satan totally legit in five years."

Stellwag paused. His face told Mickey he was having an internal conversation.

"What are you thinking?" she asked.

"The name. Walker White. So, in the service it would be White, comma, Walker. White Walker. Wow. That sounds evil, doesn't it?"

"I don't know. Maybe to a writer it does," Mickey said.

"Sorry I can't help you more, Mick," Stellwag continued. "You know I would if I could."

"I know, LT," Mickey replied. "Just keep your ear to the ground. Same for the Hardy Boys, huh?"

"How are the kids holding up?" Stellwag asked.

"Missing their daddy," Mickey said as she stood. "Stop by and stay hi some time. Take Leenie for a spin on the Royal-Enfield. Do both of you some good. You're starting to look a little too domestic there for my tastes."

"Thanks for that." Stellwag chuckled. "You know, Mick, I was thinking. I could try and fit the Enfield with a little car seat. For Michael. Wouldn't be that hard. Start'em young, I always say. Maybe get him a 'Born to Ride' tattoo. Fake one to start, of course." He rose from his chair, walked over and hugged Mickey tightly.

She tapped his back three times with her closed fist.

"Quinn Martin, huh?" Mickey said when they broke their embrace.

"*Twelve O'Clock High*, *Barnaby Jones*, *Dan August*, *Streets of San Francisco* – a show they totally ripped off from *Bullitt*. *Cannon*, *The Fugitive*, *The FBI*. And that might not even be half of them."

"He did *The FBI*?"

"They," Stellwag corrected. "Quinn and Martin are the two producers. Two different guys. Sounds like one, I know, but it's two." He grabbed her shoulder affectionately. "Be careful out there, Mickey Cleary."

Mickey gave him a little salute and walked out of the newspaper office.

The thoughts in her head were floating around like the letters in the Campbell's Alphabet Soup Michael liked so much. A psychologist at the State Police academy had taught the recruits to verbalize their thoughts as a way of clarifying them.

As she climbed into the Mustang, Mickey said a few of her newer ones out loud.

"Martin Quinn. Quinn Martin. The FBI. Quinn Martin is two people. The FBI. Quinn Martin is two people. Martin Quinn. The FBI. Martin Quinn is-"

A Surf City squad car screamed by, siren wailing and lights flashing, immediately snapping her out of the mental exercise. She fired up the GT and pulled out to follow it.

She was in the neighborhood, she figured.

TWENTY-SIX

Bombay Hotel & Casino
Top Floor Offices

THE BREATHLESS QUICKIE ON her desk, he assured Ilsa, was only a down payment.

Now, she'd actually taken him with her inside the massive vault, a space ten times larger than any bank he'd ever visited. It had taken her a bit to count out the Bearer Bonds and make sure they were all in sequence. She hadn't seemed to care when he wandered away on a little self-guided tour.

Mr. White, he used the trick to remain in character, was not prepared for what the vault contained. The straps of bills, he'd expected those, but the sheer number of them boggled his mind. It appeared there were enough of them to rival anything King Croesus might have ever possessed. Each strap, he knew, contained one hundred bills of the same denomination. Ten thousand dollars in every one, since he saw nothing but Benjamin Franklin's portrait on any of the top notes in any of the straps. He tried to count the number of straps, but gave up. There could be a thousand of them, meaning he was sharing a space with ten million dollars in cash. With that, he figured, they could bloody buy Northern Ireland from the fecking Crown and be done with it. But there was more than money within the walls.

Around one corner was a room packed cheek to gill with artwork. Another alcove had clear tubs packed full of jewelry and gems, stacked floor to ceiling.

And another had fur coats, he couldn't count how many, neatly hung on mounted racks. There had to be several hundred of them at least.

Ilsa's voice interrupted his amazement.

"They're all ten thousands," she said. She was holding a non-descript valise which was zippered shut. "So there's one thirty, not one twenty-five. You can work off the difference tonight," she said and gently cupped his crotch. "Look around some more if you like. It's not like he's keeping national treasures in here or anything."

"What's in here?" He pointed to a windowed wooden box.

"Maps," Ilsa said. "Old maps. Like extremely old. I suppose rare maps would be the proper description. The Boss is a freak for maps. The older the better. He visits libraries all over the world. Buys them from them, I suppose, because he always comes back with at least one or two. Puts on white linen gloves if he needs to touch any of them. No idea what he does with them. Kind of odd. But then, so is he. A born collector of things, I guess."

He took the valise from her.

"Thanks, love. I'll make good on the difference, don't you worry."

"Oh, he'll be glad to have his little chip back," Ilsa said as she walked toward the vault's door. "They only go up in value. Another year and who knows how much it would have been worth."

They exited and Ilsa swung the door closed with one hand. The warmth of the office made him realize the temperature inside the vault must have been fifteen degrees cooler. For the furs, he assumed.

"Don't be late," Ilsa chided. "I have something very special in mind for tonight. I hope you're adventurous as well as amorous."

"Well, then. Guess I'll plan on bein' a bit o' both," he said and kissed her.

As he descended in the elevator he wished Mr. White a fond farewell. A short stroll to The Claridge, a few more hours as Mr. Green, and by this time tomorrow he'd be somewhere beyond the sea. He began to whistle the Bobby Darin tune and figured he'd make it to Surf City around dinner time.

The hard years as a Lightkeeper's son had kept his palate simple. He knew he'd likely not be finding anywhere a plate of cabbage and bacon, a pint of warm stout, or even a slice of soda bread. But perhaps Mickey Cleary, with the Irish heritage he'd seen in her FBI file, could point them to a place with a decent pub burger. How anyone drank beer cold was still beyond him.

He slid into the front seat of the sedan Evan Driscoll had loaned him. Driving on the wrong side of the road still required concentration and the overruling of learned tendencies. But there was an upside.

It was good practice for Spain.

Surf City

Mickey took all three front steps at once.

Music was playing. Loud.

She waited. And listened. And smiled when she recognized Donovan's "Atlantis." Mercifully, she'd missed the meandering spoken preamble. Mickey liked the Scottish singer's voice but she wasn't buying his whole mystical hippie poet shtick. Peter, Paul and Mary had done well to skewer that in "I Dig Rock and Roll Music."

The refrain was playing now. Mickey opened the door so she could hear better. She recognized Bunny's, Nancy Donahue's and Eileen's voices. But it sounded like there was an extra one chiming in. She wondered if Eileen's annoying little friend Cubby had come over.

Mickey eased the door farther and made her way silently toward the source of the sound. She stopped outside the children's bedroom and stared in.

Nancy Donahue spied her, silently put a finger to her lips, and then beckoned her closer with a curled index finger. Nancy's face broke into a huge smile as she pointed to the floor.

Michael was singing.

Mickey watched in amazement. It wasn't gibberish. She distinctly heard him say "down," "she," "be," "low," and something close enough to "ocean" – it came out "osha" - to make her cover her mouth in shock. She realized she was close to tears.

"Keep singing!" Nancy shouted as she quietly backed out of the room.

Bunny mimed holding a microphone in front of her. Eileen danced like Stevie Nicks. Michael sat on the floor, seemingly awash in the whole experience. Mickey watched his mouth moving and looked at the young woman she playfully referred to as Our Miss Donahue.

"When did –"

"Who knows?" Nancy replied. "Who cares? Maybe today. Maybe yesterday. Maybe six months ago. He might not like to talk, but he sure loves to sing." She poked her head back into the bedroom. "One more time!" she said over the speakers. "Louder!"

"I know Dr. Harman said read to him," Nancy continued. "But I never thought about singing to him, did you?"

Mickey shook her head.

"I read this article in *Scientific American* one afternoon when the Reference Desk at Princeton was pretty dead. It said experts now think one side of the brain is dominant in some people and that the opposite side runs the show in others. It was pretty fascinating. The right side, I remember it said, processes music, art, all the sound and visual stuff. The left is more, I don't know, more...analytical. Math and theoretical things. So, like there are right and left-handers in baseball, there are right and left brainers, I suppose. At least now we know which way Michael throws. Or bats, maybe. Bottom line is – buy more records."

The song ended. Eileen saw Mickey and ran to her.

"Mama!" she said and hugged her around the waist. "Did you hear us?"

Bunny picked Michael up and brought him over.

"You hear him?" she asked Mickey.

"I did," Mickey replied. "I did hear him." She took the child from Bunny and kissed him several times.

"Ma," he said distinctly. "Ma."

Mickey felt the tears start to come and she struggled to speak.

"Ma," was all she could manage at first. "Yes, honey, yes. Ma." She squeezed the boy until he squeaked. "Wow," Mickey said. "Didn't expect to come home to this."

"Mama," Eileen chirped up. "I skippered the boat today. It's called a dory. Greg said tomorrow we'll search for Captain Nemo. But we rescued a raft. Way, way, way, *way* out on tha' ocean."

"Was there anyone on the raft – way, way, way out there on the ocean?" Mickey asked, leaning down.

"No. But it was scared and lonely all by itself in the big waves."

"I bet it was," Mickey said and patted her on the head.

"Greg said if no one says it's their raft, I can have it," the child went on. "I'm going to name it Maribelle."

"Why Maribelle?"

"It's a mermaid's name. Greg said it means Star of the Sea. It's Irish. Like we are."

Mickey looked at Nancy. "So, did you talk to Greg?"

"Oh, yes," Nancy said with a funny smile. "Greg."

"He didn't."

"He did."

"Was it... icky?" Mickey asked. "I did tell him that you and-"

"No," Nancy said laughing. "It wasn't icky it all. He's actually rather charming and intelligent. He didn't make a pass or anything. He simply said that sometimes situations change, and he would be very interested in learning more about me. Said he spends most of his time in the university library. Loves to look at old maps. He asked me if I was a shusher."

"And?"

"And I assured him I was not a shusher. And then guess what he said?"

Mickey shrugged her shoulders.

"Will I see you in September?"

"Wait, like the -"

"Uh-huh," Nancy said, putting the tip of her tongue on her upper lip.

"And you said?"

"I said, "Farewell. So long. Bye, bye."

"I think it's the other way around, but sorry, Our Miss Donahue, that sounds to me like a lot of verbal flirting on both sides."

"Hey," Nancy replied. "It's not like I'm married. Jeez, I'm not even engaged." She held up her ring-barren left hand. "And I'm starting to think 'engaged to be engaged' is code for the whole dairy analogy thing."

"Dairy analogy? Oh, right. Why buy the cow when you're getting the milk for free?"

Nancy Donahue nodded. "Honestly, I don't think he meant any harm and I kind of enjoyed the attention. Always nice to be noticed, isn't it?"

"Depends on who's doing the noticing," Mickey said. "But usually, yes. It is nice."

"*You* get noticed. A lot. You can't tell me you don't know that." Nancy wagged a finger at her.

"By who? The old lech's on the benches? That hardly counts as being noticed."

"Well," Nancy continued, "When we got home from the beach, Eileen ran straight into the kitchen. I walk in and all the dishes are on the table and she's got the drying thing in her hand, turning it this way and that. She looks at me and says 'I don't see what's so great about it.'"

"I'm not following."

"Couple of the LG's were talking, I guess, close enough for Eileen to overhear. One commented that you had a great rack."

Mickey rolled her eyes. "You gotta be – did you? You didn't."

"No, of course I didn't tell her. I wanted *you* to know - ya still got it."

"I may have to start wearing housecoats," Mickey said. "Anyway, I am so happy about Michael. God, I was so worried."

"Do you still have that old record player?" Nancy asked her. "I'd start there. Nothing like classical music, even it is from the nineteen-sixties."

Mickey nodded. "I'll have to dig it out. Along with the stack of 45s that go with it. Hey, do you want to go out to supper with us tonight. I'll see if Bunny can go – I was thinking McLean's over in Beach Haven Crest. A steak dinner is like five bucks. My treat."

Nancy appeared to think about. "Sure. I don't have any other engagements in my future that I know of," she said and winked at Mickey. "Meet you there or meet you here?"

"How about here," Mickey said. "We can all fit in the Brookwood, as long as you don't mind being seen in it out in public."

"The Green Dragon? I love that beast. I'll even drive so you can have a drink."

"I have to meet someone in a little while," Mickey said. "Police business –but I don't plan on letting that sink the whole night. Let's say we'll meet here around seven. The dinner crowd will have thinned out by then. Think Michael will make it?"

"Yeah," Nancy said. "He's a trooper. Just like his mom. Who cares if he falls asleep on the way home? It's part of the experience."

Mickey checked her watch.

"Tell Bunny what we're doing and tell her to call Charlie and Barbara. See if they want to meet us there."

"Will do. I love it when a plan comes together," Nancy said.

"What? What about a plan?"

"It's from *The A-Team*. You know, the show? Man, Bunny was right. You really do need to watch more TV."

TWENTY-SEVEN

Linwood, NJ

AN FBI OFFICE WAS not exactly the type of place or address a biker could ask the local populace about without getting noticed. And remembered.

Owen Pettigrew could smell the salt in the air wafting over from nearby Lakes Bay. The seemingly contradictory name, he'd learned on one of his multiple recon sojourns, came from Arthur Lake, who'd invented the submarine in 1884. Its shoreline had once been the site of the Ventnor Boat Works, builders of the first boat to reach sixty miles per hour over the water.

He finally deduced that the non-descript building sitting on the south side of Shore Road had to be what he was looking for. It appeared to be designed to hold multiple small businesses or offices. He half-expected to see signs for a nail salon, an attorney or a chiropractor, but the six spaces on the directory on the tidy front lawn were all empty. There were a few cars in its lot, which was on both sides of the building and, he assumed, extended behind it. But their engines were all cold.

Knocks at the six glass doors on both stories and on the tall, narrow windows failed to elicit a response. There wasn't even a little "Be Back At" clock-hands sign to be seen anywhere. It wasn't a federal holiday as far as he knew, but he hadn't kept track in years. He remembered Washington's Birthday and Lincoln's Birthday had somehow gotten combined and moved around, so they weren't even on their birthdays anymore, but he thought that had happened a few years ago now.

Pettigrew made another pass around the perimeter, looking for a mailbox, a door slot, or anything he could surreptitiously slip the folder hiding in his vest into. The cars in the lot were all locked and their windows were rolled up tight. He'd even tested the trunks. He thought about leaving it under one of the hoods, but realized that left too much to chance.

He felt bad about his old lady. Rhonda had always been good to him and she hadn't done anything to deserve what he was sure she'd gotten, or quite possibly, was still getting. Walker White was a ruthless bastard. Pettigrew wondered how far he'd go.

As he was about to ride south for some grub – Somers Point wasn't very far away – he saw a car slow down. It pulled deliberately into the parking lot. Pettigrew thought it was a Plymouth Fury, probably new or at least a late model. It had cop tires and cop mirrors, so he figured it was a good bet that it was a Bureau ride.

Two men in dress shirts and ties emerged, both with sport coats slung over their arms. One lugged a briefcase. They approached the building, did something complicated with the door that he couldn't see, and went inside.

His hope now was that they'd left the Fury unlocked. There was no hurry for them to see what he was giving them. He didn't want to leave it on the dash or the front seat. The file was in a plastic case and he'd wiped it for prints before sliding it in. It should slide right out. The one thing he was not going to do was hand-deliver it.

Owen Pettigrew rested in the cool suburban shade and watched for another twenty minutes, to make sure they didn't come right back out. Then he approached from the side where he knew there was only a transom window high up on the wall. Probably a bathroom, he guessed. He approached the Fury calmly and slowly. When he reached the passenger side he ducked down into a low crouch.

The lock button on the rear door was sticking up.

He opened it as slowly as he could, checking in all directions around him and listening for the sounds of doors, engines or footsteps.

In his vest he found the slit in the lining and eased the folder out.

On the back of the passenger seat, low down, there was an elastic netting kind of thing. Pettigrew slid the open end of the plastic sleeve down into it all the way. Then he tapped it, and slowly withdrew it, shaking it gently so that the folder dropped into the netting totally untouched by his hands. He closed the door and leaned his shoulder heavily into it until he heard the latch click.

Another look around revealed a clear coast. Pettigrew stayed in his crouch until he reached the Plymouth's grill. He heard a car approaching on the two-lane and pretended to tie his bootlace until it passed. Then he straightened up and walked unhurriedly back to his Harley.

Before he kickstarted the bike into life, he contemplated, once again, which direction to go. He knew he was only about ten miles from Atlantic City. He hadn't seen the Boardwalk since he was a kid, when his dad had taken them both on the Diving Bell. He pointed the front forks north and sped away.

Pettigrew didn't know if the new casino had actually opened its doors yet or not. But what the hell. All the money he possessed was in a fat roll in his pocket, and he'd already taken the biggest gamble of his life. He could get a nice hotel room, take a shower, shave off what Rhonda called his ZZ Top beard, and cut his own hair. Find something with long sleeves from a Boardwalk vendor or a gift shop that would hide his tattoos. With any luck, he'd only be a schnook in a loud Hawaiian shirt.

He thought about what was in the folder. He was doing a good thing, the right thing, for the first time in a long time.

Maybe that meant his luck was about to change.

Surf City

Mark Nepp was finishing up when Mickey rolled into the office.

"I need to pay you," Mickey said. "You've been here all day."

"Nonsense," Nepp answered. "I like it here a lot better than in my garage. Plus, you have got to see this." He pushed a button on the front of the little television. Mickey heard a soft hiss. She could see her phone was sitting in the cradle thing. The screen glowed with green letters and numbers. Nepp typed a few things and the *Irish Times* front page reappeared.

"I won the Irish Sweepstakes, didn't I?" Mickey said.

"I didn't see that. But watch this."

He tapped a button with an arrow. It looked to Mickey like a right-turn signal. The image on the screen changed.

"Abracadabra, Presto Change-O, and we have Page Two. With pictures, I might add. Here, sit."

Nepp brought over her chair. Mickey seated herself.

"Press the right arrow to go to the next page. Press the left to go back. If you can't see the whole page, press the Up or Down arrow and it will move the image for you in that direction."

Mickey tried a few tentative taps.

"Don't worry," Nepp said. "You can't break it. I'm going to use your johnny, if that's all right. Get myself cleaned up, and then I'll be out of your hair. I have to say, this is working even better than I imagined."

Mickey experimented with the keys. On page six she found pictures of recent graduates. She loved reading the names – Joanna, Eithne, Gerry, Ethnea and Ciaran. How her mother would have loved this.

There was a story about the Bray Bridge Congress and note about the Dublin Chess Club's one-day allegro-style tournament. Pushing on to page seven, she was amused to see a story about an organization named the Gingerbread Group calling on the government to introduce "a suitable form of divorce."

Down in the corner a headline caught her eye:

2 Year remembrance held for slain Garda

Mickey started to read the story when she heard the office door open.

"Detective? It's DellaDonna. You in here? Detective?"

Mickey looked up from the screen.

"Yeah," she said. "Right here. Come on back."

Margherita walked toward her. Mark Nepp intercepted her.

"Is that the uh, sound system?" DellaDonna asked.

"It's a, a test version, let's say," Nepp replied.

Mickey noticed that he had positioned himself between the young officer and the equipment. Mickey understood immediately. She got up and met DellaDonna and gently walked them toward the entrance.

"Your phone off the hook or something, Detective?" DellaDonna asked.

Mickey thought of her receiver and where it was.

"Why – you been trying to call me, Officer?"

"Not me, ma'am, but some guy is. He says you're supposed to meet him tonight. Connor or Conroy something. Would not leave a last name. Said you'd know what it was about."

"Connor," Mickey said. "Connor Kilderry. He's a, he's an associate of the two FBI agents you met last night."

"Wow," DellaDonna said. "FBI agents, an almost-unidentified associate, clandestine meetings. Sounds like real 007 stuff. I hope that's not out of line, Detective Cleary, ma'am"

"DellaDonna," Mickey said with a smile, "You shoot straight from the hip, don't you?"

"Quicker that way, ma'am," DellaDonna replied.

For a moment, Mickey did get the sense that she was looking at a younger version of herself.

"Strong accent," DellaDonna said next. "Irish, I'm pretty sure. Bit of a bullshitter, if I may speak freely."

"That basically describes every Irishman ever born," Mickey told her. "Did he leave a message?"

"He did, Detective. Said he was driving up from Atlantic City and he'd meet you in the bar of the Hotel Surf City. Hopes you can go over his information at dinner." DellaDonna paused. "He did not say if he was paying. I did ask, in case he mentions it."

Mickey had to laugh. 'Excellent work, Officer DellaDonna. Thank you. Did he say what time?"

"Yes, ma-am, he did. He said six o'clock."

Mickey looked up at the cuckoo clock.

"Well, dinner is going to be a no. I'm taking the kids and the babysitters out to McLean's. I said I'd be back at the house by seven. We're taking the Brookwood. That should prove interesting."

"Permission to speak freely, Detective, but you do have great taste in cars. I looked up every patrol car you drove during your time in Surf City. I believe the Chevelle is still the best."

"Thank you, Officer," Mickey replied.

"Although, local legend says the Brookwood has a rather interesting history as well."

"Officer DellaDonna," Mickey said. "Is there anything you don't know about me?"

"I don't know your favorite song or your favorite color, ma'am," DellaDonna answered. "Outside of that, I think I'm pretty well-versed on your particulars. I've been studying you and your career since you spoke to my high school class at Our Lady of the Angels Academy. Mr. Lipinski raved about you. I had no idea he'd ever been a law enforcement officer. That must have been, if you'll excuse the expression, a real trip."

"That it was, Officer," Mickey said. "That it most certainly was. Danny saved - well I'm sure you already know." Mickey patted her hands together. "All right, looks like I'm going to the Hotel Surf City. If Hyman Levine is there tonight, I might have my one drink on the house."

"Enjoy your evening, Detective Cleary," DellaDonna said. "And did one of your FBI colleagues, Stosh, did he by chance give you a five-dollar bill to give to me?"

"Not that I remember," Mickey said. "Should I remind him when I see him next?"

"If you don't mind, ma'am. A bet's a bet."

Mark Nepp cleared his throat. Mickey almost forgot he was there.

"Oh," Mickey said. "Officer DellaDonna, this is Mister, this is Doctor Mark Nepp. The professor kind, not the stethoscope kind. He's been installing my new sound system."

Mickey saw DellaDonna trying mightily to force back a smile.

"I'm sure he is ma'am. Nice to meet you, Doctor Nepp. Try to keep the volume down to a roar, would you? And, please, no Barry Manilow."

Nepp laughed. "I promise, Officer," he said. "We'll only play Mantovani or Percy Faith."

"Detective Cleary," DellaDonna said, "If there's anything I can do to assist you, I'd be happy to pitch in. I love a big case."

"Who said I have a big case?" Mickey asked.

"No one, ma'am," DellaDonna said. "No one at all. Well, better hurry. You'll be late for-"

The clock chimed. The cuckoo popped out of its door and gave its odd three-note chirp.

DellaDonna looked at Mickey. "Did that bird just say-"

"We think so," Mickey and Nepp said almost in unison.

"Man," DellaDonna said. "Some German clockmaker must've had a sick sense of humor. Good night on that note."

When DellaDonna left, Mickey turned to Nepp. "She's a pistol, ain't she, Doctor Nepp?"

Nepp nodded emphatically. "I'm going to place this painter's cloth I found in the closet on top of all this, if you don't mind," he said. "Industrial espionage is a real thing."

Mickey helped him drape it over the table and turned out the lights.

When they were outside Nepp remarked, "I like your car. Very sporty. I'm not a car person, myself."

"What do you drive?" Mickey asked.

"1977 Ford Pinto Country Squire." He put his hand up. "Don't say it. I know. But my equipment fits in it very comfortably."

“I’m sure it does,” Mickey said, completely at a loss for words mentally picturing perhaps the worst car design in recent memory and possibly in all of recorded automotive history.

“Oh,” said Nepp, pausing his steps. “I forgot to put your phone back. It’s still connected to the network. Do you want me to-”

“Nah,” Mickey said with a dismissive wave. “Nobody’s calling me there tonight.”

TWENTY-EIGHT

FBI Resident Agency
Linwood, NJ

WALTER STENKEWIECZ EMERGED FROM the bathroom still rubbing his eyes.

He stood at his desk for several minutes before sitting down, staring blankly at the papers on his desk as if he were looking through them and not at them. The photos Evan Driscoll had brought back from the ACPD had been devastating.

There were twelve agents assigned to the Atlantic County R.A., four very recently added to coincide with the arrival of casino gambling.

Evan Driscoll's presence made that number thirteen.

No one spoke for a long time. Driscoll made the rounds of the two person cubicles, checking on their somber occupants. He had called a meeting for six-fifteen.

When that time arrived, the twelve Field Agents shuffled their way to the spacious conference room. Making sure they all had Cokes, coffees or tumblers of water, Driscoll called the meeting to order.

"This is a day we all dread. I've spoken with Director Durkin and read him in. As you would expect, he has pledged all the resources the Bureau can muster to find and bring to justice the perpetrators."

Driscoll paused to take some water from his cup.

"I did not know Agent Brascone or Agent Tierney personally. But their files and their actions speak to what our own careers are all about. Their deaths, while tragic, give us more than purpose. They give us meaning. I will not disrespect their memories by reciting platitudes. They accepted the most dangerous work we do because they believed the risks they took made the world better. Made the world safer."

He wavered for a moment, took a long drink, and then put his hands on the polished tabletop.

"I have requested additional manpower, weaponry and ordnance, and that will be arriving later tonight. If necessary, we will utilize the assistance of our military partners at McGuire Air Force Base and Fort Dix for air and ground support. If needed, our colleagues at ATF have volunteered their tactical resources and their assault team as well. Director Durkin will be monitoring our movements from the secure Situation Room in Quantico. Agent Stenkewiecz will take lead. I'll yield the floor to him after a moment of silence for our fallen comrades, Agent Joseph Donald Brascone and Agent Johanna Colleen Tierney."

Everyone in the room either lowered their heads or stared off into space.

"Stosh?" Driscoll finally said, breaking the stillness.

Stenkewiecz stood and addressed the group. Chair rollers scuffed on the linoleum tiles as the Field Agents physically and mentally readjusted their focus.

"First, a couple of ground rules, if you will," Stenkewiecz preambled. "As far as the ACPD is concerned, the bodies at the Steel Pier have not been officially identified yet. John and Jane Does for at least another twenty-four. Captain Rodriguez, our contact with ACPD, is extremely sharp. In your notes you'll see he often provided local security for Senator Biden of Delaware, so he's already been fully vetted. Neither of our agents has a traceable paper trail, although Rodriguez somehow came up with one of Agent Brascone's previous UC aliases. But that's all he has. Beyond that it's a complete blank. Agent Tierney's record is also *tabula rasa*, a totally blank slate."

Stenkewiecz brushed back his thinning hair.

"We needed Captain Rodriguez to obtain access to the photos and reports you each have in your laps. As I said, he's very sharp. We explained the Bureau's interest by telling him we were looking for a C.I. who might be on the run. We assured him that neither of the DB's were the C.I. we were looking for. I'm guessing we'll have twenty-four hours at best until he starts to put at least some of the pieces together. We have two other assets working with us. I'll let Deputy Director Driscoll fill you in on them."

Driscoll stood again. He felt more composed now and it showed in both his voice and his body language.

"Obviously, our best working hypothesis is that our agents' covers were blown and that they were murdered by the Sons of Silence, although the M.O.D. and the disposal of the corpses remain a little puzzling. You're all familiar with the Federal RICO statutes. I'll remind you that while New Jersey has its own RICO statutes drafted, they are, as of today, still pending before the legislature. The Sons of Satan have official status as a criminal organization, so we still have a lot of leeway. Terminations with extreme prejudice are not out of the question. This is not for quotation, but I am not foreseeing a day in court for any these scumbags."

There was a general murmuring and a short but enthusiastic round of applause.

Driscoll walked to a map of Southern New Jersey that had been hastily pinned to the cork perimeter of a blackboard.

"Intel, which we believe to be highly reliable, places the HQ of the Sons of Satan MC – I'll refer to them simply as the Sons for brevity from now on – deep in the Bass River Forest in the Pine Barrens." He pointed to an area on the map. "We have a chopper on standby to do recon awaiting our signal. Obviously, we don't want to spook them too early, as they could rapidly disappear into the woods – terrain which they know and navigate far better than we do."

"What about the State Police? This is kind of their backyard," an agent at the far end of the table asked.

Driscoll cleared his throat. "For the moment, and only for the moment, we feel that involving the NJSP might represent, shall we say, too much of a good thing. They are an elite police organization, to be sure. As good as any you'll find. And they know that. This decision comes from the very top, so rest assured it's been strongly considered and thoroughly vetted. The concern is that there might be an element of competition at play and, given the aggressive tendencies we all possess, things could, um, accelerate past the point of command and control. The DOJ would like to avoid that scenario if at all possible."

"You said something about other assets," another of the Field Agents called out.

Driscoll wiped his mouth and continued.

"We have two," he said. "One is an LEO with a long tenure and deep familiarity with both the local agencies and the major players in the area. The other is a recently arrived LEO from Ireland, here on special assignment and attached to the Bureau. He has intimate knowledge of the suspected purchasers and their methods, as well as their communication strategies. For safety's sake, I will shield the name of our local LEO for the time being. This resource has had prior dealings with the Sons and may be invaluable in assisting us."

"No offense, Deputy Director," an agent piped up. "But the asset you mention has to be Mickey Cleary. Most of us have been here for more than five years. Some of us more than ten. What's the harm in saying that's who it is?"

"Thank you, Agent Callan. But for the moment, I can neither confirm nor deny the accuracy of your supposition. I stress - for the moment."

"OK, then who's the Irish guy?" Callan asked.

"His name is Connor Kilderry. At home, he's an Inspector, which is like a detective, with the *Garda Siochana*, Ireland's National Police Force. His picture and vitals are also in your folders."

There was a rustling of papers.

"Shit. He looks exactly like Han Solo," Callan blurted out. "He shouldn't be too hard to ID."

"Thank you for sharing your astute powers of observation and facial recognition, Agent Callan," Driscoll said, not unkindly.

A low ripple of laughter ran around the table.

"I am presently waiting for him to report back. He was due to meet with our other asset at about," Driscoll looked at the wall clock, "actually right about now. Gentlemen, it promises to be a long and eventful night ahead. Before we kick the tires and light the fires, let's make double sure we're ready to roll on short notice. Stosh – Agent Stenkewiecz – will open the Tactical Locker. Please remember to sign out everything you take, but be sure to take everything that you need. Better one magazine too many than one magazine short."

Chairs began to shuffle and the assembled agents stood up, talking in subdued voices to one another. Driscoll heard one agent near him end his statement with "Nuke them back into the Stone Age."

The volume of the hubbub in the room prodded Driscoll to speak louder to garner everyone's attention again.

"Agent Brascone did relate that the Sons had an impressive arsenal, although as a Prospective Member, he did not have direct access to it and so could not deliver an accurate inventory. We must assume they possess military-grade weapons, most likely ones diverted from our own armed forces. Make no mistake, though, we will fight firepower with firepower. Now, I'm not one for ooh-rah's or motivational speeches, but I would ask you to join me in one simple salute."

Driscoll stood at attention. The group fell silent.

"Tierney and Brascone," Driscoll said. "Fidelity, Bravery, Integrity."

Driscoll nodded his head.

"Tierney and Brascone," the solemn group repeated. "Fidelity, Bravery, Integrity."

"OK, gentlemen," Stenkewiecz said loudly. He held up a ring of keys.

"It is time to lock and load."

TWENTY-NINE

Lobby Bar
Hotel Surf City

HE'D BEEN SURPRISED TO learn from the barman that they did indeed have Guinness Stout as one of their selections. They even had a pint glass to serve it in.

The rather lovely Detective Cleary remarked that it looked like a beer milkshake.

Ronan Graham's function in H-Block had been to interrogate any and all new prisoners, political or otherwise, immediately after intake. The Prots and the RUC, he knew, were sending in a steady stream of imposters in a weak attempt to infiltrate their ranks. They were a sorry lot, with easily refutable stories, some of them ludicrous in nature. There were simply too many to kill them all, so they'd come up with a fairly workable strategy to thin their numbers right out of the gate.

After they had been deloused, Graham would see that they were immediately - and painfully - tattooed. He specified that "OUR DAY WILL COME" be inked at the same spot on each of their left shoulder blades, the blacker the better. It was no "Red Badge of Courage," but the idea was to mark the proddy *tout* forever, presumably removing him from further infiltration attempts at other prisons. It also made them tempting targets for any street sniper who happened to get a gander at it.

On the third day, the buggering would begin. Usually, the *tout* would be rather promptly removed with a grand dramatic show by the screws, to undergo "questioning," never to be seen again The lads were not particularly fond of doing their parts, but war was always a dirty business.

The detective had ordered a Miller High Life, to his eye, a rather pale excuse for a gargle. Their tab had been made nil by the hotel's owner, a sheeny who said he was an old friend of Mickey Cleary.

She'd made it clear she'd not be sharing his company long, so in the guise of exchanging information and theories, he'd probed her knowledge of the present complications. It was not unlike his knack for questioning a new prisoner. Often, a bit of hooch would loosen a tongue, but she sipped her beer slowly and kept an eye on her watch.

What interested him most was her rather intimate knowledge of the bikies. That had worried him most until she'd made the chance remark that one of his inside men had been a superior officer of hers when she was what she called a state trooper.

This, he knew immediately, was going to be a problem.

A problem, he now figured, that presented him only one solution.

FBI Resident Agency
2000 Shore Road, Linwood, NJ

Evan Driscoll sat in the now-deserted office. The pot of coffee he'd brewed twenty minutes earlier for only himself was half-empty. He hadn't had a cigarette in twenty-three years. He thought if there were one within arm's reach, that streak would most certainly come to an end.

Six phone calls to Mickey Cleary's office had been met with six busy signals. She should be meeting with Kilderry, not talking on her phone. He also hadn't heard from Kilderry, which bothered him. The light outside was fading. The Fury didn't have flashers or a siren. Even at breakneck speed, the drive to Surf City would take forty-five minutes.

He grabbed a phone book off Stenkewiecz's desk and rifled the pages until he found the listing for the Surf City PD. They were landing people on the moon, he thought. Why couldn't they make a phone that stored numbers?

He dialed, drumming his fingers while it rang.

"Surf City Police Department," an unfamiliar voice said. It had the sultry husk of a mature woman.

"Agent Evan Driscoll calling. I'm trying to get in touch with Detective Mickey Cleary. Is she there, by chance?"

"This is Arlene Shields at Central Dispatch. I can connect you to her-"

"I've tried her office multiple times," Driscoll interrupted. "All I get is a busy signal. Could you connect me with the Surf City Police Department instead? I believe it may be a matter of some urgency, Miss Shields."

"It's Mrs. Shields, and I'll patch you through to SCPD directly. Hold on."

Driscoll chuckled at the patch-through term. Even real cops were talking like television cops, he thought.

The line clicked several times and then picked up.

"SCPD, DellaDonna," a female voice said curtly.

"Officer DellaDonna," Driscoll said. "This is Evan Driscoll. I wonder if-"

"Yeah, listen, Agent Driscoll, FBI or no FBI, you need to get a new card. I called the number on it ten times, and all I got was a prompt to leave a message. Have you heard from Detective Cleary?"

"No, that's what I was calling you-"

"Well, something's not right here, Agent Driscoll. Her babysitters called here looking for her as well. She was supposed to be home at seven. They were all going out to dinner in Beach Haven Crest. Even had a reservation at McLean's. They haven't heard a freakin' peep from her since she walked out the door. Something's going down. Don't tell me it's not."

"I assure you, Officer DellaDonna, that –"

"And I assure you, Agent Driscoll, something is not right. I was with her at six o'clock, standing in her office. She was leaving to meet this Conway or Conroy buddy of yours at the Hotel Surf City for one drink. That was it. Now she's

MIA. I've got officers on their way to the hotel now and scooping the loop in Surf City. Where are you?"

"I'm at our Resident Agency in Linwood. I was waiting for her call as well."

"Well," DellaDonna said, "I would strongly suggest, Agent Driscoll, that you fire up that Fury and put pedal to the metal and get here as fast as you can."

"Have you checked her office? Her phone has been busy."

"She's not in there. There's a weird little light coming from her office, but it's locked up tight. And her car is not in her spot, either. Whatever this mess is, I'm pretty sure you guys got her into it."

"I'll – "

"I'm hanging up now, Agent Driscoll," DellaDonna said. "Pedal to the metal, sir. Pedal to the metal."

Driscoll remembered the Fury's broadcast function didn't work. He went to the radio room and used the base station to contact Stenkewiecz.

"Stosh," he said when Stenkewiecz clicked on. "What's the sit-rep? Over."

"Mobilizing, Deputy Director," Stenkewiecz answered. "Gotta hand it to the Bureau, sir. Some heavy-duty help on hand here. Dix trailered over a bulldozer and an APC. It's like frickin' D-Day, sir. Over."

"Stosh," Driscoll replied. "I'm not worried about the dirtballs. We know there are women in their compound who are anything but captives. But do we know for certain if there are any children? Over."

There was a burst of static. Driscoll adjusted the Squelch level.

"There are no reports of any children on or near the site. Repeat, no children on or near the site. The APC came with a flamethrower. Sir, are we authorized to use that if needed? Over."

The image of a snowball rolling down a hill at ever-increasing speed appeared in Driscoll's mind.

"Negative. I repeat. Negative on the flame-thrower. Only we can prevent forest fires, Stosh. Over."

"Copy that, Deputy Director. No firestick. Over."

"I'm on my way to Surf City, Stosh," Driscoll said into the microphone. "Hold position and hold fire. Repeat. Hold position and hold fire until ordered to advance. Copy? Over."

"Copy that," Stenkewiecz answered. "Holding position and holding fire and awaiting further orders. Understood. Copy five-by-five. Over."

"Roger that," Driscoll said. "Over and out."

The room was cool, but Evan Driscoll noticed he was sweating. He grabbed an old ESSO gas station map from one of the agents' IN boxes and hustled for the door.

He just prayed none of the bikers decided to fire the first shot.

Hotel Surf City

Four Surf City police cars sat idling at various angles outside the Hotel's elegant portico. Their asynchronously flashing light bars made for a carnival atmosphere as the red, blue, and white beams strobed and caromed in all directions, dancing on and bouncing off every reflective surface.

Margherita DellaDonna sat in her cruiser, door open and radio in hand.

"Roger, Chief," she said. "What's your 20?"

Charlie Higgins and his wife were on their way back from Toms River, the Seat of Government for Ocean County, after putting the final touches on Bunny's adoption paperwork. She had interrupted his quiet dinner with his wife at the Old Time Tavern. His instructions had been crystal clear.

DellaDonna got out and gathered the other officers around her.

"Chief Higgins is on his way. He's driving his personal car, so no Code 4, but he says he's not stopping for anything. Here's what he wants. I'm to meet FBI Agent Driscoll and search Detective Cleary's Office for anything that might indicate a second destination. Jenetta, you searched the Mustang thoroughly. Nothing, I assume?"

Chris Jenetta shook his head. "No keys, no purse, no badge, no creds. Holster and sidearm were in the glovebox. I secured those."

"She wouldn't leave her weapon in an unlocked glove compartment," DellaDonna said.

"Um, I may have, um, tapped on it once or twice and, you know, and it just popped open," Jenetta replied sheepishly.

"I can see how that could happen," DellaDonna said without blinking. "OK. McNally. Shoot."

"Garbs and I did a grid search starting at opposite ends of the municipal line. Nothing."

"You checked her house?"

"They're worried, but they're OK," Sammy Garbarino said. "I told them to all stay put and call us immediately if they heard a word from her. From Detective Cleary."

"OK. All the other PDs have the BOLO out. Ditto for the OC Sheriff's office. Chief Higgins' ETA is thirty minutes or less. Let's try to have something for him when he gets here. Let's saddle up, gentlemen."

In less than a minute, three patrol cars screeched off in three directions. DellaDonna walked up to the hotel's brightly lit entrance and into its beautifully appointed lobby. Even the pedestal ashtrays looked like little works of art. Her presence was not unnoticed by the well-dressed patrons.

Hyman Levine walked over.

"So, Officer, you've certainly given my guests something to talk about."

"I'm sorry, Mr. Levine," said DellaDonna. "I hope this won't be bad for business."

"Bad?" Levine laughed. "On the contrary, young lady. You've given the place an air of mystery—a Raymond Chandler feeling. Let the guests think what they want. I'll be discreet, but, eh, I might make it seem like they're in a scene from a Hollywood movie. Who knows? Maybe Tony Rome will walk through those doors next. It could happen."

DellaDonna understood Mickey Cleary's tight bond with him.

"You're sure they left together?" she asked.

"What I know," Levine said, "What I saw, is that they walked though those doors at the same time. The same time, but not exactly together. Walked like they were headed different places, if such a thing can be gleaned from gestures and postures. I comped their tab, which was only one Guinness Stout and one Miller High Life. Maybe they noshed some bar snacks, but that was it."

Hyman Levine looked at DellaDonna intently.

"I would know this man, the one she sat with, I would know him again in a heartbeat if I saw him. I've seen men like him before. Met men like him before. From all my years in Miami Beach. Something about him. Something hard. Something secret. I watched Mickey's face. She saw it, too. I know she did. You find her first. Then you find the man. Bring him here. All my years in Miami – all the friends I made. All the friends I still have. I promise I can solve your problem faster than you can."

DellaDonna had no doubt he could. But she knew he was right.

First, she had to find Mickey Cleary.

THIRTY

The Pine Barrens

WALKER WHITE RAN THE scenario in his head again.

A prospect and his Property were gone. His Sergeant-at-Arms, whose personal responsibility the Prospect had been, had ridden out and not returned. Problems, to be sure, but not insurmountable problems.

He'd sent the remaining crop of Prospects out to complete the mission, promising them an accelerated path to patching in if they performed well. The Members and their old ladies were restricted to the compound until the Prospects returned. Most of the Prospects had never set foot off dry land, but the prize of the patch dispelled any trepidation they might have had.

They had the bodies of brutes, the morals of reptiles, and possessed the brainpower of lower primates, he calculated. No sense, no feeling, a summer job boss had once advised him after posting him to the back of a garbage truck.

If they happened to get caught with the cache of weapons on their way, the MC could and would simply disavow them as hangers-on and wannabe badasses masquerading as Sons of Satan.

He marveled at the simplicity of the whole thing. How the MC was strictly a middleman, barely connected on either end. The missing RPGs, well, the Staff Sergeant, would have some 'splainin' to do there if anyone checked. The money was the real kick. One hundred large in exactly ten sheets of bona fide Bearer Bonds. No checks, no marks, no exploding dye canisters, no bulky suitcases stuffed with bills like in the movies. And no one to complain. The money wasn't even going to be stolen, Scooch had explained.

The purchaser had taken care of the monetary transaction details. The supplier, or their registered agent as it were, was paid off with a double-cut bag from the MC's house supply of low-grade cocaine. The legal tender certificates would be locked in a safe only he knew the combination to. One he had recently changed.

The rocket launchers would be off American soil for good within the hour. Two dark offshore rendezvous' later and they would disappear forever, although he fully expected to see the fruits of the transaction on *The ABC Evening News* in a report from Belfast.

Walker White was an avid follower of international politics. He found it irresistibly ironic that a raging civil war had been reduced to an innocuous non-sequitur. He couldn't help but think of the prescient lyrics of an old song. They had their Troubles. He certainly had his own, but their Troubles were nothing but opportunities for him.

He had no visions of ever making an honest living, but weapons to overseas buyers seemed like the perfect business model. It would free him from the constant fighting with the street dealers and the tiresome negotiations with the ever more demanding and, recently, more threatening South Americans. If they wanted his drug operation, they could have it. One big buyout and it would be done.

He looked around at the ramshackle clubhouse. He sniffed its ever-lingering potpourri of sweat, vomit, stale beer and urine. They lived like animals and for most of them, that was fitting. They behaved like animals on most days. On its present line, he figured, the MC's days as a viable business entity were numbered. But as society evolved, so did the crimes against it. He wanted the MC to follow that curve.

They could maintain their image, their swagger and their talent for intimidation. Maybe still do a hit every now and then, strictly for looks. But beneath that, he intended to install a new infrastructure that would do everything but print money. And he hadn't completely ruled out that possibility.

Where do you see yourself in ten years?

A college recruiter from Swarthmore once asked him that question, sitting in a plush admissions office chair. His answer would not have been the spot he now occupied. But his business plan also included a personal plan. He'd closely studied the Las Vegas casino models and had perfected his own version of The Skim. He had personal accounts under various aliases in nine different banks in three different states. He had the various identity papers he might use when the time came in a safety deposit box at Jersey Shore State Bank, along with a list of countries that did not have extradition treaties with the U.S. Government.

There was money in the safe. There was also a poorly disguised false floor, so that if he disappeared into the wind, they would think they'd found his secret stash when they eventually drilled the lock.

But there was no hurry. They were tucked away in the center of a trackless and, for most people, forbidding wasteland. They had enough firepower to defend a fortress. His favorite part in old movies was when some villain uttered the line "You'll never take me alive!" It wasn't his plan, but if it did ever come to that, he was prepared to go down in flames. Even as a child, Walker White was always the hero of his own stories.

During one of his early stabs at drug rehab, a counselor had described him as possessing "an almost messianic complex." It wasn't far from true, he later thought. He was surrounded by men who could snap him in half or beat his brains out with their bare hands. And yet they didn't. They listened to his ideas as if he were preaching a sermon. He kept them flush in money and drugs, he never touched their women, and for this they paid him back with unquestioning loyalty.

One day, they'd wake up or they'd turn around and wonder where he went. Because one day he would do what his parents had unknowingly destined him to do.

He would walk.

Barnegat Bay

Jack Rigger had seen nothing but good luck since the day he arrived in Atlantic City.

Twice the money the State of New Jersey had ever paid him. More free trim than the visiting celebrities were getting. And side gigs that, given enough time, would make him a rich, rich man well before he turned sixty.

The *Southern Cross* was moored at a slip in Brant Beach. He'd signed for the spot using Darwin Schassau's name and a duplicate of his casino ID.

Barnegat Bay was dotted with one-hundred-and-twenty-nine separate islands, many of them unmarked, some submerged, and most of them invisible in the dark. The *Southern Cross* was perfect for the job. At twenty-four feet, its closed bow was easy to see over when underway. It was a Black Jack Sea Skiff, built by the Hubert S. Johnson Boat Manufacturer company in Bay Head, New Jersey, just south of Manasquan. The boat under Rigger's feet had been constructed in 1960, twelve years after Hubert Johnson's untimely death. His company would survive another eight years. The Sea Skiffs were popular, if fairly utilitarian boats. The *Southern Cross's* amenities, such as they were, included a rudimentary cabin in the bow, a long bench seat attached along the transom, and a rectangular padded seat centered amidships, which doubled as a cover for access to the bilge and the engine compartment. A 270 horsepower diesel provided the power. The helm resembled a student's writing desk. There were four rudimentary gauges and a single throttle on the starboard side.

Rigger found it surprisingly nimble, although it was debatable how it would fare in a more than mild chop. The offshore forecast called for light winds and smooth to moderate seas of two to three feet.

He'd left the Bombay early under the pretext of a dental appointment in Absecon. The drive to Brant Beach had found a window in the usually snarled traffic, and he'd made the trip in slightly less than forty-five minutes. He checked the tide table and shoved off as the sun was arcing downward.

His route took him inside the southern half of Long Beach Island and he'd negotiated several clusters of grassy islands until he cleared the southern terminus at Holgate Beach. He'd turned inland at the site of the old Tucker's Island Lighthouse, past the abandoned Fish Factory known for generations as the Stink House, and then motored across Great Bay until he reached the mouth of the Mullica River. The Mullica was a serpentine waterway, and he followed it as far as the boat's shallow draft would allow.

And then he waited.

When he heard the distant rumble of a truck, he flipped on the navigation lights and tooted the air horn.

Twenty minutes later, four scraggly bikers came tromping up, swearing and swatting at mosquitoes and no-see-ums as they lugged a heavy olive-drab box with white stenciled lettering.

Rigger maneuvered as close to the bank as he could. He ordered two of the bikers onboard. The other two stood knee-deep in the brackish water. They hoisted the heavy box onboard. The added weight increased the boat's draft to the point that the keel was resting in the muck.

Rigger had the bikers, he noticed all four of their jackets said Prospect, center the box and then hop out. He slowly backed the engine and had them push him and the *Southern Cross* into deeper water. Only when they were chest-deep did he let them back on board, hauling them one by one up and over the transom. Because he was an avowed prick, he told them there were gators lurking nearby just so he could watch them scramble.

Rigger ran the *Southern Cross*'s engine astern until the Mullica widened enough for him to turn around. Once he was pointed toward Great Bay, he had the sodden Prospects sit with their backs against the gunwales, two to port and two to starboard. Even with the weight of the weapons, the boat felt sure and centered.

One of the Prospects asked where the life jackets were.

That made Rigger laugh.

If something had to go overboard, he figured, it wouldn't be the weapons.

Surf City

Margherita DellaDonna was waiting outside when Evan Driscoll pulled up.

"Do you have a key?" he asked her.

"Jesus, of course I don't have a key," she said. "Would I be standing out here like a mook if I had a key?"

"So what do we do?"

"I think the FBI should do the B & E—I'm a beach cop. I don't have the U.S. Attorney General's number in my Rolodex like you do. But I will swear to your story that we had the plausible concern that Detective Cleary might be inside, injured or maybe even unconscious."

"OK," Driscoll said. "Is there anything that we can use to do it?"

"Hey, is that Jimmy Hoffa over there?"

Driscoll turned to look. An instant later, he heard the sound of wood splintering.

When he turned back, the door hung open, and DellaDonna was already halfway inside.

"Well, that's one way to do it," he said.

"That's why there's a B in B & E, Agent." DellaDonna shot back.

They hustled to the back, past the first divider. A sickly green glow suffused the otherwise dark room. DellaDonna reached the credenza by Mickey's desk and whipped off the drop cloth.

"Jesus H. Christ. What the hell is all this?" Driscoll asked.

"A BOSE 901 sound system, if you believe Detective Cleary and her Ph.D. pal who built it." DellaDonna touched the plastic keyboard. The screen on the little television hissed and came to life.

"Is this, like, closed circuit TV or something? Surveillance footage from somewhere, maybe?"

"I don't think so," Driscoll responded.

DellaDonna pulled Mickey's desk chair over and sat down. Driscoll leaned in and over her shoulder.

"Looks like-"

"A newspaper," DellaDonna said. "And it sure as shit isn't the *Philadelphia Daily News*."

Driscoll leaned in farther and reached over her shoulder. He tapped an arrow button, and the image enlarged and shifted downward.

"OK, seriously now," DellaDonna said. "What is this thing?"

"It's a computer," Driscoll said.

"Great. There's my tax dollars at work. I know it's a computer, Mister G-Man. But where is this feed coming from? There's no antenna. Not even Rabbit Ears or a...a UHF thing."

Driscoll peered in. "This is *The Irish Times*, Officer. The biggest circulating newspaper in Ireland. Looks like yesterday's edition. So what was she - "

"This," DellaDonna said, pointing to a corner of the screen. "Do that thing with the key again and see if you can center it."

Driscoll tapped a few more times until the article appeared closer to the middle of the screen.

They both began reading the copy out loud. Driscoll tapped the key again, and a grainy black-and-white photograph jerked slowly into view. A dark-haired man in a police uniform stared directly at them. He had a trim mustache and piercing eyes. A photo credit in one corner read ***Courtesy Garda Siochana/PubAff***.

The caption underneath the picture was small but legible.

"Insp. Connor Kilderry 1949-1976"

"Holy shit," DellaDonna blurted.

"Holy shit," Driscoll repeated. "Holy, holy, holy shit."

"Sorry, Agent Driscoll, but your guy is obviously not your guy. Connor Kilderry was killed by an IRA bomb two years ago. So how the hell did-"

"Holy *shit*," Driscoll said again. He seemed paralyzed by the revelation.

"We gotta find her," DellaDonna said, almost leaping up from the chair.

"Where do we even start?" Driscoll asked.

"Where do we start?" DellaDonna asked incredulously. "Shit, man, how 'bout we start by calling the FBI."

THIRTY-ONE

Atlantic Ocean

1.2 NM SSE of Barnegat Lighthouse

THE *VIRGINIA JEAN* ROCKED gently beneath her.

Rescued by the Coast Guard from beneath the Causeway Bridge, it was returned to its berth in Viking Village, assumedly having simply come unmoored.

Connor Kilderry, or whoever he truly was, was at the helm.

And he appeared to know what he was doing.

"Sure, and it's a grand night for a sail, wouldn't you agree, Detective Cleary?"

He'd tricked her into going with him to the docks to see the boat. He said he wanted her to be able to describe it in detail when the time came to call in the cavalry. He'd even shown her on the chart where the pickup point was supposed to be and complimented her on her nautical knowledge.

Mickey looked at her wrist.

He'd tied one hand behind her back and used a shackle to secure her wrist, looping the brass fitting around the anchor rope, which he'd pulled into the boat from the foredeck.

There wasn't any mistaking what the sequence of events was going to be.

Her error had been getting distracted by his mellifluous language and his tales of her ancestors in the Irish constabulary. He'd jammed her radar, and she felt incredibly stupid.

"I don't understand what possible threat I pose to you," she finally said.

"You're a loose end, love," he replied as he steered them farther into the blackness. "A loose thread is probably more like it. But there's no denyin' that your single thread is woven right close and tight with so many others that one bleedin' tug and –"

He waved his left hand to illustrate unraveling.

"I'm bettin' you were maybe a few hours from figuring the whole thing out, more or less. You must understand, we're talkin' about the fate of a nation here, not some bleedin' bank heist or dirty drug deal. What you're smack in the middle of here is nothing short of real international diplomacy. You Americans might call it gunboat diplomacy, seein' as it involves guns, well actually rocket launchers, and boats. I do love a good seafaring yarn, don't you?"

"And you're a seafarer," Mickey said derisively.

"That I am, dear," he said and checked the chart again.

Mickey heard the engine throttle down.

"The only son of an Irish lighthouse keeper. Could row a twelve-foot dory before I could ride a bike, don't you know. The Irish Lights are wonders of the world, our lovely coast having more boulders than beaches. Moved six times before I turned fifteen. Before the last move me ma' was polishing the glass when a rogue gust of wind caught her skirt and blew her off the promenade. Almost kil't Da as he'd told her to leave it be. They transferred us immediately, of course, this time to The Great Light, just upriver from the Belfast Docks.

"I started workin' the light with Da. Few years go by he remarries, this time to a lovely Protestant woman. Then The Troubles arrive. The Prots, they don't care much for one of their own shacking up with a *taig*. One night, they come to the door, hoods and masks, and drag her out. Next time we see her, she's on the marble steps leadin' up to our flat. Dead as your fecking doornail. Pinned a note to her, they did. Six months later, Da' was dead from grief, and I was in as deep as you could get."

He killed the engine and looked at the sky.

"Give me a tall ship and a star to steer her by. That's John Masefield. A bloody Brit, but we'll overlook that for the moment."

Mickey wanted to keep him talking while she scanned for anything she might use to disable him or the boat. So far, she saw nothing. The anchor sat at her feet. A new Danforth. The flukes were pointed and sharp, but the chances of wielding it like a weapon appeared weak. She did notice that the braided line, the anchor rode Helly called it, was attached directly to the anchor shackle, which fit through the eye of the shank. The rode, she thought, looked brand new. There was no chain.

In Hostage Negotiation School at the academy, they taught recruits to keep the captor talking and to use their own name and his own name. Make it personal as quickly as you can.

"Since it doesn't look like it's going to matter" – she raised her shackled wrist and the rope – "what is your real name? And who is or was Connor Kilderry?"

"Ah, ya do think like a true detective. I respect that. And since the chances of a return trip on your part are rather sketchy, I suppose there's no harm."

He shut off the engine, checked the chart, and perched himself on the wooden captain's chair.

"I was born Ronan Innish Graham. Named after me da' and me great grandda'. Four generations as Keepers of the Light, we were. Could rightly have been five. But it's not. No. I'll not mount a lighthouse staircase again until Ireland's free."

"You seem to know a lot about the Cleary Clan," Mickey said. "Things I didn't know."

"Your FBI, now that's one fine information-gathering organization. Your file is quite thick, actually. But one thing we've learned about America is that your many police forces are like wee toddlers with their toys—they don't like to share."

"Who was Connor Kilderry?" Mickey asked again. "Was he *Garda*?"

"Indeed he was. Indeed he was. And a fine one. He poked at the wrong package is all. One we'd left was a present on the doorstep of a *tout*. Y'ever heard the phrase 'pink mist'?"

His nonchalance infuriated Mickey, but she kept pushing.

"And how did you manage to magically become him?" she asked.

A swell rippled under the boat. Ronan Graham waited until it went on its way.

"A bit of Irish luck and ingenuity," he answered. "The lads set a fire, a right toasty one, in H-Block one evening. That's where they put us political detainees at Long Kesh Prison. Chaos and confusion like you've never seen. We made sure one of the *touts* got, what's your phrase, burned beyond recognition? The lads, they all swore to a man it was me.

"The screws, they were more'n happy to be rid o'me, so they didn't do a whole lot in the way a' checkin'. I only weighed about eighty pounds back then. A starving sow'd turn her snout up at what they fed us in there. So I snuggle myself into a body bag, the lads, they lay a blanket over me, and then they shovel in what was left of the feckin' tout.

"Two skeletons in that bag, there were. But only one was still breathin'. I spent nearly two years shufflin' between safe houses. This opportunity presented itself and, well, document forging has come a long way. And your FBI, they jumped at the chance to make a big splash. So here we are. I must say, they were right accommodating."

He cocked an ear toward shore.

"They'll be approaching us on a line from the south," Ronan Graham said. He paused and scanned the empty sea around them. "Your ma', she ever tell you stories about *Tir na nO'g*?"

She had, but Mickey was not going to give him this one.

"Can't say that she did."

"Magical stories, they are. I used to think I might see it from the top of the lights, just as the sun set." He tapped on the wheel. "Your ma'," he said, "Says in your file she left you and your da' when she was still young. As did mine. Both of them. I hold to the belief that when I see them again, they'll still be as lovely as a Spring day. Maybe you'll have the same luck."

"We make our own luck," Mickey said.

"Indeed we do." He reached under his shirt for something. Mickey heard a ping as something fell to the boat's wooden floorboards. Graham hopped off his captain's perch and began looking around for it. After several minutes, he gave up. "No interior lights on this tub," he said. "I didn't think to bring a torch."

"Bad luck," Mickey said.

In the time he'd prattled on, she'd made a mental inventory of the things that might be reachable. She wiggled the hand behind her back, turning her hips so he wouldn't see. There wasn't much slack, but there was a little. Then she looked at the brass shackle that encircled the anchor rode.

Ronan Graham stood before the helm. He craned his neck around and then stayed still. Mickey could hear the sound of an approaching engine. They were too far from shore to see the top of the lampless and lensless Barnegat Light. She would have to gauge her position from the direction the boat approached. She looked again for a radio at the helm. There was none.

Helly had taught her a little bit about Dead Reckoning.

She looked at Ronan Graham with a hatred as intense as anything she'd ever known.

I reckon we'll see who ends up dead, she thought.

Mickey shifted her hip and felt something rub against her leg. Looking down, she saw the edge of what looked like a religious medal sticking up between two boards.

St. Christopher was always around her neck.

She wondered if he'd brought a friend.

THIRTY-TWO

Viking Village
Barnegat Light

HELLY HANSEN STOOD AT the end of the pier.

The whole Island seemed to be ablaze with what had to be every police cruiser in service. He'd been readying equipment on the *Hans N* when he heard the first siren scream by up on Long Beach Boulevard.

A lost child, perhaps. There weren't many high-speed car chases on LBI, there being only one road on or off, and that was over a bridge. The lights and the sirens continued. Helly walked back toward the *Rachel*, which sat nestled comfortably in the lee of a larger boat farther down the dock. He did notice, with some surprise, that the *Virginia Jean* was gone. He wondered if the owner had returned or if someone had formally claimed her. He thought he'd make it a point to ask Lars Roellke, the Dock Master, in the morning.

Helly made a brief visual inspection of the *Rachel* and found everything ship-shape. The sirens and lights persisted. As he returned to the *Hans N,* he passed Steve Levy, a retired Coastie who wasn't ready to be done with open water just yet.

"Any idea what's going on up there, Captain Steve?" Helly asked.

Levy shook his head. "Seems like whatever it is, it involves the whole Island. If the lighthouse wasn't closed, I'd hike up to the top to see. You're not going out, are you?"

"No," Helly said, "I was getting the gear ready. Long run tomorrow. Be a good night to take the *Rachel* out, though. Don't see many like this. Damn near flat."

Levy nodded his agreement.

"How's the *Skipjack* holding up?" Helly asked him.

"Trying to get her to the end of the season," Levy said. "Her overhaul is way overdue, and I'd prefer to do it myself at a leisurely pace."

"*Uff da*. Good luck with that," Helly told him and kept walking.

He looked out at the black ocean. Without a moon, it was hard to tell where the water ended and the sky began. He saw the glow of the navigation beacons.

It would have been a good night to take Mickey out on the boat.

Surf City

Charlie Higgins blew into the PD like a Nor'easter.

"Anything?"

"Nothing," Margherita DellaDonna said. "We've established our shop as the Command Center. Must be forty units crawling over every street on the Island. If it's got light bars, it's looking for her. I'm going back out again, now that you're here, Chief. With your permission."

"Go," was all Higgins said. DellaDonna hustled out the back door.

"Anything on your end?" he asked Evan Driscoll.

"My guys in the Pine Barrens report no movement. Doesn't seem like he's taking her there."

"It's a small island, but there are a million places to hide," Higgins said.

"Nooks and crannies," Driscoll replied.

"Nooks and what?" Higgins asked.

"Nooks and crannies. You know. Like that English Muffin commercial. That's how DellaDonna described it."

"That's as good a description as any, I guess. Bureau cars are meant to blend in, I assume?"

"Not completely," Driscoll said, "Otherwise, the budget bosses in D.C. would have us driving VW Bugs."

The Base Station radio crackled. It was Stenkewiecz hailing Driscoll. He looked over at Higgins.

"Hope you don't mind," he said. Then he keyed the microphone. "Driscoll here, Stosh. Any action? Over."

"All quiet on the Western Front. Over."

"Copy that. We don't think our boy is headed your way, so keep the safeties on for the time being. Over."

"Roger that. I don't think the flame thrower has a safety, though, sir. Over," Stenkewiecz said.

Flame thrower? Charlie Higgins mouthed.

Driscoll shrugged and shook his head.

"Sir?" Stenkewicz said.

"Yeah, Stosh, what is it? Over."

"You know Paul Revere, right? Over."

"I do, Stosh. Are you suggesting we should take a Midnight Ride? Over."

"No sir," Stenkewiecz radioed back. "I was thinking, sir. One if by land. Two if by sea. Over."

Driscoll was lost in thought for several seconds before he keyed the microphone again.

"Copy that, Stosh. Except this time it's the Irish that are coming. Driscoll over and out."

He set down the microphone.

"What was that about?" Higgins asked.

"Shit!" Driscoll said through gritted teeth. He turned to Higgins. "Chief, redirect all units to concentrate on parking lots and streets directly adjacent to any dock, pier, or wharf capable of launching a boat. And you can reopen the bridge."

"On it," said Higgins. He seated himself in front of the radio.

Driscoll had read Mickey Cleary's updated file on the ride from the jet. She'd been on an Island for eleven years.

And she still couldn't swim.

THIRTY-THREE

Atlantic Ocean
2.0 NM E of Barnegat Light

MICKEY WAS STILL SCANNING the boat's interior for anything usable she might have missed.

She'd managed to loosen the rough, braided line that Ronan Graham had used to tie her right wrist to her belt. It felt like it might be the plastic kind Helly didn't like. Poly rope is what she thought he called it. He said it got slippery when it got wet and could untie itself. She remembered what Rodriguez said about the fibers in the ligature marks.

The sound of a boat motor was getting louder.

Graham flicked the navigation lights on and off three times.

The inboard aspect of the boat was rather sparse. A wide bench seat ran along the stern rail, and the rectangular engine box sat like a legless dinner table in the center. The helm was open, but it was guarded by two wide wooden seats. Mickey noticed that the two windshields opened out from the bottom, like an outfielder's flip-up sunglasses, except independently. And both had been cranked open about six or eight inches.

She knew the anchor was meant to take her straight to the bottom, meaning Graham wasn't planning on remaining on the vessel. And if there were duffel bags stuffed with cash anywhere on board, she didn't see them.

"Fine little skiff, isn't she?" Graham said. "One of your American Chris-Crafts. The ID plate says she was built in 1960, and she's twenty-four feet long. That's a bit shy of seven-and-a-half meters, which is how the rest of the civilized world measures things. All wood, too. Beautiful to view but a bleedin' bear to take care of. Leave'er outta the water too long, and the boards will shrink. About have to sink her to get 'em to swell tight again. Otherwise, she'll leak like a feckin' sieve."

"I'll try to put that knowledge to good use," Mickey said. She wanted to spit on the deck to accentuate her point, but her mouth was too dry.

Graham whipped his head around to starboard. Mickey saw the blink of navigation lights in the inky darkness. Graham blinked the *Virginia Jeans in response.* She watched him start the engine and noticed something she'd missed. It was a push starter, not a key. The *Virginia Jean* started to move. As Graham shuffled his feet, Mickey noticed him pushing a small toolbox, or maybe it was a tackle box with his foot—another detail that had initially escaped her.

She figured there was at least fifty feet of anchor rode, most of it coiled sloppily several feet out of her reach. She couldn't see how much remained on the bow and wondered how deep the ocean was underneath her.

The approaching boat's engine grew louder and then quit.

Graham backed their vessel until its rub-rail kissed the other craft. She felt and heard their boat shift into neutral.

A flashlight beam raked the deck. It fell first on Graham, then around the interior, finally coming to rest on her.

The light was directly in Mickey's eyes. Her night vision instantly evaporated.

She heard a coarse belly laugh. Then, a voice boomed out of the darkness.

"Man. Just when I thought it couldn't get any better."

She knew the voice.

Jack Rigger.

Surf City

Evan Driscoll sat in the passenger seat of Charlie Higgins' patrol car.

"How many boats do you figure there are docked on Long Beach Island?" he asked.

"Jesus," Charlie said. "A thousand? I don't know. Could be several thousand. Never even thought about it, really. Deputy Director, we are looking for one cranny inside one nook inside a whole bag of English muffins. I hope you know that. Our only real chance is to find the car you loaned this guy. What's his name again?"

"We're working on that," Driscoll said. "But it is not Connor Kilderry. I am praying this does not turn into the mother of all clusterfucks."

Higgins chuckled. "The mother of all clusterfucks," he repeated. "I do like that. I do. Permission to repeat...with attribution, of course?"

"Permission granted, Chief," Driscoll said. "If we can just locate the car, we'll at least have identified the correct bagel."

Higgins' radio crackled. It was Billy Sievert, the new Chief in Barnegat Light.

"I think we might have found it," he said. "Viking Village. West Eighteenth and Bayview for you out-of-towners. We're approaching with caution."

Driscoll looked over at Charlie Higgins.

"How far away are we?"

"Ten minutes, Code 4," Higgins replied. "Should we tell him this guy was a bomber?"

Driscoll looked straight ahead.

"Just punch it," he said.

Bombay Hotel & Casino
Room 2512

The champagne bottle was sweating, and so was she.

She looked at the digital clock radio glowing amber on the nightstand.

Archie Graham was not coming. Not in the sense she had planned for him, anyway.

But Ilsa Schoenweiss was not someone who was easily discouraged. She was going to celebrate one way or the other. Benno Bruxelles had kissed her when she presented him with the ivory chip. And then he did something wholly unexpected.

He told her to keep it.

She'd already opened the champagne and poured herself a congratulatory glass. After savoring it, she'd taken matters in hand to, as a favorite song might say, get her motor running. Standing naked in front of the windows, she noticed how utterly black the night was. The sky and the sea were indistinguishable for as far as she could see.

She walked to the bedside table and picked up the phone.The hotel operator answered immediately.

"Chief Concierge, please," she said. "I'll hold."

She stared out the window again as she waited. When she heard the line pick up she spoke only two words.

"Five minutes."

Then she hung up

Ilsa returned to the window, wet with anticipation. Beyond the haloes of lights on the boardwalk, there was nothing. It was if the world beyond had simply ceased to exist. The 1968 *Moet & Chandon* was chilling in a silver bucket on top of a pretty cabinet. She poured another glass for herself and one for her soon-to-be-arriving guest. The blackness was OK. In fact, it was more than OK.

Who needed moonlight, anyway?

THIRTY-FOUR

Atlantic Ocean
2.5 NM ENE of Barnegat Light

RONAN GRAHAM HOPPED OFF the *Virginia Jean* and onto the vessel Rigger was piloting.

They were rail-to-rail, starboard to starboard. The dull silver Danforth anchor now sat perched on the *Virginia Jean's* stern rail, parallel to the transom. Rigger lit it up with his flashlight. Mickey recognized it as a New Jersey State Police issue. He'd stolen it even as he was getting kicked to the curb.

There was a little more of a swell now, and the anchor wobbled precariously.

Graham stood near the adjoining hulls. Rigger's boat looked like a carbon copy of the *Virginia Jean* but with a white hull. And it didn't look like it had any helm seats, she noticed.

"As with most things Irish, 'tis truly tragic, what's about to transpire," he said. Jesus, he loved to hear himself talk. "You can at least be comforted by the fact that you've got a wee boy to carry on the line. And, since we're not far from a gamblin' town, you've also got a bit of a sportin' chance."

"Piss off," Mickey said to him. "You're no patriot. You're a murdering shitbag with a poor excuse."

"Ah, darlin'," Graham said. "How I do love a lass with spirit. But as I said, it's not a pat hand. So perhaps not all is lost. If that anchor would choose to fall into the boat, then you've got yourself rather a fighting chance and maybe we'll meet again for a *cuppa tae*. If it tips over the side, well, then I pray you'll be lucky enough to catch a glimpse of *Tír na nÓ'g* on yer way down. I am truly sorry, for what it's worth. *Slan leat a Ghraidh*. Farewell, my lovely."

He tapped Rigger on the shoulder. The two boats drifted slowly apart.

Mickey saw Rigger grin. "Yeah? Well screw that," he said. He walked to the stern, reached across to the *Virginia Jean*, and heaved the anchor overboard.

Mickey watched as the anchor rode slid overboard and out of sight. It seemed to uncoil in slow motion and before Mickey could even utter a sound, it tugged hard on the shackle and pulled her toward the transom.

Mickey kicked with both feet as she reached the stern. She managed to wedge a knee against the seat, but the waterproof upholstery was smooth and slippery and with only one hand to work with, she quickly found herself head down, jackknifed over the transom. Her sneakers struggled madly for purchase, but the offshore current was pulling the boat in one direction and the anchor was falling in the opposite.

One foot lost its grip. Then the other.

In what seemed like less than a heartbeat, Mickey was head down in the cold black water.

And she was sinking.

Viking Village
Barnegat Light

Billy Sievert was standing outside his patrol car when Charlie Higgins pulled up.

To Charlie Higgins' chagrin, so was, Margherita DellaDonna.

"I won't ask how you managed to get her so-"

"Probably best if you don't, Chief," DellaDonna answered.

"Do we have somebody posted at the detective's home?" Higgins asked.

"Jenetta's there," DellaDonna said. "I told him to keep them calm but to keep them there. This could be a hostage situation for all we know."

"What have we told them?"

"That her meeting was lasting longer than expected and that she'd be home later. They were supposed to go out to eat over in Beach Haven Crest. The babysitters are making macaroni and cheese now for the kids. Bill Kuriakos' nephew Nick is bringing over sandwiches and Cokes."

"God, I hope it isn't Greek cheesesteaks," Higgins said with a wince.

Evan Driscoll came trotting up, slightly out of breath.

"That's it," he said. "That's the one we loaned him. Wasn't even locked. I've got a van coming to dust for prints and look for anything that might help us."

Charlie Higgins surveyed the flotilla of vessels within sight.

"Helicopter?" he asked Driscoll.

"A lot of black ocean out there," Driscoll answered. "A sure bet he's running without lights. Could you get as many uniforms down here as you can? Let's see if we can figure out if any boat that is usually here is missing. Maybe know what needle we're looking for, at least."

"On it," said DellaDonna. "Arlene Shields is manning Dispatch for this. She only works one day a week anymore. Glad it was today."

"Have them check aboard all the boats," Driscoll said. "See if there are any captains or deckhands around who might have seen something. Anything." He pointed to his nose and sniffed. "I don't think any young lovers come down here to make out."

"You have any pull with the Coast Guard?" Higgins asked Driscoll as DellaDonna headed up the wharf.

"I'll make a call to the OOD – one friendly federal bureaucracy to another. Any time I've had to work with them, and it hasn't been often, they always rise to the occasion."

"There's also McGuire AFB," Higgins added.

"There is," Driscoll said. "But we'd need a chopper with Search & Rescue experience on the open ocean. A needle in a haystack is easier to find than a boat on the ocean. In the dark. And specialized personnel. They have guys known as Rescue Swimmers. They'll jump out of a helicopter in a wetsuit, with only a mask and a snorkel in the middle of a hurricane. That narrows it to the Coast Guard and the Navy. U.S. Coast Guard Station Barnegat Light is right around the corner. Literally. I don't know what resources they have on-station. But I'll ask."

"How dangerous is this guy?" Higgins queried. "On a scale of one to ten."

Driscoll's head gave a little shake.

"Chief," he said, "He's blown up women, children, old people, infants in strollers, people on buses, nurses at hospitals, and clergy in their churches without shedding a tear or breaking a sweat. One-to-ten? I'd say twenty."

Helly Hansen was in the bowels of the *Hans N.*

The bilge.

There was always water in it, but that's not what was bothering him. The raw water had more oil floating on it than usual. When he'd shined his flashlight down through the open hatch, he'd seen the little black rainbow swirls that meant there was a leak in a line or a crack in a filter. It might also mean that the fuel separator had gone bad. Marine diesel gas had a high component of oil in its mix. He knew they couldn't afford to miss a whole day of fishing. Not now, with notes and loan payments coming due.

It was hot and cramped where he was and he didn't have his tools. They were in the truck. He wanted to spend a little more time inspecting before he went to get them.

THIRTY-FIVE

Atlantic Ocean

2.1 NM ENE of Barnegat Light

JUST BEFORE SHE HIT the water, Mickey heard what sounded like three shots. They were followed by the gurgly rumble of an engine revving at high rpms.

They were leaving her.

The anchor rode was taut but at least she wasn't being down dragged any longer. It had twisted around her wrist but with a kick of her legs she had solved that problem. The shackle was around the rope. With a few more kicks she realized she could slide along it. At least it would keep her from drifting away from the boat.

The slippery knot behind her back was slowly loosening. It was poly rope, she was sure now, and it was flaying her wrist. But she kept wiggling. Finally, her hand slipped free

She'd had enough time to take a big gulp of air when she was pulled overboard.

Now, though, Mickey's brain was shouting at her to breathe.

The water was so dark she couldn't tell how deep she was. Swallowing a bucket of seawater wasn't the problem, she knew. Inhaling a lungful was. A thousand voices in her head were screaming at her now.

Take a breath! One breath! Take it! Take one breath!

Mickey desperately fought the urge to follow their advice, although the drumbeat chant was becoming almost irresistible.

Breathe. Breathe. Breathe.

The ocean current was twisting her around the anchor rode like bait on a hook. She shook the tangled pieces of the Poly line off, reached up with her right hand and watched them float upwards. Her left hand was useless, so she let it go limp. The shackle was sliding slowly up the line. She had no idea how far it was to the surface.

Breathe. Breathe. Breathe.

Mickey felt like she was inching up the line. Helly said it was the carbon dioxide in your blood that told your brain to make you breathe. But you had to let it out to get rid of it. It was the "bad air" in the old exhortation.

But she knew if she dared breathe out she would immediately and automatically breathe in. And that salt water would flood her windpipe and in the space of a heartbeat, her lungs. The air in her chest was keeping her buoyant. She reached up again and pulled, like a one-armed mountain climber hanging over a precipice.

Mickey realized it was getting harder and harder to think straight. A single second felt like an hour. Her mother's face flickered in her mind, and she could hear her voice.

Right here by your side. Always.

The chant immediately tried to drown her out.

Breathe. Breathe. Breathe.

Reach and pull. Reach and pull, Mickey told herself.

Step by step. Inch by inch.

Breathe! Breathe! Breathe!

They were right in her ear now. And they were screaming louder than ever.

Reach and pull. Reach and pull.

I think I can. I think I can. I think I can.

Her thoughts were muddled. She wasn't going to make it. The book. The book she read to Michael. His face looking up at her.

I know I can. I know I can. I know I can.

Now! Now! Now!

Breathe! Breathe! Breathe!

Reach. Pull. Reach. Pull.

The cords in her arm and shoulder were on fire.

Reach. Pull. I know I can. Pull. Pull.

A shape appeared. Or maybe it was one final apparition. The last thing she would ever know.

One more reach, she told herself. One more pull.

The chorus of voices reached a crescendo, and she knew she had to obey.

She took a breath.

Just as her head broke the surface.

Surf City

Evan Driscoll took off his sport coat. The heat, coupled with the lack of any significant breeze, suddenly made the night feel oppressive. Chief Higgins had driven him back to the Surf City cop shop. He'd picked up his Bureau car and, with directions from Higgins, was now at the Central Dispatch office. He wanted to check in with Stosh and did not want the conversation to be broadcast on the police band that was now being closely monitored for twenty miles in every direction. The chief had assured him Central was equipped with access to more frequencies, even some marine bands.

Driscoll knocked on the door and was buzzed inside. An attractive woman in her fifties sat in a small office, surrounded by several telephones and a desk stacked with radio equipment.

"Arlene?" Driscoll asked.

"You must be Agent Driscoll," Arlene Shields replied. "Chief Higgins said I should expect a gentleman caller."

Driscoll smiled. "Are you a fan of Tennessee Williams?"

"I enjoy a little drama now and then. What do you need from us?"

He withdrew a slip of paper from his pocket.

"Can you put me on this frequency?"

Shields looked at it. She spun in her chair, adjusted the dial on her consoles and pointed to the microphone.

"There might be sensitive aspects to this conversation," he said.

"I'll take a few minutes to, um, powder my nose," Shields said demurely. "Take all the time you need."

He keyed the microphone three times.

"Stenkewiecz," a scratchy voice responded.

"Driscoll here. How do you read, Stosh? Over."

"Copy that. Five by five. Over."

"Any activity? Over."

"Negatory, Big Ben. The lights are still out in Georgia. Over," Stenkewiecz said.

"Roger. I'll check back in an hour. Over."

"Copy that. One hour. Sir? Any advice if this becomes a live fire exercise? Over."

"Rules of engagement apply. Repeat, rules of engagement apply. Stosh. If they shoot at you first – shoot back. Everybody on our side goes home tonight. Everybody."

"Copy that. Understood. I'd much rather see them walk out than see us go in, but we will respond with a level of force appropriate to the situation. Over."

"Copy that, Stosh. Driscoll out."

Arlene Shields came around the corner.

"Need anything else?" she asked.

"No," Driscoll said. "Thank you. You've been very helpful."

"Buzz on the PB if you do need something. I'll be here until Mickey – until Detective Cleary is home safe and sound."

"Let's hope that's soon," Driscoll replied.

He grabbed his sport coat and walked back to the Fury. He noticed the right rear door wasn't closed all the way. He opened it and was ready to toss in his coat when he spied something on the back of the passenger seat. It looked like a file folder, but it wasn't like anything the Bureau used.

He reached into the little elastic netting and slipped it out.

A soft breeze finally blew up. Driscoll didn't want to lose anything in the folder, so he sat in the back seat and rifled through its contents.

After scanning the first few pages, he thought there might be more than twenty, he grabbed the folder, hopped out and went straight back into the tiny dispatch office.

"Arlene," he said, "Can you tune me in again? It's kind of urgent this time."

The dispatcher fiddled with the frequency dial and turned in her chair.

"There you go. Different Bat Time, but same Bat Channel. Should I-"

"No," Driscoll said. "Stay right here, if you don't mind. This is a conversation I'd like to have somebody witness."

The Bombay Hotel & Casino
Atlantic City

He wouldn't even recognize himself, Owen Pettigrew thought.

The room was pricey, but not as pricey as what they wanted for an Ocean View with a King Bed. His room looked out over a construction site, and his view was mostly of a huge crane dangling a cement bucket at the end of its hook. Clumps of long hair and a medium-sized forest of whiskers lay in the sink. He scooped them out and tossed them in the trash.

He couldn't remember the last time anyone would have described his appearance as "respectable." The hotel Gift Shop also sold tiny spritz bottles of aftershave. Old Spice, the brand he'd used when he was a teenager. The kind his dad had used. He sprayed himself with what seemed like a generous amount.

The Hawaiian shirt was cruise ship ugly, but it was the only one in his size. The hardest thing to find had been something long-sleeved to wear underneath it to hide the tats.

"Permanent proof of temporary insanity," his father had said when he got his first ink at sixteen. He'd found something cheap and comfortable on the boardwalk.

The room had a full-length mirror. He hadn't looked in one in a long time, either. He was a little rounder through the middle than he remembered. He wouldn't cut a dashing figure, but from what he'd seen of the men milling about in the lobby, he might make the Best Dressed list.

The Harley was parked in a City lot and he'd walked the three blocks to the glittering edifice that was the Bombay. Tomorrow, after a free, all-you-can-eat complimentary breakfast in his belly, he'd walk the three blocks back, mount up and find a way to keep heading south.

The only subject he'd excelled at in high school was Spanish. It just sort of came to him naturally.

One summer he'd read *Diarios de motocicleta,* "The Motorcycle Diaries," written by Che' Guevara, in the original Spanish. The English translation didn't do it justice. The memoir had been published well after Guevara's execution as a revolutionary in Bolivia in 1967 and detailed a long motorcycle sojourn through South America he'd taken with a friend when he was a medical student. The idea that Che' had been a person before he became a poster had meant something to him back then. Owen Pettigrew reflected that while he hadn't been a poster, he had been a poster boy for very bad behavior.

If he could make it the seven thousand miles to *Tierra del Fuego*, the Land of Fire, maybe, with any luck, he could become a person again.

THIRTY-SIX

Atlantic Ocean
2.0 NM E of Barnegat Light

FOR SEVERAL MINUTES, MICKEY bobbed like a cork. She'd heard one of the Rescue Squad guys use the term "air hunger." Now she understood exactly what it meant.

She willed herself to take slow, controlled breaths. Overbreathing, the academy had taught her, was as dangerous as underbreathing. And there wasn't a brown paper bag in sight.

She'd been yanked over the transom, but the anchor rode was tied off in a locker at the bow. The V-shaped hull came to a sharp point directly above her. It looked like it was a mile away. One more mountain to climb. But, she realized, although she still only had one arm to pull with, now she had two feet and two legs to help propel herself upward.

Half of doing something, Sergeant Wolf had told the recruits repeatedly during Physical Training at the academy in Sea Girt, *is thinking you can.*

If there was any humor in her present predicament it was the small mistakes Ronan Graham had made, likely in haste, that allowed her to be alive to think about it.

The bow above her was not unattainable. But she couldn't climb up the hull. It was too steep and too flat. It would have to be the anchor rode.

But that would only put her on top of the bow. From what she recalled, she wouldn't be able to reach the crank-out windshields from that far forward. The Danforth was meant for offshore anchoring. She figured it might weigh twenty pounds. If the flukes were stuck in the sandy bottom, it would be unlikely she could dislodge them without the boat moving under power. If they weren't, it would still be a Herculean effort to haul it onboard all by herself. Helly said some boats had a motorized windlass, a toothed gear that pulled up the anchor, but that it was mostly on newer boats. The *Virginia Jean* was not a newer boat.

Mickey looked up again. It was likely her imagination, but the bow seemed a bit further away. She remembered the three gunshots.

She hoped all of them had been for Rigger.

Then she started climbing.

Steve Levy rapped on the open hatch cover with a wrench.

Helly Hansen poked his head out.

"Whataya got going on down there?" Levy asked.

"Water separator went bad. Almost done replacing it." Helly looked around. "Where'd all the cops go?"

"They didn't say," Levy answered. "One was making the rounds down here on the docks. You must'a been below. Asked if any boats were missing."

"Missing?" Helly asked.

"Yeah, like, were any unaccounted for."

"You tell him about the *Virginia Jean*?"

"No," Levy answered. "It's abandoned, right? I figure somebody must've claimed her or maybe the owner came back and sailed off with her. Good little boat. Doubt it drifted away on its own. Hey, I'm all done. You need a hand? We could get a beer afterward."

"Ah, couple more screws to put back and I'm all finished. But I want to run her for a bit. Try and meet you, though. Where were you thinking?"

Levy rubbed his beard. "You can't beat Kubel's. They've been getting fishermen drunk since the nineteen-twenties. The new owners, I think it's gotta be five years now, they've kept it pretty much the same, but they've done a few new things. You ever had an Anchor Steam Beer?"

Helly shook his head. "Nope. Sounds like a fisherman's beer, though."

"Indeed it is. It comes all the way from San Francisco. I don't know how the Stavish's manage it, but they have cases of it in their cooler. The first one's on me if you can tear yourself away from this rusty bucket."

"Hey," Helly protested. "Christian Hansen, Senior, hears you call her that you'll be pulling a boat pole out of your ass quicker than you can blink."

"OK, OK. How's it going with that pretty policewoman?"

"There isn't any it," Helly said. "Simply enjoying each other's company now and again. Trying to teach her the basics of boat handling."

"Helly. Come on. She's a widow. You're a widower. You've both suffered knockdowns, that's for sure. But you've both righted yourselves. Comes a time when you need to sail on, sailor."

"Yeah, well, thanks for the advice, there, Captain Ahab," Helly said with a grin. "Go save me a seat at the bar. As long as you don't plan on dispensing any more relationship advice. I can get that for free on the radio now. Fishing and the Phillies. That's it, shipmate."

"Deal," said Levy. "I'll save you a stool."

THIRTY-SEVEN

1.6 NM ENE of Barnegat Lighthouse

THE FINAL TWO FEET had been exhausting.

Mickey lay sprawled on the foredeck, almost unable to move. But even from her pinned position, she could tell something clearly wasn't right.

The *Virginia Jean* was down at the stern, which could mean only one thing.

She was taking on water.

Extending her shackled wrist, Mickey managed to get herself into an uncomfortable semi-sitting position. Then she noticed something else.

The boat was drifting.

There was a soft glow in the sky off to the port side. It had to be the lights of Long Beach Island, even though the glow was all she could see. Up in the sky, there was no moon to help her get oriented. But the boat was definitely drifting. Which meant the anchor hadn't caught.

Yet.

It could be dangling in the water like a fishhook, or it could be dragging along the bottom, just waiting for something to snag on it. She had to get it up.

There were cleats on either side of the bow. If she could bring up enough of the rode, she could tie it off on one of the cleats with a fancy loop Helly called a hitch. She would only need enough to allow her to crawl through the open windshield and into the cockpit. Ten feet might do it, she figured. Maybe fifteen, tops. Even if she couldn't get all the way inside, she could still drive the boat with one hand.

Mickey tried to remember the rhythm of the tides. Two sets of highs and two sets of lows, separated by about six hours. She thought Helly had mentioned that a new moon meant the difference between them was larger. She forced herself to try and remember the tides they'd encountered the night before and what times they had occurred.

A swell that seemed to come out of nowhere, rogues Helly called them, rocked the *Virginia Jean.* Mickey realized that had she not been tethered to the deck, she would have been dumped right back in. Once the boat settled, she set her feet and started to pull.

The Danforth felt like it was intentionally fighting her.

But then the boat swung a little bit to starboard, and the pulling suddenly got easier.

Mickey found she could haul up about a foot of line at a time. She used her shackled but functional hand to hold the wet rope, then reached with her free arm to grab it as far forward as she could.

It was miserable. With each pull, her shoulder felt like it was ready to pop out of its socket.

But it didn't, so she kept hauling.

Finally, she had what looked like it might be enough rode and allowed herself to rest. She noticed the hazy glow seemed farther away. Mickey knew that meant she was drifting out to sea.

In a boat that was slowly sinking.

Although she couldn't see them, she figured either Ronan Graham or, more likely, Jack Rigger must have fired one, two, or three shots down into the deck. The seawater would bubble up slowly until the edge of the transom dipped underwater. Then it would sink much faster.

Mickey didn't think she had the strength to pull aboard any more line. Grabbing as much as she could, she made the loop Helly had taught her, under and around the cleat. She desperately wanted to rest a little longer, but the uneasy sensation of the boat sinking by its stern dispelled any notion of that.

Mickey crab-crawled over the foredeck until she reached the starboard windshield. She managed to get her head and shoulders through the aperture. Then she pushed up with as much strength as she could muster. The crank mechanism groaned. She managed to raise it maybe six more inches.

She wiggled and squirmed until her elbows were on the helm. Mickey looked for anything she could use to cut the anchor rope, but there was nothing.

Then she noticed the box on the floor again, almost completely hidden in the darkness. It was a metal toolbox, she saw now, not a tackle box, with a rusty hinged handle on top. Maybe there was a knife inside. Two hands would surely be better than one. And she'd be free to stand in the cockpit or even climb back to the bow if the *Virginia Jean* started to sink by the stern. Without a knife, without getting free of the anchor line, she would still go down with the ship.

There was a knife in there, she told herself. What kind of sailor didn't have a knife on their boat? And surely it was the serrated kind like Helly had. A blade designed specifically to cut anchor lines. Or maybe, maybe, it had a shackle key, like Helly's did. Then she wouldn't have to saw through the line at all. She'd unscrew the pin, something that could not be accomplished with a bare hand, no matter how strong, and she'd be free. She tried to picture those things in her mind.

But Mickey realized that if she wanted to reach it, she would have to go back and haul up another five feet of anchor rode. The thought of doing that about made her cry. But if that's what it took, that's what she'd do.

She summoned all her resolve and wiggled her hips again. She was able to move back a few inches when another universal truth was revealed to her.

She was stuck tight in the windshield.

Helly wasn't sure he was up for a deep, personal conversation with Captain Steve. He'd refurbished and rechristened the *Rachel* so that she would always be with him. Whether sitting quietly in port or rolling with the swells, they would still be making their voyage together.

He'd told Mickey Cleary this the first time he'd invited her aboard. He shared their story and asked if she thought this meant he was breaking his promise. Mickey told him that she'd felt exactly the same way the first time she'd let another man ride Ronnie's Royal-Enfield Interceptor motorcycle. But she'd decided that their lives together had meant something and that the Enfield should never become a museum piece. Should never become a shrine.

What good was a bike if you never rode it? She'd asked him. *What good was a boat if you never sailed it?*

They'd agreed that both their late spouses would be happy that, whether by land or by sea, their memories would remain alive, and their journeys would continue.

When Helly had renamed the boat after his wife, his soon-to-be-stood-up drinking partner, a college and Service academy graduate, was the one who pointed out to him its literary significance. He'd never actually read *Moby Dick*. But he'd read the Cliffs Notes, and he always looked for the old movie on the late, late show.

He sat in the *Rachel's* helm and thought of her. She was with him. She was all around him. He turned on the tape player.

CCR's "Sailor's Lament" was finishing up. It was more about losing at cards than it was about sailing, he'd always thought. Next came Looking Glass and "Brandy," the one-hit-wonder song he'd mistakenly recorded twice. He found the song silly but still always listened to it all the way through. Once more, he told himself. There were several seconds of tape hiss. Not so bad, considering he'd done the transfers himself. He was certainly no sound engineer.

Bobby Darin's "Beyond the Sea" came on, with its familiar muted trumpet intro. On their first boat trip, Mickey told him it was actually a cover of a French song, "*La Mer*," and that the original lyrics were about the sea, not a woman. An American had rewritten them as a love song. Helly liked the idea that it was both.

He also liked the idea of someone waiting for him and decided he'd let the song finish.

THIRTY-EIGHT

0.6 NM ENE of Barnegat Lighthouse

MICKEY PUSHED FORWARD INTO the cockpit on the helm side.

She had her shackled arm as low as it would reach, and her free arm extended as far as her shoulder tendons would allow. She thought about intentionally dislocating her shoulder but quickly dismissed the idea as being genuinely stupid.

Her fingers crawled over what she'd called, to Helly's amusement, the dashboard.

She willed them to full extension, said a silent prayer to Saint Jude, and pressed the starter.

The engine coughed and then quit.

She tried it again. Same result.

Third time's the charm, Ronnie liked to say. Next to the starter, she spied another knob. She managed to reach it and tried pulling it instead of turning it. She was right. It was the choke. Mickey hit the starter again and the boat's engine turned over. She let it run for a minute then eased the choke back in. There was one major problem, she quickly realized.

The throttle was still in neutral.

The boat's gauges glowed weakly, so at least the electrical system was intact. Which meant the steering was intact. Mickey didn't think there was any way she could reach the throttle with her fingers. Then an answer to two of her prayers appeared. It was only a shadow in the captain's seat, but she knew what it was.

A boat pole. Maybe one with a hook like she'd seen on the *Rachel.*

Mickey managed to get two fingertips on it and tried gently teasing it toward her. Then a prayer she hadn't yet sent up was answered anyway. A swell rocked the boat, and the pole rolled into her curled fingers.

Mickey made sure she had it securely and then pulled it all the way out. The effort required was enormous, even though her movements were small in scope. She was able to carefully reorient the pole without losing her grip. With a grunt, she used it to push on the throttle.

It didn't budge. She had no leverage.

She pushed the pole's much smaller diameter tip into a corner of the helm, hoping it would wedge. Then she pushed on the thicker handle end in her fist.

The throttle nudged forward. The *Virginia Jean* lurched.

She grunted and pushed again.

The throttle eased forward a little more, and the boat began to move, although it seemed to be swinging around the anchor line in a slow circle. She wondered if the rudder was what Helly called hard over to one side or the other. Taking care to maintain her grip on the boat pole, she tried turning the wheel to port.

It wouldn't move.

So she turned it in the opposite direction. The vessel seemed to slowly straighten out. But now it felt like she was steering it out to sea. The compass was still illuminated and Mickey peered through the bubble-shaped glass, reminding herself she was looking at it upside down. Making the mental adjustment, it read just shy of 090. She thought hard about the navigation pearls she'd learned and said, "Due East" out loud.

Then she said "Wrong way, Corrigan."

She turned the silver wheel slowly, making sure not to lose the boat pole, which she still needed for one more task. The *Virginia Jean* responded sluggishly, fighting the tug of the anchor. But it did respond. Mickey didn't even look up. She watched the compass, floating in its bath of oil, as it very slowly started to rotate. She was steering to port, so the heading numbers decreased until it reached 000.

"Due North," she said out loud.

The turn was gradual, but the boat was making it. Even the Danforth seemed to get the idea.

The *Virginia Jean* lolled and rocked as the swells now hit her broadside. Mickey kept the boat turning to port, her eyes locked on the compass.

As it approached 270, she eased the wheel back. She tried to remember the tilted Compass Rose on the chart. 270 wasn't actually 270, she thought. She needed to be more like 300, maybe even farther. Wedged as she was, she couldn't look back over the bow. It'll never lie to you, Helly had told her about the compass. She hoped he was right. She let the boat come about a little more, and straightened the wheel when the compass dial bounced a little shy of 330. Then she went to work on her next job.

It was going to be a race. The boat was, hopefully, heading in the general direction of the shore, but the water was seeping in. If she lost propulsion or steering before she could beach it, all was truly lost.

But the *Virginia Jean* soldiered on. It even felt like she might be picking up speed. It took Mickey a minute to figure that out. Helly had said that even if a boat was taking on water, the best strategy was to keep it moving forward, that some Italian effect she couldn't remember would actively force it out behind. And the stern did now seem to be riding a little higher in the water.

If only she could see where she was going. That, again, meant cutting the rope.

She turned her attention to the toolbox. Carefully, she flipped the boat pole around and began trying to pull the handle on the toolbox up. The boat was bucking a little, making that task harder. On one bounce, through the Grace of God, the metal handle flipped up, and she hooked it with the gaffe.

It teetered precariously on the hook as she pulled it toward her and, disappointingly, she could feel that it wasn't very heavy. It sounded like there was at least one thing inside it, maybe more. Finally, she brought it to rest atop the helm. The simple latch was rusted, but she opened it easily.

Payoff pitch, like the baseball announcers said when the count was three and two and the bases were loaded.

Tilting back the lid, she saw three things inside - a dry bottle of *Aqua Velva*, a foggy mirror that was probably meant to go on a sun visor, and what looked like a revolver.

But it wasn't heavy enough to be a revolver. Then it dawned on her.

It wasn't a revolver. It was a flare gun. She turned the box so she could see the barrel. There was one flare loaded. There weren't any spares.

There was still hope. Maybe only a sliver, but a sliver would have to do.

She bent her neck to look at the cabin roof above her. She could aim a flare off the stern, or maybe aft to port or starboard. But she didn't think it would ever have enough altitude to be seen by anyone on shore, even if they were looking.

Mickey checked the compass again.

She had drifted off the 330 line, so she adjusted the wheel until she was back on it. She tried wiggling out of the window again, but it still wouldn't budge. Mickey took the mirror and slipped her hand through one of the stretched-out elastic straps. She tucked the boat pole under her chest.

The *Virginia Jean* was still making headway. The stern had stopped rising, but at least it wasn't sinking, as far as she could tell. If she had to slow down, that might change. Mickey adjusted the mirror until she found something to look at. The warm summer glow of Long Beach Island was behind her, which meant it was actually ahead of her. She saw a white flashing light, bobbing in the swells. She counted the flashes.

One short. One long. One short. One long.

Then she heard the mournful sound of a bell.

It had to be the striped marker. She knew she had to be on one side of it. But which one? Facing backward made everything so much harder to visualize

The *Virginia Jean* was picking up speed. She was sure of it. The incoming new moon tide was sweeping it toward shore. Between the aching in her arms and hands and the now increased rocking of the boat, it was hard to keep the mirror steady. She thought she caught glimpses of what looked like the illuminated lower half of Barnegat Lighthouse.

She was being pulled toward the Inlet.

Mickey felt the boat swing hard and then self-correct. Eddy current, she guessed. She must be getting close.

She looked in the mirror and saw another flashing light—flashing Red. This one wasn't bobbing. It had to be the aid marking the tip of the jetty on the north side of the cut. Mickey steered the *Virginia Jean* toward it as best she could. When she had the compass heading and the light in the mirror lined up, she grabbed the boat pole again and tried the same maneuver to lever the throttle. After several failed attempts and a stream of profanity, the boat surged forward.

Mickey checked the cloudy mirror one more time and dropped the gaffe. It clattered on the floor of the cockpit and rolled away. The boat picked up even more speed as the invisible moon sucked it toward the swirling mouth of the Inlet.

Suddenly, the *Virginia Jean* rolled hard to port. Then, in the next instant, it seemed to roll hard to starboard. Then it seemed to rise as if lifted from below by some unseen hand. It took Mickey a minute to realize what had happened. Then she knew.

The anchor had broken loose.

If she hadn't tied it off to the cleat, she thought, she'd be free. But there had been no other choice. The mirror dropped from Mickey's grasp and shattered on the cabin floor. The boat swung again, and Mickey lost all sense of direction. She was looking at a black horizon again.

The *Virginia Jean* shuddered, rose up again, and then came down with a splintering thud. Mickey was tossed violently upward and then down, her chin stuttering hard on top of the helm. For a moment she thought she might pass out. She looked at her hand. The flare pistol was still in it. Mickey could hear waves lapping at the hull, but the little boat didn't move. It took a few more seconds for her to realize something else.

The impact had splintered the windshield's wooden frame.

Mickey backed herself out from the cockpit and surveyed her surroundings. The boat was aground at the tip of the jetty, the red navigational beacon flashing close by, silently mocking her. She flipped over, pulled herself along the anchor rode until she reached the cleat, then released the hitch. She slid the parted end of the line through the shackle, returning her left arm and hand to her.

She almost cried. Then, the glow of the flasher put a thought in her head. She was in a Red Light District. The absurdity of it seemed somehow comforting.

The *Virginia Jean* rocked gently as the swift incoming tide swept over the giant granite boulders inches beneath her keel. Mickey moved backward toward the cockeyed windshield. She could see that water was flooding the stern of the boat at a faster rate. She also saw two bullet holes in the decking. But only two. Barnegat Lighthouse loomed so close it looked like she could walk to it

Mickey knew there would be only a short period of slack tide when water wouldn't be moving in or out. Then, this tiny tongue of the Atlantic Ocean would come roaring back out the mouth of the Inlet, sweeping her and the slowly submerging *Virginia Jean* back out to sea and, this time, down to the bottom.

Mickey braced herself against the windshield.

She'd have just enough time to take her shot.

"Beyond the Sea" was followed by Leon Russell's languid ballad "Back to the Island." It wasn't Helly's favorite, and he clicked the tape player off halfway through. He made sure the boat's "house" battery was off and got ready to hop out of the *Rachel*. He heard footsteps approaching as he gave the mooring lines one last tug.

"Hey," a voice called. "Hey. You work here? You a captain? Is that your boat?"

Helly recognized the Surf City PD uniform but not the woman who wore it. Up the dock he could see a cruiser with its roof lights strobing and bouncing off the water in the harbor.

"Yeah," he said. "Helly Hansen. We run a fishing business. Lot of hubbub for a weeknight. Can I ask what's going on?"

"Any boat go missing from these docks that you know of?"

A small swell rocked the *Rachel.* Helly grabbed the cabin roof to steady himself.

"Yeah. There is one," he said to the officer. "The *Virginia Jean*. It's been abandoned for at least a few weeks. We figured either the own-"

Helly saw surprise register on the policewoman's face.

"Stay right here," she told Helly. "You stay right here. *Vagina G* did you say? You can name a boat Vagina?"

"*Virginia Jean*," Helly corrected her. "Virginia, like the state. J-E-A-N."

The officer repeated the name to herself several times, loud enough for Helly to hear. Then she headed back up the dock.

"You stay right there!" she called back over her shoulder.

Helly rested his back against the captain's seat as the swell subsided. The water was very still. He looked at his watch.

Slack tide. Right on time.

He took a look up the dock but did not see the police officer returning yet. Helly decided to check the flying bridge for any loose gear. He clambered up the wooden ladder and stood at the high-perch helm, gazing East toward the ocean.

It took him a minute to realize what he was seeing.

Because a moment was all it lasted.

THIRTY-NINE

Barnegat Inlet, North Jetty

THE GREAT GRANITE BOULDERS that had cracked and now cradled the *Virginia Jean* sat atop a bed of medium-sized rocks. Those rocks rested on a layer of small stones that had been poured onto the seabed from flatcars high up on a temporary railroad-tracked trestle. The boulders weighed between five and ten tons each and had been hauled overland from quarries in Lambertville and Kingston in flatbed Fords. The construction project, completed in the fall of 1940, cost the State of New Jersey a sum upwards of three-quarters of a million dollars and was an overlooked engineering marvel.

There had been heated debate about allowing the boulders to be awash at high tide, but the Army engineers had stood firm. Their solution was the navigation beacon mounted on a heavy steel cylinder which blinked uncaringly at Mickey as she stood inside the boat for the first time since she was dragged overboard.

She'd worried about shooting off the flare from the rocking bow and had tiptoed along the outside of the cabin on the narrow and slippery port rail to reach the aft deck. It wasn't a far distance, but there weren't any real handholds, and the boat's motion had nearly pitched her off twice.

Mickey had mentally prepared herself for the flare to misfire or, more likely, not launch at all. She even imagined the *pffffffft* sound it would make when she squeezed the trigger.

When it popped and whizzed skyward into the blackness, she had actually jumped for joy, whooping and screaming like, as her friend Loretta LaMarro was wont to say, "some kind of crazy woman."

If help did not arrive in time, or did not arrive at all, Mickey thought her only remaining hope would be if the outgoing tide somehow took pity on the *Virginia Jean*, who had fought so hard to bring her this far and this close, and allowed the little boat to spend her final hours at rest on the rocks. Even if she flooded, she would provide Mickey with a refuge until the sun lit up the horizon before making its grand entrance.

The fishing fleet went out early. One of them would spot her. She tried to picture Helly Hansen piloting the *Hans N* past her and the look on his face as he sailed by. She decided she'd wave and smile. Maybe even salute.

This scenario seemed less likely as she listened to the tide slowly turning, as the Moody Blues song went. The *Virginia Jean* was rocking more and rolling harder. She and the boat would be washed away long before her sorrow. Mickey calculated the odds of reaching the navigation beacon as being extremely low. The water was already moving, and once she left the admittedly precarious safety of the hull, the moon, and the tide would surely sweep her seaward before she even got close. The three convicts who paddled their raincoat raft away from Alcatraz probably took less of a risk. She wondered if federal prison raincoats were Helly Hansens, and laughed out loud at the idea.

Mickey patted the rail of the *Virginia Jean.*

"Hang in there," she said. "We're almost home."

Helly slid down the ladder with his feet barely touching the side rails.

The engine was idling, and the navigation lights were blazing. If the officer didn't return momentarily, he was going alone. Helly assumed someone on watch at the Coast Guard Station had also seen what he'd seen, but he wasn't taking the chance.

The female officer returned as he turned to use the radio.

"You know anything about boats?" he asked her.

"My dad graduated from the U.S. Merchant Marine Academy. So yeah. I know something about boats."

"Climb aboard," he said. "I'm going to hail the Coast Guard. Then I'm going up top. You're going to cast us off. Do it in the order I tell you."

Helly was surprised at the ease with which the woman went from the dock to the deck.

"Standing by, Cappy," she said and gave him a crisp little salute.

"What's your name?" Helly asked.

"DellaDonna," she said.

"Got a first name?"

"Just DellaDonna."

Helly made sure the *Rachel's* marine radio was tuned to Channel 16. The Uniden Oceanus unit was old but reliable. He lifted the microphone from its notched mount and keyed it.

Then he set it down.

The movement of the tide was becoming more evident now.

Mickey could feel it. She could hear it. When she looked down over the rail, she could see it, working its way past the wounded hull on its journey back out to sea.

The lights on the gauges had gone dark, meaning the electrical system had probably shorted out after being flooded with saltwater. She was standing barefoot in about four inches of the decidedly uninvited Atlantic. Even if she could float, the *Virginia Jean* wouldn't start, and she wouldn't steer. And after the splintering sounds Mickey'd heard when she hit the rocks, she was pretty sure she wouldn't float—at least not for very long.

Mickey thought of all the people on shore right now, laughing, drinking, playing with their kids - all blissfully unaware of her dire plight and her likely fate. If she thought of her own children right now, she knew she might lose herself to despair.

One of the local restaurants, Mickey couldn't remember which one, had the Breton Fishermen's Prayer printed at the bottom, right below the beer selection. Bretons, Ronnie had said, were Celts who settled in France. She remembered that part of it read,

O God, thy sea is so great, and my boat is so small

She wondered if God tested his believers. She wondered if He would let her sail within sight of salvation, only to watch her drift away before it arrived. She slipped the St. Christopher's medal Billy Tunell had given her when she'd first arrived on LBI out from under her shirt and let it dangle on her chest. How many times had he intervened on her behalf, she wondered? Then she remembered something.

Mickey ran her foot along the submerged deck until she felt it. She reached down into the dark water. It was still wedged between two of the boards. She got on her knees in the water and somehow managed to pry it out. The inscription was hard to read in the blackness, but she held it close and thought she could make out the words.

Saint Brendan the Navigator
Patron of Seafarers & Voyagers

It was either another answered prayer or a cruel celestial joke.

The *Virginia Jean* rocked alarmingly now. Mickey thought of the time she and Ronnie had stayed up late to watch *A Night to Remember*, the old black-and-white movie about the *Titanic*. She didn't feel panicked, and there was nowhere to run. They should make another movie about that, she thought. Maybe in color this time.

She held up the St. Brendan medal.

"Can you ask your boss to get me off the hook? For old times' sake?" she said to it.

Then she slipped it deep into the pocket of her pants. When they found her - *if* they found her – they'd know she'd called in every marker she had.

Maybe you know a Saint who knows a Saint? She laughed out loud.

The Virginia Jean gave another shudder and then pivoted to starboard. At least the bow would be pointing out when the rocks released her.

Mickey knew she could probably tread water for a while. She'd already searched the boat twice. No vests, no cushions, no carved coffin to use as a life raft. She was good at accurately assessing situations. She understood the present one completely. Mickey decided she'd better get used to the ocean temperature. She sat down with her back against the rail. The water was at her hips now. If she made it out, she thought, she'd have to get a new driver's license. And she hated going to the DMV.

The boat shifted again.

Mickey wrapped her arms around her legs, laid her head on her knees, and started to pray out loud.

"Oh my God, I am heartily sorry," she said, then added. "Really sorry. Like so sorry, you would not fricking believe it."

The water started lapping at her waist.

FORTY

Barnegat Bay, 39.76N, 74.10W

THE OLD SCANDINAVIAN FISHERMEN knew what they were doing. The docks and piers that eventually became the commercial fishing enterprise known as Viking Village were at almost the shortest distance between two points—the harbor and the Inlet.

Henry Hudson, of Hudson Bay and the *Half Moon* fame, was given credit for discovering the inlet mostly because he was the first European to name it. A native Englishman, he sailed for the powerful Dutch East India Company, and so he called it by a Dutch name, *Barende-gat*, which translated to "inlet with breakers." Mapmakers being mapmakers, liberties with the spelling were quickly taken, and it next became Barndegat, and then, for reasons unclear, the "d" was dropped, and the modern name of Barnegat became standard on nautical charts and land maps.

"It's a pretty cool view from up here," Margherita DellaDonna said.

Helly had pried her first name out of her with some difficulty.

"So why'd you name her the *Rachel*?"

"My wife's name," Helly told her. He didn't feel the need to elaborate.

"That's sweet of you," DellaDonna said. "She's a nice boat. You take good care of her. It shows. You ever read *Moby Dick*?"

"No," Helly said. He decided to leave the part about the Cliffs Notes out.

"You should," DellaDonna told him.

"OK," Helly said. "I'm going to have you climb down in a minute. I'll steer from up here because I can see the eddy currents better. If there are people on board, I'll need you on the deck. Do you think you can throw a rope if you have to?"

DellaDonna just looked at him.

"You drive the boat, there, cappy. I'll do my part."

"Can you steer her for a minute?"

"Seriously?" DellaDonna asked.

"Yeah. Two minutes. Keep on this heading. I gotta make a call."

The tide was with them but a breeze had kicked up, making the Inlet a bit wavier, as the fishermen liked to say. Helly zipped down the ladder and back to the radio.

"Coast Guard, Coast Guard, Coast Guard," he said quickly. "This is the power vessel *Rachel* moored at Viking Village. Over."

There was a burst of static.

"Roger, Rachel. This is Station Barnegat Light. Over."

"I wish to report what I believe was a distress flare. Fired from somewhere beyond the Inlet I think. Over."

"Roger, Rachel. Possible distress flare spotted Barnegat Inlet. Confirm? Over."

"Confirm. Heading out to investigate and render aid if needed. Over."

"Roger, Rachel. Be advised we do not recommend that course of action. Tide is imminently outgoing, and conditions are likely treacherous. Repeat. We do not advise you take that course of action. Station Barnegat Light vessel and personnel will investigate and respond as necessary. Please confirm your understanding, Rachel. Over."

"Copy that. Rachel understands and confirms. We will, um, we will stand by. Over."

"Roger that. Station Barnegat Light over and out."

Helly banged the microphone back in the mount and slid over to the ladder. DellaDonna appeared next to him.

"Who's steering?" he asked.

She pointed to the wheel.

"You said you're the captain. You steer. I don't know this water. And I certainly don't know how to turn around in it."

"We're not turning around," Helly responded

"Wait. What? We're still going?" DellaDonna said. "But the Coast Guard told you not to. I heard what they said. And you told them-"

"You follow every piece of advice somebody gives you?" Helly asked

"No, but-"

"I told them I understood. I didn't say I agreed with them. Standing by can mean a lot of things. Plus, technically, we're closer than they are."

The base of the lighthouse was off the beam of the *Rachel* along her starboard rail.

Helly started up the ladder again.

"Just get ready to do what I tell you. Unless that gun you're wearing changes things, I'm still the captain."

"Aye, aye," DellaDonna said. "Hope you like the food they serve in the brig."

They rounded the point and entered the Inlet. DellaDonna was on the second step of the scuttle ladder, scouting the surroundings.

"Ever heard of binoculars?" Helly heard her say.

"There!" Helly said and pointed off to port. "On our side of the Marker 2. Gotta be somebody who ran aground on the rocks. Usually one too many margaritas or someone who should never sail at night." He turned the wheel on the flying bridge helm slightly to starboard. Then he slid down the ladder.

"You asked about missing boats," he said to DellaDonna. "Did somebody steal one? PD's don't usually get involved in that stuff."

"Yeah. We think a boat theft might be involved. We're looking for someone who could be on a missing boat, though. Kidnapping maybe," DellaDonna answered.

"Not an actual kid, I hope," Helly said.

"Nope, not a kid," DellaDonna replied.

"So, who got kidnapped?" Helly asked.

DellaDonna had moved up the ladder, her head and chest now above the cabin roof. She said something, but a wave smacked the hull at the same time, and Helly missed it.

"Say again," he called to her.

"You familiar with the name Mickey Cleary?"

When Helly was sure he'd heard correctly, he gunned the *Rachel's* throttle and headed her straight for the blinking beacon.

The *Virginia Jean* was now broadside to the swells and not faring any better for it.

Mickey thought maybe the keel had settled in one of the large gaps between the black boulders, as the rocking motion had lessened. But the water was now approaching the gunwales. She had hopped up on the captain's chair. Her last refuge would be on top of the helm or out on the bow deck. She'd found the crank for the port windscreen and had been able to open that window all the way, so she had one last egress route if she needed it.

She felt like she was sitting at the bedside of a dying friend.

The wind had picked up. She'd heard some sounds earlier coming from the Island, but now it felt like it was coming in from the ocean.

Mickey decided she'd keep her gaze toward the horizon. She did not want the lights of LBI and the shadow of Old Barney to be the last things she saw.

She closed her eyes and prayed again. She asked God to look after her children, and that's when the tears started to trickle.

A loud horn sounded. Probably from some frustrated driver on the Island, Mickey decided.

"Goddamn tourists," Mickey said to the helm. "Probably a New Yorker."

Then the horn sounded again.

Only louder this time. Mickey heard voices.

Shit, now I'm hallucinating.

But the horn and the voices persisted. Mickey snapped herself back to full alertness and turned around.

The *Rachel* was coming straight toward her.

Helly put the throttle in neutral, slid down the ladder, and went right to the cockpit helm.

"What's our plan?" DellaDonna asked.

"I'm going to try to back her," Helly said. "I'm afraid an eddy will drive her bow into the jetty. You'll have to work from the stern. Not much to hang on to back there."

"Don't worry about me," DellaDonna said. "Just get us close."

Helly watched as she grabbed a line. He'd noticed when they were heading out that she'd placed all the free lines in Flemish coils, which made them look like flat circles or spirals. That impressed him. He was turned halfway around, the wheel in one hand and the throttle in the other.

As he approached the end of the long rock jetty, he recognized the lines of the *Virginia Jean* even in the dark. Helly reached under the helm and tossed a large waterproof flashlight to DellaDonna. She caught it with one hand, clicked it on, and shined it toward the stricken boat.

"We gotcha, Chief!" Helly heard DellaDonna yell. "Hang on! Cavalry's coming!" She looked over at Helly. "We're good. We're good," she shouted to him. "Thirty yards. Try to keep this line."

A swirling eddy attempted to catch the bow, but Helly was ready for it.

"Yeah, yeah," DellaDonna said. "Twenty yards. A little hot, maybe."

Helly throttled down slightly. The stern swayed but kept moving. If he slowed down too much, he knew, he'd lose steerage.

"We're good, we're good," DellaDonna said. She kept the light on Mickey. "Ten yards. Almost there."

"Get ready to heave it," Helly told her.

She dropped the flashlight and put the free end of the line in her right hand. The rest she held in loose loops in her left. *Perfect technique*, Helly thought, wondering what divine hand had put her on his boat on this night.

"Five yards!" DellaDonna shouted. "Now or never!"

Helly gave the motor a little puff of gas and then clicked the throttle into neutral.

The *Rachel* jumped.

DellaDonna heaved the line.

After such an extended period in the pitch dark, the flashlight in her eyes had about blinded her. Mickey thought her night vision was taking its sweet time coming back.

When it finally did, she was shocked to see Margherita DellaDonna, in uniform, shouting at her.

A mooring line from the *Rachel* landed with a splash.

"Wrap it on the cleat," DellaDonna yelled. "On the cleat."

She pointed to the stern cleat in front of her to drive home the instruction.

Mickey gave her thumbs up and sloshed her way to the stern. She had to think again about how to make the hitch Helly had taught her. There were more breakers now around both boats, and Mickey struggled to keep her feet.

"We'll back up and pull you across. Don't try to jump, OK? Do not jump!"

Another thumbs up.

Mickey saw the water churn and bubble at the *Rachel's* stern as it moved slowly toward her. The newly arrived set of breakers seemed intent on preventing the rescue in any way possible. The sterns of both boats slipped and swayed, pitching both Mickey and DellaDonna to their respective decks more than once. The line connecting them sagged and then pulled taut with a groan in repeated cycles.

Mickey made her way back to the long bench seat that was up against the transom.

She was going to have to jump across. She simply couldn't see any other way.

A large breaker, another one of Helly's rogues, lifted the *Rachel* high on its crest. The stern line snapped tight and remained that way. There was a moment when all the sound around Mickey seemed to go away. What broke the silence was the sound of wood cracking and then splintering. The cleat tore out and whipsawed back toward the *Rachel* and Margherita DellaDonna.

Mickey didn't see it hit her, but in the next instant, she watched in horror as the young officer tumbled headfirst over the rail.

FORTY-ONE

Atlantic Ocean, 39.60N, 68.88W
8 NM E of Barnegat Light

FOR A BUNCH'A BLEEDIN' badass bikies, they weren't so feckin' tough, Ronan Graham thought as he motored the Black Jack ocean skiff forward.

Up on plane, it was almost flying. Most of the keel was out of the water.

The gas gauge bounced on and off the "E" mark. His simple Dead Reckoning calculation told him it would be enough.

The second after he'd shot Rigger in the back of the head, he'd opened up the throttle. The sudden acceleration pitched two of the bikie bastards straight over the transom. The other two would be even easier. Near paralyzed by the shock of what they'd just witnessed, they now stood dumbly near the rail, peering into the black after their lost mates. One stupid cur even tried calling out to them over the roaring diesel engine.

Graham kept the throttle wide open. He turned the wheel hard to port and then immediately back hard to starboard. The rudder responded, and the boat cut the water sharply, first one way and then the other. It listed hard enough in each direction to bring the beam gunwales barely a hand's breadth away from the ocean's rolling surface. Although they were on opposite sides of the deck, the two taggers went over and out almost simultaneously.

There was probably a mile of water between the boat's keel and the ocean floor, Graham figured. These buggers certainly wouldn't be floating up to any amusement pier. Sharks roamed these cold depths. Big ones. The Prospects' prospects were looking pretty feckin' bleak, he thought with a small laugh. His Da' would have liked that one. And the sharkies, they would teach them a thing or two about what it means to be a predator.

He'd already decided to give Rigger the captain's honor of going down with his ship.

Graham flipped on the boat's lights. He held the chart close to the glowing gauges. If he wasn't already there, he figured, then he was bloody well close. The heavy crate of weapons had barely budged despite the rapid shifts in the boat's center of gravity—a well-thought-out benefit of having it ride squarely amidships.

The skiff's engine was starting to sputter and cough as it became starved for fuel. Navigation lights winked on and off perhaps a hundred yards off his starboard bow. Graham looked down at the lifeless Rigger.

"Sorry mate," he said to the corpse, "That's my ride."

The engine sucked its last sip of gas and quit. The skiff settled and then glided until it sat dead in the water, rocking rhythmically in the ceaseless swells.

The approaching navigation lights now burned continuously. Graham turned the skiff's lamps off and killed the electrical power. He was now a black shadow bobbing on a black ocean.

The water churned, and propellers turned as the other vessel drew closer.

Something was off, though, Graham suddenly thought. The positions of the lights were all wrong for the vessel he was expecting. They were too high and spaced too widely apart. Whatever this boat was, it was much bigger than it was supposed to be.

Ronan Graham reached for his pistol.

That's when the spotlight blinded him.

Bombay Hotel & Casino
Top Floor Business Offices

Gus Galliardi had possessed all the flair and all the fire of a Sicilian lover, even if he did fall short of the size and the stamina of the Irishman.

Still, Ilsa was satisfied. What Gus had lacked in girth, he'd more than made up for in technique. Rarely could she come to climax without penetration. Gus showed her that perhaps more pleasure was always possible.

She held the ivory casino chip in her hand, turning it over and over. Where to secure it was going to be a question. There was not one place in the entire hotel and casino that Benno would not have access to if he suddenly decided he wanted it back. In the morning, she would open a new account at a new bank and rent a safety deposit box. It would hold only one object.

She placed the chip in her clutch purse. Ilsa noticed that one of the file cabinets had a drawer that wasn't fully closed. She found that odd. She got up, walked over, slid the drawer out, and studied its contents.

Ilsa Schoenweiss was a detail person. She had a compulsion, bordering on an obsession, about symmetry. And she was definitely looking at some asymmetric corners. Off by only millimeters perhaps, but still off, catching her eye among her carefully arranged folders. She knew Benno would sometimes take one of the folders, the ones he referred to as his top secret documents, and just look at the papers it contained. Many of them were in German. A few were in Dutch. Not uncommonly, he would ask her to translate the wording and read it aloud to him. Only the words. The numbers always spoke for themselves. He said he liked the sound of *Deutsche marks* so much better than the dull term dollars. Ilsa would never dare say it, but in such moments she reminded him of Gomez Addams when Morticia would speak French. The humorous thought allowed her to ignore the fact the figures on some documents were annotated with the abbreviation for *Reichsmarks*.

Nothing seemed to be missing, so Ilsa chalked it up to one quirk of Benno's among so many. He was like millionaire child in some ways, jealously guarding his collection of toys. He was content to look at them most of the time. What good was a toy if you never played with it, she wondered.

Ilsa readjusted the folders so their crisp edges lined up perfectly and pushed the file drawer shut until it clicked. The cabinet didn't have a lock. It didn't need one. Only she and Benno Bruxelles had access to the top floor warren of offices and storage spaces. Not even Rigger could get in.

She clicked off the lights and moved toward the door.

Ilsa silently wished her Irishman *Gute Reise. Bon voyage.* Then she left the offices, feeling rather happy.

And why shouldn't she?

After all, her own *Reise* had only just begun.

The Pine Barrens

Walker White knew it was over in less than a minute.

Some of the hard cases had pleaded to fight it out. And he knew it wouldn't have taken much goading at all to get the militarized force that surrounded him to create a PR nightmare for themselves and make cult heroes of the MC's less than heroic members.

The flamethrower had changed his mind.

Agent Stenkewiecz had been more than cordial, immediately recognizing that Walker White was possessed of both natural intellect and education. Stenkewiecz had simply and calmly explained the competing narratives and their more than certain outcomes. Then, in what Walker White still regarded as a consummate act of political theater, he'd summoned a tactical-gear clad agent to light up a pine tree with the one weapon he hadn't counted on.

It was more dramatic than a cross-burning. Especially with the sizzling resin and the popping pine cones. And Stenkewiecz had the decency to have the flames extinguished right after he'd made his rather direct point.

Pettigrew had given them everything they needed in one slim volume, as his English teachers used to say. But they'd never get him for murder or even manslaughter. The time he'd do would be significant, but the money and the ID's would still be there when he eventually got paroled for good behavior. He'd claim he'd found Jesus, maybe start a prison ministry, and teach classes to the other inmates. Maybe help them get their GEDs. Hell, he figured, he'd tutor them for the SATs or the MCATs if they'd let him.

In a life that allowed for few kindnesses, Walker White found room for one. He requested that Rhonda Petty be allowed safe passage out of the compound and maybe some unofficial help in managing a strategic, and distant, relocation. Stenkewiecz hadn't even blinked before granting the ask.

Walker White did not look back as he was led in handcuffs to the waiting sedan. That part of his life was over now. A silly song from high school popped into his head, "I Fought the Law," by the Bobby Fuller Four. He remembered reading that Bobby Fuller was found dead outside his Hollywood home not long after its release.

Walker White had indeed fought the law. And, for the moment anyway, he'd lost. But he decided that at least he'd lost graciously. And he was still young enough to picture what lay ahead.

He thought of himself now as not unlike an American grizzly bear. An apex predator that hibernated for a long stretch, then emerged – hungry, motivated, and unafraid.

He'd be in hibernation for a while.

But not forever.

FORTY-TWO

Barnegat Inlet

THE DECISION TO JUMP, Mickey realized, had been the wrong one.

But she hadn't tried to jump into the *Rachel* to save herself. She'd jumped into the water to help DellaDonna. It wasn't even a decision. It was simply a honed instinct.

Now, it was very possible they both might drown.

A foamy breaker had pushed her toward the dazed officer. Mickey had the stern line wrapped around her forearm. In her other arm, she had DellaDonna. The dislodged cleat had come off. She probably hadn't tied the hitch correctly, she thought.

Helly must have put the boat in neutral, which meant the propeller wasn't turning underneath them. But without propulsion, the *Rachel* was now at the mercy of the outrushing tide and the complicated currents. Helly was scrambling on the deck, attempting to deploy a boarding ladder that would hook on the rail and hang over the side.

Maybe they weren't dead yet.

Helly finally got the ladder hooked on, just as a swell rolled under them and knocked him down. Mickey was keeping DellaDonna's chin above the water, but not by very much. Helly made it back to the rail and started pulling them toward the boat. But the Inlet, it seemed, had other ideas.

A smaller breaker spun the two women around. The stern line on Mickey's arm instantly became a tourniquet. She knew her ability to grip wouldn't last long now. Mickey thought of the saying, "All is lost."

DellaDonna was starting to come around. But they were being pushed farther away from the ladder by the Inlet's conflicting currents. Mickey's arm muscles were failing, and her hand felt like it was on fire. The stern line was the only thing tethering them. She knew she couldn't let go of it.

In the next instant, they were surrounded by a dazzling white light. The ocean seemed suddenly calmer and Mickey wondered if this was the end of the line. There were splashing sounds coming from somewhere. She hoped it was dolphins and not sharks. In the sudden brightness, Mickey couldn't tell if Helly had fallen from the arms of the *Rachel* as well. It was like they were in a dream.

Suddenly, Mickey felt arms around her. Then, a black shape that looked like a creature from a deep-sea nightmare appeared. She realized the creature was speaking to her.

"I am Coast Guard Rescue Swimmer Salvatore Campisi. Let's get you both to safety. Do not try to swim or assist me. I will get you there. You both are going to be OK."

Her vision was still hazy but Mickey could feel that she and the slowly awakening DellaDonna were now being propelled toward the *Rachel* rather forcefully. Before she knew it they were at the ladder.

"You first," the swimmer told Mickey.

"No, her first," Mickey said.

The swimmer shook his head forcefully. "You first. This is not the time to argue with me, ma'am."

Mickey let go of DellaDonna and grabbed the bottom rung of the heaving ladder. Helly reached over and pulled her in. She wanted to help get DellaDonna aboard but realized she was too weak. The line was still wrapped around her arm. She peeled it off with some difficulty and looked at the deep indentations it left in her skin. They looked like the pale tattoo of a snake.

Helly was hauling a now more coherent DellaDonna onto the *Rachel*.

After she spit out a mouthful of saltwater, DellaDonna looked at Mickey and Helly.

"Well, that was pretty goddamn embarrassing, I gotta say. Shit. Do not *ever* tell my dad about this."

Before they had time to laugh, the rescue swimmer clambered on board. He pulled off his oversized swim fins and raised his mask. Then he addressed Helly with no trace of humor or goodwill.

"Captain, I'm Coast Guard Rescue swimmer Salvatore Campisi. I will direct you to Station Barnegat Light. We will proceed there directly without any intervening stops or diversions. Do you understand me, Captain?"

"I understand," Helly replied. "And thank you."

"The Coast Guard Motor Life Boat will remain on station to attend to the damaged craft. We will try to salvage her if possible, but our primary mission will be to prevent her from becoming a hazard to navigation. Do you understand that as well, Captain?"

"I understand," Helly repeated.

"Very good. Then let's get underway and out of this Mixmaster. I can pilot if you'd prefer to focus your attention on the two female souls aboard."

"I know the way," Helly said, heading for the helm. "I'll take us in."

Mickey could now see the whale-gray rescue vessel with its distinctive orange stripe. It had to be forty feet long. As the *Rachel* passed wide of the open cockpit, the rescue swimmer gave a thumbs-up to its crew. Mickey gave one as well. The huge searchlight swung and trained its beam on the *Virginia Jean*, which, although sunk almost to her rails, was definitely still above the water.

Don't give up now, Mickey thought as they passed her port-to-port.

"Excuse me, ma'am," the swimmer said. His mask and snorkel were completely off, and his swim hood was bunched around the zippered neck of his wetsuit. "But what in the world were you doing out there tonight?"

Mickey thought for a second.

She didn't know where to even start and somehow wasn't surprised when DellaDonna started for her.

After sketching in the details each of them knew, the swimmer went to the helm and got on the radio.

Minutes later, as they rounded the lighthouse point and headed for the docks at Station Barnegat Light, Mickey saw a much larger Coast Guard vessel making its way out with some haste.

It wasn't a rescue vessel, Mickey quickly understood.

Rescue vessels didn't have mounted guns.

FORTY-THREE

Naval Station GB
1138.0 NM SSE of Barnegat Lighthouse

THE FLIGHT HAD BEEN incredibly noisy and he hadn't slept at all, slung as he was like a sack of potatoes in some cargo netting instead of sitting in a proper seat.

They'd kept the hood on him the whole time, shoving metal canteens up under it and forcing the water down in a way about like to drown him. Sweat was pouring off his nose.

Wherever he was, Ronan Graham thought, it was bloody fecking warm.

A powerful grip seized his shackled wrists and walked him along what felt like baking asphalt.

"Where the feck are we?" he asked through the hood.

"Welcome to the tropics, Mr.," there was a pause, "Mr. Graham. We certainly hope you enjoyed your flight. We'll be taking you to your lavish accommodations after a quick and routine debriefing. Shouldn't be more than two hours or so."

The voice was definitely American, and it spoke in a clipped military cadence.

"Two hours!" Graham protested. "I've gotta use the jacks, then."

"Ah, you're a big boy, Mr. Graham. I'm sure you can hold it that long."

"You'll want to treat me nicer," Graham said as he was marched along. "I know a bloody lot of things you'd like to know. A bloody lot. I can give you what a lot of others would be willin' to pay me for."

"We're sure you can, Mr. Graham," the clipped response came. "That's why you're here."

"Ya," Graham grumbled. "And I'm done feckin' around with your feckin' FBI. Bloody bunch'a wankers that lot is. What I got has international ramifications. You get me in touch with somebody in your feckin' CIA. And right quick, 'fore I change my bloody mind and decide to shut the feck up for good."

"I do believe the agency you mentioned will be delighted to talk to you. Excited. Maybe even giddy with anticipation, you might say. They're always looking for a few good men, same as we are. Why else do you think they would have brought you all this way?"

FBI Field Office
Newark, NJ

J.J. Durkin gently hung up the phone.

The conference call with Washington had gone well. Extremely well.

Sunlight was streaming into the room from over the Passaic River. Evan Driscoll considered putting on his sunglasses, then thought better of it.

Durkin went to get the coffee pot to pour them each a third cup.

"Let me get that, Director," Driscoll said immediately and started to rise from his chair.

"Evan, sit," Durkin chided. "You've taken what could have been one of the biggest possible political turds and somehow made it look like a marble sculpture. And that standoff with the bikers in the woods had all the earmarks of a fiasco. How you defused that should be taught at Quantico. You've bought me some valuable and some high-placed markers, Evan."

Durkin poured the two cups. "Have you ever been to Ireland, Evan?"

"No, sir. I have not."

"Driscoll is an Irish name if I'm not mistaken," Durkin said. He replaced the glass decanter and seated himself.

"Yes, sir, it is. It comes from the Gaelic word that means messenger or go-between. Some say the Driscolls can trace themselves all the way back to the 10th Century. My family says we came from County Cork. Cork, as I'm sure you know, sir, is in the far southeast, on the Irish Sea."

Durkin sipped his brew.

"It's not every day we're lauded personally by the Attorney General of the United States. It's a shame neither of us could record that call for our children to hear someday."

Driscoll nodded and drank from his cup.

"Permission to speak freely, sir?"

"Always, Evan. What's troubling you?"

"I still have the sense we were played somehow. Even if it did all come out right at the end."

Durkin considered the statement and set down his cup.

"We're always players, but, you understand, that's different from being played by a country mile."

"But the Coast Guard found no boat, found no weapons, and more interestingly, they found no Ronan Graham."

"It doesn't matter who found what or whom, Evan," Durkin said slowly. "Consider this hypothetical. Someone has the weapons, and someone has Ronan Graham. Again, hypothetically. Someone, let's use MI6 because they're always such fun, wants Ronan Graham, and they're willing to trade something for him. Something that we might want. The weapons are all present and accounted for and awaiting an appropriately selected recipient. Someone who, for the sake of argument, could use a little help in achieving a mutually desired result somewhere on the globe."

"I feel the Agency's hand in all of this," Driscoll said.

"Their unseen hand, you mean. And, after all, they are, first and foremost, a covert organization. Are you familiar with the saying 'The enemy of my enemy is my friend'?"

"I am," Driscoll said. "Are you familiar with the Grateful Dead?"

Durkin smiled. "Only to the level of what our informants tell us about their dedicated followers."

"They have a song that . . ." Driscoll paused. "Anyway, it begs the question. What do we do when your friend is the Devil?"

Durkin raised an eyebrow but did not answer.

"NEED TO KNOW, I assume, on the, um, hypothetical details?" Driscoll asked.

"EYES ONLY, I'm afraid, Evan," Durkin responded.

Driscoll nodded his understanding. "I'm glad I could attend the services for Agents Brascone and Tierney. Please reassure me Ronan Graham doesn't get to skate for their murders."

"What I can tell you," Durkin said, "What I can assure you, rather, is that there will never come a sunrise when Ronan Graham doesn't pray to Almighty God to put him back in the H-Blocks at Long Kesh. And at the moment, I don't think he has any Coppertone lotion, which is going to be a problem for him."

"And why is that, Director?"

"Evan. The Irish. You know. We don't tan. No. We just burn."

FORTY-FOUR

MAY 1979
ONE YEAR LATER

Off Island Beach State Park
Berkeley Township, NJ

"YOU COOK GOOD BURGER, pilgrim."

Helly Hansen almost choked on his soda.

"Says The Outlaw Mickey Cleary," he responded. "Too bad there ain't no grizz hiding in them thar dunes. And it wasn't me. It was the girl at the concession stand."

"Come on, admit it. It's a great movie," Mickey said.

"OK. I just don't know if Clint Eastwood is a Hollywood director," Helly replied. "We'll have to wait and see how that plays out."

"I reckon," Mickey shot back. Then she spit over the rail.

"OK, that's enough Josey Wales," Helly laughed. "And speaking of Hollywood, did Mr. Sinatra keep his promise?"

"Yes, he did," Mickey said. "He most certainly did."

Helly gazed toward the beach and the splashing children.

"You want to go gather them up?"

Mickey looked at her watch.

"Eh. Tide won't start going out for another hour," she said. "Let them play a little longer. Michael is having the time of his life. I have this nightmare where I have to go to court to fight Bunny for custody."

"Well, aren't you the master mariner now," Helly kidded her. "Memorized today's tide table and everything. Should I get you a sextant?"

"Not sure I'm ready for that step yet," Mickey said.

"We're talking about celestial navigation, right?" Helly asked.

"I am," Mickey answered. "You can speak for yourself, sailor man." She tapped on the wooden rail. "We did all the steps, right? We didn't miss anything?"

"We did all the steps," Helly assured her. "I even checked with Dad, and several of the old codgers, including the oldest living captain in the fleet, and they all agreed. They said squaring it with Njord was a good idea, even if we are a long way from the Norwegian Sea."

"Hey," Mickey said, "I'm not taking any chances. Not since I found out what a big deal it is to rechristen a boat. We appeased Poseidon, we checked in with your Norse God of the Sea. We didn't overlook anybody?"

"We did not," Helly said.

"But what about the transom?" Mickey asked. "Does it matter that we didn't burn it?"

"First of all, Poseidon claimed the original transom for himself," Helly explained. "He basically reached up and grabbed it. So burning it wasn't an option unless you want to hire Jacques Cousteau to go look for it. So the old trident flinger, he's more than satisfied. Now Njord, well, he's happy that you even knew his name." Helly pointed to the boat's rebuilt stern. "This new one is all teak. I picked it out myself."

Mickey hopped up and jumped into the flat, green water.

"What are you doing?" Helly asked her.

"I want to look at it again," Mickey said. "Can you believe how calm it is today?"

"There's a big high-pressure system right on top of us. It won't be like this two days from now."

"Says Channel 6 Weatherman Helly O'Brien," Mickey teased. She backed up a few more steps. "It looks great," she said. "And to think you hand-painted it yourself. Who knew?"

Mickey stood in the knee-deep water and regarded what had once been the *Virginia Jean*. Michael and Bunny came splashing up.

"We saw dolphins," Michael said. "I like dolphins. Dolphins swim fast." He paddled his arms to accentuate his point.

"Yes, they do," Mickey said. She picked him up and kissed him. "Where's Leenie Beanie?" she asked Bunny.

"At the concession stand," Bunny replied. "She wanted another hamburger. She's a skinny girl, but she eats a lot. I like your new boat."

Mickey put Michael down. He ran up to play on the beach. Eileen toodled down to join him, a spray of white sand marking her every step. She waved at Mickey and Bunny.

"It's actually an old boat, Bunny," Mickey said. "But she has a new name."

"Helly fix up good."

"Bunny," Mickey scolded.

"Helly fixed...Helly fixed it up very good," Bunny said slowly.

"Much better. And it's not an it. Boats are called she or her."

"Her has a funny name," Bunny said. "What does it mean?"

"Mmmmmm," Mickey answered. "It means...it means something like...heaven. A place where people never die and they never grow old. Some say it's an island paradise. Some say it's under the water. Some say it's both. Either way, it's very hard to get there. So we keep sailing around in circles until one day we find it."

"This island looks pretty good," Bunny answered, motioning to the long, unbroken stretch of beach. "And it's easy to get to. But if Mickey-san says so, it must be true. Hey! I think Michael found a crab. I'll go see before it pinches him."

She splashed away to where the children played in the shallow tide pools.

Mickey made her way back to the boat and joined Helly. Two aluminum beach chairs with sun-faded yellow and turquoise straps served as their deck chairs. There wasn't room for anything bigger.

"At some point," Mickey said, "You gotta tell me what it cost to restore her."

"Not that much," Helly answered. "Probably a lot less than you think. And I enjoyed the work. I did a pretty poor job of rescuing you, so let's say we call it even. Plus, it gave me something to do every day over the winter. Even Dad came to the shop with a few pointers. He remembers when his dad and his dad's dad built their first boat. I'm not in their league, but your nice librarian, Miss Croce, or is it Miss Donahue? Anyway, she found some great books for me. Is she still dating that lifeguard? Anyway, I'll be a proper shipwright one of these days. I even learned how to use an adze."

"Well, you're a pain in the adze, that's for sure," Mickey said and punched him in the shoulder. Helly shook his head and laughed.

"I saw that Kase fellow again," Helly said. "He's a persistent sort, I'll give him that. But I do think he's just trying to look out for you in his own way. Lot of money for a salty piece of sand."

Mickey momentarily considered telling him about the checks from New Age Nepptronix, LLC, that arrived every month. She decided against it.

"Has the local Coast Guard forgiven you yet?" Mickey asked.

"They've boarded the *Hans N* six times and issued seven citations. Does that sound like forgiveness to you?" Helly responded.

"Yes," Mickey said. "Actually it does. See, your sin is forgiven - but this is your penance. That's how it works in the Catholic Church."

"Snapping mackerel is not one of the fish we usually catch," Helly said with a tiny smile.

"Yeah, well, you won't make any friends around here serving lutefisk," Mickey chided him. "Do you really cook it with lye? *Uff da.*"

"It's brined with lye. But then it's soaked to remove it all. It's just steamed cod, for God's sake."

Mickey started to chuckle. "Hey, if it's not fried flounder, I'm not interested."

"OK. Now. This is probably top-secret stuff," Helly said. "But did you ever figure out exactly what happened out there? I mean, after they tried deep-sixing you?"

Mickey adjusted her Wayfarers.

"My two good friends in the FBI have been pretty tight-lipped. Jack Rigger, the slimeball who tried to force me into screwing him when I was at the Academy, they figure he sleeps soundly with the fishes. They believe the poor bikers, who were just along for the ride, met the same fate. Five souls, all still missing. No bodies. No boats. No debris. But who actually whacked who out there remains a mystery. They did give me one very useful piece of information, though. I could tell you, but, then, you know I'd have to drop *you* overboard."

Mickey pictured the ivory chip, carefully wrapped in felt cloth in a safety deposit box at Jersey Shore State Bank.

"And what about Mister Irish Spring?" Helly asked. "Lost at sea, as well?"

"Nobody, and I do mean nobody, is talking about him. Like not one word either way. Casper is less of a ghost than he is. Give me the local hoods and the leftover wiseguys any day over someone like that. If he is alive, I sincerely hope he's in a deep dark hole somewhere. Handgun diplomacy - that I understand. This other stuff is above my pay grade. And, it would appear, above my security clearance."

Mickey shifted in her lawn chair which let out a metallic squeak.

"The thing is - I hadn't put it all together. Sure, I probably would have, but when we were at Hyman's hotel, I said something about the Sons of Satan, and it was like he all of sudden changed channels. Normally, I would have sensed that right away. But my mind was on the kids and not being late to take everyone out for supper and, to be honest, on his lovely Irish accent and his stories about the Cleary clan. Plus, I had no frickin' idea he wasn't really Connor Kilderry of the *Garda*."

Mickey checked her watch again.

"I suppose maybe we should gather up the brave island explorers before we're marooned. They won't come willingly."

Helly popped up first.

"I'll get them. After we load up I'll pull the stern anchor out of the mud. Nice job on the anchorage, by the way. Seen that go south more than once."

"I had a good instructor," Mickey said.

Helly hopped out. Mickey collapsed the chairs and stowed them. She could see that the tide was starting its seaward creep. If they stayed where they were, the hidden moon would suck the water right out from under the boat, stranding them high on the sandbar. They could wait for the next high tide to refloat them, but it would be dark by then.

She thought about Ronnie and the beach fire they'd shared not long after their first meeting. She thought about Helly and all he'd done for her. She wondered if the unfilled spaces in both their lives would remain unfilled forever.

Helly called from the beach as Bunny and the children made their way to the boat. When they were safely aboard, she gave him the high sign. He dislodged the flukes of the small Danforth out from the soft sand and began walking it toward them, gathering up the slack as he did.

Mickey went to the helm. She touched the large St. Brendan of Clonfort medallion, which was permanently glued next to the compass.

As soon as she saw Helly was on board, she pulled out the choke and pushed the starter.

The fully refitted engine responded and thrummed contentedly.

Mickey patted the compass and eased the throttle forward, taking time for one last look at the beach.

Then she pointed the bow of the *Tir na nO'g* toward home.

FORTY-FIVE

Editorial Offices
The Philadelphia Inquirer
North Broad & Callowhill, Philadelphia, PA

JEFFREY SILVERMAN'S KNEES WERE pumping like pistons as he sat in front of the famous reporter's desk. He slid the large, accordion-style file folder farther away from his lap to quiet them.

On the wall behind the desk was the Pulitzer Prize certificate. A gilt-edged wood frame with a narrow cream matte held it. The museum-quality glass that protected it caught the fading afternoon sun but, Jeffrey noticed, did not reflect much of it.

The glass-paned office door rattled open.

"Gotta go to the can," Mike Gannon said, poking his head in. "Be right back. I promise. Truly sorry about the long wait. We're finishing up a huge investigative series."

He was gone before Jeffrey could respond. Jeffrey leaned forward to peek at the jumble of papers, clippings, and pictures strewn about the oversized desktop. They all had something to do with Agent Orange, American soldiers, or the Vietnam War.

The glass rattled again, and the door swung open. Gannon shuffled in, lit a cigarette, and installed himself in a chair that looked like a prop from *The Front Page,* a comedy currently being performed at the Walnut Street Theatre. He took a couple of quick puffs and then stubbed out the barely burned Lucky Strike.

"L.S. may M.F.T., but I'm still trying to cut down," Gannon said, by way of explanation. "So, my secretary tells me you've got something—in that rather fulsome folder, I assume—that you think I and my readers might find interesting."

"I believe so," Jeffrey responded. "But, first, may I ask you a personal question?"

"That's usually my job," Gannon shot back, "but, sure. Ask away."

"Your name is Gannon. But you're not Irish."

"That's a statement, not a question. You have red hair and fair skin. But you're not Irish either. Now, I'm going to assume you've done your due diligence and you already know my birth surname was Ganon. It's not exactly a secret. You could say that Mike Gannon, my reportorial *nom-de-plume* and glittering literary persona, is one highly observant Irishman. But Mischa Ganon, well, I'm afraid he is a rather, and sometimes completely, non-observant, non-Irishman. Much to the regret of his beloved *bubby*."

Jeffrey smiled and nodded.

Gannon pulled another Lucky Strike from the pack. This one he did not light.

"Does my observational status have anything to do, perhaps, with what you're about to share with me?" Gannon asked.

"I think," Jeffrey said as he unwound the elastic loop from the button on the front of the folder, "That it has literally everything to do with what I'm about to give you. It's why I chose you."

Gannon sat back with a puzzled look. He cupped the side of his lined and whisker-stubbled face in one palm and narrowed his gaze.

"Jeffrey, if you're about to tell me that you've found Josef Mengele managing a McDonald's in Moorestown," he said, "I must regretfully inform you that you'll be the third person this month. Please, please don't say you've found Mengele in Moorestown."

"I have not," Jeffrey replied. He grasped the thick folder with both hands and set it on Gannon's desk. "But after what I can truthfully describe as a year of painstaking research and perhaps some personal risk, I think I may have found something even more elusive."

"Let me guess," Gannon said. "Jimmy Hoffa. If so, that would make you the sixth person this month."

"Mr. Gannon, I am confident that what you'll find inside," Jeffrey pointed to the folder Gannon had not yet touched, "is evidence that the story of one of the great American family fortunes, a story gracing the pages of this month's issues of *Fortune* and *Forbes* I might add, is an utter and complete fabrication. A fractured financial fairy tale."

Gannon leaned forward.

"You've piqued my interest, both literally and alliteratively. Not such an easy thing to do," he said. "Should I look, or are you going to tell me?"

"I've typed up a one-page summary. It's the first piece of paper inside." Jeffrey leaned back in his chair.

"OK," Gannon said. "You've strung me along me this far." He flipped the fold-over flap open, removed a sheet of heavy bond typing paper, and began to read.

After a few minutes of intense perusing, hmmm'ing, and brow-knitting, Gannon looked up at Jeffrey.

"You can - you can document all of this?" he asked.

"I can document almost all of it. I'm hoping you'll have sources and resources that will connect the remaining dots, as well as verify and possibly even flesh out some of the murkier details."

"Hmmm. I see you've even given your little project a title," Gannon said. "Very good. Very clever. Actually, quite clever indeed. He reached for a silver Zippo lighter. "*Riechsmarks* Roulette."

"Heidi, my wife, she's the one who actually came up with it," Jeffrey said. "It was originally 'Casinogate,' but she said that was too trifling, too...too derivative, given the seriousness of the subject matter."

Gannon stared at the page again. Then he reached for his phone, pressed a button, and waited, holding up his index finger.

"Candy, would you step into my office? There's someone in here I'd like you to meet and something I'd like you to read. Yes. No. What? The law student? Um, um, um, Durkin. Katherine, no, Karen - Karen Durkin. She's working with Sam Santaspirito in Surf City. Call his office. OK. Right away if you can."

He turned to Jeffrey.

"My assistant, Candy Catan. Nee` Catanzariti, as long as we're being transparent. She'll be joining us momentarily." He picked up the pack of Lucky's. "Do you smoke, Jeffrey?" he asked.

"I do not, sir," Jeffrey replied.

"Well," Gannon said with a wry smile, "Given the very dangerous ground we are about to tread, you might seriously consider starting."

Acknowledgements

I hear you. You're saying, "Again with the Jersey Shore?"

The problem with having "sand in your shoes" is that you can never get it out. So, thank you for indulging me (and my Top-Siders) one more time.

Writing a novel involves conjuring up a lot of words and applying them one at a time to a blank page. Creating a book requires more than that – the cover that catches your eye, the layout, the details, the ads that let you know it exists. For those aspects, I have several people to thank: Alicia Dean, who once again took on the job of editing and proofreading the manuscript; Jim Zach, at *zGrafix*, who continues to amaze by taking the caveman drawings and nebulous cover ideas I send him and turning them into works of art, and who also designed the world's coolest logo which is now officially Trademarked; Terry Persun, who formats the manuscript for publishing so it turns out looking like a book; critical reader Kate Galluzzi; Doug McCarthy and Ryan Martz at Fire and Pine, for the use of their lovely coastal map; Kellie Jo Heimer at Control-Print Creative who designs the advertisements; and Raul Carolus, overlord of the BandageMan Press website.

Note should be made of the gracious assistance of the United States Coast Guard Office of Public Affairs and the Office of the Historian for details about Station Barnegat Light; the Federal Bureau of Investigation's Historian for details about the Bureau's New Jersey offices in 1978; Steve Levy, USCG (Ret.) for his Boater's Ed and technical advice; Neil Pignataro, Education Officer, and the Cape Coral (FL) Power Squadron for their excellent courses on Boat

Handling and Marine Navigation; and my mostly silent writing partner, Blaze the Wonder Dog.

I would like to thank the old and new friends who generously lent their names to the purely fictional characters in this story: Timothy Mulholland, MD; Steve Feder; Darwin Schossow, DO; Michael Ganon, DO; Mary Beth Harman, DO; Mark Nepp, DO; Arlene Shields, RN; Mrs. Nancy (Miss Donahue) Croce; Dan Lipinski; Daniel Ragone, MD; Joseph Bottalico, DO; Mike Kase; Jim Frichionne, Fixer of All Things Florida; Bob Rocca; Jim Filisky; Mike Garufi; Bill Sievert; Marianne Carlton; Louis A. Petroni, Esq.; April Eberhardt; Dale Andres, DO; Mike Andreas; F. Gregory Gause, III, Ph.D.; the Hon. Karen Durkin; Gary Levinson, MD; Bendheim Architectural Glass (NYC); Capt. Steve Levy; Melissa Summerfield, MD; Barbara Tomalino; and Gene Galasso, *pizzaiolo straordinario*. A nod to those whose names live on although they are no longer with us: James C. "Juice" Giudice, DO; Fr. Joseph Feeney, S.J.; William P. Tunell, MD; John. J. Durkin; and Mrs. Loretta LaMarro

As always, a heartfelt thanks to those who nurtured and encouraged my writing career: Joe Marquart, Bob Rocca and Anne Marie Donahue at Bishop Eustace Prep; Fr. Feeney at St. Joseph's College (PA); the amazing Professor Laura Hope-Gill at Lenoir-Rhyne University's Thomas Wolfe Center for Narrative in Asheville, NC; and my writing "posse" in the MA program at LRU who helped me in so many ways. And last, but by no means least, prolific author, friend and mentor Bob Dugoni, who continues to provide sage advice and baseball analogies. Apologies to anyone I may have missed. So, enough with the acknowledgments already! I hope you enjoyed reading this story as much as I enjoyed writing it.

DJW
March 17th, 2024

About the author

Daniel James Waters, D.O., M.A., was born in Philadelphia and grew up in southern New Jersey. He attended Bishop Eustace Preparatory School, St. Joseph's College (PA), and the University of Medicine and Dentistry of New Jersey. In addition to a medical degree, he holds a Graduate Certificate in Narrative Healthcare along with a Master of Arts in Writing from The Thomas Wolfe Center for Narrative/The Center for Graduate Studies at Lenoir-Rhyne University in Asheville, NC. He published his first story as a medical student in 1981 and has been writing and publishing steadily ever since. His work has appeared in major medical and surgical journals as well as in the literary magazines of major universities and medical colleges, including Intima (Columbia University), The Examined Life Journal (The University of Iowa Carver College of Medicine), the North Carolina Literary Review (East Carolina University/University of North Carolina Press), and The Missouri Review (University of Missouri), along with several collections and anthologies of the best medical writing.

He has contributed to online platforms and served as a Writing Fellow for the medical professionals' website Doximity.com from 2019 until 2021, producing a widely read series of "Op-Meds." He sits on the Editorial Advisory Board of *The DO Magazine* and is a regular columnist. Along with an array of scholarly and scientific articles, he is the published author of two oft-quoted books of surgical advice, numerous essays, six other well-received novels, and several poems. He was the recipient of the Pacific Northwest Writers Association's prestigious Nancy Pearl Award for Best Book (2020) and also took First Place in PNWA's 2020 Literary Competition in the Creative Nonfiction/Memoir Category. He was Runner-up in The Missouri Review's 2021 Jeffrey E. Smith Editors' Prize for Nonfiction. He retired from clinical practice in 2019 after an award-winning thirty-year career performing open-heart surgery. He is the founder of BandageMan Press, Inc., and now devotes his time to his family and his writing.

VISIT OUR WEBSITE: www.bandagemanpress.com
CONTACT THE AUTHOR: drdan@bandagemanpress.com

Books by Daniel J. Waters

A Heart Surgeon's Little Instruction Book

A Surgeon's Little Instruction Book

Threshold

Surf City Confidential

Ship Bottom Blues

Barnegat Dark

Shore Crimes

Dunes 'til Dead

Boardwalk Babylon

All Books

Available in Paperback and eBook formats at Amazon.com

Also at Select Local Booksellers

Or Visit: www.bandagemanpress.com

Surf City Confidential

Long Beach Island, 1967

Mickey Cleary is the new Police Chief in Surf City. Just before the Memorial Day Weekend, the traditional start of the tourist season, a body washes up on her beach – the son of a Philadelphia mob boss. Advised to call it an accident and close the case, Mickey presses on with an investigation that sets in motion a series of events that takes her deep into the foreboding Pine Barrens, where she finds herself in a fight for her life.

"A gripping debut. Waters brews a cauldron of colorful characters simmering in an intricate plot. The revelations come in a wild, tense finish. One of the best books I'll read this year."

—Robert Dugoni, #1 Amazon, Wall Street Journal, and New York Times Bestselling Author

Ship Bottom Blues

In the year 1969...as the August sun beats down, things in SurfCity,NJ are heating up.

Police Chief Mickey Cleary is ready to put another hectic tourist season on Long Beach Island be hind her. But just as the days of Summer and the events of her own past seem ready to slip further away ,old ghosts and new monsters are on their way "Down the Shore" – and heading straight toward her.

"This Vietnam era thriller works well on many levels. The book is well-written, with tension-driven suspense. The structure is taut; the plot is solid. There's tension in every line, making it a page-turner.

The musical references and the cars add to the real-life details that make the reader part of the scene. It's a great read, hard to put down, and comparable to John Sanford, Robert Dugoni, and Jeffrey Archer.

—***Writers Digest*** Judges' Review

Barnegat Dark

Summer 1971. The Jersey Shore. America is a country at war – abroad and at home. An entire nation is clamoring for change. Over a sweltering Independence Day weekend, a sea of simmering tensions is set to boil over in the shadow of an iconic landmark. And for Surf City Police Chief Mickey Cleary, a new kind of threat and a new kind of enemy will imperil both her and those she cares most about.

The sleepy little towns up and down Long Beach Island are about to wake up.

"The characters and the tightly woven plot were believable.You had me turning the pages to find out what happened next. Definitely not a book to start at night if you want to get any sleep."

—***WritersDigest***Judge'sReview

"Another great read about LBI, Chief Mickey & Old Barney. The war is wearing on our favorite characters as well as some newbies to the Jersey Shore. The Surf City police are busy as always. A lot of action, crime, & camaraderie plus a surprise!"

Shore Crimes

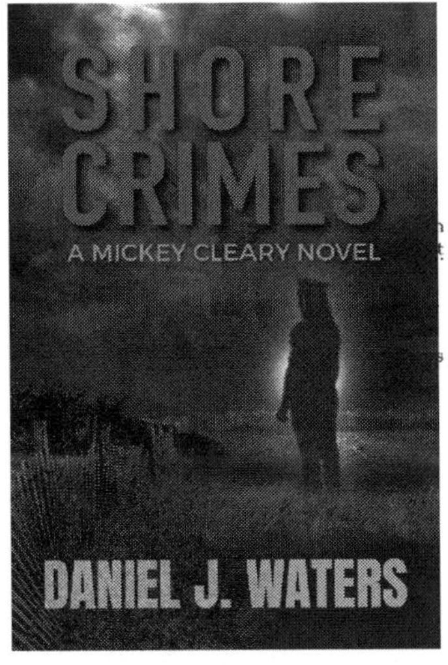

SURF CITY, LONG BEACH ISLAND, NJ
SEPTEMBER 1974

The casino gambling referendum has failed. Another hectic beach season has ended. Police Chief Mickey Cleary is ready to throttle back and focus her attention on her husband Ronnie and their little girl, Eileen. But Mickey quickly discovers that assuming anything is the ultimate longshot bet. And treasure isn't the only thing that ends up buried in the sand...

AMAZON READERS LOVE "SHORECRIMES"!

"Great book. Love that it is based on LBI."

"I love the characters!"

"A must read for anyone familiar with Long Beach Island. Numerous references make what is already a very good storyline even better."

"I have enjoyed this series of police stories set on LBI. I'd love to see how Beach Baby turns out in 20 years!"

VOTED "BEST SOUTH JERSEY THRILLER SERIES"
by SJ Magazine, October 2021

Dunes Til Dead

Down the shore, it's America's Bicentennial Summer. But not everyone is celebrating with sparklers and bottle rockets. The bodies of two young women have turned up in the dunes at the southern tip of tourist-packed Long Beach Island, NJ.

Mickey Cleary, Surf City's Police Chief for the last ten years, has just embarked on a new challenge when she finds herself pulled back to LBI's white sand beaches to help hunt down a killer. As the investigation unfolds, she uncovers a horrific truth.

Mickey is about to learn that sometimes the devil you know can be much worse than the one you don't.

"A SMART AND FUN DETECTIVE STORY WITH A NEW JERSEY ACCENT."

—Kirkus Reviews

Threshold

One heartbeat — and the world changes forever.

Dr. Johanna Roberson, a former Olympic rower, is a resident in cardiac surgery training at Seattle's most prestigious hospital, The Cutter Clinic. She believes she has stumbled upon a lucrative medical device scam to implant cardiac pacemakers in wealthy Middle Eastern patients. What she has unwittingly uncovered, however, is something far more sinister and terrifying. Enlisting the help of Homeland Security Agent Triplett "Trip" Collier, the pair track a mercenary madman from the top of the city's iconic Space Needle to the maze of underground hallways beneath the world-famous medical center in a desperate race to avert a catastrophe that could plunge the country into global armed conflict.

"A terrific read. Taut, timely, and, at times, terrifying. Engaging characters, intensely high stakes, and a plot that hurtles to a stunning denouement. Highly recommended!"

—SheldonSiegel,NewYorkTimes Best Selling Author of the Mike Daley/Rosie Hernandez Thriller Series